sex drink & yellow FISH

JASON BLAKE

A Star Paperback

Jason Blake was born in 1970 and studied Graphic Design at Loughborough College and York University. He works in advertising and lives in South Leicestershire with his wife and son. *Sex, Drink and Yellow Fish* is his first book.

First published in Great Britain 2009
by Star Publishing, Leicestershire

A CIP catalogue record for this title is available from the British Library

ISBN 978-0-9561237-0-1

Special Edition

ISBN 978-0-9561237-1-8

Printed and bound in Great Britain by
Athenaeum Press Ltd, Gateshead, Tyne & Wear

Printed on Munken Print White 80gsm from sustainable sources.
FSC Accredited.

To Trac, old pals, The Yellow Fish and to the part of my life where the only things I believed in and wanted were love, vodka, music and The Beast.

Prologue

Jay parked his backside on the nearest bench within the grounds of the church, happy that the graves were far from reaching it. It was a peaceful British summer, not a cloud in the sky and the distant sounds of birds, children playing, lawn mowers and an ice cream van in the distance all layered perfectly and subtly.

He took three swallows of Coke, wiped his mouth, and before he could offer his girl a taste she had laid down across the bench with her head positioned neatly into his lap so that the sun could shine directly onto her face. He thought how beautiful she looked and suddenly he felt warm and ever more joyful. He gently brushed his right hand through her big curly blonde hair that he adored and meticulously pushed loose strands behind her left ear just to see her cute round face and wide mouth smile all the more.

Sipping at his Coke he took time to study the different shades of green surrounding him and enjoyed the effect the sunlight made as it passed through the leaves to the ground where the added breeze made an interesting dappled effect on the grass. Time, it seemed, had somehow become immaterial.

Shelley's smile had not wavered in hours, fuelling his carefree glow by the minute. He watched her loosen the buttons of her shirt and as they slipped from their holes the material gaped open revealing the nape of her neck invitingly. The Body Shop's White Musk perfume lifted into the air even more so, mixing with the smell of flowers and freshly cut grass. This, he thought, was his very own female. She fascinated him without her realising to what extent she actually did. With no hesitation he gave in to her every whim and couldn't understand why. She was headstrong, bossy and domineering; the exact kind of person he had an unstoppable urge to retaliate and defy against. Yet for some unknown reason he gave himself to her. He allowed her to experiment by perming his hair without question; even knocking him out with a tennis racket had not swayed his devotion. She taught him the simplest of things like making popcorn or how to play draughts. She had filled him with a depth of emotion that he had never felt before and he craved everything from her unique strength of character to the mascara marks she left on his pillow... even her woolly tights seemed to spark the animal in him. He couldn't help but wonder if this was love?

'What are you thinking about Jay?' she murmured studying his thoughtful brow.

'Nothing much,' he replied. 'You know, just thinking.'

Glowing with a smile she said, 'I'm hungry, shall we walk back?'

He didn't respond, he was happy to stay there, where life had never been more wonderfully simple. Shelley then lifted herself up, squinted slightly, and brought a hand up to shade her eyes.

'You okay Jay?'

He stood and put his hand out, 'yeah,' he smiled, 'come on, let's go.'

She took his hand in hers and they wandered down the pathway leisurely.

1. Fishes in the sea

The end of January 1989

Jay did not want to get out of bed, he wanted to wait until something happened. After twenty minutes snoozing he managed to pull open the curtains slightly from his lying position to allow the strong bright daylight to warm him. The alarm went off and his eyes flew open. He hit the clock really hard with his left hand and then hurled it across the room.

'Damn. Forgot what I was dreaming about,' he whined, rubbing at his eyes.

He lived in South Leicester, had done all his life. The city was ever expanding and his house was about seven miles south, in a village called Narborough. Two popular public houses and a train station were the only items of interest to him, although the village offered a great deal more.

His mum and dad had been separated for several years. His feelings on the matter were unconfirmed, it was something he chose not to dwell on and, as they still saw each other regularly, that seemed the best way to handle it. His brother Shaun, a few years older, was away at college in London studying to be a building surveyor while his sister Nicola, a few years younger, lived with his mum too. They used to fight like cat and dog when they were kids but by now they had either run out of energy or become bored in their relentless teasing and bickering with one another. Their dog Sam, a cross between a poodle and a yorkie, was the spit of Gnasher from *The Beano* yet he only ever seemed devoted to his mum, spending all day looking out the window or asleep on her bed, waiting for her to come home. He only ever barked and bit at Jay's trousers whenever he left or returned to the house.

He started to feel a little hungry so he dragged himself up out of bed reluctantly. Squinting and stumbling he assembled his clothes and slowly put them on. Right; plan for today he thought, whilst drinking a sweet cup of tea in front of the TV. I think I'll stay here, then I might stay here a bit longer, okay I think I'll piss off back to bed. He smiled happily to himself, this was typical of his lazy disorganised lifestyle, 'oh sod it I'll do it tomorrow' was his general attitude, only ever cowering into submission or effort when his mum began her 'you treat this house like a bedsit' routine. He simply assumed that cooking, cleaning, washing and ironing was what every good mum did for their offspring. An image of his mum bearing down on him firing off a series of nagging statements was enough to prevent him from returning to his pit.

He arrived at Loughborough College of Art and Design late as ever and blamed it on a delayed train. In the classroom there was a good deal of muttering going on. The sun shone brightly through the windows and the air smelt stale. He made his usual barged entrance, slamming his art box down onto his desk just to let everyone know he had arrived. Nobody seemed to be doing much in the way of work. He became agitated and immediately bored. Moving over to the far corner of the classroom he sat down on a desk in the sunlight, he got a better view of the class from there. With one hand on his knee and the other supporting his head he pulled out a record from his bag and and thought what a great title The Left Legged Pineapple was for a record shop.

'Alright Jay?'

The guy approaching him was Andy; an avid rugby player, short hair, flattish nose and a generally easy going kind of guy, he got on with everyone.

'What have you got there then?' he asked politely.

'The Wonder Stuff,' he grinned, waving it in the air. ''Give, Give, Give Me More, More, More'.'

'Is it good then?'

Jay gave a slight chuckle, 'fucking magic.'

'I guess it's another fast guitar song you'll go mad to in the near future.' He held that thought in his mind and smiled broadly, 'most definitely.'

He had moved away from pop to indie music, it seemed to somehow mean something. Songs he liked had harsh guitars, fast metal that you could lose yourself to and pump you full of adrenaline, generating attitude and immense energy.

He sat there silently, he was always subdued and quiet in the mornings, the day woke him up as it went along and by night he came alive. He decided to drift off to the college library to attempt some research into his latest design brief. On his return Adrian was seated at his desk; dark-haired, soft eyes, and full of enthusiasm for art and alcohol, he jumped up and marched gingerly towards him in one swift move.

'Lend us thirty pence Jay,' he uttered, jangling a few coppers under his nose.

'Don't you mean give you thirty pence?'

Adrian didn't respond to that so he reluctantly dug a hand into his pocket, 'here, there's fifteen.'

'Cheers mate,' he said following it with a loud rasping fart, a regular occurrence.

'Awwgh, fucking hell, do you have to?'

Adrian beamed a smile as he wafted his smell about for all to appreciate.

'There's something wrong with your insides mate,' muttered Jay shaking his head and leaving his current location in search of fresher air.

Adrian ignored the protest and simply proceeded to pester Andy for money.

At lunchtime they wandered over to the student union building to play pinball and have some chips and beans. Dave arrived in time to join them at the Purple Pit, the student union's resident snack bar.

Dave tutted loudly as he approached them.

'Look at you dossers,' he chuckled.

All three of them looked up at the tall figure of Dave, he was well built with blonde hair, it was easy to see why all the girls went for him. He was the kind of guy who liked dinner dates, buying his lady a gin and tonic, insisting they never drank anything else.

'Where have you been?' quizzed Jay abruptly.

'At home finishing off that drawing for Ruth's lesson.'

'Would ya?' Interrupted Adrian as he spotted a young blonde female with fair sized breasts stroll past.

'Marks out of ten?' asked Dave.

'I'd give her one,' droned Jay. 'Can't you two think of anything else?'
Jay merely glanced at the girl and took a mouthful of chips and thought about getting a pint of lager.

'I might go and see *Young Guns* at the cinema tonight,' mumbled Andy before sinking his teeth into a chip cob.

'Yeah I went the other week, it's a good film,' said Jay.

'You go with your girlfriend?' whispered Dave following it with a smirk.

'Yeah,' Jay muttered with his mouth still full of chips.

'How is your girlfriend? What's her name again?'
Dave never usually showed any interest in the girls he dated and his behaviour struck him as rather odd.

'Okay,' he smiled. 'What's going on? Don't try and wind me up.'

'Oh come on Jay, why would we do a thing like that,' teased Dave.

'Her name is Sue, alright?' and with that he scrunched up his empty chip paper and threw it in the bin shaking his head in the realisation of what was about to unfold.

'Erm,' murmured Adrian, 'I think her name is Tangerine Dream isn't it Jay?'
She had been dubbed the nickname by Adrian because Jay, on one of his sexual adventures, introduced a tangerine into the fun of foreplay and confessed all in drunken confidence. However Adrian was clearly about to take much delight in giving Dave the low-down.

'Aargh, no! You're joking,' laughed Dave looking at Jay. 'You never told me about this, is it true?'

'I don't believe this,' Jay replied reluctantly.

'When did this happen?'

'Why is everyone on at me today?' and with that he shook his head. 'It's old news Dave.'

'Not to me it isn't.'

'Well for your information it just kind of happened,' he said calmly as he wiped his hands on a serviette. 'Why is it always my fucking love life that's the point of conversation?'

'You just confess to things when you're pissed. Besides, we ain't got love lives.'

He grinned, then gave a chuckle as his brain began to hatch a plan to tease them with more titbits.

As he collected up his coins from his pocket hoping he had enough for a beer he said calmly, 'she likes being treated...'

Adrian moved to the edge of his stool, closer so as not to miss anything and Dave followed suit with equalling curiosity.

'Treated how?'

Jay smiled craftily as he began to count the money in his palm of his hand.

'Come on tell us,' spurred Dave.

He snapped his hand shut and shoved the coins into his right pocket. 'Tell you what Dave,' he said, 'treat me to a pint and I'll tell you.'

By late afternoon Jay still couldn't settle down to work, he just wasn't in the mood for drawing. Some days he couldn't put a pencil down, but today he didn't feel creative in the slightest. He sat idly, throwing screwed up bits of paper at Dave, who in turn threw them back at him. Adrian sat with the headphones of his personal stereo clamped over his ears, in the bored silence you could just about hear the tinkle, tinkle of his music. Jay began to nudge him until he took his headphones off.

'What's up?' snapped Adrian.

Jay nodded forwards to the door, 'let's go.'

He shook his head and put his headphones back on.

Jay, not one to take no for an answer, carried on pestering him over the next twenty minutes or so until he agreed. They left quietly, slipping out of the classroom without being seen.

That evening he was glued in front of the TV set, *Mission Impossible* was on BBC2. Let the dinner get cold he thought as his mum began to nag at him to sit at the table in the kitchen. Still in his restless state he became bored with the TV, bored with conversation and bored with Monday's regular mashed potato, pork chops and beans and retreated to his bedroom where he paced up and down trying to decide what to do.

He hated wasting time doing nothing, each day had to consist of something exciting. He pulled a few faces at himself in his mirror and that seemed to amuse him for all of a minute. He decided to phone Sue to see what she was up to. They had known each other from school and over a period of time a series of encounters took place, usually from bumping into one another down the pub. They had ended up together at New Year's Eve and had regularly seen each other since. She had a round face, black hair and dark eyes packaged with dark make up and a wardrobe that was exclusively black. The slight gothic aura she and her friend gave off had them known as the spooks. Sue's relaxed easy going nature was what made her so likeable.

Disappointed that she had gone round to see her fellow spook for the evening he pondered on the idea of phoning one of his ex-girlfriends, Sharon. She'd phoned and left a message for him only a few nights ago. He found her number in his diary and began to dial, but stopped halfway through. He replaced the receiver thinking it probably wasn't a good idea, he was just desperate for company and things between them were far from great. He dug out the coins from his pocket and counted them out twice, there just wasn't enough to make a trip to the pub. He thought momentarily about asking his mum for a fiver but quickly opted not to as he remembered he already owed her fifty pounds and she certainly didn't need reminding. A search of his room for emergency stashes of cash he may have placed in peculiar places resulted in just twenty eight pence and an old half pence coin from behind his desk that was long since useable. In defeat he put some music on and slumped onto his bed. He faintly heard something along the lines of 'turn it down.' He scrunched up his face and increased the volume. As he lay staring at the ceiling his thoughts turned to the first girl that had really emotionally and physically meant anything to him, Shelley. It had been a while since he had removed all trace of her and confined it to a box at the base of his wardrobe, yet her cute round face, big cheeks, long blonde hair that hung in curls and wide smiling mouth with spongy lips came flooding back all too easily. Their relationship was doomed from the start with her family's plans of emigration to Australia. This inevitable separation was probably the catalyst for their quick devotion to one another. Time was short and their feelings developed so fast it had made his head spin. The whole relationship was like a rollercoaster of emotion. He knew it was going to end in tears but being broken hearted somehow seemed hopelessly romantic. As her emigration grew nearer she pulled away from him, hoping it would make it easier to say goodbye. Seeing her for the last time was never going to be easy. He made her a compilation tape, wrote a letter, placed a photo in with it and went to the school youth club to meet her. She spent the night surrounded with her friends and he had found himself keeping his distance, with his stomach in knots he never even spoke to her. Then, just as he was about to get onto the bus home, he looked across at her group and she quickly jogged towards him but stopped, and fell short leaving the length of the bus between them. He went into auto pilot, walked briskly up to her and gave her his gift, kissed her cheek, smiled and got on the bus. It wasn't how he wanted or pictured saying goodbye, but then again he wasn't calling the shots, and if he was honest it killed him to underplay it the way he did.

During the months leading up to and beyond her departure, the only other person who felt somewhere near the sorrow that he did was her best friend Tracey, Trac for short, who happened to live in Leire, the same village as Jay's dad. It was a quiet village about six miles further south, with two pubs, a garage and a post office. Apart from the time when his brother tried to blow up the village phone box, nothing of great importance ever seemed to happen there. Trac was slim, attractive looking with eyes that gazed like a cat and a smile that caught people a little off guard. With long straight hair she had high raised cheekbones drawn to a narrow chin. They had formed a strong bond since October and phoned each other on a regular basis. The first time he went over to see her was the week after Shelley had gone. She had taken him down under a bridge on Jubilee Walk where, in the dark, they had sat on a bench and talked.

Back at her house he had studied her room, impressed by her stereo, Sony with a CD player, and noted that she was a Cure and Prince fan. She placed an LP on by a band called The Wonder Stuff which instantly captivated him. 'This is brilliant,' he smiled with a nod. Towards the end of the night he had swamped himself in her teddies, it had become somehow easier to open up more about Shelley hidden in the half dark behind a wall of stuffed bears. He found Trac to be warm and funny and it totally deterred him from his first materialistic, 'I'm the it girl' impression he had of her.

At Christmas they had danced and kissed and told one another their secrets and problems, they were becoming close. As time went by he ended up visiting her more and more and as a consequence Sue was drifting from his mind slowly. He knew he was falling for Trac like he had Shelley and feared it. This time he could feel himself fall gradually. She was radiant and desirable and above all made him feel overwhelmingly confident, vibrant and happy. He told her everything, his pure pursuit of alcohol and the exploits that inevitably followed made her laugh. Her first view of him was that of a rebel, but then there was so much more to him than that. Sure, he was irresponsible, deliberately so, impulsive and reckless but she had made other more positive notes about him too. He was charming, witty, cheeky, creative, and unlike most guys she met, he could talk about his feelings, yet it was his carefree and rebellious attitude that appealed to her the most.

'You like getting out your face then?'

'Yeah I do,' he grinned. 'Sometimes I get this buzzing feeling, the excitement at the thought of getting drunk. It's an adrenaline rush, it pumps right through me.'

'You're a piss artist,' she smiled at him.

'Of course,' he smirked. 'You should come down The Bell sometime, it's mad down there... my second home.'

His modest and sarcastic humour often set her into fits of giggles. Saturday lunches in town and Sunday afternoons together at his dad's house were fast becoming the norm.

Friday, February 3

He rolled the bottom of his jeans up to display a little of his baseball boots.

He tucked in his new shirt, black, and unscrewed the top to a tub of Shock Waves hair wax unsure whether the new hairstyle he was about to create was going to work or not. His hair, waxed back with a slight quiff, looked pretty good he thought as he winked amenably at himself in the mirror. He pulled on his new black jacket that he had acquired from the Lighthouse in Leicester's Silver Arcade and had to agree that it was the smartest he had ever been, if you discounted the baseball boots. He picked up his keys and left the house feeling magnetic.

He hurried to The Bell Inn, the wind fighting him all the way. As he got closer he could hear the muffled laughter and voices spilling out into the night. He was in good spirits and his expression of manic eagerness could easily be read. Once at the bar it seemed almost empty. Maybe it was because he was the first out of his local mates to arrive. He sat with a draught beer, staring at the rinsed glasses until a voice shook him from his day dreaming.

'You alright?' asked Rob.

'Yeah not bad.'

The six foot, well built, short curly dark ginger hair shape of Rob leant down on the bar next to him. He had a cheeky grin surrounded by designer-stubble and was dressed in denim. He was clever with words, even having failed his English O'Level, spitefully funny with a cackle of a laugh and a passion for vandalism. The tall lanky figure of Nick arrived next. With light brown hair parted in the middle, in a bright red jumper, he had the same kind of spiteful humour. He gave a welcoming jeer and patted the Foster's lager pump hoping it would goad one of them into buying the next round. Then there was Aidy, a bit of a Sylvester Stallone character. Well built, he attracted the girls all too easily. Not that he was picky – he was only ever interested in one thing. They had all known each other for some time now and had become regular pub drinking pals sharing an acute sense of humour making one another laugh with a single wisecrack.

Slowly the place began to fill with people, a lot he knew, but they were nothing more than pub acquaintances. Getting bored with the conversation which revolved around cars and football, Jay went to get something stronger, a snake bite, which guaranteed severe drunkenness within a very short space of time. On his return, Rob's voice drifted across to him and they started to discuss their past holiday in Corfu. They studied each other like knives ready to strike on someone, any chance to take the piss out of each other could not be missed. All of them together drunk was a lethal combination of ill respect for anything or anyone including themselves.

The pub became more and more crowded, particularly with under age drinkers, so it started to get a youth club feel. Further pub friends began to waltz over to join the general chatter, someone would say, 'did you see that programme on...?' and launch the weekly TV review.

Jay squinted from the brightness of the bar and at that point he decided to get drunk, purely out of boredom.

'Whiskey... Jameson loaded with ice please.'

He leant on the bar and fingered the ice in his glass and stared at the amber liquid.

'Jay?'

He had drifted into thought, he didn't recognise the voice and turned to its direction without thought.

'Karen!' he chirped after a short pause to allow his brain to put a name to the face. 'It's been a long time.'

The next question was obvious so before she had chance to ask he went straight into what he was currently doing in his life. Karen used to sit next to him in art class at school. Although they never officially went out with each other, they did spend a lot of time in each other's company. She talked dirty to him and allowed him to feel her legs in full stockings and suspenders which was great for a fifteen year old and was probably why art quickly became his favourite subject.

'Lived out any of your fantasies yet?' he mused before taking a sip at his drink as if he quickly shied away from the question.

'What about your black cherry yogurt one?' she smiled.

'No I haven't,' he grinned, 'I'm saving it for you.'

'Oh but I hear you're married to the bar and have a mistress.' And to that he smiled as he glanced over to see Trac before him, so perfect too, his smile widened further. This was the makings of a great night.

He wandered up to Trac and passed her a small glass of creamy light brown liquid and a few cubes of ice popping out of its surface.

'Here I got you a drink,' he smiled.

'What is it?'

'Baileys. You'll like it, trust me.'

She didn't look too convinced until she had taken a sip.

'Like it?'

She gave a polite nod and said, 'it's busy.'

'Yeah it usually is. Who are you here with?'

'Boyfriend.'

'The Doctor.'

'Student Doctor.'

'Well, it's what he's going to be that counts isn't it?'

She didn't respond to the question. He figured she either didn't hear him or he was stepping on taken territory.

'Did my sister give you my letter at school?'

'Yeah,' she replied and gave a little nod again.

'So where is he?'

'At the bar,' and she nodded to her right.

He could see a dark haired chap wearing a blue and white striped top. When he noticed his hands move around the glasses in front of him and begin to turn it was time for him to go.

'I guess I'll see you Sunday?' he asked.

'Yeah,' she replied.

He moved back and gave a half hearted smile to the guy coming towards them and he did the same in return.

Near closing time he sat chewing a straw from his empty glass. The barmaid nearby was wiping the black veneered bar top with a wet folded rag. One more for the road, all he seemed to picture was a crystal cut glass loaded with whiskey glittering as it bounced off the ice in all directions. When it was placed in front of him it bared no resemblance to his dream, it looked somehow limp compared to his refreshing thought, but he knocked it back all the same. Drunk with his mates, the euphoria of it put a exuberant smile across his face. Well life doesn't get much better than this he though as he eased himself off the bar stool.

'And now... pissed from The Bell,' he jeered as he staggered towards the exit.

As they spilled out into the street the noise increased as they were briefly entertained by a huge argument involving a bloke and two women. Jay was too pissed to work out what it was all about, but burst out laughing when one of the girls shouted to the other 'You fuckin' slag!' and grabbed at her hair.

'The Bell,' he chuckled, 'never short on quality entertainment.'

It was events like this that gave The Bell Inn its bad name, even people fifteen miles away had been known to have said, 'you don't want to go there, it's rough.'

The small upset ended in tears, apologies and hugs. Aidy had disappeared with a short dark-haired girl with 'large fun bags' as he called them, while the remaining three staggered off towards home, but not before desperately trying to jam two pence and five pence pieces into the newsagents' bubble gum vending machines. Rob couldn't leave it without trying to prise it off the wall, 'The fucker's nicked my money,' he roared kicking and pulling at the steel box desperately.

'Rob, what the fuck are you doing?' said Jay softly trying to calm him.

'It's fucking robbed me the bastard!'

'Shit you're pissed... leave it.'

A single flash of blue light turned their attentions to the two men climbing out of the abruptly halted car, adjusting their hats they approached them with swift ease. The first police officer looked them up and down 'What are you guys up to?'

Jay smirked, 'we're not up to anything,' he said adopting his best sarcastic tone.

Rob had no love for the police, despite his girlfriend's father being a chief constable. He tried every opportunity to get their backs up, taking pleasure in pushing as far as he could without ever getting arrested, somehow he always succeeded.

'Bollocks,' he roared.

'Stop swearing,' grunted the second officer firmly.

'Fucking hell,' he mumbled.

'If you don't calm down I'll be forced to arrest you.'

'What for?' spat Rob. 'I've got a disease... I can't stop swearing.'

Jay glared, waiting for a chance to strike, but Nick pulled him back and they crossed the street with swaggering impertinence. Rob frowned, lit a cigarette, smiled at the officers and followed silently, concentrating on his footing.

Wednesday, February 8

'Nice of you to drop by,' said Jay.

His sister looked up from her kneeling position and felt uneasy about being caught sifting through his music collection as if it was indexed for public use.

'I was just looking for that song you were playing the other night.'

'And there's me thinking you were returning something.'

'God,' she snapped in response. 'I only want to tape it,' and jumped to her feet.

'Record,' he said putting out his hand to retrieve it from her thieving mitts.

'I don't mind if you borrow any of mine,' she said calmly handing it over.

'Umm, Bucks Fizz,' he said laced with sarcasm.

'Yeah right! I haven't listened to them since I was about ten.'

He chuckled and put his art box on his desk and noticed a small blue handmade envelope, it looked like a tiny parcel, 'what's this?' he asked picking it up.

'Oh, Tracey gave it to me.'

He sat down on the edge of his bed flipping the mini letter between his fingers pondering as to its importance.

'Are you going to read it then?'

With that he rose to his feet and muttered, 'what you got to do round here to get a little privacy.'

His sister scuttled off out of his way, in a blink of an eye she had disappeared into her own room. He leaned into his chest of drawers and thumbed his way through a few tapes before choosing The Adventures' 'Sea of Love' album. He eased back down onto his bed and opened the letter. As the first song fizzled out he'd read it a number of times... she had fallen out with her boyfriend, unsure as to how she was feeling about it all in between the crying and being glad. He massaged his brow in thought wondering if there was any significance as the remaining part of her letter informed him that her mock exams had now finished and how well she had done in commerce, geography and chemistry washed over him. She'd asked if he could get over, that it would be good to see him. With muted eyes he folded the letter back up and pushed it into his back pocket.

The sky was the colour of lint, white, grey and limp. The wind came in gusts, it numbed his face and whipped his hair. He pulled his collar up on his leather jacket to ward off the chill. The cold of the day made him miserable and he longed for a blue sky with a bright sun. Frosted grass made a pleasant sound he thought as he trundled along, head bowed with his art folder under one arm. As he walked briskly up Trac's drive, he began to feel a warmth seep through him. He rang the doorbell and saw her silhouette through the patterned glass come towards him. The lock made a click and she appeared wearing a long sleeved grey T-shirt, faded blue jeans and thin black socks. She looked as though she had been crying and was clutching a clear mug of tea and a scrunched up tissue.

'Hi,' she smiled pleased to see him.

'It's freezin' out here,' he mumbled. 'You okay?'

She nodded lightly and welcomed him with a half smile.

'What have you got there?' she asked sizing the large black folder in his right hand.

'This,' he said waving the video in his left, 'is *Friday the Thirteenth Part 2*. I picked it up on the way home from college. We can watch it later if you want.'

'No, silly, the folder.'

'Oh right, my portfolio.'

She frowned at him, distracting him for a second or two. '...erm well you said you wanted to see some of my work so I thought well...' and he gave a shrug.

She wandered to her room and over to her stereo. As he followed he looked about, waiting to feel a point in which he could relax. Like him she loved music. He watched her for a while, toying through her selection of CDs as if she was in a trance or just unsure of what to put on.

'Thanks for lending me these CDs,' she said, 'do you want them back?'

'No,' he smiled, putting his folder down. 'I haven't got a player anyway.' She frowned at him again as that struck her as a bit odd. He noted her confused expression and offered up his reason.

'I'm getting one for my birthday and Christmas so at least this way I'll have built up a collection. I just tape them at my dad's for the time being.' She put Deacon Blue's 'Raintown' on and sat down on her bed looking fragile as he took her through his work, hoping to cheer her up or at least distract her for a time. Not knowing any of the famous artists or designers he mentioned didn't stop it from becoming interesting.

'Botticelli,' he said with surprise, 'you don't know who Botticelli is?' She looked at him blankly waiting for an insight.

'Well if you saw some of his work you'd recognise it, say *The birth of Venus*?'

She shook her head vaguely.

'The naked lady standing with a huge shell behind her,' and used his hands in order to simulate the shape.

'Oh I think I know what you mean,' she agreed still looking slightly vague. 'I see the point of old paintings but I don't really understand all the modern art.'

'It's just a case of whether it's a piece that is aesthetic to the eye or whether it's a piece that makes you think, question it, or is making a point. Therefore it becomes interesting on that level alone, which is pretty much where most of modern art falls. A lot of it looks on the dark side of things, which I guess all art that intends to be fairly serious does.' He smiled, 'I don't know, I'm no expert but I love all the bright, positive artwork. I'm biased I know, but I love anything that's creative; TV, music, design, architecture, fashion. The thing with graphic design is it has many crossovers into those fields, so it never really gets boring and to be fair I get bored so very easily.'

'Sounds like a lot more to it than I thought.'

'It's all about the ideas,' he said. 'Being resourceful.'

She smiled profoundly. 'Well it's good that you're doing something you enjoy.'

'It's just in me. I guess the only thing with design is that self expression is restricted. That said, if I did stuff that was really personal I'd have to be torn away from it to let it go.'

'I don't know how you come up with the ideas.'

'Reference, inspiration... you get a brief.' He smiled, pleased that she was showing a keen sense of interest. 'Sometimes I just carry a pencil and pad around in case I get ideas or see something of interest.'

'Have you always wanted to do this?'

'I pretty much decided to become a graphic designer without ever having met one, or any real idea of what was involved. I realised that I didn't have the artistic ability or patience to spend months on end alone in a room working on a painting or whatever. I saw record sleeves and movie posters and thought this is good, it's like art and it was New Order's 'True Faith' record sleeve that really helped me say yeah I want to do this.'

'Who designed it?'

'Peter Saville.'

'You just made that up.'

'No, I haven't.'

'Hmm,' she said quietly, looking up at him with a bizarre expression from the poised sitting position she still held on her bed.

'Really... Okay I admit that the only reason I know that is cos, as well as taking a folder of my art stuff from school to my interview at Loughborough, I took a few items that inspired me at the time. One of the things was the cover to New Order's 'Blue Monday'. It went down really well, apart from the fact the guy asked me the same question and didn't know so I found out a few days later and phoned him up and told him.'

'Really?' she queried.

'No, not really,' he whistled.

'You sod!'

He chuckled 'No, it's true, I wasn't having you on. My bullshit answer could've been Neville Brody who's in at the moment as an influence, but I chose to be honest, that's all.'

'Who's he?'

'He's the wizard behind that,' and he pointed across to the small table at the end of her bed.

'What?' she quizzed looking about her.

'*The Face* magazine.'

'Oh,' she paused for a moment then said, 'this is all new to me.'

'There's a good article in this week's *NME* on sleeve design. I'll have to show it to you,' he smiled. 'It would be cool if I got to do one for a real big band.'

'Maybe you could do one for Kylie and Jason.'

'Not a chance,' he sneered.

'You might get paid a fortune,' she smiled.

'Irrelevant,' he shook his head in disdain. 'Wouldn't do it. I'd rather die.' She chuckled, 'maybe that's what you could end up doing?'

'I'd have to go and live in London and I don't want to do that,' he shrugged blithely. 'Besides it's supposed to be really badly paid, and truth be known, it's the fans of the music that make the covers more special than they really are.'

'Like you and New Order.'

'Probably... but you should know from a sleeve what kind of record it is and I think that's not always achieved. But they're simple, modern and yet classic all at the same time... timeless.'

'Mmm.'

'It's only a shame that vinyl is fading out cos CD covers are too small, you don't get the same impact.'

'So might that be why you still have my Wonder Stuff album? Must be getting on for what... four months?'

He chuckled softly, 'really is it that long?' and scratched at his head. 'Well it does have a cool Andy Warhol style cover.'

'Mmm,' she frowned and returned to his folder. 'I like the cartoons you've done.' She smiled, picking one up from his folder.

'Yeah, my mum likes the cartoon stuff, everything else just seems to wash over her.'

'What about your dad, I bet he's impressed?'

He chuckled. 'Don't be daft, he's a businessman. He doesn't care about stuff like this.' He gave out a shrug. 'Apparently if I want to be creative I can do that in my spare time so I figure it's okay to have my mum on side.'

'That's good. I'm sure my mum wants me to go into nursing but there's no way of telling her that it's not going to happen.'

'Well it's a case of saying I know where I'm going and I don't have to be what you want me to be.'

'You make it sound so simple.'

'It is.'

'So you're going to be this rich designer, driving around in a flash car?'

'I don't know... money, careers, material things, I don't get it, all I want to be is happy and independent. Idealism over materialism. That said though a Harley Davidson would be cool.'

'Well I'm very impressed,' she said positively.

'You're about the only person who is. I sketched Shelley a couple of times but it didn't seem to get her interested in what I did.'

Trac wasn't sure what to say to that so she reached for her boots. 'I don't think Mum and Dad are going out now. Can we watch the movie at your dad's?'

'Yeah, he's not in anyway.'

He zipped up his folder and leant it against her wardrobe and put his jacket back on.

'Here, you've forgot this one.'

'That one's for you,' he smiled.

'I can't take that.'

'Yes you can. I want you to have it.'

'Why?'

'Because... it won't quite make it to my end of year show,' he gave a lethargic shrug, 'and you're the only person believing in me right now.'

'Are you sure?'

'Yeah I'm sure.' He smiled and tapped at his chin in thought and looked around her room for where it could be placed. The Cure's 'Boys Can't Wait' poster would have to stay, so that meant the Spencer Rowell L'enfant poster would have to go.

'Maybe...'

'No,' Trac replied jumping up in front of it.

'But it's just a guy holding a baby?'

Trac remained in her protective position with a stern looking brow.

'Okay,' he smiled. 'I'll leave it with you.'

Trac loved movies and Jay thought it was a big plus for a girl to not confuse *Star Wars* with *Star Trek*. She had jumped several times during the film and that made him enjoy the movie all the more. They lay back to back on the floor and found it effortless to talk freely when there was no eye contact. She asked him if he had written to Shelley and he replied with a 'no.'

'You miss her though?'

'Sometimes,' he replied. 'But she's gone and there's nothing I can do.'

'Do you feel bad... you know, about how it ended?'

'Not really. At the end of the day it was nobody's fault. I don't see the relationship as a failure, she just had no choice but to go with her family.'

'I'm glad that you've got over her, and to do that you haven't had to forget her completely.'

'Yeah... me too.'

'And Sue?'

'What about her?' he replied vaguely.

He guessed she wanted to talk about his relationships so she could put hers into perspective, not that he had seen much of Sue recently. It was nearly Friday, so he figured their paths would cross in The Bell. In the comfortable silence that followed he sat on the couch as she sat on two sofa cushions on the floor, one of his calves at either side of her, her back against the sofa, neck and shoulders supported by its front edge, her head bent back, resting between his thighs. He played with her hair, taking up strand after strand and curling each around a finger, pushing four fingers under a section of hair, lifting it up and pulling it gently away from the skin, rubbing a small area of her head at a time, his hands moving slowly across her head, over and over.

'I suppose I'm just a romantic, dreams of being in a relationship like in those stupid books.'

'There's nothing wrong in that,' he smiled.

He wanted to look after her and found it was good to feel needed. So he comforted her and gave her the support she needed, just as she had been there for him even before Shelley had gone.

'I'm sorry but I best go home,' she said quietly.

She went to thank him but he stopped her midway, 'shhh!' he whispered putting an index finger to his lower lip. 'You don't have to thank me,' he said faintly and she smiled, content with her friend.

'Come on,' he smiled. 'I'll walk you back.'

Thursday, February 9

A young slim slender girl approached and rested her elbows onto the rolled edge of the wooden bar and leaned forward.

'Hi,' she smiled.

Jay looked up from slicing a lime and replied, 'hi,' and glanced across to his fellow barmen.

'Are you serving?'

He studied the girl for a second or two, taking in her mousey blonde curls that fell about her face. He placed the cut lime to the side and ran his hands briefly under the small brushed steel tap and wiped them to the sides of his apron.

'Sure,' he smiled. 'What you after?'

The girl bit the bottom of her lip and seemed to lean further towards him clutching a black leather purse in both hands as she did so.

'Not really sure...' she murmured looking at the list of cocktails on the chalk board behind him.

'After a cocktail?'

'Yeah, three... but I'm not sure what though?'

'What do you girls normally drink? Gin, rum, vodka?'

'Vodka,' she smiled.

'That's easy... You've got your Black Russian which is vodka, Kahlua, ice and Pepsi, or Blue Pacific which is Blue Curacao, vodka, bit of a shake with a splash of lemonade and floated with cream.' He made a circular motion with his right hand. 'Then,' he continued, 'there's the classic Harvey Wallbanger, vodka, fresh orange juice topped with Galliano. Or the Japanese Boat which is melon-flavoured Midori, shaken with vodka, cream and Galliano.'

'Which three do you recommend?'

He waved his hand slightly and said, 'forget about the Japanese Boat.'

'Okay,' she beamed and he set to work.

The Helsinki bar was one of the top bars in town but that didn't concern Jay, it just made it harder work. But free drinks, entrance to a nightclub and a cab home did support his truer vocation. He engaged the girl with small talk as he swiftly sliced, poured and shook away as he made sure each one looked every bit the perfect drink.

'So... do you get to go out after work?'

'Yeah, most times we finish up and pop in the Bear Cage.'

'Tonight?'

'I'm not sure?'

She sucked some of the Black Russian up through the straw and said, 'I think you should go tonight.'

He placed the last cocktail on the bar and studied her eyes momentarily before lightly nodding. 'Maybe,' he said with a smile.

Saturday, February 11

Jay squinted hard then drew back, his face taking in the cartoon he had drawn onto a near perfect letter he had written out a second time in order to look as neat as possible. It had taken several hours but it was worth every bit of effort as Trac seemed to be occupying his mind most of the time. He got change and made his way into town. Trac worked in the Western Jean Company near the clock tower on Saturdays and he made a point of calling in to see her whenever he could. As he trundled down to the lower level she was behind the till leaning on the counter with her head in her hands looking totally bored. Great eyes, terrific legs and a cute bum he thought as he reached the bottom step. She sprang to life with a big smile as soon as she saw him and he felt instantly glad he had made the trip.

'Hi,' he said smiling back at her. 'I'm sorry if I look a little rough.' He rubbed his hands briskly over his face to try and give it some colour. 'I had a bit too much to drink last night. Getting up this morning wasn't easy and I've got a bit of a sore throat too.'

'What happened to your face?'

He felt at his chin until he came to a graze, 'oh that?' and wondered if her concern was merely confirmation as to whether he'd fallen or been in a fight. 'I sort of fell out of a moving car,' he smiled.

'What do you mean, sort of?'

'Well, all my mates were off from the pub somewhere without me, so I tried to dive through one of the windows as the bastards were leaving. I guess at some point I just fell back out.'

'While it was moving?'

He gave a shrug. 'Yeah I think so.'

'You're crazy,' she said scrunching her face up a little.

He continued to feel his graze and mumbled, 'I guess it's what you call an occupational hazard.'

'Hmm,' she murmured, not convinced with his somewhat aloof statement.

'Anyway, talking of cars, I put in for my driving test Thursday. And,' he grinned, 'I wrote you a letter.'

Her face became open and friendly once more. 'Can I read it now?'

'Sure,' he said and passed her the small letter from his back pocket and she almost snatched it with excitement.

'So, how's school?' he asked trying to hold onto her attention.

'Boring as usual,' she replied with a sigh, 'you just get treated like a kid.'

'I know what you mean. I couldn't be doing with all that authoritarian bullshit,' he said with a wry smile.

School for him had been an uncomfortable union. 'Still,' he continued 'I did have some good times, usually involved in some kind of mischief or other.'

She smirked, 'you haven't changed then!'

'Nope not much,' he replied. 'You got time for a coffee or something?'

'Yeah,' she smiled positively, 'just give me two minutes.'

Sunday, February 12

For the first few hours, Jay enjoyed having the marathon driving lesson from his brother Shaun. It had highs such as how to do a handbrake turn, and lows of being reminded, just as most things since birth, that the car was being handed down. For some reason though it felt as if there was some kind of debt with this one, or maybe it was the realisation that his brother wasn't ever coming back from London and this would be the last item to be passed over. Even on the way to get a tank of petrol he felt a sense of responsibility, but became more preoccupied with who was going to pay. It wasn't so easy to convince your brother you were skint.

At the garage Jay, after filling the tank, was relieved at the sight of Shaun thumbing through an open wallet and proceeded to hand him the money.

'I'll get it off Dad,' he said as he retrieved the *Highway Code* from the open glove box. Jay wondered whether he was now about to methodically go through a stream of questions?

'Don't worry about that,' he smiled. 'I'll get Trac to test me later.'

'Okay. I'll drop you off.'

'Yeah, fine,' he replied and wandered off to pay.

Jay stared out into the street, watching the corner and waiting for Trac to appear. His face slowly illuminated as she made her way towards the house. Bag over her shoulder she took small steps and walked with a swing of the hips. He padded his khaki green shirt to his chest and then darted to the front door.

'What can you do for kicks around here then?' he said as he opened the door to greet her.

'You've started to notice then,' she replied sticking her bottom lip out, 'it's dead boring.'

He made her a drink and they sat on the large beige comfy curved sofa listening to some music of his dad's and supping tea.

'U2's 'Joshua Tree'?' he suggested and she shrugged as if to say 'whatever.' It was fairly easy listening that agreed with them both, they also had use of a half decent Chris Rea album and some Roxy Music. The rest of his collection failed to impress, there was only a Hot Chocolate LP that had a slim chance of getting a play.

By now they had spent quite a number of Sundays together. Even though it was supposed to be the day he had time with his dad, he decided that seeing Trac was much more fun. Making an open fire for her to ward off the remaining wintry chill wasn't as easy as first thought and he soon gave into Trac's keenness to take charge of the situation. As she sat cross-legged in front of the fire, she was waving her hands about screaming as they were fast becoming as black as the coal. He couldn't remove the smile from his face. Covered in dust, she was as cute as could be.

As the day drew to a close he spent the last hour or so at her house. He played with her teddies as always, using them as a barrier to shield his vulnerability. He didn't like Penny the Panda much but the small beige bear was his favourite. He brought him to life easily, making him climb up her shin to her knee then slide him down her thigh.

'Weeee,' he sang and made her giggle and occasionally look at him inquisitively as he continued to make the bear run about her body and up to her chin.

'How come you can be so soft one minute and a bad boy the next?'

'Me bad?'

'Making me assist you in taking the car out for a spin.'

'Mmm... okay I'm bad, but you could've stopped me,' he smiled comfortably.

He knew she had enjoyed being bad too, he noted the wild look in her eyes as she allowed the excitement to rise within as he grabbed at the keys. He loved her energy, she sparkled with curiosity and it charged him even more. He loved to run free and, being eighteen, he got away with it, and he knew it.

'I really enjoyed today, spending time with you,' he said in a mild way, still toying with the small bear.

'Good... and I'm glad I'm not quite what you imagined.'

'And me... soft and bad?'

'Yep,' she nodded positively. 'And you make me laugh too.'

'That's good then, isn't it?'

She nodded again. 'It's nice to feel so close and comfortable with someone even though there are no bonds. It's like I'm not worried that I'm making a fool of myself with you.' She treated him to a smile, 'next time you can get your hands covered in coal dust.'

He let out a big enough yawn for the two of them and stretched out all four limbs at the same time before ruffling his hair.

'Sure... anytime,' he smiled expansively as he stood up. 'I better go, Mum's picking me up from my dad's.'

'Okay,' she said with a disappointed tone.

'I'll catch you later...' he said with a burst of energy hoping to lift one last smile from her. 'Write me a letter or something.'

Wednesday, February 14

Jay and Sue sat at a corner table next to the window in the Helsinki supping their drinks. Sue had a rum and cola and Jay had a can of Red Stripe, which he drank straight from the can. The moon shone down elegantly through the buildings of the city, beneath which the black street lay flat and pretty much deserted, except for the odd taxi pulling up at the International Hotel opposite. There he sat in front of his girl while thinking about another, not good for his mindset for an evening out on Valentine's day. He couldn't deny that he cared for Sue, but she was so strong-minded, she lacked the openness and subsequent closeness he had with Trac. It played over and over in his head while he flipped the beer mat off the edge of the dark wooden table. His face looked almost contorted as he did battle to dumb down the issue, otherwise Sue would be in for a mediocre night and he knew that would be unfair of him.

A few cans into the evening and the place began to fill up.

'They'll probably ask you to work in a minute if it carries on like this,' said Sue as a group of about ten people flooded in. Her comment fell on deaf ears so she asked if he was okay, concerned with his manner.

'Yeah,' he said defensively. 'Why do you ask?'

'You seem a little distant, that's all.'

'Nope I'm okay,' he smiled. 'You want another drink?'

'It is a week night.'

He picked up her glass anyway and said, 'rum and Coke.' She approved. The music went up a few decibels as he approached the bar to the kind of level that made it difficult for conversation unless you were millimetres away from someone's ear. This suited him, he wasn't really in the mood for conversation. He put a double rum in her glass, hoping that she would get to the point at which she would oblige and do enough talking for them both without realising.

'You coming out after work Saturday night?' asked the guy mixing the records. Jay never really spoke to him and couldn't even be bothered to remember his name on account that he was Leicester born and bred yet had adopted a London 'cocky style' accent after spending only a single weekend down there DJing. He wondered as to whether this was somehow supposed to be the ideal DJ persona. He studied this baggy clothed individual with greasy hair, whispery moustache and bad teeth, that seemed to grab at his nob every five minutes. He had the misfortune to catch part of his banter, 'yeah I tell ya man she was on her knees sucking me. Fucking birds can't get enough of me man, I tell ya... get yourself some decks, the chicks fucking love it,' and he motioned a feeble gyrating movement with his hips. Worst still, he thought, was the catchphrase he had picked up that seemed to be doing the rounds, for Jay it was unbearable. Far from impressed he tried not to engage in any conversation and began to slide away down the bar slowly.

'Going out Saturday?' came the voice again.

'Yeah sure,' he mumbled back and looked round for someone... anyone so as to make good an escape.

'Yeah same again for me,' he said to the barmaid impatiently.

'Eh what's up man?' came the voice yet again.

'I said yeah sure. Where's everyone going?'

'Just up to the Bear Cage.'

'Oh right.'

The guy nodded back at him, holding one half of a large headphone to his left ear. Please don't, thought Jay looking into the rum and Coke desperately, please don't say it... please he pleaded and began to get agitated waiting for change.

'Yeah, top banana man. Top banana.'

Jay cringed, grabbed his beer can, and the rum and Coke and fled back to the relative safety of Sue's company.

Halfway through the can a veil of warmth hit his face and he looked pleasantly animated and resolved to be more in tune and attentive to Sue. Once he had drained the can and half of Sue's rum and Coke she detected a slight slur and flicker of loss in his eyes that meant he had reached the point of drunkenness.

'You're going to look at Northampton College tomorrow aren't you?' she asked wondering if it was about time they left.

He waved his right hand in the air as a gesture that said 'I'm alright don't worry about it'.

'It's getting late Jay,' she continued.

He looked at his bare wrist as if he had a watch and muttered something along the lines of 'yeah you're right, best only have a couple more.'

Sue pulled the straw to her lips but before she could drain her glass he was up and swaggering towards the bar, assuming the round was still the same.

'I'll just have a Coke,' she called after him.

Out of earshot he had been engulfed by the sea of people.

Thursday, February 15

'Come on you, I haven't got all day. I've got work to do,' said Jay's mum as she threw open his bedroom curtains.

Five minutes later and another shove from her and he was in the shower feeling and looking like a zombie. He turned up the temperature to as hot as he could handle and sat in a fairly uncomfortable cross-legged position with elbows resting on his knees and head in hands, slipping shortly into a foetal position as he waited for the water to do its magic and bring him back to a reasonable level of life.

'Come on,' came his mum's voice and a tap on the door. 'I've got to be in Bedford first.'

He slid out of the bath tub and onto the mound of towels he had gathered on the floor. Slowly he managed to emerge from them dry and fresh looking.

He made his way down the stairs, wrestling a black T-shirt on as he went to find his mum sitting at the kitchen table with a coffee and what seemed to be a pile of college prospectuses.

'I've been looking at some of these colleges as well.'

'Mum, you're going to college? That's great,' he chirped as he reached for a mug from the cupboard.

'Look, do you want to end up working in a warehouse six days a week?' she snapped.

'It's only February.'

'Then it will be March, then it will be April,' she moaned. 'You have to start applying now.'

'Maybe I'll take a year out,' he smirked.

'And do what exactly?'

'I don't know,' he responded in an amusing tone.

'Not while you're under this roof. You can go and live with your dad.' He repeated her words in an almost silent mumble and she glared at him as he did so, so he frowned back and took a sip of his tea.

'I thought I could drop you off at the college for an hour and then take you into the centre of Northampton for some lunch.'

She passed him the Nene College prospectus and he took it without a word giving into the day ahead. He appreciated that she was only trying to steer him to carry on with his education because she cared, yet he couldn't help feeling a lack of motivation. September after all, he thought, was a lifetime away.

'I thought you could come with me tomorrow, then you could look at the college in Derby.'

Again he decided not to retaliate too strongly and just said, 'yeah alright, I'll think about it.'

'Maybe your dad could find you a nice office job?'

'Look,' he replied to that sternly. 'I'm not one of those guys in a suit... I'm not a corporate body... that's just not me and you've got to let me be me.' She seemed relatively pleased that at least he had some direction in which to take his life.

'Have a look at these colleges too.'

He took the pile from her, 'okay I'll read them in the car.'

Northampton wasn't too bad and the visit to Derby on Friday opened his mind up to the fact that going to another college was going to be better than getting a job at least. Truth was, he wanted to stay at Loughborough, only trouble was, he didn't even have a slim chance of remaining and besides both Adrian and Dave were leaving too, so it wouldn't be the same anyway.

Saturday, February 18

Jay didn't get out of bed until about two pm and lazed about until it was time to head off to the Helsinki. With little in the way of communication and a sluggish manner he made his way through the evening before floating off to a club without much thought.

The twenty five year old accountant that had spent the last thirty minutes making a play for him in the Bear Cage seemed to slowly blur in front him. He could see her lips move but nothing she said seemed of interest anymore and he began to wonder what he was doing. He made a conscious note that he was going to leave, none of the people he was with seemed to matter to him, they all seemed way too pretentious and none of them were on the same page as him as far as humour went. His booze fuelled disdain for Top Banana did not go unnoticed and besides, he was starting to get frowned upon for giving out too many free drinks. He scrawled down his plan of action on the back of a beer mat so as not to forget his drunken decision; *Leave the Helsinki, they're all cunts!* and placed it in his back pocket. Half an hour later he still wished he was a long, long way away from here, lying still, peaceful and warm, drifting to sleep in another's arms.

'Can't do this... sorry,' he chuntered and he retreated to the pavement outside and hailed a cab.

Sunday, February 19

Jay was removing the L plates off the car and thanking his dad for the lesson as Trac came round the corner. She smiled at him and asked, 'how'd it go?'

'Born natural,' he smiled.

'Not too hungover from last night?'

'No, not too bad. I didn't stop much after work.'

She followed him into the house studying the *i-D* magazine she was holding.

'Do you know that Iceland have some jelly sweets called spunk!'

'Really?'

'Yeah, they come in four colours and are tadpole shape.'

'And you buy that mag for stuff like that?'

'Nooo,' she smiled, 'it's fashion. It says in here that flares are coming back in.'

'Yeah right,' he chuckled. 'I for one am not going to be wearing them.'

'Well I'm at least going to have to get you into a pair of Levi's.'

'Okay,' he said. 'You sort me a pair out and I'll have them.'

'Righty o,' she smiled as she wriggled her feet out of her shoes.

He noticed for the first time how attractive her neck was as she took her coat off and adjusted her top to get comfy. When he complimented her upon it she said it was too thin and pointed to the slight hollows either side where her neck met her shoulders, 'Mum calls them my salt sellers.'

'Did you watch the Brits?'

'Yeah, it was awful.'

'I mean I know Sam Fox has big... you know, but she can't present, stick to-'

'Showing your tits?'

He nodded with a smile lethargically and said, 'okay what do you want to do?'

'Don't mind, whatever.'

'I've brought *Nine and a Half Weeks* over, I thought we could watch that.'

'You've seen it though.'

'Yeah, but you haven't.'

'Good o,' she agreed positively.

She sat erectly on the edge of the sofa, palms upwards in the air, her face expressionless yet somehow emitting a relaxed glow.

'Guinness?' he asked.

She gave a shrug and said, 'don't know whether I like it.'

He passed her his can and she took it. It looked quite large in her hand as she brought it to her lips and took a taste. Her face initially scrunched up but then seemed to mellow out somewhat.

'Not convinced are you?' he said.

'Umm no... it's okay,' she smiled, taking another sip.

'You sure? I can make you a tea or something?'

She licked the brown stout residue from her lips as she passed him the can back. 'I'm okay, put the movie on.'

Folding his arms, he sat back on the sofa and extended himself outward and she joined him. As the film started the atmosphere in the room was instantly cosy.

Thursday, February 23

The sky was dull and rain swept down the street, whipped up by a swirling wind. It was a miserable night. The rain increased its speed as a shivering Jay and Adrian repeatedly burst into short runs as they reached the final stretch down to Loughborough railway station.

'Fucking hell,' shouted Adrian, 'there's the fucking train.'

Jay huddled his art box and folder close and decided not to break into another run, there was no way they were going to make it. Adrian's body had changed into a silhouette and all he could see was his folder bumping against his hips as he ran. Jay entered the station and made his way across the footbridge and down the slate coloured steps leading to the sombre looking platform that looked more gloomy than he had imagined. He saw Adrian pull his long grey coat heavy in rain around himself tightly, cursing in defeat.

'Didn't quite make it then?'

'I'm fucking frozen,' wheezed Adrian.

'I could do with just going to bed, I'm knackered.'

'Well gutted you went clubbing last night and didn't invite me.'

'I wasn't planning to, besides they were old school mates.'

'Yeah, and all three of them women.'

'Well I got a party coming up if you fancy it?'

'Where?'

'The Cove.'

'Cove?'

'Yeah it's a pub, they've got a bit in the basement for parties and that.'

'Sounds good.'

'Yeah it's not a bad place to meet girls and get really pissed. You'd love it.'

'Who are you going with?'

'Sue, it's one of her mate's birthdays.'

'Gives me something to look forward to, cheers.'

'Just one thing.'

'What's that?'

'Don't mention tangerines... in fact don't mention any kind of fruit.'

Adrian chuckled, 'no problem.'

'So when's the next train?'

'Half an hour,' muttered Adrian.

'Don't worry, you'll be back in time to see Dirty Den get shot.'

'I'm not watching it now he's out of it.'

'I hardly watch it anyway.'

They positioned themselves at the far side of the platform and leaned uncomfortably against the wall. Jay was hugging himself helplessly as the wind came in gusts and chilled his pale face. 'I can't wait till I pass my test,' he muttered.

His soaking wet jacket began to slowly dampen his jumper and seep through further to his skin, making his teeth chatter and goose bumps break out.

The rain became heavier and heavier, pelting forcefully and attacking the station. He watched the increasing flow of water run along the dark dappled platform and gurgle into a drain. Damming the flow with his foot, water leaked under his boot. Transfixed by this image, he managed to let his imagination take him away from the cold until Adrian started swearing again. He was sat on the damp bench, water saturated his jeans and the stench of burnt oil and urine was tipping him over the edge as he manically flipped his young persons rail card between his fingers .

'I hate missin' the train, especially when it's fucking like this.'

The smell of bacon wafting in the air from the food hatch on the opposite platform set Jay's stomach rumbling. A flurry of water then dripped on him from above making him wince as a trickle ran down his neck.

'You want a cup of tea?' he asked abruptly pushing himself from the wall.

'I got no money.'

'Don't worry, I'll get you one.'

'Yeah, cheers.'

His mouth began to water as the lights of the hatchway became brighter and closer. As soon as he held the bacon roll in his hand he studied the photo of this fine looking food behind the counter and realised that what he held in his hand was a very pathetic imitation. He held the cob in his mouth, picked up the two styrofoam cups and made his way back to Adrian. The warm, greasy butter melted and oozed out, dripping down his chin as he approached Adrian who raised a smile as he clutched the warm cup with steam still emanating from the hole in the lid.

'Cheers mate,' he said.

The announcement of their train gave further relief, and as it bounded into the station and halted with a long drawn out eerie screech, their hearts and spirits lifted.

Saturday, February 25

Jay spent the morning working at the bar. As soon as he finished the shift at one, he smartened himself up as best he could and went to see Trac at the jean shop.

He crept up behind her and said, 'hello' loudly, making her jump slightly.

'What you do that for?'

He gave a shrug and watched her continue to fold some jeans up, looking very tight lipped.

'Tough morning?'

'Yeah it's been real hectic, one of the girls is off sick.'

'Will you allow me to take you away from it then?'

'Can you manage to entertain me for an hour?'

'Absolutely,' he smiled positively as he pulled out a small brown envelope. 'Just got paid, ten hours work. I figure there's enough in here to have a good time. Arcade?'

'You've not left yet then?'

'No, but I will... soon. Just need another job, preferably not a Saturday night.'

Trac was wearing her black polo neck jumper, and a pair of jeans that were terribly ripped at the knees and bum, she had some sort of tight black shorts underneath. She informed him of how much she loved those jeans as they strolled across the road towards the arcade.

'Yeah, you look good in them,' he said and resisted the temptation to give her bottom a squeeze. 'Pinball?' he suggested.

Jay could hardly contain his desire at watching Trac get excited by the steel ball, flashing lights and ping ping of the machine. She jumped up and down and clapped her hands with joy as the digital score clocked higher and higher. He pulled coin after coin from his pocket pleased to watch her take it from his hand and feed it into the slot.

'You did well then,' he said with pleasure.

'I'm worn out,' she smiled and leaned her body to him to catch her breath.

The two of them strolled back towards High Street and headed for a nearby café. Finding a table at the back they nestled comfortably into the padded wooden chairs.

'I had a good night last night,' he mused as he added an extra sugar to his tea.

'Did you go down The Bell?'

'Yeah. I nipped in the Arms too, it was real busy.'

'Drunk?'

'Of course,' he said proudly.

Snippets of the night came back in flashes and made him raise wry smiles that made Trac merely peer at him oddly in wonder of his thoughts.

They talked and talked, about all kinds of things, Shelley, parents, alcohol, music, love, sex, school, anything and everything.

'It's fun to be with you, you cheer me up.'

'Thanks.'

'And you enjoy spending time with me?'

He smiled lightly and sipped at his tea, she could clearly read his 'yes' reply expressed only in his eyes and she liked that about him. Jay took a mouthful of his tea and watched her with interest as she swirled the remaining liquid in her cup. She looked at him in a pleasing way and said 'Do you...'

'Do I what?'

'Doesn't matter.'

'No, go on.'

'I just wondered if you think you will be as happy with someone else again?' she asked.

'You find the right person and anything is possible,' he murmured and gave a slight lift of his shoulders.

'And love?'

He returned to his occasional attractive smile, rolled his eyes, but said nothing.

'You're always smiling,' she said.

'Smiling... I wasn't aware of that, if it bothers you I can stop,' he said softly.

She shook her head lightly, 'I like it when you smile.' Shyly she prompted him again, 'so are you going to answer my question?'

He pondered further and said, 'I hope so.'

An opportunity to open up, to put himself out there, but his heart pounded as a wave of fear immersed him. He suddenly felt awkward so he said nothing, just rolled his eyes upwards and then back down to her, 'I'll see you tomorrow yeah?'

2. The perfect kiss

Thursday, March 2

Jay came to the conclusion that the best thing about being eighteen was that all the mates you had gone to school with were also turning eighteen and that meant parties, a lot of parties, so many that his own eighteenth do at Lutterworth Rugby Club seemed a distant memory - apart from the part where it turned into a full scale bar brawl in which his father thrived. Hmm Jay thought, a black eye for your birthday, picturing his dad patting him firmly on his back, 'now you be a man my son.'

The picturesque setting of the Stoney Cove, sunk deep in a valley by a small lake, had become a popular location for such functions. The only problem Jay seemed to be having was getting invites, particularly for Adrian.

Jay sat on the concrete wall by the lake idly throwing pebbles into the water in silence. Once he had ran out of the small stones he allowed the moon's reflection flickering on the water to captivate and somehow transfix him, so much so that he had forgotten the dilemma he had been questioned about on the journey over.

'The ticket is for me and a friend,' moaned Sue.

'I know it is, you've made me read it a million times.'

'Then how the hell is Adrian going to get in?'

'I don't know, I'll think of something,' he chuckled.

'Go on then!'

'Look, don't you worry about it, you've got an invite you can get in,' he sneered. 'If they don't let me and Adrian in we'll get pissed in the bar upstairs.'

'That's typical,' snapped Sue and put a cigarette to her lips and looked away from him across to the queue so he returned his gaze to the water.

A tap on his shoulder brought him back from his short daydream. He turned from the moonlit water to Adrian's blank face. He could see Sue's silhouette pacing up and down some way off behind him puffing away at her cigarette and getting more and more agitated by the second.

'I wonder if there's any fish in there,' said Jay plainly.

Adrian frowned at him, 'what's going on Jay?'

'Fish in the lake?'

'Erm... probably... maybe Carp.'

'Right,' he said clapping his hands and launching himself off the fence. 'This is what we are going to do.'

He marched towards Sue and put his arm tightly around her shoulders and gave her a couple of positive squeezes. 'Me and you hand over the invite. The bouncer looks at the three of us and refuses to let us in, but...' he grinned holding his index finger up in the air, 'this is the best bit right.

We all stay perfectly calm and hand over these,' and he produced two cards and a pen.

'What are they?' asked Adrian.

Jay shook his head, 'they're birthday cards,' he replied and followed it with an impatient sigh. 'If the answer is still no then we make our apologies and say we will be upstairs and could he pass the cards on.'

'And...' quizzed Sue.

'It's charm isn't it... He'll feel sorry for us and let us in.'

'Where did you get the cards?' asked Adrian taking one.

'Does that matter?'

Adrian nodded buoyantly as he read the inside of the card he had selected.

'My mum works for a card company.'

Adrian nodded again positively, he liked the plan. Sue on the other hand was less impressed. 'You're unbelievable,' she muttered.

He handed her a card and pen with a broad grin, 'your best hand writing now.'

'This is not going to work,' she complained taking them from him reluctantly.

'Lighten up, of course it's going to work, trust me.'

'And if it doesn't?'

'Okay, I'll buy the bouncer a drink and if that fails, then we can all go to the bar upstairs and get pissed.'

Jay quickly signed his name next to hers and passed Adrian the pen.

'Got the invite ready?'

'You know I have. I've made you read it a million times.'

'Oooh,' he chuckled, 'do I detect an attempt at sarcasm?'

She ignored him and searched in her bag for another cigarette.

'Ooo-kay,' he smiled, 'are we ready?'

Adrian acknowledged him enthusiastically. 'Let's go,' he said confidently.

'Sue?'

Such was the infectious nature of his heightened spirits she gave him a nod. He adjusted his black jacket, checked his hair and smiled again at her before heading for the basement entrance.

Jay's grin seemed to get wider when his plan worked moderately well. The downside was having the bouncer accept his offer of a pint.

A smooth hand over the bar surface and he felt immediately comfortable and got into position swiftly thrusting a ten pound note into the air like a flag, impatiently waving it hoping to get noticed.

'Yes?' asked the barman.

'Erm, give me a double Pernod and black and a pint of Guinness. Adrian what do you want?'

'Lager.'

Jay felt even more relaxed and happy when his hand was finally wrapped around a glass. Adrian adjusted himself on a stool next to him and they began to race through their first four or five rounds of drinks, during which time Jay occasionally made idle chat with old school friends and enemies that drifted his way.

After a few more drinks he started to circulate in a sort of stagger with a dazed expression on his face. He managed to find Sue and fondled with her in the corner leaving Adrian making slurred conversation with anyone he bumped into. All the beer Jay had consumed finally put enough pressure on his bladder for him to make the decision to relieve himself. On his way to the toilet he bumped into an old girlfriend and proceeded to follow her into the ladies and was weighing up her breasts when the bouncer came bursting in.

'What's going on?' the bouncer bellowed and puffed out his chest in order to appear larger than he actually was.

Jay splayed his arms open and shrugged his shoulders innocently as if to say 'I don't know?'

The doorman pointed his thumb towards the door, 'wrong toilet'.

Fair enough he thought. With the night still young he didn't want to offer any resistance and eased passed the bouncer with his hands up in the air smiling apologetically.

Glass empty, and no sign of his drinking partner, he weaved through the crowd of people. He stopped occasionally at a face he recognised but walked off as soon as they asked, 'So what are you doing now?' which by now was becoming boring but clearly showed an intolerant side of himself. Eventually finding Adrian nestled in the corner of the bar they reunited and continued drinking. He was now on gin and orange. Normally a pint man, he'd allowed himself to be encouraged by Adrian and was fast becoming a master spirit drinker.

'That was nice,' he smiled after a swift gulp, 'I'll have another.'

They continued talking over each other, knocking back spirits until they were both clean out of money. Worse still, Sue had refused point blank to buy him any more drinks. All they managed to do now was to swagger all over the place feeling ten feet tall as if it was their party, grazing on any loose drinks they came across.

As the night began to draw to a close, the noise level had shrunk and a few people lingered on the dance-floor. The pair's exhibition of fairly outrageous dancing and incoherent singing ended when the lights came up; music alone wasn't enough to keep things going, the night was over but at least they were proud to be both legless.

'What about 'Who Wants to be the Disco King'?' jeered Adrian.

'Yeah,' sneered Jay spitefully, 'play some fucking Wonder Stuff!'

As much as they wanted the night to go on, it was over. Sue had chosen to avoid him for most of the night, clearly not particularly overjoyed with the state he was getting in, yet somehow she still felt obliged to control him.

'Come on Jay it's time to go,' she yawned.

He frowned at her, eyes glazed, hair collapsed, 'which way?' he slurred.

'Just grab Adrian and we'll go.'

Adrian was slumped in the opposite corner to him, the two of them laughed at each other, rasping tongues and pulling faces like eight-year old children.

'You look terrible,' Sue informed him as she tried to help him to his feet.

'Oh beautiful,' he said and made a kiss with his mouth. As he slumped forward to use some kind of body language he simply smacked his head on the table and passed out. Annoyed, she began pulling on his jacket firmly until he came round and rose to his feet which took him a considerable amount of time as he refused her help.

'You go...' he kept muttering, 'leave me... save yourself,' he chuckled.

'What about Adrian?'

'I'll... I'll get Adrian,' he mumbled with a slur and made an effort to rise. It seemed to take forever to get the pair of them out of the club. After shouting 'goodbye' more than half a dozen times and wandering round in circles they finally began to leave.

'Oh, look Adrian it's a bar,' shouted Jay.

'Great I'll have a drink,' drawled Adrian.

'Two large Gins please,' he grinned followed by a chuckle.

He could see Sue thought he was joking, which was probably for the best. He was ready to surrender when the bouncers decided enough was enough, it was time to step in and escort them out the door, paying little attention to their excuses.

'Thank you and good night,' roared Jay as he stumbled towards the edge of the water and fumbled with the buttons of his jeans.

He stood there making his contribution to the Stoney Cove lake with a perplexed grin.

'A good night,' he croaked to himself and gave a few nods of his head before wandering over to Adrian who was leaning in the back window of a taxi talking to a girl.

'Have you got some paper Jay?'

'Yeah, here,' and passed him a beer mat from his pocket.

'Your cock is still hanging out,' came a giggling voice from within the taxi.

'It's not is it?' he replied looking down.

He laughed at the sight of his cock sitting quite relaxed out of his flies, 'it looks good doesn't it.'

'If you come over here I'll sort it out for you,' shouted another one of the girls.

'I bet you'd like that,' he smirked back at her and nodded his head slightly as he swayed about pushing it back inside his jeans.

'Yeah right,' she sneered sarcastically.

'Well I can manage,' he mocked and turned his back to the cab.

'It's not big enough for me anyway,' she called after him.

'Oh really,' he said raising his hands to the sky and turned back to the taxi and smiled, 'I can always tell a class lady when I see one,' and stumbled off.

As the taxi pulled off and drove passed him the girl shouted something offensive at him out of the window but he only heard 'wanker'.

'Sexy,' he muttered to himself and rambled onwards towards Sue.

Adrian walked alongside Sue's friend quietly while Jay tried his best not to argue with Sue by totally debunking the suggestion that he had drank too much.

'I don't know what the fuck you're talking about? It's a party isn't it,' he paused. 'You're supposed to get drunk.'

'There is a difference between drunk and paralytic.'

'It's not... it's not,' he stumbled and then clean forgot what the hell they were arguing about and pulled a confused face.

'I mean... I mean whatever,' he uttered.

Their taxi finally pulled up and he got into it without any fuss, all four of them beginning to feel tired. Jay watched the orange lights of the street lamps pass and felt a comforting hand run through his hair.

'How's your head?' came Sue's soft voice.

'It's fine,' he whispered softly, 'it's just fine.'

He wound the window down a little and shut his eyes and fell asleep as the empty conversation Adrian was having with the driver faded.

Jay woke to feel his head tapping against the window and wasn't quite sure if Sue was nudging him or trying to find some money in his pockets. Adrian opened his door and he slumped out onto the pavement breaking his fall with his forehead.

'Fuck,' he uttered.

'Jay... you okay?'

He pulled himself up, 'I'm fine... I haven't got any money,' he muttered as he tapped at his pockets lightly.

'Adrian?'

'No sorry I haven't.'

The two of them were still apologising to the girls as the taxi pulled off.

'Tell you what, I need some food.'

Once inside the house they began to cook a feast; pizza, Marmite on toast and a large pot of tea.

'Jay,' whispered Adrian, 'how do you switch the TV on?'

'Press the on button,' whispered Jay with a giggle.

Happily bloated in front of the small TV they watched Tom Sellick as *Magnum*. Once the food had been eaten Jay put on The Adventures' and they fell asleep to it.

Friday, March 3

At five am they both woke to begin a short pre-dawn conversation. Adrian began rubbing his face and groaned quietly as he rose into a sitting position leaning against Jay's chest of drawers.

'Jay?' he mumbled.

'Yeah.'

'Are you awake?'

'Not yet,' he said.

'Rewind the tape.'

He sat up in bed and leant against the headboard, his fingers laced together behind his head.

'I spent quite a bit last night,' droned Adrian as he rubbed at the tight knot of pain in his stomach.

'Yeah me too. I can't remember much either.'

'You got your camera.'

'Yep got it right here and no doubt it'll tell us at least some of what went on last night.'

'You going into college?'

He mulled it over for less than a few seconds, 'what do you think!'

Sunday, March 5

Trac sat on the edge of the sofa sifting through her bag looking for what? He didn't know, but her small grey suede bag seemed to be full of just about everything possible.

'I take it you've got everything you need for an afternoon with me?'

Biting at her lower lip, mooning up at him blankly she had registered he'd spoken to her but hadn't caught a word. He stood pondering as to what might be going through her mind and took half a step back, dipping his head further to gain better eye contact and asked, 'you okay?'

'Sorry, miles away,' she replied and her mouth returned to a doubtful smile.

'If you've got other things to do that's okay.'

She shook her head and said, 'no.'

He raised his eyebrows in thought for a second then suggested 'tea?' and she smiled as if it pleased her that he had said the perfect thing.

He meandered into the kitchen to find his dad sitting at the table with a mug of tea, some biscuits and a pile of Sunday papers to get through. He was looking his usual laid back weekend self; Lutterworth rugby shirt and a pair of comfy tracksuit bottoms. Jay found this more reassuring and approachable than seeing him in a suit. His dad turned as he moved to the fridge and removed his reading glasses, looking beyond him he said, 'hello Tracey.'

'Hi,' she replied shyly and slotted in behind Jay.

'What are you two up to?'

'Not much, listening to some music. Maybe watch a film.'

'Sure,' replied his dad returning his glasses and his attention back to the papers. He licked at his thumb and turned the next page of the Observer. As Jay opened the fridge his dad uttered, 'now you're not going to drink all my Guinness are you?'

He replied, 'no, just going to do some tea,' and Trac supported him with a slight nod of her head.

'Want one?'

His dad pawed at his cup lightly, concentrating on the article he was reading and uttered, 'no.'

Halfway down the cup, and a few grumbles about the amount of revision she needed to get done for her exams, Trac began to relax. She eased in between the cushions on the sofa, happy to watch him flip through the *Highway Code*, muttering occasionally to himself as he wrote down on a pad something she figured he struggled to remember. They were comfortable just being in each other's presence.

'Do you want me to test you?'

'Nope, I'm okay,' he replied casually and increased the width of his smile momentarily.

'What shall we do then?'

'I don't know if my dad's going out.'

'Well if he doesn't we could always walk up to mine.'

'Okay,' he agreed leisurely.

She studied him as she sipped further from her tea and then asked him if it bothered him that his mum and dad were separated.

'I don't really think about it,' he replied lightly and gave a slight shrug. 'I guess they both look better for it, I don't know... younger perhaps.'

'Yeah your dad seems okay.'

'Hey,' he suddenly asserted slapping his thighs. 'You've got to see these photos from college, they're brilliant.'

He disappeared and reappeared with an almost strange urgency as though she had to see the pictures right now. Sizing the folder in his hand she asked, 'how many photos?'

'Well there were a lot of parties. We notched up something like twenty in one month. It was all good fun until we got barred.'

She frowned slightly and put her cup on the floor and rested the A4 binder on her lap while he buzzed about her energetically. Opening and flicking through the sleaves the first observation apart from the drunk faces was they were nearly all in black and white. She remarked on this and he began to fidget as if she had sparked his enthusiasm again.

'Yeah good aren't they. I develop them myself at college which means I can blow them up or cut bits out I don't like. Okay, okay,' he said excitedly 'these ones are from Halloween last year. We all went as ghosts.'

'Original then?'

'Yeah,' he nodded positively, 'we made smiley masks, look... they went down really well.'

She studied a photo of him appearing through a crowd of people with a inane grin as if he'd been up to something or was about to be.

'What have you been up to?'

He nodded with a smirk urging her to turn to the next page,

'Jay!' she exclaimed, 'where are your trousers?'

He began to chuckle at her astonished face he had no shame and only offered her an innocent shrug.

'This is in a night club?'

'Yeah, Sammy's,' he mused, 'on stage.'

'And you didn't get thrown out?'

'Course not, besides my arse isn't that offensive is it?'

'No but...'

'Well...' he frowned and continued to chuckle to himself.

'Don't you care what people think?'

'No,' he replied shaking his head.

'So this is the kind of stuff you get up to when you're drunk.'

'Yeah, I suppose... I do hear loads of stuff that people said I've done that's not true but I can live with that.'

'God if I got that drunk and did something like that I'd so regret it.'

He replied positively, 'regret the stuff you don't do.'

'Even so I couldn't live that down.'

'Live it down,' he said, 'you should have heard the huge cheer that went up, I was the highlight of the night, plus I got a bottle of champagne from the DJ.'

'Well worth it then?'

'Definitely,' he replied. 'Now, I know you're keen on my bum and that but you can come back to that photo later, I could even run you a copy off if you want.'

She leant a shoulder on him and replied, 'yeah right whatever!' and they chuckled together.

Thursday, March 9

Jay and Adrian's return to the Cove was a gin and Jack Daniel's frenzy, the high volume and rapid consumption of spirits had become more like an Olympic event. This time it was Sue's eighteenth birthday party, and the moment she walked up to Jay at the bar dressed in a tight black dress with big long black gloves he joked, 'you look like fucking cat woman.' Not surprisingly, their relationship seemed to go down hill from there.

Reaching a stage where the music took over was a joy but short lived, their exuberance diminished rapidly as the spirits had their way. So drunk they weren't capable of calling a taxi, Jay had just walked away from the phone looking bewildered, leaving its receiver hanging.

Sue had no intention of waiting on him this time, realising he was unstoppable. They had no choice but to walk back, which given their state, made the likelihood of getting run over a high probability. Adrian's only concern was getting back for *Magnum* while Jay grumbled about being cold as he simply yearned for his bed.

Friday, March 10

Jay sat in the dark room keeping a low profile and developing the Cove's photos. The Leicester Citizens Guide had been printed and delivered and, although he quite happily admitted that his effort to win the competition to illustrate the front cover was poor, he thought Adrian's was far superior to the one that was chosen. The winning cover featured a badly drawn fox head and a wonky portrait of Bradgate Park's Old John, staff politics he figured. Well at least Adrian had got third place and fifty pounds so he was buying the drinks and paying back some of the money he'd borrowed.

To ease the disappointment and on behalf of Comic Relief he had managed to raise a few quid for charity by setting fire to a copy of the design. Hailing how rubbish it was to the rest of the class, he elicited a small round of applause for his protest. The softly spoken guy who designed it sat muttering and cursing but clearly didn't want to confront an angry mob.

He plunged the coiled negatives from the developer into the fix and set the timer. Slouching back to a seated posture, he decided that once this task was done he was off home.

Saturday, March 11

Leicester's town centre dispersed from a centre point; the clock tower, which was where Jay sat comfortably waiting for Adrian. He glanced up at the time, two thirty, and caught sight of Adrian marching towards him in his long grey overcoat clutching a carrier bag from the Another World store and panting quite heavily.

'New comics?'

'Yeah just a few,' he nodded in reply. 'What you listening to?'
Jay pressed stop on his personal stereo and removed his headphones. 'New Order,' he said.

'You get up to anything good last night?' he asked.

'Yeah went to the Fan Club,' he replied with a wry smile.

'Drunk?'

'Absolutely arseholed,' he grinned. 'I didn't get back till about half three, feel a bit worse for wear, but I'll live.'
Adrian sat down next to him and continued to catch his breath. 'You been

waiting long?'

'Nah, I was just in the jean shop.'

'Oh yeah,' replied Adrian with curiosity. 'That girl you've been on about works there.'

'I don't go on about her.'

'Come off it,' smirked Adrian.

'Okay, maybe I've mentioned her once or twice,' he chuckled, 'but, really we're just mates and I don't want to lose that...' Adrian didn't look convinced. 'Besides if I make a move on her and she backs away,' he gave a shrug of his shoulders that gestured 'What then?'

'Yeah, it's a bit tricky,' muttered Adrian. 'Mind you, if you don't make a move some other bloke will come along and snap her up. Then where are you going to be?' and he offered Jay a swig from his can of pop.

'You know,' said Jay taking the can, 'I've been friends with all kinds of girls; fat ones, thin ones, ugly ones, old ones, young ones, but Trac... I don't know?... She makes me feel happy all the time.'

'Well that's good, they're not easy to find,' nodded Adrian. 'Wasn't she mates with that other bird... What's her name... Shelley?'

'Yeah... well I still do miss her from time to time but Trac, she has all the things I loved Shelley for but somehow more.'

'And what about Sue?'

'I don't know? Since I apparently ruined her eighteenth she's been avoiding me, which I don't understand.'

'Well you did say she looked like cat woman.'

'Yeah,' he agreed, 'there was that.'

'Why don't you go round and see her... make up?'

He gave a doubtful smile. 'I like Sue a lot... more than a lot it's...'

'You'd rather be with Trac right.'

'Awwgh, I don't know... I'm just thinking about Trac all the time and what could be I guess.' He smiled, 'I tell you, she's... cool, intelligent...' he shook his head slightly, 'she's not going to want a twat like me.'

'Is she pretty?'

'Yeah she's pretty,' he said exhaling expressively. 'The kind of pretty that gives you butterflies... you know what I mean?'

'So what's the plan?'

'I honestly don't know. All I do know is I love being with her.'

'Look Jay, in my experience you don't come across that many girls with the ability to give you butterflies... You got to talk to her or something.'

Jay let out a huge sigh, passed the can of pop back, and began to scratch at the side of his head.

Adrian shrugged, 'as I say what's it going to be like if she gets a new bloke. Nothing ventured nothing gained.'

Something told him inside that it wasn't going to happen, the real issue was he had already become attached to her and the fear of getting hurt again was what worried him the most. To take it further meant he had to put his trust in her and he just wasn't sure whether he was ready to do that.

They moved away from the clock tower towards the shop and Jay leant on the glass and pointed her out to Adrian who cupped his hands against the glass and stared between the hanging garments.

'That one there in the black top?'

'Yeah, that's her.'

'She's fit,' he said and turned to wink and give him the thumbs up. Jay stuck his hands in his pockets and looked to the ground thinking about Adrian's comment. How long would it last, if every guy noticed her in that way?

'One minute I'm happy being mates, then the next I really want to start kissing her.'

'Shit, you've got it bad and that can only mean one thing, I'm going to have to put up with your sad drooling until you do something about it.' He put his arm around Jay and pulled him close, 'What you need is vodka,' he smiled.

'Right...' Jay nodded vaguely. 'I ply her with drinks and take advantage.'

'Not for her, for you. It might calm you down a bit, although now you mention it that's not a bad idea.'

Jay rubbed at his chin pondering on what Adrian had suggested.

'Que Sera,' replied Adrian.

'Eh?'

'You know the song, *Whatever will be, will be*. Come on let's go and get a beer.'

Sunday, March 12

'I've got to do something with my hair,' Trac moaned, 'it's annoying me.'

'It looks nice how it is,' Jay said looking up from a magazine.

'I think I'll put it up.'

She pulled her hair and pinned it back, it tightened the skin around her eyes and made her look slightly Chinese. He went off into a trance, she looks so beautiful he thought as she jumped up and down playing with her hair. He frowned as he got a glimpse of her smooth skin. As she tied a knot into her loosened shirt, she looked absolutely, entirely perfect.

'Do you want to watch a film then?' she asked.

'Yeah, okay,' he nodded slightly.

'Cool, I'll just tell Mum.'

Her mum was a nice lady, soft spoken, very caring and Trac looked a lot like her. Her father was grey haired and slightly chubby with a deep voice, her sister was always in and out so he had not met her properly. Her brother was married and lived down south somewhere. Their dog was a character and the cat was shy and ran off whenever he tried to introduce himself.

'Bloody moggie,' he'd jeer. This could quite possibly be hereditary on his father's side, his great grandad was a notorious piss artist who lived on stout and by all accounts hated cats. His great grandma had to retrieve kitchen utensils and pans from the garden on a regular basis, but it was unconfirmed as to whether any of the items ever made contact with a cat, it was almost as if he was a throw back from the past.

'Film then?' he prompted her as she seemed lost in her hair. 'My dad will be leaving for the rugger club soon.'
With a hair clip in her mouth she nodded, 'I got Fatal Attraction.'

'You've seen that.'
She smiled, 'but you haven't.'

He felt so much warmth for her, he wanted to reach out, pull her close and kiss her. He lay stroking her hair behind her ears, their friendship was already turning into something more. After the film Trac was a little disappointed that the bath scene in the movie's climax didn't make him jump.

'I've watched too many movies I guess,' he said and gave her a light shrug. They had a can of Guinness each and talked, he tickled her feet and enjoyed seeing her toes scrunching up as she pulled them away fast and then back again to get tickled some more.

'It tickles,' she giggled softly wiggling her feet frantically.

'Of course it does,' he said with a smile and whispered, 'you'll like this... this little piggy went to market. This little piggy stayed at home. This little piggy had roast beef,' he paused.

'And this little piggy had none,' she continued for him.

'And this little piggy,' he roared, 'went we we we we we we we we we we,' moving his hand his hand up her thighs tickling her as he went, 'all the way home.'
He laughed, catching himself having a good time. 'Do you want to go to the cinema?' managed to blurt its way out and before he had a chance to panic about the rejection she simply replied 'yes' without pause.
He perched himself on the edge of the sofa. 'Maybe afterwards we could have a drink and then you could come back and have a cup of tea and something to eat,' he suggested.

'You can cook?'
'Sure I can cook, bacon sarnies that's about my limit,' he smiled childishly.
'Mmm,' she paused, 'give me a ring.'
'I'll have to dig out that Prince album too.'
"Under The Cherry Moon'?'
He gave a slight nod of his head. 'Trac,' he said softly looking at his hands, 'There's something else...'
He wanted to tell her how he felt about her but struggled to find the words.

He began to feel awkward and found himself knotting his fingers together as his eyes began to shine and lips tighten together. Once his eyes began to roll and gaze up and down and to the side, anywhere but straight.

She asked, 'what's up?'

'Erm... I've... got,' he took a deep breath, ' I've... I'm going on holiday next Sunday so how about making it Friday?'

'Okay,' she replied happily.

Friday, March 17

Friday night had not come soon enough. He stood dressed neatly in front of the mirror, eyes narrowed he scouted for spots; all clear. He had spruced himself up, changing his clothes several times and walking back and fourth past the mirror until he was elevated with his look.

He heard a car and his heart began to race as he quickly hid the unused clothes under his bed. He swiftly squirted out a palm full of mousse and rubbed it through his hair as he ran down to the front door to let her in. With her bag over her shoulder and to his delight, bum wiggling slightly as she made her way up the driveway.

'Hi,' he said casually, 'come in.'

Trac just smiled elegantly as she stepped into the hallway. She dropped her bag to the floor and nudged it to the side with her grey suede boots and stuck her hands into her favourite jeans.

'Right,' he smiled. 'This is my house,' and panned his arm around the small hall. 'This is where I live, the lounge is in there,' he said pointing through the nearest door, 'the kitchen.'

Flashing a boyish smile, he sloped up the stairs and she followed.

'And this,' he said, 'is my bedroom,' and he splayed out a hand again.

She braced herself as she ventured into his room. 'You can tell a lot about a person from their room,' she murmured softly as she studied the grey and blue decor, a white painted fitted wardrobe, chest of drawers and desk.

'This is my TV, guitar... art stuff... records... my stereo,' and patted it as if it was a best mate.

'Oh cool, you've got a video, I'm not even allowed a TV.'

'Yeah,' he nodded. 'This is my Cult poster... 'Electric'... great album, the window and my bed, that's where I sleep off my hangovers. Any questions?'

She felt nervous as she looked around the room, it smelt of pencils and paints and she glanced at his desk. A copy of *NME*, a bottle of Grolsh, a couple of photos, a cartoon, a few sketches, camera and set of brushes laid across it in no particular order.

'Is this where you do all your drawing.'

'Yeah pretty much. I can get away from college if I do the work at home.'

'They don't mind?'

'Yeah, sometimes, but as long as I make up a good excuse and meet the deadlines I get away with it.'

'I wish school was like that... What are they?'

'Magic Markers, they're like expensive felt tips, good for doing concepts and visuals.'

'What's this you're working on?'

'It's packaging for a baseball, just at the idea stage.'

He put on some music to help her relax and sat on his bed smiling expansively.

'What are you smiling at?' she asked quietly.

'Nothing.'

'Come on, what is it?'

'It's just you,' he continued with his smile.

'What about me?' she gave a slight sigh.

'It's just you being in my room after all this time,' he shrugged lightly. She gave him a soft nod of agreement.

'You've got quite a lot of records.'

'That's not all of them. I've got a stack in the wardrobe and all my tapes are in the drawer.'

'Your music's very...'

'Very what?'

'Mixed.'

'What can I say?' he said in a laid back manner. 'I love music.' She nodded nervously as she placed herself down onto his bed.

'Do you want to see some other bits of work?'

'Okay,' she agreed with a blank expression, still studying his room carefully.

He placed a folder onto the bed next to her and spread some pieces out. 'Look, do you recognise her'.

'God,' she said sounding impressed. 'Shelley, that looks just like her.' He smiled. 'Yeah, pleased with how that turned out. It's the eyes that sell it.'

He put 'Under the Cherry Moon' on by Prince while he made his last minute adjustments and double checked he had enough money. As he came back into the room she was lying across his bed in deep thought, listening to the music.

'How do I look?' he asked pulling his jacket on tightly.

'Great,' she smiled.

'Cheers.'

Did she like his room he wondered? More importantly did she like him? And could he stop his escalating feelings for her? Thoughts like these raced about his head randomly as she flung her hair back over her shoulder and moved closer. He could smell the Body Shop's White Musk perfume mixed in with the smell of her hairspray. Closing his eyes for a second and taking in the scent with much appreciation, he felt a strange feeling of comfort.

The evening was great, the company, the mound of popcorn, the drinks at the Helsinki afterwards, it was heading towards perfection and maybe even about to get wonderful as they returned arm in arm to the darkness and sanctuary of his bedroom.

Jay, ever the romantic, used his Minilite, a road repair light he had acquired once during a journey back from The Bell, to give out a cosy orange glow.

'How romantic,' Trac commented.

And he replied with, 'well I try my best.'

He sat on his bed and Trac lay back, her head resting between his thighs and he played with her hair as usual, taking up strand after strand and curling each around his finger pushing it gently away from her skin in a slow sequence to the music that seemed to fill the room and shut the rest of the world out.

She whispered, 'I like this one, what's it called?'

"Sometimes it snows in April',' he whispered.

Slowly she drew in to him. Wrapping her legs round him she pulled him in close, so close a sensation of falling spilled over him, the anticipation of a first kiss was upon him and he couldn't help but move that one centimetre further and place it onto her lips. She responded and began kissing him back. Everything around him became hazy and the only thing in focus was him and her and for a moment he felt an intense overwhelming feeling, a combination of excitement, passion, fear and relief, so lucky he found it again yet instantly scared that it would go. It was as though the last six months had been building up to this moment and now he wished it would never end.

Saturday, March 18

The next morning he ate his breakfast quickly, he had a vague feeling of joy, triumph even. His mum and sister were in deep conversation about Portugal, they were set to fly out in the early hours of the morning but Jay had other things on his mind. He'd packed his case in about ten minutes flat and shot off into town. He felt sure that Trac's view of the night had been romantic, maybe even the most romantic of her life so far? He imagined her thinking of nothing more as she shuffled about the jean shop just waiting for her lunch break and for him to come smiling through the door.

He strolled into the Western Jean Company, face alight with a gleaming grin as he leaned over the counter, 'I'll let you take me out to lunch today,' he whispered softly into her ear.

She led him to a corner table in a quiet café. There were only two older women hunched over a long polished bar and a man working a coffee machine behind it, otherwise the café was empty. He sat there propping his

42

elbows on the table and sipping at his tea trying to ignore the fact his heart seemed to pound heavier all the time. After staying seated for a long time, unable to dislodge what he had done from his head, he gave in to the thought of kissing her again, he couldn't stop thinking how good her lips had felt on his. He found himself with the urge to reach out and touch her hand, when he did so she looked up from her glass of milk and that was when he first allowed himself to admit she was the most beautiful and attractive girl he had ever met and leant forward and kissed her softly.

'Do you fancy me then?' he smirked trying to lighten the tone.

'You're weird!'

'Weird?' he frowned in puzzlement.

'Yes weird,' she exclaimed.

'I'll take that as a compliment then.'

'Of course.'

'So do you like me despite that?'

'Yes I like you, even though you're not a normal guy.'

'Oh... okay I can live with that.'

She informed him that he was different, interesting, and that his face turned attractive when he talked, even more so when he smiled and that his bum is perfect hand grabbing size.

'So it's my bum you're after then?' he mused and went to stand so that she could give it a squeeze.

Smiling she stopped him with her hand and said, 'you make me laugh too.'

'Well that's good isn't it?'

She gave a nod.

They sipped their drinks in silence for a moment or two, allowing things to sink in a little further.

'Why are you smiling at me?' Trac asked staring with curiosity.

'Smiling at you?'

'Yes.'

'And there's me thinking I was giving you my come-to-bed eyes,' and she nudged him under the table with her foot.

'Why don't you come to dinner when you come back from Portugal?'

'Mmm come to dinner? Come to bed?' he pretended to ponder and she gave him a second nudge with her foot. 'Dinner, with your mum and dad?'

'Yes,' she said.

He dropped his head to the table with a thud and protested humourously. 'I don't think so. I'm not too good at that sort of thing,' he mumbled.

'You'll be fine,' she chuckled.

He looked up at her and smiled, 'okay then, but I'll probably embarrass you.'

'What are you smirking for now?'

He gave her a slight shrug, 'I don't know... sometimes things just pop into my head.'

'Like what?'

'Like kissing you before.'

She gave him a puzzled look, 'when?'

'At the youth club! We danced and then we kissed.'

'Christmas... that's different.'

'Suppose.'

'And...' her tone changed slightly, 'you started fighting I seem to remember.'

'Hey, I didn't start anything, that lad just bopped me on the nose.'

'And after all the effort it took getting you to the hospital to get it straightened the first time.'

'Now that definitely wasn't my fault.'

'Well you shouldn't have fights.'

'How many did Muhamid Ali have? And he's a millionaire!'

'Jay, that's not the point.'

'Yep, that's exactly the point.'

'Stop wiggling it,' she said, 'it looks alright now, nobody can tell.'

'Are you looking forward to Portugal?'

'Well, apart from my fear of flying, wanting to be with you and not being able to buy 'Fire Woman' The Cult's first release in eighteen months. I'm sure it will be great'

'Poor you.'

'I suppose I do have the option of sampling a lot of the local booze.'

'So getting pissed is the plan.'

'Getting pissed is always the plan.'

'You don't have to drink, you can sunbathe too.'

'Yeah, but I like to. You know me.'

'Yeah, but you get into trouble most of the time.'

'No, only sometimes and never anything serious. Besides you're only young once.'

His energy obviously intrigued her and she whispered with a smile, 'you're a bad boy.'

Is that why I'm unusual he thought, troublesome, maybe a good weapon to wind her parents up?

'Am I bad?' He replied softly.

'Yeah.'

'I just want to do stuff that excites me.'

'Getting into trouble isn't the way.'

'That's why you like me.'

'I know, but just be careful.'

He tapped his temple slowly with his index finger. 'There doesn't look like there's anything going on up there, but there is. I'll be fine.'

'Hmm and what about your career?'

He shrugged, 'I've not thought about that too much, as long as I do what I want and I do what's interesting to me.'

'And prove your dad wrong?'

'Not bothered, the idea of proving anything to anyone is just weird to me.'

'And what do you want from me?'

'To spend time with you... you make me happy. I feel I can talk to you,' he responded. 'I just don't want to interfere with you studying for your GCSE's.'

She tilted her head to the side slightly and asked him how many exams he had passed and he replied a confident 'six.'

'Six?' she exclaimed with surprise. 'Are you sure?'

'Yeah,' he replied forcibly, 'I got six' and nodded enthusiastically.

'How did you manage that?'

'Easy,' he smiled. 'I cheated.'

Jay drew to a halt outside the fresh fish shop with Trac in tow a pace behind him. He peered through the open doorway and said in a low voice, 'I just want to nip and see Adrian, catch him before I go away.'

He sprang to life once his eyes registered on his mate emerging from a large freezer, frosty air surrounding him.

'You alright?' asked Jay looking agitated as he entered the shop.

Adrian responded, 'yeah, you?' as he wiped his hands on his apron and came from behind the counter.

'No,' muttered Jay still looking a little agitated. 'It stinks in here,' he said looking around him.

His mate looked at him with a confused expression. 'Jay, it's a fish shop,' he replied. 'It stinks of fish.'

'It's not very nice is it?'

'I get used to it.'

'Come outside, I want you to meet somebody.'

The two of them strolled over to a nervous and curious Trac. She quickly moved her hand away from her mouth.

'Hi,' she smiled shyly.

'Hi,' replied Adrian, then turned to Jay. 'Don't forget the duty free.'

'Forget? That's the only reason I'm going,' he chuckled.

'Alright, see you later,' replied Adrian. 'Bye Trac.'

'Bye.'

Jay noticed Adrian's eye twitching with a slight jarring of his head.

'What?'

Adrian moved back to the shop doorway nodding as he went in order for Jay to follow him.

'What's up?'

'So are you shagging her then?'

'What is the matter with you, she's standing right there?'

'She can't hear.'

'Look, it's purely platonic.'

Adrian stared at him, sure he could see a glint in his mate's eye. 'Fuck... fuck,' he began to babble.

'What is up with you?'

'It's this fucking jonny, I've had it in my pocket for so long... the fucking thing goes out of date in May.'

'Put it away... fuck.' Jay backed away. 'Look I got to go. I'll see you later.'

'Yeah,' Adrian nodded, 'have a good time.'

Jay and Trac wandered up High Street and sat down by the clock tower for the last few minutes of her lunch.

'So how do you feel about us then?' she asked.

'I don't know, I guess it's all still sinking in.'

'You look almost happy.'

'Come here,' he smiled.

She leant forward and they kissed.

'I am happy, just a little apprehensive maybe. What about you? You happy?'

'Yes,' she smiled, 'I am.'

'I wish I didn't have to go away.'

'I'll see you when you get back. It's only a week.'

'I'll write you a letter before I go.'

'Okay.'

Dear Trac,

I am really lost for words which is not like me at all. I needed you to kiss me on Saturday, it was so much like a dream on Friday night it was so hard to put it into reality. I don't know why it seemed a dream, it was just so good to hold you and kiss you, I wanted you. I wanted to kiss you when we had watched so many films together, but I always had my doubts, I thought you might have backed away from me and I'd have lost a close friend. I knew that when and if I kissed you it would be in the heat of the moment, I wouldn't think shall I, I'd just kiss you and I did and it happened. You felt so warm and fragile. I am sitting on the edge of my bed now thinking how to explain how I feel and I just can't find the right words. I just know that I want to be with you, spend time with you. I'm enjoying myself, I enjoy you, I don't want to lose that and there's nothing I wouldn't give to be in that situation again. Your exams are very important and the idea of you getting attached to me flatters me and I'd love to get attached to you, I don't want you to walk away from me either. I'll be back in a flash and we can talk. It needs time to sink in, my head is just in a spin.

Love from Jay. xxx

Sunday, March 19 - 26

The week in Portugal flew by fairly quickly considering he was thinking about Trac. He spent most of his time in shorts, shirt and a nasty battered straw hat he found on some rocks. With his headphones clamped to his ears, he was content to relax and daydream to The Adventures' album.

The place was fairly quiet, isolated and the time of year meant there were not too many people even in the local town. He took the hire car out a few times for a spin but that became boring fairly quickly. He made conversation with four sunbathing Portuguese girls, all of which had dark brown hair, eyes as deep as coffee with chocolate brown topless bodies gleaming in lotion. Their small perfect pert breasts seemed to catch him off guard as he pondered as to whether this was really happening or not.

A few nights spent getting drunk were thrown in the mix of being idle, the better of the nights being a cocktail session with his sister. Altogether it had not been a bad decision giving into parental pressure to go on this family holiday.

Returning with an Easter egg, miniature bottle of Baileys for Trac and a bag full of duty free booze he found a crisp white letter with his name, he recognised the writing; Trac's. He opened it feeling a little unsure as he sat on the edge of the kitchen table. When he found that her words mirrored his, he was overjoyed.

As he sank effortlessly into Trac's arms, a self satisfied smile tugged at the corners of his mouth. The four and a half hour flight of nerves and stress seemed to float away with ease and be replaced with an uplifting glow.

'Okay,' she smiled patting his back, 'that's enough.'
He drew back from her slowly and smiled, 'glad to be back.'
Trac tugged on his black shirt and allowed himself to be pulled into the privacy of her bedroom. His dream of finding new romance had broken into reality. Suddenly all the pain of Shelley emigrating had been worthwhile... he'd found Trac.

3. And you smiled

Trac often quizzed Jay about Shelley and he was always quick to respond to her, after all she had helped him when he was sad and wistful. His path of thought was funny, he just summed up what he had loved about her the most.

'I think the two main things I remember about her with a certain degree of fondness was the way she used to sneer at me and boss me about.'
He twirled Trac's small beige bear in his hands and chuckled.

'She used to wear woolly tights. God those were sexy,' he smirked.

'Woolly tights?' she giggled.

'Yeah,' he exclaimed, 'crazy isn't it.'
He laid back on Trac's bed and fumbled with the rest of her bears. He turned his head and glared at her. She pulled a strange face and she asked him what he was staring at.

'You,' he replied, 'because you're beautiful.'

'Creep.'
She leaned her head to one side and smiled 'well come over here and kiss me then,' she said.

'I'll have to think about it.'
She pulled a sad face so he leapt off the bed and jumped on her in a frenzy, smiling continually as he bent over and kissed her hair just above her left ear.

'I guess now I'm kissing you.'

'Well why should she always get the best guys?... it's my turn.'

'Mmm, that's one way of looking at it.'

'So, you working at the Sink tomorrow night?'

'Why?'

'Because I want to see you.'

'I've quit.'

'Really?'

'Yeah, finally.'

'Just like that.'

'Yep.'

'What about money?'

'I don't want to work Saturday nights anymore, most of them were wankers... and for money?' he gave a shrug, 'I'll get another job, besides it means I can spend more time with you.' He beamed as he arched his back and pulled an envelope out of his back pocket.

'Here, I've written you another letter,' and he dangled it above her hoping to tease her with it but she was too quick for him, snatched it and made good her escape. She sat reading it quietly and just smiled profoundly a few times while he carried on fumbling with her bears.

'Oh you,' she hugged him with surprise.

'I wanted to kiss you for ages,' he said.

'I know, you took your time.'

'See that's because I'm a gentleman and really not that bad.'

He watched her from the corner of his eye as she folded up the letter. He lifted himself up from her bed, holding both her hands as he crouched in front of her.

'How do you feel about me?' he asked softly. 'I want to know what you feel.'

'I feel that maybe I'm falling in love with you,' she whispered but squeezed his hands to emphasise what she had said.

He paused as his heart began to race unexpectedly. He became hot, it's what he wanted to hear but instead of feeling full of joy, he suddenly felt fear. His hands began to clam and he released her as he stood slowly avoiding her eyes. He folded his arms and swept his eyes around the room with a worried complexion.

'Jay,' she whispered.

He turned back to her, bent to his knees again and leaned in close to her.

'You're so beautiful,' he said softly.

A vain of worry still on his face, he ran a finger over her cheeks and lips. Her eyes began to well with tears and they twinkled like crazy. He could tell by her reaction that she had put herself on the line, and regretting so. Now she wasn't going to talk to him again... maybe that was a good thing? He rubbed at his brow and was about to say 'sorry' when her eyes left his face.

'Trac... I'm... I...' he paused. 'I just can't do this, I need some time... I best go.'

Thursday, March 30

The phone was ringing, by the fourth or fifth ring Jay tutted and moved in closer to the TV and turned up the volume. He heard the muffled thuds above as his sister gave in to the phone and it made him smile.

'Jay!' she yelled. 'It's for you.'

'Typical,' he muttered and darted into the hall and snatched at the phone so quickly he dropped it and swore.

'Yeah.'

'It's me,' came Trac's voice.

'Yeah?' he snapped.

'Just ringing to let you know The Cult are on Top Of The Pops.'

'I know I'm... was watching them.'

'Okay, okay, don't bite my head off.'

'Got to go,' he said and replaced the receiver.

Watching his heroes mime 'Fire Woman' he found, was not actually that great. Dance bands he thought can get away with miming but a rock band?

He decided he wished he hadn't seen it, he'd rather they had performed live and sounded great, even sounding awful would have been better than miming, failing that just show the video.

Friday, March 31

The party was a disaster for the football club but Jay found it fun, only because he and Rob were so heavily intoxicated and therefore oblivious to the reality of the situation. The lack in numbers was embarrassing. Most of the other people were drunk and merry but the two of them had passed that stage and were in a state of dissolution, confusion and totally unaware of their poor behaviour, which was mainly down to Jay's encouragement. Nobody could understand a word they said, their comical conversations appeared as drunken babble. This was the same night that Jay had invented his ideal drink, a cocktail known as 'A Bastard!' The name was derived from drinking it down in one, you would gasp sharply and could not fail to utter the word 'bastard' as it took your breath away due to its potent and poisonous content. The lethal concoction was surprisingly simple, three drops of Angostura Bitters, a shot of a good single malt scotch whiskey and one single cube of ice. The idea was simple; to finish the drink before the ice melted, then order another followed by another and another and so on until you passed out and dropped to the floor in an unconscious mess. As the party wore on their only dance was passing drinks back and forth and knocking some back before passing it on again. When that soon fell apart at the seams they staggered about, falling over drunk, joking, ribbing and laughing. They had spent most of the night at the bar, consuming their cocktails. Shirts untucked, jackets falling off shoulders, it wasn't long before they were being helped home.

'I've never seen you so drunk,' mumbled Nick shaking his head at Jay. Tonight, the Newtownions Rugby Club had sacrificed for Enderby United Football Club's party. The idea was to raise money for its funding. Jay couldn't play football to save his life but he could sure down a drink or two. Clutching his souvenir of the evening, an orange Beacon Bitter beer mat that recorded his drink intake; three pints of Guinness, seven straight whiskeys, three vodkas and thirteen bastards. He burst into life and stumbled into his lounge at a funny angle. With several crashes he ended up in a pile in the middle of the room.

'More scotch,' he babbled.

Nick grinned, 'I'd hate to have your head in the morning,' and pulled the front door to and left him to sleep it off. Meanwhile Rob was leaning out of the window of Nick's van, laughing and trying his best not to throw up.

Saturday, April 1

'It's me.'

'Hi me,' came Trac's quiet voice. 'Are you coming over?'

'Bit tired.'

'Trying to tell me something?'

'No, just still hungover I guess, I got the football thing in the morning so...'

'So, you're okay to talk.'

'Sure, why?'

'I don't know, maybe there's something on TV you want to watch.'

'No not really,' he replied.

'Really?'

'Oh I get it,' he jabbered, 'Thursday. Hey, look I'm sorry about that I... well, you know it was The Cult.'

'So there's nothing else going on?'

He sat on the third from bottom step of the stairs and ran a hand through his hair and rubbed at his eyes. Open as he could be he wasn't so sure he liked being put on the spot like this.

'No nothing, I was just grouchy is all. College was shit... I missed the train, you know...'

There was a brief silence before Trac said, 'I'm sorry about the other night what I said, I shouldn't have said it. I've really cocked things up haven't I.'

'Don't say that,' he stammered. 'It was all me.'

'I'm rubbish at trying to say how I feel, it just makes me feel vulnerable someone knowing so much about me. It means you know how to hurt me... scares me.'

'I don't want hurt you... just need to talk I suppose.'

'I want to, but my mind just goes blank and I just become... I don't know more frustrated. Anyway, it looks like when I do finally say something nice I just make things worse. All I've done is pushed you away.'

'You haven't, look do you want me to see if I can get over.'

'No,' she sighed. 'Tomorrow's okay.'

'I feel bad now.'

'Too much alcohol.'

'Drowning in it, but you know what I mean.'

Sunday, April 2

Jay jigged about on the spot yawning continuously and looking at the patch of flattened grass he had made with his feet. 'Come on, for fuck's sake' came a shout and he did a small star jump and moved to his left a bit, then to his right, and thought how much he wished he had stayed in bed instead of running the line in a football match. Physical exercise after a night out on the beer was not a good idea. He wasn't even sure he knew what he was doing despite Nick's rather lengthy explanation, interrupted on numerous occasions, regarding the offside rule.

'Can't Northy run the line?' he'd protested.

'Jay, he's playing.'

'Can't I play instead?'

'You're shit.'

Jay nodded his head lightly, eyes downcast.

'So you'll do it?'

'No, I was just agreeing that I'm shit, not to being a linesman.'

'Look, just for a bit and I'll get someone's dad to take over.'

'Can't I go on for ten minutes at the end?'

'Rich ain't here and neither is my brother, the team's already shit. Besides, you're hungover.'

'So's Daz.'

'He's the fucking goaly.'

Jay studied his kit for a moment before nodding again and started to change.

The ball flew passed his head so close it made him wobble. Concerned by the near fatal bruising he held a delayed flag up and pointed.

'Fuck off,' barked Nick.

'Huh?'

'You fucking twat!'

Jay noted a smile on one of the opposition's faces and realised he had placed the flag up incorrectly, it was his team for a throw in.

'Are you watching the game?' ranted Nick.

He made a face back at him that he hoped said, 'I didn't want to fucking do this in the first place.' Nick's competitive streak was huge, maybe it was because he was half Italian he wasn't sure, but one thing he was sure of, he was going to suffer in the post-match debate.

He gave Nick a slight shrug as if to say 'calm down, it's only a game' as he handed the ball away.

Relief came as a direct result of the throw in. A stumbled pass and their star player Steve somehow managed to connect his head to the ball and push it into the back off the net. Cheers and swearing of a positive nature erupted and as Nick jogged passed him he muttered 'lucky fucker.' Now if he wasn't so hungover he could afford to be smug about his part leading up to the goal, but was happy enough just to slope off and let one of the dads take over.

He put on his favourite black shirt and talked his mum into giving him a lift to Trac's. He was finding out that the feeling of being terrified and excited all at the same time was a confusing state to be in. It had, at moments, scared him so bad he almost lost his nerve and quit before they had even began. He pondered on the way over how he was to put the way he was feeling into a coherent and meaningful sentence that she could understand and also not get upset with.

When he arrived at her place he found her sitting on the end of her bed warming herself in a strip of sunlight in a pair of blue jeans that hugged her thighs and a small black top. She looked up at him blankly as if she were waiting for him to speak first. He mumbled how sorry he was as he made his way across to the stereo and began to toy with the CDs. A full minute went by with him sliding out a case, flipping it in his hand, and replacing it in the silence before she spoke. 'Put Otis Redding on' she said softly.

He looked over at her still in the same position, arms down her side, hands under her bum. He twirled the LP in his hands a couple of times before positioning it on the turntable. He waited until the opening crackle of the vinyl turned into the sound of the first track, and then eased himself next to her. He sat in the same position and from there began to mimic her every move no matter how slight. Moments later he got the desired effect, and her face began to illuminate with a smile. Her body dropped its perched position to a more relaxed state and slowly but surely she nestled herself into him and folded her head downwards onto his shoulder. Once they had reached this point he felt at ease to talk and after a short while he crouched down in front of her so he could look up to her bowed head.

'Talk to me,' he said.

'I thought I'd lost you,' came her whispered reply.

'No such luck,' he smiled a little. 'Trac I'm...' he looked lost for a second, 'I'm... I'm scared that's all,' he said and smiled coyly.

She suddenly became aware of his keen blue grey eyes upon her taking her all in and opening himself up to her.

'I don't want to hurt you Jay,' she said softly and stroked at his hair.

'I know you don't, nobody wants to hurt anybody, but it happens. It's just that...'

She eyed him wistfully, 'Just what?'

Her eyes shining and fine hair falling about her face brought him closer to her still, 'It's just that...' he whispered as he brushed her hair gently with his right hand, 'I'm afraid that one day, I'll wake up and you won't be there anymore.'

'I feel like I've ruined everything,' she murmured.

'No, you haven't, it's just me.'

His head was aching from too much thinking. He had asked himself a thousand times 'am I ready?' but the memory of the pain he had felt over Shelley was still fresh.

'Trac,' he said softly, 'just give me some time to at least accept what I feel for you in my head.'

She nodded slightly with what he accepted was her understanding face. He moved to her side once again and playfully leaned on her until she gave way and allowed his head to fall into her lap and she began to play with his hair.

'I love Otis Reading,' she said.

'I know,' he whispered and later decided that it wasn't first rate stuff but well worth listening to nonetheless.

Tuesday, April 4

Jay swung open the door of the college common room and charged in followed by Dave and Adrian. He stopped suddenly and both Dave and Adrian barged into the back of him.

'I think it's time for one of Molly's cobs,' he said positively.

They formed an orderly queue and as they got closer to the counter Jay reached out an arm and took a cheese and tomato bread roll. He then glanced back and forth, then swiftly put it into his pocket.

'What are you doing?' exclaimed Dave.

'It's called stealing Dave. What you do is this.'

He took a second bread roll and this time put it into Dave's pocket and started to whistle.

'Jeez,' uttered Dave immediately fidgeting.

'Don't panic,' smirked Jay patting Dave's cheeks lightly.

To Dave it was the crime of the century, looking racked with guilt even before he had made his escape, but to Jay it was just a game, it wasn't serious. Adrian smiled innocently he had already stuffed two large sausage rolls and a Cornish pasty down his jumper and to him he deserved them unquestionably.

'You'll be fine,' mused Jay picking up a Mc Cowan's Highland toffee bar and a Curly Wurly.

Dave's cold sweat had disappeared once they had made it back to the relatively safe haven of the classroom and Adrian had pulled out a dog-eared copy of yesterday's *Sunday Sport*, the newspaper for the perverted, he called it. They had a giggle over the daft stories and for amusement decided to write their own story.

They completed it in less than an hour, fully illustrated as well. It read as a short article about aliens coming down to earth:

We were at college and a group of us decided to stay behind to do some work as we had to get a project in by the next day. As usual, we weren't concentrating and ended up messing about in class. Everyone started throwing things about when Dave shouted, 'look at that!'

We all turned around and to our disbelieving eyes saw a large saucer like thing hovering over the university building. Our classroom is on the second floor and we could clearly see the student union building which is almost like a block of flats from our room. None of us could believe it. We were shouting and swearing with our excitement, just staring at it. Then the thing started to move towards our building and we started to panic! Then there was a terrific buzzing humming noise, the windows were shaking, we had to cover our ears from the noise. Then it stopped. It had gone. We talked about what we had just seen for about half an hour, Simon left the room to go to the toilet. He was doing the business staring at the wall when he felt that someone was watching him, he turned around shaking his manhood to be confronted by three humanoid figures dressed in silver suits, Simon screamed which is all he could remember. This is where we pick up the story, we were still talking when the three figures came out from the dark and said in a very deep voice of which we could just make out.

'We would like to see your portfolios.'

We all screamed and tried to get out. They then said, 'we won't hurt you, your friend is downstairs.'

We were all panicking, they then picked up Jay's portfolio and left.

'What do you reckon Jay?'

'Absolutely fantastic,' he smiled, 'only one slight snag'.

'What's that,' giggled Dave.

'Well I think it needs a little bit more sex in it.'

'Really?'

'Yeah, pep it up a bit.'

'Like what?'

'Erm maybe... the aliens... were bollock naked and they had gigantic testicles.'

'Now that's not a bad idea,' smiled Dave.

'We can title it *Alien's with Bulging Lallies*.'

Adrian laughed, 'alright,' and began drawing a cartoon of an alien creature with extremely large testicles.

'Simon could even get buggered by them,' muttered Adrian.

'No,' Dave replied, 'that's going too far.'

'No it's not,' chipped in Jay, 'how do you know that wouldn't happen?'

'We want them to print it don't we.'

'Okay then,' said Jay. 'What about some kind of rectal probe.'

Dave's face looked stressed by the situation, he began rubbing at his head most probably wondering how the two of them seemed to go that one step further than he could or would allow himself to.

'Jay, have you got that photo of the spaceship over the uni.'

'Yeah,' he passed him a black and white photo he had set up of a UFO.

'Perfect,' Adrian smiled. 'One story, one photo and one cartoon.'

Proud of their constructive afternoon, Jay and Adrian decided to skip off early.

'You're dossers you really are,' Dave muttered as they collected their art stuff up.

Jay's excuse was that their tutor was Welsh and getting on his nerves, while Adrian just picked up his art box said, 'see you,' and marched off, only pausing at the doorway to peer down either end of the corridor, before giving Jay the thumbs up to show it was all clear.

Friday, April 7

'Jay.'

'What?'

'Go get some more Red Stripe.'

'Fucking hell, has it got back round to me already? I don't even feel slightly drunk.'

Propping The Bell's bar up with Nick and Rob after an eventful day mooching about the town, going to the cinema and fuelling up on pizza, he wondered if the Red Stripe promotion was going to be the ideal way in which to round off his day.

'Three cans cheers,' he said and then slid fifty pence over to Rob. 'Put something good on the jukebox Rob.'

Pushing round what was left of the day's change in his palm he realised he was going to have to pull out the folded ten pound note from his back pocket and break into it knowing full well that once he had done so it was as good as gone. It would be worth it though if he got back to his pit, in possession of one of the promotional posters, drunk and happy.

Saturday, April 8

Minutes inched by and the sky began to darken, rain was imminent. At six o'clock, as promised, he stood by the grey shutter of the shop waiting for it to lift and make its usual clatter as it rose to let Trac out. By ten past six he moved round the side and squashed his face up to the glass trying to see where she was through the racks of clothing. He could see her by the counter with two people. She was standing with her hands on her hips. He couldn't quite work out whether she was grumpy or confused, maybe both? He looked up at the clock tower and then moved back to where he was before and stood leaning against the wall. She appeared next to him in a matter of minutes and the two of them wandered out into the street.

'Hard day's work was it?'

She sighed, 'I'm a bit pissed off.'

'Don't worry I'll cheer you up,' and he placed a comforting arm around her shoulder and lightly kissed her neck, cheek and nuzzled her ear as she tilted her head so he could better explore the tender skin below.

'You smell good,' he whispered softly and gave her a reassuring squeeze.

'I thought we could go for something to eat?' he suggested and she nodded with agreement.

'What do you fancy? A pub meal, or say pizza?'

'Pizza,' she said quickly.

'Okay, pizza it is,' and took her hand in his.

Trac found them a table at the back of Pizzaland, it was warmer, quiet and smoke free. She wiggled her bum into the seat and positioned herself neatly opposite him, looking positively excited.

'What would you like to drink, wine?'

'A pot of tea,' she smiled widely.

A young female waitress attended to them and asked for their order politely. Studying the menu he looked up at Trac. 'If we have a cheese and tomato base, a ten inch size one we can share it and you can pick some extra toppings at the bottom there,' he pointed.

Trac simply nodded with agreement and he placed the order.

'A pot of tea, a can of Foster's, then we'll have a ten inch pizza with...'

'Chicken and sweetcorn,' suggested Trac.

'Yeah that sounds good,' he agreed.

'Anything else sir.'

'Two glasses of wine?' he suggested looking over at Trac.

'I don't know whether I'm keen on wine,' and she gave a shrug then shook her head. 'Just one glass of red wine,' he smiled.

Trac held herself in a posh posture and readjusted her cutlery, she was enjoying herself.

'Well this is good,' he said and gave a soft chuckle.

He held his can of beer in both hands. 'Aah... nice and chilled,' he said smiling with delight.

'Oh, I got Deacon Blue's new CD today. I can't wait to listen to it,' she said retrieving it from her bag.

'That will give us something new to listen to tomorrow then.'

He watched her in close detail studying the back of the CD case, with a wrinkled frown upon her face. He gave her a gentle smile.

'Sorry,' he said when he registered her bemused look. 'You just make me smile.'

He poured his beer into a long glass and sipped at it slowly.

'I don't want you flirting with the waitress,' she said firmly.

'What me?' he shook his head at her. 'I never flirt,' he said.

'You do, it's in your nature.'

'Okay I flirt a little, but I'm loyal.'

They sat gazing at each other, he studied her and felt enriched. She had a lovely complexion with little in the way of make up which appealed to him. Firm features, bright and beautiful he thought as he put his thumb diagonally across her lips, his fingers cupping her left cheek.

'Leave your mouth open,' he said softly.

He withdrew his hand from her face and ran his thumb round the edge of his wine glass before submerging it into the deep red liquid. He noted its colour turn almost clear on his skin as he returned it to her lips. She allowed him to glide it over her teeth as a combination of lust for her and alcohol surged through him. His fingers cupped her cheek once more as his thumb came to rest on her tongue which prompted her to suck on it. He chuckled lightly as she did so and he gave her a roll of his eyes to let her know where his thoughts lay. He was still smiling when he retrieved his thumb, eyes looking at her tentatively he said, 'you do terrible things to my mind.'

'Umm, this tastes quite nice,' she said licking at her lips.

Soft and aloof he said, 'try some,' and tilted the glass for her to drink from. He spotted the waitress heading towards them holding a large plate aloft. Mouth watering with anticipation Jay muttered, 'I'm starving,' as the plate dropped down before him. Trac smiled widely as she cut her slices up into small pieces before consuming, while Jay raced through the first few mouthfuls until his stomach had stopped aching. When their plates were clear he found himself still hungry.

'Do you fancy a pudding?'

'No I'm full,' she said feeling her stomach bulge. 'You have one.'

Leaning forward, eyes wide at the sight of a strawberry fool, he managed to consume one in a matter of seconds.

'Well,' he said wiping his hands on a serviette, 'that was gorgeous... but not quite as gorgeous as you.' he said strongly.

'Kiss me,' she said.

'Where?'

'There,' and she pointed to her mouth and he obliged.

Sunday, April 9

A short powerful surge of wonder and excitement rushed through his whole body as Trac leant up to the stereo and her shirt lifted to reveal her bare back. Ideal he thought and slipped onto the carpet and crawled up behind her placing his hands on her back gently massaging round to her stomach.

'Do I excite you?' he whispered cunningly into her ear.

'Yes,' came her soft reply.

Her skin felt warm and soft to the touch. Burying his head into the locks of her hair he was unbelievably elated.

She murmured, 'do I turn you on?'

'The very thought of you does things to me,' he replied, nuzzling into her shoulder.

Pulling back on her hips they both stretched out on her bedroom floor.

'Do you miss her though?' she gently whispered, 'Shelley, that is?'

'She pops into my head from time to time,' he sighed.

He rested his head in his hands and squashed his cheek thoughtfully.

'I used to bike thirty miles to see her in the cold and the wet, no lights on my push bike. It was freezing, loads of hills and stuff. The wind used to drive me absolutely crazy.' With a sigh he ran a hand through his hair, 'I wonder what she's up to... if she's happy? I want her to be, but I guess when she finds out about us she won't be,' and gave another sigh.

'Are you going to write and tell her?'

'Yeah I suppose one of us should before someone else does. It'd probably be best coming from you.'

With his left hand he was making circular motions on her stomach, not brushing her breasts but coming playfully close. He had a deviant smile and a sparkle of fun in his eyes. Trac in turn ran a hand from his back to his front and felt the scar run down his stomach, 'Does your scar bother you?'

'No,' he said faintly. 'Does it bother you?'

'No. What did you have done?'

'They just took a small part of me out.'

'Was that the only sane bit of you.'

'That might not be as daft as it sounds,' he mumbled, 'when you're eight years old surrounded by doctors who after two months in hospital can't figure out what's wrong with you, and you're worse than ever, you think your time's up. It has to have an effect on the way you look at things.'
She pulled him close and hugged him, 'well I'm glad you're here. Are you going to stop for lunch?'

'Oh I don't know, I told you, I'm not too good at that sort of thing. Me and parents don't tend to get on. I can't relate to them, adults are like aliens to me.'

'Okay I'll bring it in here so you don't have to sit at the table with Mum and Dad.'

'I can't do that,' he said.

'I don't want you to go though. She won't mind while my brother's here with his girlfriend, there's no room at the table anyway.'

'Okay then,' he whispered.

Jay felt increasingly uneasy when it came to her parents, in particular with her mum, who was less reserved than her father. He had to give in to being judged. A rebellious piss artist was never going to make the right impression, especially with her mum being a nurse that so well matched Trac's ex; the Doctor to be. He sat staring with these damning thoughts at the clear cup with tea stencilled on the side. He was deflated at the fact that he was never going to measure up, and as a consequence, it was as though he had to accept this, even programme it into his head that they disapproved of him. He was not much more than a bad influence, ready to bring out the worst in their daughter.

He dipped his hand into the hexagonal glass biscuit jar and yawned. When his biscuit broke off and disappeared into the depths of his tea he let out another long sigh and stretched along the floor and yawned loudly. He took note of the small row of footwear along the bottom of her chest of drawers her mum had so neatly arranged; cowboy boots, baseball boots and greasy dock shoes he asked if she had any high heels.

'Yep,' she jumped up and shuffled through her wardrobe. 'Here,' she slipped them on and tottered around her room.

'Oh yes, very sexy,' he grinned, 'and red too. You'd better take them off, they're getting me going.'

She scrunched her face up at him debunking his sarcasm, stuck her tongue out at him and rolled her eyes making him laugh out loud.

Monday, April 10

At four minutes past nine Jay stood outside the entrance of HMV with his little piece of paradise in his mitts, The Cult's brand new album, 'Sonic Temple', on CD. Looking down at it he was almost bursting with excitement. He glanced at the clock tower then up and down High Street, totally blinkered by what was upon him, this fix of music meant only one thing... College was out! Somehow he had to get to Trac's or his dad's or somewhere, anywhere as soon as possible in order to play it over and over again, that was his only goal for the rest of the day.

Tuesday, April 11

Snow began to fall like a blanket, he watched from his front window and became absorbed in thought. As the glass steamed up with his breath, he wrote his name, the phone rang and he wiped it away abruptly and picked up the receiver.

'Hello.'

'It's me,' came a voice.

'Who's me?' he teased.

'Trac silly.'

'I know. I was joking.'

'Guess what?'

'What?'

'Look at the weather.'

'And?'

'It's snowing,' she said, 'thicko.'

'What?'

'What month is it?'

He rubbed his forehead and yawned. 'April.'

'Our song.'

'Eh?'

'"Sometimes it Snows..."'

'Oh yeah... first kiss,' he smiled to himself, 'sorry, half asleep.'

'Don't worry, you're male, you can't help it.'

'So sweet of you to phone though.'

'Are you being sarcastic.'

'Nooo... must be true love then,' he said, 'you ringing this early?'

'Mmm,' came her distracting voice, 'must be.'

'My Cult album safe?'

'Yes it's safe, I've been giving it a listen... quite like it.'

'Okay, I'll see you later then.'

'Mum won't be able to bring me over tonight if the snow's too bad.'

'Okay, I'll ring you later.'

'Bye,' she chirped.

'See you,' and he replaced the receiver.

Just before he had time to sit down and relax with a cup of tea his mum came in.

'Are you going to college,' she asked, 'or are you going to sit around the house all day?'

'I'm just going to sit round the house all day,' he droned sarcastically.

'You're bloody not,' she roared.

'I'm eighteen I can do what I like, when I like,' he smirked.

'Not while you're under this roof you can't.'

He mouthed her exact words at the same time.

'Moan, moan, moan,' he uttered lightly.

'Oh, do what you bloody like,' she yelled and stormed off to work. He frowned, leant forward and released the TV from its standby mode.

Wednesday, April 12

Jay sat cross-legged in the middle of Trac's room, surrounded by records, cradling in his hands a cup of milky tea and trying not to focus on anything other than the task in hand. He leaned forward and pulled a sheet of blank writing paper to him, poised with pen in hand ready for thoughts to pass down to it. Trac lay on the bed propping her head up with her left hand. Flipping through *The Face* magazine she casually informed him tit bits of gossip about some celebrity or other. He found it dull, to be truthful it kept breaking his concentration, so he made a light tutting noise that Trac didn't seem to pick up on.

'Have you recorded anything onto tape yet?'

'You know I haven't,' he said flippantly.

'It's only a mix of songs Jay.'

'Ahh, see that's where you're wrong, it's more than that, you have to blend the songs. Besides, I'm doing this mix for us so I've got to take your taste into account.'

'Well I can help then,' she smiled firmly and picked up a record. 'My mate leant me this Deacon Blue EP, maybe you can chose a song off it.'

'Which one?'

'Don't mind,' she replied and gave a slight shrug 'I like them all.'

'What is your top three albums?'

'Not sure... yours?'

"Eight Legged Groove Machine', 'Sonic Temple'... 'Sea of Love."

Trac was now frowning at the speed in which he delivered. "Raintown'... 'Under The Cherry Moon' and... 'Staring at the Sea."

Jay rubbed his forehead for a moment and muttered, 'I'm not sure a best of album counts?'

She didn't reply just pulled a face to let him know he was being way too serious.

'Okay, okay,' he said taking note. 'I just need to have a rough outline on paper first and then we will be away.'

'Did it take you this long to do your Cult mix?'

He held a finger in the air and corrected her. 'The Fucking Cult mix,' he uttered with a rising frown. Which somehow made his personal best compilation of The Cult into something more magical than it actually was. Trac frowned at him, 'yes, and why is it called that?'

'Well,' he replied giving her lazy eyes, 'the thing was, I designed the tape cover with The Cult mix in big letters but there was a space that looked a bit odd so I scrawled in fucking and it all pulled together nicely.'

'Right,' she nodded at him, pulling a face that said 'you're weird,' so he stuck his tongue out at her and returned to the blank sheet in front of him. Once the pen hit the paper the list had started, that was the next couple of hours or so mapped out, and that was that. Trac had found herself his second ear along with tea making duties. Conversation was reduced to, 'you will love this song,' or, 'shall I put this one on?'

Friday, April 14

Jay heard his name being called and turned away from his thoughts.

'Hi,' said Trac.

They had arranged to meet outside the Tie Rack near the town centre, now their usual meeting place.

'Hi,' he smiled raising himself from the bench, 'Who's this?'

'Oh, this is Johnny,' she smiled.

Yeah, fine thought Jay staring at the lad standing next to them. He waited for him to leave. Trac then took Jay to one side.

'I can't get rid of him, I've tried dropping hints,' she smiled sweetly.

'Oh right.'

'It will be okay, he'll go in a bit.'

'Great,' he muttered sarcastically.

His rudeness was only superficial. While Jay stood mulling over whether to go or adopt this guy for a while he watched him, hands dug deep into the pockets of his jeans frowning under his mousey and slightly curly fringe. He looked fairly plain thought Jay. The only outstanding feature he really noticed was he was a lot shorter than him, a little below Trac's height. Rubbing at his chin he decided to settle for the fact that Trac had befriended him so therefore he must be okay, for a while at least.

They wandered round the town, window shopping, they had a cup of tea that went okay. Jay actually had exellent manners, he just deliberately acted like a slob, when he wanted to be he could be a remarkable conversationalist too. Trac was hungry and decided on pizza, but Johnny was still tailing them, with a slight huff of breath Jay turned and walked off, she followed him half way across the road, she waited looking at him while a few cars passed between them. A gap came and she walked towards him, her hands together and her head tilted slightly. She reached the pavement and stopped a few feet away.

'Jay, come back.'

'I'm going home.'

She then stepped forward two steps and stood with her small feet together.

'I'm sorry, I tried.'

He tutted and rubbed at his face, 'I came to see you.'

'I thought you'd like to meet some of my friends.'

He mumbled softly, 'I don't want to meet anybody else... I just want to be with you,' and continued to rub at his forehead.

She bit her lip and moved closer still, holding his hand for a few moments.

'Are you alright?'

'Yeah I'm fine,' he sighed again.

'Come on please, he'll go soon, promise. I'll share a pizza with him.'

'Okay, okay,' he smiled, 'you win.'

He followed Trac into Pizzaland with Johnny shuffling behind him. Trac came to a halt at a corner table, next to a large rubber plant.

'Right,' she said removing her purse form her bag, 'I'll order the pizza as it's my treat,' and sat down with a wide smile.

'I'm pretty thirsty,' replied Jay sinking into his seat.

'I'll get these,' said Johnny. 'What do you drink?'

'Almost anything,' he replied, 'usually Irish.'

'Irish?'

'Yeah, Guinness, Jameson... Baileys,' and gave a shrug, 'but I'll be happy with a can of Foster's.'

With two slices of pizza consumed without much room for intake of breath Jay suddenly found himself perking up and feeling... well a little more relaxed and comfortable as he took another gulp of fresh, cold sparking lager.

'Have you been worrying about your driving test?' Johnny asked him.

He looked at Trac who smiled at him. 'To tell the truth I haven't given it much thought.'

'You'll pass easily,' Trac informed him.

'Yeah, of course I will. I've got lessons all week.'

'When is it?' asked Johnny.

'Err, Thursday at Welford Road... eight forty in the morning though, too early,' he replied. 'A couple of vodkas will get rid of the nerves.'

'I don't think that's a good idea,' said Trac gloomily.

Halfway through, still feeling a little put out by this guy he chimed, 'fuck it, let's do a runner!'

The blood drained from Trac's face. 'No way,' she said. 'Absolutley no fucking way.'

He smirked, 'it's just one of those things you have to do in life.'

Trac looked at him sternly as he glanced at the door behind him.

'Okay,' he surrendered and with a swish of his hand the topic was dropped allowing the conversation to seep into pets where Johnny was in his element. He had started talking about his pet snake. Jay had to agree it would be interesting to see the snake, only later that day when Johnny produced the five foot reptile he only felt comfortable observing from a distance, it was now Trac's turn to see the blood drain from his face.

Saturday, April 15

Leaning back Jay rested his head against the wall of his bedroom. With a cold beer in hand he felt like he had all the time in the world. Staring at the ceiling, the radio was playing faintly. The doorbell rang some moments later and with a determined push he moved away from the wall to answer the door. Trac elegantly received a kiss on her forehead from him as he held her hand for a moment or two before returning to his room. She followed and was happy to lounge across his bed and let him entertain her.

'I recorded this off the radio for you,' he said picking up a tape from his desk.

'What's that?'

'"Lullaby',' he smiled but she gave him a puzzled look. 'The Cure... their new single.'

'Oh cool,' she smiled back sinking her head deep into his plumped up pillow.

As he crawled along the base of the bed towards her, he stretched an arm and touched the back of her neck. From that instant his feelings were confirmed, he loved this girl.

She responded and ran a palm across a small bump to his forehead 'how did you do that?'

'I tripped, it was an accident,' he replied calmly.

'You weren't fighting were you?'

He replied with a faint chuckle.

'It's not funny you know. I worry about you.'

'I don't fight. I'm no fighter,' he said softly.

She looked at his eyes, not too sure if she believed him or not and he recognised that.

'No seriously,' he shrugged, 'a slight miss judgement of some steps, that was all.'

She had come to expect a certain amount of his irresponsibility. 'You've got to look after yourself,' and she kissed his bump lightly.

'Maybe I've not had enough parental guidance?'

'No, you've just chosen to ignore it more like.'

'Anyway I've got you to look after me now.'

'Mmm.'

He held up his hand and with his finger and thumb he made a small gap. 'I'm that far from loving you.'

She smiled as it became a battle between them both, they drew comfort and confidence from the gaps getting smaller each time, he was smiling with delight at this subtle form of communication. It made it fun and all in under five minutes.

'So do you then?' she asked, with a warm smile.

He gave her another shrug and frowned at her as he changed the music on his stereo, returning closer to her he whispered, 'I'll think about it.' Smiling he ran a finger down the centre of her face and then began to unbutton her shirt with a kind of careless elegance to reveal her bare chest. Noting her gold heart shaped necklace, he toyed with it momentarily. He had when he could trust himself a strange gentleness and loveableness.

'Come on, tell me,' she said, but he just replied with a wider smile. 'I don't know whether I should let you do that?'

'Oh I think you should,' he said softly.

'Why?'

'Because Trac,' he pulled her to him closer still and whispered, 'I love you.' Her face beamed all the more, 'now I've been waiting for you to say that for the last half an hour.'

'So do you love me then?' he whispered coyly.

She looked into his softened eyes, 'I thought you already knew I'm wild and crazy about you.'

Detecting a little sarcasm he gave her another one of his frowns and waited.

'Of course I love you silly,' she beamed.

He gave her a lopsided boyish grin and collapsed onto the bed backwards, overjoyed that the belief that nothing beats the high of a first time had been shattered. He rolled onto his front, rubbed his face into his pillow and murmured, 'tickle my back.'

Trac happily sat on his bum and removed his top. 'The nerves in the back are farther apart than the nerves in the finger,' she said.

'What?'

'Have you got two pencils?'

'Yeah, on the window sill.'

She lightly touched his back with the two pencils at the same time yet it only felt like one, only able to feel two when she moved the pencils further apart.

'You learn something new every day,' he mumbled.

Upon his second request she scratched at his back until it was red but he still pleaded her to continue.

They talked, kissed, brazenly eyed and touched each other. Trac rubbed her nose companionably with his and they held each other tightly. They kissed for a long time, they wanted to be there in the dark all night and so allowed the evening to pass tranquilly away.

Sunday, April 16

The large triangle shape of grass before them was Jubilee Park, but somehow lay barren and uninviting, the under used patch of land had little in the way of attracting kids and held no park furniture, no swings, no slide, no goal post or any kind of sporting activity markings on the grass. With not even a single bench, it just looked like a field.

Jay looked at Trac and said, 'at least it's nice and quiet.'

'I can't believe how warm it is.'

'Global warming,' he muttered as he looked around. He had to admit it was the ideal place to walk a dog, yet there was not a soul about, maybe a loose dog sniffing in the hedge rows would suddenly appear... no, only the sound of a horse could be defined among the rustle of the trees as the wind passed through them.

'Yeah it's quiet,' agreed Trac nodding her head and taking his hand, 'no adults.'

'True.'

'Come on,' she said lively and yanked at his arm, 'let's go down onto the old railway track.'

They entered by a smooth mud slope about two metres wide which led down to a grassy dirt track. Immediately to his left, the arched bridge made of dark blue bricks covered in the occasional faded splatterings of graffiti, protected a pub style bench from the elements. To the right, the path lead away as far as your eyes could see before reaching another bridge above it. In front of him stood a large boulder with a small plaque and he eased closer to read it.

Leire Nature Walk. This nature reserve generously donated to the village of Leire by Mr and Mrs J.A. Redfern was officially opened 1st May, 1988.

'Well, it's not been here long then.'

'No,' she smiled. 'You remember coming down here before don't you?'

'It was dark then, wasn't it.'

'Suppose.'

'It's a shame about all the graffiti, makes the place look run down.'

'Oh, I thought you'd be into graffiti.'

'Well it is art, self expressive art, if it's good I do... this kind of scrawl it's just damaging.'

'It's supposed to get up people's noses and maybe that's the point of it?'
He gave her a shrug, 'I guess that knackered building used to be something.'

'Yeah but I don't know what?'

They wandered up the path leisurely, listening to the flutter of wildlife in between the bushes. Jay jumped up and along the large moss covered bricks that were dotted along one edge of the embankment. Fields to the left and right, the transformation from a quiet park to this peaceful nature driven secluded footpath seemed like the ideal pocket in which to escape. The whole path from start to finish took about ten to fifteen minutes to walk depending on the pace and you could venture beyond if you hopped over the wooden fence and ignored the signs to keep out.

Halfway or so back down the footpath he broke away from her and disappeared up the embankment among the trees. A moment or two later Trac followed him unconvinced it was a good idea and cursed under her breath as she grabbed onto the odd tree trunk or branch for support as she went. When she reached the top he was sitting on his leather jacket smiling.

'Not a bad view from here.'

'Really,' she panted. 'I've got muddy shoes now.'

'Oh no! It's the end of the world,' he smirked and she clipped him across the shoulder in retaliation to his sarcasm.

'Let's sit here for a bit seeing as the weather's pretty good.'

'Okay,' she mumbled as she plonked herself down next to him, half in the hedgerow and half on the field. She tucked her thighs close to her chest, arms looping round them and lacing her fingers tightly together. He looked at her; hair straight, cut below the shoulders, her skin clear... she was pretty he thought. He ran an arm round the base of her back and she fell into him effortlessly. He pushed a hand through her hair and kissed her forehead. As she looked up he pressed his lips to hers fingers now slowly unbuttoning her top and trying to tease out one of her breasts to the open air.

'Jay, what are you doing?' she chuckled.

'I was... err, sort of,' he stopped there, smiled, and gave her a light shrug of his shoulders. 'You can't blame a bloke for trying.'

'Someone might see.'
He looked around, 'but there's no-one around.'

'Yeah there is,' and she pointed over to the entrance.

'Oh, he can't see all the way over here.'

Further kissing and a compromise had been reached with the one breast and Jay was more than willing to stay exactly like that for the rest of the afternoon but Trac had other ideas.

'I'm hungry,' she moaned as she buttoned up her top. 'Let's go back to mine, grab something to eat and watch TV.'

The small spare bedroom upstairs had a slanted roof dominating it. He rolled onto the single bed while Trac put on the small portable TV sitting upon a small dark wooden chest of drawers.

'It's black and white,' he muttered.

She responded by putting her hands to her hips and blurting, 'we can always go downstairs and sit with Mum and Dad?'

He scrunched up his face at her and shook it slightly, much happier to be laying in the half light of the TV close together.

'Well then,' she said as she flicked through the channels, 'looks as though there's nothing worth watching anyway.'

He pulled at her left hand and she gladly fell back onto the bed.

'Maybe it's time to get my own back,' she whispered as she swept a teasing hand up between his thighs.

Tuesday, April 18

Jay gave his thin spectacled driving instructor a bundle of five pound notes and began to apologise for all the loose change that was slotted in between. The instructor counted the money, allowed his face to rise into a gleeful smile and accelerated harshly away. The two hour lesson was a breeze. The only thing that had become recently annoying was using his paid time to fill the vehicle with petrol, still he thought, only one more lesson before the test and it will all be done and dusted.

He returned to his room which, apart from his bed, resembled a designer's studio with paper, pens, brushes, Spray Mount, card and a pile of work littering every surface including the floor. With Monday having ran the same course, his enthusiasm for getting his portfolio ready for his HND interview had finally disappeared. He slouched onto his bed, hands slotted behind his head and wondered if he could wait out this period of time until he had the urge to finish off what had so far been a very productive couple of days. He pondered as to what Trac might be up to, sitting in a class doodling his name onto her folder, too tired or bored to concentrate for the last half an hour perhaps. The image of her in her short navy blue skirt brought a smirk to his face and he decided to finish recording the mix he started on Sunday along with designing its cover.

'Cartoon,' he muttered to himself as he rubbed at the side of his head and moved from his bed to his desk and set to work.

Wednesday, April 19

Jay was pumped up ready to deliver his positive, enthusiastic passion about all things arty as well as his own contribution when he entered the interview room clutching his portfolio protectively.

The first thing that struck him was how small the room was, the bare walls displayed none of the feeling of excitement or energy he had anticipated. The guy behind the worn desk had wiry hair, thick black national health glasses behind which sat a pair of bulging eyes both pointing more to the side than straight ahead. Dressed in a dark brown suit and tie with an off white shirt he looked in his mid forties and more like a history teacher or librarian. He thought about what Trac had told him... 'just look at life as though everything is fate. If you were meant to pass the interview you will, if you were meant to be a brilliant graphic designer then you will be.' A slow and negative aura washed over him and he found himself switching off, whatever the bloke was jabbering on about, Jay simply wasn't interested. All he wanted to do was pick up his folder and leave. He tried to nod and desperately regain eye contact but he found it hard to focus, his disinterest only mounted. 'This is a load of fucking rubbish this,' ran through his mind as he found himself looking at the clock on the wall, 'ten more minutes and I'll be on my way home.'

Retreating back down the bland corridor from where he came Nene College didn't seem to have the lift it had when he had visited. He suddenly felt pissed off, he made the wrong first choice college and the only consolation was he knew the interview was far from good and his application would be rejected, in other words 'fate' as Trac would say, had let him know Northampton wasn't the place to be.

Another two hour lesson left him bored with driving. With his limbs free and the fresh air blowing, he enjoyed the walk up from his dad's to Trac's.

'Driving lesson went well.'

'Don't worry about tomorrow, you'll sail through,' replied Trac.

His eyes fluttered a little and he smiled with a slight nod.

'And the interview?'

He retained a warming expression as he brought his index finger to his mouth, he didn't want to be taken back there and allow that to dampen his upbeat mood. Trac sat speechless on the edge of her bed. A full minute passed while he pawed the row of ever growing CDs that were making their way across the back of the chest of drawers. Another minute passed before he looked up and noted her expressionless face, smiled and said, 'come here and I'll give you a big kiss then.'

As they kissed he felt a warm explosion in his head, the pleasure was grand. He was in love again and he felt on top of the world. 'You're my little baby,' he said holding her to him. He held up 'Under The Cherry Moon' and said, 'this?'

Trac's eyes narrowed as she smiled and floated to her bed, fingers lingering in his until he followed.

He lay relaxed, happy to be quiet, to soak her up, to listen to her talk. He slightly nodded or raised the corners of his mouth so that she didn't stop or feel as though it was too much of a one way conversation.

'You blokes have it easy, women have it way harder,' she sighed. 'We have to deal with periods... babies and stuff. And if a girl sleeps around she's a slag. How unfair is all that.'

Jay gave her another light nod only she was looking directly into his eyes as if wanting him now to engage more. He rubbed his face into her pillow and replied softly, 'erm... I suppose but then again as weird as it is, the whole baby thing is really special... well bigger than special. You know what I mean.'

'Mmm,' she responded.

'That's one of the reasons women fascinate me.' He lifted her top up and kissed her stomach. 'It's amazing you can have a real live person growing in there,' and he massaged her stomach lightly before blowing down into it making a loud rasping noise and she shied a little.

'What's up?'

'Don't you think my stomach's a little podgy.'

'Perfect.'

She smiled happily and pulled her top down.

'You'll always be perfect compared to me,' he whispered.

'Well women usually look rough by the time they're forty... figures go, hair goes grey. Men seem to age better,' she yawned and cuddled nearer, 'wrinkles suit men.'

'Mmm,' he murmured placing his hand on the back of her thigh, where it became her bum. 'I'd better go... early night an all that,' and squeezed her bum as he rose. 'If I pass I'll take you wherever you want to go.'

Thursday, April 20

The sound of synthesised punk music blared out the window of a red half black vinyl-roofed 1600 S registration Chrysler Avenger as it came flying round an S bend at a seemingly ridiculous speed. He had finally passed his test.

Trac stood at the top of her drive waiting for him. As he pulled up smiling, he beckoned her over with his hand and she jogged down the sloped driveway to him, arms still folded.

'You passed then. Well done,' she commended him.

He grinned, 'shall we go for a spin then?'

She approved and skipped to the passenger door.

Backing down the drive with a screech he jeered, 'here we go' and turned the music up.

She frowned upon his unsound driving but was excited about him passing. He had the biggest smile of self achievement beaming across his face which she knew would take some time to dissolve. The straight road ahead urged him to drive faster, he broke into an even wider grin, a disquieting grin.

'Slow down.'

He slowed a little but there was still the untrustworthy playful smile about his eyes. He could see Trac was slowly losing herself in him, losing her normal bounds of reality. He wanted to show her that life was never dull with him. He didn't like rules and he didn't like being held down. He always wanted freedom to see how much he could push, and push. A free and easy lifestyle, he seemed to feel this great positivity and presence amongst people.

'Where are you going to take me then?'

'I don't know,' he said in a humourously sarcastic voice.

He indicated into the garage to fill the car up with petrol. He then drove round a small car park off Shuttleworth Lane in Cosby, spurting gravel everywhere and with a handbrake turn he brought the car to an abrupt halt.

'Shall we go for a walk?'

'Okay,' she smiled.

They walked along a small country path at the back of Cosby village golf course and decided to edge their way down the slope to the old abandoned railway line. Trac went first, she was being really careful, but too slow in his opinion so he gave her a little nudge. Turing she slipped down the dirt hill. Sliding down most of the way on her backside to his delight. It was almost as if she was sledging.

He quickly ran down and picked her up trying to hide his amusement.

'Look at the state of my jeans,' she groaned.

Her glum face made him break into a light chuckle, 'they're not too bad,' he replied, impishly peering round at her bum.

'Mum will go mad,' she muttered tersely. 'It's not funny,' and pushed him away once she had gained her balance.

'Smells a bit,' he smirked.

'Don't you dare laugh,' she harked and began to hit him in a frenzy.

He began to chuckle at her outburst, 'Calm down... why don't you just calm down.'

She stopped and took a couple of deep breaths, 'take me home.'

He teased her a little by saying she couldn't sit in his car with her muddy jeans.

'Oh don't,' she whined, 'take me home. I want to go to the loo as well.'

He gave a meek smile. 'Come on then,' he replied and he put his hand out. She paused and glared at him unsure for a moment before taking it.

Her mum was not at all happy, 'I've just washed them,' she snapped. Typical mum thought Jay trying to hide behind her bedroom door.

He stayed with her until dinner time and then went home. Later he met his mates in the pub and dropped his keys in the middle of the table so they all knew he had passed.

4. Wild and free

Dressed in his black shirt, sleeves rolled up and the top button undone, Jay sat on the bonnet of his car sipping at a can of Coke and enjoying the sun. He wondered what time it was and became increasingly impatient. He finished the can and wandered into the grounds of Lutterworth school to find Trac. She could be anywhere, he thought dropping the can into the bin and surveying the school building. He cast his mind back to when he skulked the corridors of the place and chuckled softly to himself. The school seemed somehow smaller and less daunting than it had when he first started there, yet its familiarity was warming. He looked at the decor, nothing changes he thought, painted in such uninspirational colours, a dull green or battleship grey giving off a suppressing atmosphere except perhaps the art department which had a lighter feel and felt more like home. It brought back good memories. He pondered for a moment wondering if he should have perhaps stayed on to do A levels... Nah, he shook his head, wouldn't have lasted five minutes, too head strong, anti authoritarian and only ever saw the system as something to upset. It brought back memories of detensions, crisp sandwiches and nasty tight fitting trousers that were all the rage but so uncomfortable around your privates. He wandered through the half circle bus lanes glaring at the building as though it was a relic and headed towards the S block. Trac spotted him and waved frantically at him along with her friends from a classroom window, snapping him from his thoughts. He gave them a smile and walked into the building. She jumped off her stool, excused herself from the class and approached him, feet squeaking as she walked quickly along the freshly waxed floor, with so much delight on her face she had a spring in her step.

'Hi,' she whispered.

He grabbed her and began to kiss her once she had reached him but she pulled away from him.

'Not here I'll get done,' she said quickly and furtively glanced about for hidden teachers on the prowl.

'Come on,' he smirked, 'that's what makes it exciting,' and reached for her again. She quickly scoured the corridor making sure it was all clear before allowing the embrace.

'Lucky you found me.'

'Well I remembered you said you were doing science so...'

'So you do listen to what I say?'

'Sure, I just look as though I don't,' he replied softly. 'I spent most of my time hanging about here,' and he looked around.

'Why aren't you at college anyway?'

'Well... it was a choice of tracing out eight point lettering in a typography lesson, which would have taken eight million years, or spending the day cruising about in the car in the sunshine listening to music and seeing you in your school uniform.'

'Mmm... where are you parked?'

'Just round the side there,' and he pointed.

'Look,' she said, 'it's nearly home time anyway so I'll see you in a few minutes.'

He tapped his fingers on the steering wheel to The Wonder Stuff's 'Eight Legged Groove Machine' that roared from the car's speakers. He didn't hear the school bell sound but realised the end of her day had arrived by the army of kids that swept out of the gate. He sat studying a group of girls all dressed in a similar attire; navy blue skirts and summer blouses, two of which were wearing thick black tights which began a warmth and stirring in his loins. There was something about schoolgirls he thought, maybe it was due to the fact they seemed so much of a tease when he was at school. Trac opened the passenger door and woke him from his daydream.

'You don't mind giving Craig a lift do you?' she asked.

'No, no, get in,' he mumbled more concerned with the fact he had an erection.

The short curly haired lad still had the remnants of boyhood, a round face and freckles about his cheeks. He leapt excitedly into the back of the car and began to yank at his blue stripped school tie, freeing it from a badly creased light blue shirt.

The screeching tyres of the car left rubber marks on the tarmac as he put his foot to the floor.

'So, what kind of day have you had?'

'Boring,' she moaned.

'Arrh, poor little baby,' he chuckled, placing a comforting hand onto her knee.

Jay suppressed a smirk as Trac sighed grumpily, slung her bag to the floor, kicked her shoes off and headed for the kitchen to make a large pot of tea.

'I always drink no end of tea when I come round here,' he said, now allowing himself to smile fully while she was preoccupied.

'So you don't want one then?'

'No, I didn't say that,' he replied softly. 'It was merely an observation.'

'Mum,' she called. 'Do you want a cup of tea?'

'Yes please,' came her mum's voice followed up with, 'you're home early.'

'Yeah, Jay picked me up.'

He sat himself in front of the TV and began watching the cartoons, contented to half listen to Trac's out pouring of her day.

Saturday, April 22

Jay leaned over, wiping droplets of water off the car's engine block. His toes were beginning to go numb, his predicament merely a result of over excitement. He watched Rob to his right mirroring his actions only with the constant mutterings of, 'I told you to slow down. Now you've soaked the engine and the spark plugs.'

Jay, naturally, thought it was the end. Goose-bumps peppered his arms and he exhaled a large amount of air. All elation of passing his test had gone.

'Go and give it a go now,' Rob spat as he hopped up and down trying to keep his feet from freezing.

Jay returned to the driver's seat noting the water was only just below the rim of the cills, a few millimetres higher and the foot wells of the car would have flooded. He twisted the key in the ignition, desperately trying to revive the engine for it to make only a few feeble groans. He heard Rob shout something so he stopped and sat there babbling. 'What the fuck are we going to do?'

He'd felt exhilarated tearing down those country lanes at speed, the sound of the revving engine spurring him on, practicing some quality handbrake turns combined with rear wheel spinning accompanied by the screeching tyres and burning rubber, it had all been at the top of his agenda. There was no let up in the constant boyish banter as he screeched the car from corner to corner snaking down the narrow lanes. On taking a hump back bridge at speed he hooted, 'woooo hoooo!' as it launched off the top momentarily before slamming back down onto the tarmac. In much the same way he charged towards the ford, only it had to be said Rob did look slightly panicked with his left arm out the window clutching the top of the door where it met the roof, the other hand squeezing on his knee. He had to be fair to Rob and admit he had jabbered slow down a number of times but his observations clearly did not register, Jay was too focused on the job in hand. He envisaged a triumphant splash and spray of water from either side of the car as he ploughed his way through with a wild cheer, only it didn't go down that way. Within seconds of the car making impact the vision fizzled away as the car came to an abrupt halt and stalled slap bang in the middle of the flowing water.

Rob just said one word that summed up the situation. 'Twat!'

Now he felt drained, even slightly sick, as he sat there looking at his pale toes trying to stop them from cramping and listening to the constant mutterings that his mate made.

'Try it again.'

It groaned again with not much life. He looked down at the flowing water not sure if he was transfixed by the water or was waiting for the onset of panic. Even though his pal was a mechanic his faith was dwindling as he felt himself go limp wishing the river and ground would open up beneath him and swallow him up. He tried not to picture his mum and dad exploding in front of him and instead took his mind off the situation and scoured the water for fish.

'Again.'

This time the dull groan turned to a wheeze and sparked, the engine had life. The relief that rose up through his body was truly amazing. Rob slammed down the bonnet and waded round to him, hands covered in black grime and his socks loose over his shoulder.

'Now get the fucking thing on dry land,' he said looking more relaxed.

It took a bit of skillful manoeuvring as the wheels slipped on the slime on the bed of the ford. Once it caught grip it shuddered forward up the concrete slope and rose from the water. With the panic over, Jay cheered, 'thank fuck for that.'

That was more than enough excitement for one day, he dropped Rob off and had accepted with ease that the next time he was down the pub with the lads he was going to have to take some stick. The feeling of guilt about the abuse he'd inflicted on his vehicle appeared to be far harder to accept, so in an effort for that to pass he spent the next three hours of his afternoon lovingly cleaning and polishing it from bonnet to boot before setting off to see Trac.

Trac gave him a welcoming smile as he wandered into the jean shop looking sheepishly as he did so.

'What have you been up to?'

'You don't want to know,' he said with a rye smile.

'Here,' she said, 'I got you something,' and passed him a small parcel.

'What for?'

'It's just a little pressie to say well done for passing your test, I said you'd do it.'

He held up a toy car and turned it in his hands a few times before returning a smile.

'I couldn't find an Avenger,' she said.

'That's okay, cheers.'

'So have you come to give me a lift home then?'

'Yep, I'll be going out with the lads later on, vodka and cards night,' he shrugged 'But I'll be all yours Sunday.'

'Good o,' she peeped, 'but you'll have to ring my sister for me and tell her not to pick me up then.'

'No problem.'

He spent every spare moment engrossed in the car; it offered freedom and independence, and it was as if the car began to have its own personality. Okay he thought, so maybe it wasn't quite as cool as the 1968 highland green GT390 Mustang from *Bullit* or as iconic as the 70's Ford Gran Torino from *Starsky and Hutch* or even the British equivalent copper brown Mk1 Ford Consul GT from *The Sweeney*, but it was however a little closer to the General Lee, the orange Dodge Charger from *The Dukes Of Hazard* and he liked the idea that it had been named. He smiled to himself as he tapped on the steering wheel, the name popped into his head, from here on his car was to be known as 'The Beast'.

Monday, April 24

An early spring morning was ruined by the pollution of the train station. He caught the train on time but somehow arrived at college late. His form tutor looked at his watch and then at him and simply said, 'you should have been here at nine o'clock.'

'Why what happened?' he replied sharply and followed it with a sneer. He sat down at his desk and continued to listen to the lecture about how important punctuality is and that his work would suffer.

Paul stood over him chewing on a stubby pencil which left lead residue on his lips, he was finding it difficult to give up smoking. He was a short stocky bloke with a crew cut and pale skin. Jay had felt uneasy in this guy's presence ever since he had routed through his drawers when he wasn't around in search of some white paint. He'd found news clippings of various murders in particular pictures of Mira Hindly and Ian Brady, it spooked him enough to feel a cold shudder.

'You can't go through your life being drunk and stupid,' Paul informed him in a dull tone.

'Why not?' grunted Jay followed by, 'don't you worry about me, if he doesn't like my work then it's just too bad, but as it is I'm getting some good marks so you see stupid doesn't really come into it... Well not unless I've had at least a half bottle of vodka, then you may be privileged to see high quality performances of stupidity,' and his eyes dilated as he grinned mindlessly.

That was the one thing that annoyed half the class. If Jay and Adrian were not studying at college they were drinking themselves into oblivion and no-one knew how they did it, how they could drink and carry on like drop outs and still attain good grades?

Twenty minutes later and the class was listless with boredom, putting Jay straight into one of his 'I don't give a shit' moods.

The photography tutor finally arrived to give them a briefing of their new projects, Jay still found his stutter amusing. When the class had first met him Jay had laughed and was the first to be told off. The thing about people with a stutter is you try and help them finish a word if not out loud then certainly in your head Jay thought as he glared at Dick in mid stutter.

'F... ff... for your next pp... p... project.'

This is going to take bloody ages thought Jay as he shook his head, why doesn't he just write a brief out? Sometimes he had little or no patience. Adrian sat grinning at him trying his best to make him laugh out loud so Dick had further reason to go on disliking him.

That afternoon they spent with Leslie Marshall, their typography tutor, an elderly gentleman with wire-rimmed half moon spectacles and a posh voice that was easily impersonated. Adrian and Jay had picked up on this and had hours even days of amusement simply being Leslie. He always asked 'How are you getting on?' And muttered, 'thirteen and a half pica ems,' incessantly, most of the class stuck to millimetres when measuring a design layout, the pica scale was prehistoric and only kept itself alive by its reference to the size of type.

The class was hit with critical assessment, which meant all the work they had done had to be pinned to the wall and supposedly receive constructive criticism from Leslie. Dave had not displayed any of his work, he only had one page of drawings done in pencil that looked very poor indeed. Adrian snuck up and pinned the sheet up on the far wall of the classroom without him noticing.

'And whose is this work here?' asked Leslie.

Jay sat on the edge of the table eating a bag of KP pickled onion Space Raiders. With a smirk he said, 'eh up Dave... isn't that yours?'

'Arrgh, you bastards,' mumbled Dave stirring forward from his seat.

'Whoever's it is, it's well below standard.'

'Yeah that's yours Dave,' said Adrian trying to contain his amusement. Jay added, 'God is that all you've done Dave?'

'David is this your work?'

'Yes,' he muttered. 'Sorry but I've spent most of my time collecting reference from the library.'

'Umm,' vibrated from Lesley as he rubbed at his chin as though waiting for Dave to further explain his lack of productivity.

'I err... had a bit of a mind block.'

'Mind block my arse,' coughed Adrian.

Dave put his right hand to his forehead. 'Awwgh,' he groaned and with that he shuffled across the room towards the wall at speed and pulled it down in haste only fuelling the pair's amusement.

'I'll have to see you about that first thing tomorrow.'

Dave nodded and glared at the two of them still in stitches of laughter.

'Arrgh, you bastards,' he complained. 'I'll get you for this,' he said with a sneer, immediately planning his revenge. Dave's revenges where normally of a high standard; Jay had found a dead fish in his coat pocket once instead of his train pass, the ticket inspector wasn't amused either. Fellow passengers glared on while Adrian was struggling to breathe for laughing so much. All was fair in love and war and, just as Adrian had helped Dave pull off this wonderful stroke of tomfoolery, Jay had instigated in one of Dave's finest performances of revenge. The scene had been set for Adrian's eighteenth birthday. They had wrapped up an array of stupid items for presents and held a presentation in front of the whole class. First up was a roll of used masking tape followed by a packet of scampi flavoured Nic-Nacks. The show in front of the class continued and Adrian was thoroughly enjoying the attention as he unveiled each of his pointless gifts. The last gift was heavily wrapped as he picked at the paper trying to prize enough away to get a good rip from it, Dave already had started to laugh uncontrollably.

'Have you farted Dave?' grunted Adrian sniffing at the air.

This set Jay off laughing too as he turned to Dave and made a thumbs up sign. When he had removed all the paper Adrian held the container up trying to figure his gift out. The clear perspex had clouded up from the inside which had made immediate identification difficult, but there was a label with the words scrawled across it in blue and red Magic Marker pen that read; *That's showbiz.*

The awful smell that was in the air had notably become stronger and, to his horror, Adrian realised at the same time as just about everybody else in the class that what he held in the air was Dave's freshly produced turd, lovingly encased in a cotton bud container. His mouth fell open and he dropped it straight away in disgust. Jay laughed out loud as Dave whooped with enjoyment.

'Arrwgh you sick bastards,' he muttered squirming on the spot.

As it had hit the floor the whole class turned away in revulsion. Jay and Dave continued to laugh until tears came to his eyes.

'That ain't funny you know,' moaned Adrian. He exhaled mid-sentence, trying to force an expression of amused tolerance as he shook his head at them. 'You disgusting pair of twats.'

Wiping at his eyes Jay uttered to Dave, 'brilliant'.

Most of the class for the first time began to support Adrian in this moment of repel. One girl snorted, 'I can't believe you would do something as disgusting as that David, I thought you had more maturity than those two.' Someone else sighed, 'Oh, David.'

The class it seemed had expected nothing less from Jay but as for Dave, it was as if he had let them all down as well as himself.

Dave felt all eyes burning on him and an increasing sense of shame. He tried to apportion blame onto Jay the best he could. 'It was his fucking idea,' he said pointing away at Jay desperately trying to fend off the disappointed looks as the entertainment broke apart.

Jay gave the best innocent shrug he could possibly manage, 'Dave don't blame me... it's your shit.'

Eventually someone had managed to hurl it out the window, only the tale didn't quite finish there; Adrian had to try to even things out a little. Two days later the turd made a reappearance, this time in Dave's desk drawer along with half a dozen rotten fish, some taped to the underside of his desk and some were even in his photography folder slotted into the negative holders, gutted and giving off such an awful stench that it took most of the day before the smell had receded and Dave could see the funny side.

Shortly after tea that evening Trac's sister dropped her off at his house and he was delighted to see her.

'What did you do at college?' she asked.

'Not much, just had a laugh.'

'What did you get up to?' she asked seeing the mischief in his eyes.

'You know me, I specialise in having fun.'

'I worry about you.'

'You worry too much,' he yawned and stretched out his arms to the sky.

'And you don't worry enough. You're a bad influence.'

'What me?' he smirked.

'You give good kids bad ideas.'

'Never,' he stated innocently.

'And you shouldn't listen to Adrian, he only makes you worse.'

He simply smiled and said, 'yeah whatever you say.'

'Where's your guitar?'

She looked at him carefully.

'No, I didn't lose it at cards.'

'Don't know what you mean?'

'Yeah you do, I can see your brain ticking.'

'So where is it?'

'Sold it... pain I know but I needed the cash.'

'You need to get another part time job.'

'Yeah I guess,' he mumbled. 'Tea?'

He stood squeezing the teabag with a small spoon against the inside of the cup and watched the water change colour. He was thinking about his hands exploring her body. Tonight he could begin with his hand underneath her T-shirt because her breasts were previously explored. He smiled widely to himself as he had made a point of memorising their size and shape. The thought of what lay between her attracting thighs, and for her to explore in his jeans a little more than previous fumblings, caused a rising effect in his energy levels as well as elsewhere. Total removal of jeanwear may have to wait a little longer. That was the point he longed for, to have her press her naked body to his.

'You're taking your time,' came her voice.

She startled him from his thoughts and he felt a sense of shame, it was as if she knew what he had been thinking.

She smiled. 'you okay?'

'What? Oh yeah fine just errr... there you go,' he passed her the mug.

They lay on his bed close to each other watching the TV. Trac finished her tea and shortly began to fumble with the fly of his jeans. She continued to struggle with the buttons so he offered to help but she insisted on doing it herself. She felt his erection through his underwear, slipping her hand inside, she began to play with it, not particularly right but he enjoyed it all the same. Besides he didn't want to discourage her curiosity.

'I know I've always got stuff going through my head, but I do love you,' he said and gave her a warm squeeze.

'Love you back.'

'What do you love?'

'Everything... the way you hold me, the way you kiss... touch me.'

'Good,' he smiled as he swirled his hands lightly round her stomach creeping downward, gliding a palm between her thighs.

'Does this excite you?' he whispered.

'Yes,' she replied.

A little further and her hand stopped him, his eyes narrowed and studied her face, taking its time to read into any movement she made.

'I don't want you to think...'

'Think what?'

'That, that I'm easy.'

He smiled as a reply.

'But I don't want you to think you have to ask every time you want to.' Propping his head up with his left hand, his eyes soft he responded faintly as he ran her hair behind her ears with his right hand.

'When things are ready to happen... they will.'

Tuesday, April 25

Having read an open and love-filled letter from Trac he felt his heart sink for having dreamt of Shelley. It confused him, not so much that it made him miss her more, it just reminded him of the hurt. He took a sip of tea and, finding it was now only lukewarm, drained the cup slowly, stalling for time and trying to work out what his next move should be if the guilt did not dissolve soon. The worst of it was not being able to explain how he felt, but unknowingly allowed his body language to do the work. Trac asked him a number of times if he was feeling okay. He replied with 'fine' or 'okay,' but the tone with which he said it told a different story and therefore he found it more difficult than he had expected in turning the conversation round, to the point where he could be more casual and aloof with her. Becoming increasingly frustrated and trapped by the situation he blurted out how mixed up he was feeling.

'Jay you've got to put your trust in me.'

'I'm... I'm not sure what's going on with me?' he mumbled before making another pathetic excuse.

'Where's that leave us?'

'You can't promise me you won't ever go.'

In a matter of seconds he knew by her expression that it was the wrong thing to do. To make matters worse he made another poor excuse with which to escape the uncomfortable situation. He would deal with it another day if the feelings of doubt surfaced again.

Wednesday, April 26

The morning moved too slow, they were supposed to be studying broadsheets which created nothing artistic. It was only when they chose to rearrange some of the famous cartoons in the *Sunday Times* with scripts of their own that any amusement was had. Adrian took the prize for the most amusing, it was the small poster he had created on a tree that read *'Big Bert, £30 for a good hard arse fuck!'* and the cartoon character studying it with a pondering face. Once they had laughed at that nothing was going to match it, at least not for that day, so Jay and Dave sat in the common room both with long glum faces munching on sweets in silence.

Just before they both got into a serious mode of depression Adrian burst through the double doors clutching a pamphlet in his hand with enough enthusiasm for the three of them.

'Look at this,' he roared thrusting the small pamphlet at the two of them, 'I found it on the library notice board.'

Jay stretched out a hand lethargically and took the pamphlet.

He mumbled, 'Doctor Who on stage in Birmingham.'

'Let's have a look,' chirped Dave.

'Come on lads, let's go. It's got a laser show and everything.'

'How much does it say for a ticket Dave?'.

'Three pound fifty.'

'Let's go then,' announced Jay smiling widely.

'When... when?' asked Adrian still with an abundant amount of enthusiasm.

'Now is a good a time as any. I've got The Beast,' and he dangled the keys.

'There will be loads of kids there,' exclaimed Dave.

'So?'

'Jay, I'm over twenty years old, it's totally unthinkable of me to go and see Doctor Who.'

'Don't be average Dave... Come on... show some impulse.'

'Come on Dave,' bubbled Adrian nudging him.

Dave did his utmost to brace himself for the bombardment of goading he was about to receive. He clamped both hands to his knees 'No... No... No...' he muttered softly as they bounced around before him pointing at the leaflet excitedly like a pair of energetic children.

'Come on Dave, it's only a laugh.'

'I can't afford it,' he mumbled, 'it's my girlfriend's birthday today.'

'So,' laughed Adrian, 'we'll be back before tonight.'

'I said I'd take her out for a meal.'

'Just tell her you went to see Doctor Who with us and you'll take her out at the weekend or something,' suggested Jay.

Dave's posture had slumped, he'd become confused, even disorientated. His hands lifted to his face, he was struggling.

The Beast's door slammed. Dave was sat in the front seat still looking slightly bewildered and unsure. Jay and Adrian couldn't help but laugh, they could spur poor old Dave on so easily.

'It'll be alright Dave... trust me,' smiled Jay as he stuck the leaflet in pride of place slap bang in the middle of the dashboard; nothing else was in his head other than acting out this new plan of the day.

'Adrian that stinks,' roared Jay. 'Did you have to wait till we got in the car.' Adrian just chuckled as the windows got wound down.

The bracing smell of gas and oil filled The Beast as it started.

'It will be character building Dave you'll see,' said Jay and gave him a friendly nudge before pulling off.

'Do you know how to get there?'

'Erm, I've got a rough idea of the direction.'

'What music is this?' asked Adrian leaning forward between the front seats.

'Various indie stuff,' he replied and turned the volume control up some more notches while Dave sat swigging gulps of brandy from a bottle he had found in the glove box.

'Help yourself Dave.'

'Phew, it's pretty strong stuff,' gasped Dave wiping his mouth.

'It's only forty percent proof. Adrian, look on the back shelf there's some vodka that's fifty percent.'

Adrian turned round and picked the bottle up and admired it. 'Fucking hell, blue label Smirnoff.'

'Don't open it,' said Jay quickly. 'That's for a special occasion... there's a house party coming up.'

'House party... where?' Adrian asked.

'I don't know too many details at the moment but when I do you'll be the first to know.'

Forty minutes later they had just passed the spaghetti junction and got dizzy driving around the same roundabout while Adrian studied the map of Birmingham and waited for Dave to acquire a traffic cone.

It wasn't too long before all three of them were wandering up the road looking for the theatre.

'There...' pointed Adrian with an unsure tone as he studied the rectangular building that didn't have the grand feel they were expecting.

'Is this it?' said Dave flatly.

'Well it says Alexandra theatre.'

Adrian looked at the pamphlet in his hand then back up at the sign and followed it by a three hundred and sixty degree turn in search of a more dramatic piece of architecture.

'Let's just go for a beer,' suggested Dave.

A wave of disappointment was about to wash over them when Adrian's eyes glided over the interior displays, 'look, there's the Tardis.'

'I don't think it's *The Tardis*.'

'Erm... it might be,' he replied excitedly and marched towards the double doors waiting for no-one.

As soon as they had their tickets they wandered into the large auditorium. Dave's vision of children in school parties running around was absolutely accurate, they stood towering over them like giants. Jay patted Adrian on the back and he looked back at him with excitement, both clutching their tickets. It was as though another level of friendship had been added to their growing bond that came from design, separated parents, booze and music. They both nudged into Dave hoping to project their glee and he responded by saying, 'What have I come to watch this shit for?' flatly. 'I can't believe you guys didn't say you had no money.'

'Look Dave, it will be magic,' grinned Jay.

'Yeah it will be brilliant,' chipped in Adrian.

'This is crazy,' he said.

'Dave, in ten years time you'll one day remember this and you'll laugh.' At two thirty, Jay moved along the aisle to seat D29 as the lights came down and the infamous music started. Dave continued to mutter looking down at his ticket, 'I don't believe I've spent ten quid on this shit.'

Jay's sister passed him a letter that Trac had penned in which it outlined her love and confusion, the uncertainty to his distancing, toying with her emotions instead of being straight or even pushing her to be the one to say 'it's all over.' Why did he keep letting momentary feelings of insecurity escalate to this... worse still, did he have to tell her each time? You idiot, he thought, standing up from the couch. 'I'm going to have to go over and straighten this out.'

'Where are you going now?' snapped his mum.

'To see Trac.'

'Your dinner's nearly ready.'

'I'm not really that hungry.'

'Can't you go later?'

'No. I've got to go right now!'

'You can't carry on like this.'

'What are you on about?' he muttered as he pulled on his jacket.

'Burning the candle at both ends.'

'Mum... I've got far more energy now than I'm ever going to have.'

'What's so important that it can't wait?'

'Everything,' he said snatching at his keys. 'I'll microwave it later,' and disappeared out of the front door.

Thursday, April 27

He missed the train by a good fifteen minutes so he wandered down to the station at a leisurely pace rather than his usual brisk walk with short bursts of running. The platform looked twice as busy. As a train pulled in, it became a push and shove contest to get on board and locate a free space. Jay managed to get a seat, the only trouble was he was wedged between the window and a big black woman with a child on her lap that said nothing but glared at him. As if I'm that interesting, he thought. Still clutching the Nene College letter between finger and thumb, its content was simple, *we regret to inform you that your application has been unsuccessful*.

When the train arrived at Leicester he didn't feel so bad because Adrian was in high spirits and cheered him up, it was a gift that happily worked both ways.

'Don't worry about it mate,' he said patting him on the back.

'Yeah but the thing is I've put Loughborough as my second choice.'

'What for? they're never going to let you back in.'

'I don't want to move too far away that's all.'

'So what's your third choice?'

'Derby.'

'So Derby it is then,' said Adrian returning his letter back with a sneer. 'Besides,' he continued 'you said the bloke that interviewed you looked like a chameleon.'

Jay chuckled and folded up the letter and popped it into the inside pocket of his leather jacket and thought nothing more about it.

Friday, April 28

Jay sat on the corner of his bed aggressively pushing the channel changing button on his small portable TV, going round and round in circles between the four channels hoping something would develop. He grumpily gave up and began to make his way through his video collection impatiently. He stopped at the *Comic Strips, Mr Jolly lives next door* a favourite influencer, but he had to admit to seeing it more times than was healthy and so replaced it. Perhaps the *Dangerous Brothers*? No he put that back too. He gazed around his room and yawned widely, an air mail envelope poking out from under a copy of the *NME* reminded him of the request Trac had made of him, to write to Shelley 'to explain things.'

He reluctantly picked up an A4 pad of lined paper and immediately started chewing on the lid of the biro he was holding. Shaking his head despairingly from time to time he occasionally managed to jot a few things down but struggled to get any kind of flow going at all.

An hour later, dressed in his favourite shirt, jeans and baseball boots he closed the front door of the house behind him and headed down the road towards the local pub, wondering if he would ever send the letter he had just written, opening with a sarcastic *'thanks for all your fan mail'* dig about her lack of feedback since she left. Passing his driving test, a pathetic attempt to explain how he and Trac went from friends to becoming an item, a glorified summary of his drinking antics and finally reducing to remarking on the weather; *the English weather is so unpredictable as usual, the other week it snowed in April and now it's baking*. The comments regarding his future were vague to say the least; *a year out to travel maybe?* The only decent thing was asking her not to hold a grudge against Trac; *don't stop writing to her or anything* and finished it off with a cartoon. A couple of pints he thought and he would be too merry and carefree to worry about the letter's destiny.

Saturday, April 29

Jay started to act funny, he was beside himself, he was falling deeper and deeper in love with Trac by the minute. He was eighteen years old and in his sexual prime. Trac, on the other hand, was quite willing above and below the waist but still felt uneasy about being totally naked. It was okay when she had a few drinks, but whilst sober sometimes she would let him touch her and other times she wouldn't.

He kissed her for five or more minutes before he tried to drop his hand further down, when he did she grabbed his wrist.

'What's up?' he said using the most innocent and astonished tone of voice he could muster.

His look of hurt surprise relayed to her what he was thinking as plain as day, she informed him that it was one of the good things about him, that he had the ability to convey exactly what he was thinking or feeling with just a slight expression. Sometimes he could just communicate through his eyes and not say a word and she let him know she adored that, it was as though there was no secrets, he was honest and true.

He tried again and this time she dug her nails into his wrist.

'Oh you,' she said firmly.

He was fumbling with her buttons at any given opportunity but Trac had other ideas to make things as difficult as possible for him. Jay was never one to give up and continued on with the battle until she finally got to her knees and belted him with the pillow.

'You pest,' she cried.

He smiled at the state she was in, her shirt was pulled out, hair a mess, it was like she had been pulled through a hedge backwards. Before she had a chance to hit him with the pillow again he dived for her waist and they scuffled in a playful fight, half giggling they fell off the bed.

'I'm sorry, you just excite me that's all.'

'You're so weak.'

'It's not funny.'

She pulled a sad face to tease him further and then followed with a smile in response to his frowning.

'Okay,' he said holding up his hands in surrender.

'Look if you had asked me plain and simple why I won't let you, I'd have told you.'

'Eh?'

She sighed deeply, 'Jay it's that...'

'Oh yeah,' he interrupted, 'your friend's arrived.'

'My friend?' she looked puzzled.

'That's what I thought you girls called your periods'.

'I wouldn't call it a friend.'

'Maybe it's sarcasm then. I know plenty of other names for it.'

'Jay, I don't want to know.'

'Anyway,' he said, 'why didn't you tell me.'

'What, and spoil all my fun?'

He smirked, 'that's it, you just go right ahead and tease me.'

Sunday, April 30

Upstairs in the spare room at Trac's, the black and white TV offered junk entertainment but they had no trouble in making their own as he collapsed onto the bed and moaned, 'my back's really itching.'

'Hint, hint,' she smirked and moved her hands up and over his shoulders. 'You're not very subtle are you?'

He gave her a smug grin, 'we've passed that stage haven't we?' and buried his head into the pillow and began humming softly.

'Looks like it... I'm getting hungry.'

'What do you fancy?'

'I don't know? I suppose I'll have to wait for dinner or Mum will have a go at me for snacking,' she yawned. 'Do you like Chinese?'

'Yeah, it's okay.'

'Shelley loved it.'

'You're more of a pizza girl.'

'Yeah, have you had Indian?'

'No.'

'Mum made a curry once and it didn't go down very well.'

'Ah well at least you've tried it.'

'I wish I hadn't believe me.'

'I'll try anything once.'

'Snails and frog's legs?'

'Sounds horrible but I'd give it a go.'

'So you'd try anything?'

'Yeah.'

'What about sex?'

'Oh, I'll always be happy to try that,' he chuckled.

'No, you know what I mean.'

'No?'

'Weird stuff.'

'What's that then?'

'God do you have to make me spell everything out,' she tutted.

'Yeah,' he smirked.

'Well stuff like being tied up.'

'Yeah I'm game if you want to.'

'No not us,' she tutted again then followed it with a chuckle.

'What now?' he sighed.

'Oh nothing.'

'No, what?'

'Well would you sleep with a bloke?' she smirked.

He chuckled, 'yeah sleeping is no problem.'

She nudged his shoulders firmly, 'you know what I mean.'

His face scrunched up in repulsion at the thought and it made her chuckle further. 'I don't think I'll ever be that way.'

'I thought you said you'd try anything.'

'Well... I,' he paused. 'Are you taking the mick out of me.'

She giggled lightly, 'I just thought you were sooo open minded about stuff.' Jay stammered again but halted his dialogue once she carried on giggling, her shoulders bent forward cupping a hand over her nose and mouth.

'It's not that funny,' he scowled.

'I know,' she chuckled, 'just your face.'

'Ha, ha,' he uttered sarcastically before chuckling lightly. 'If ever I had the urge to I would and it wouldn't bother me, but I don't okay.' And with that he rolled onto his back to face her. 'Perhaps if I turned really camp it would be a bit of a shock.'

She smiled, 'yeah that's weird when they're like that. You're arty though.'

'So.'

'So a lot of them seem to be that way.'

'No,' he said shaking his head. 'Anyway what about you?' Not wishing to miss the chance to move onto the topic of lesbianism.

'What about me?'

'You and another girl?'

'Yeah right,' she smiled 'you'd love that.'

'Maybe,' he said rubbing at his chin thoughtfully, 'it's worth considering.'

'No, don't even go there,' she smiled and he chuckled.

'Can't you make something up?'

Eyes narrowing she replied, 'no, and it's my turn for a massage.'

'I'm too relaxed.'

'Oh come on, it's my turn.'

'Look something interesting has just come on the TV.'

She turned her head to look then quickly snapped back to him, 'no there's not.'

'Yeah,' he said positively, 'it's err... you know.'

She waggled her left foot in front of him and he turned his head away, 'no I'm not interested,' he said.

'I thought you liked my feet?'

'I do but...' he craned his neck to get a better view of the TV screen.

'What parts of me are you interested in?'

He leaned back and his eyes squinted as he grinned, this sounds a little more interesting he thought.

'Oh I've got your attention now have I?'

He looked down to his groin and chuckled, 'you're starting to.'

'Mmm.'

He leaned forward and gave in with a yawn, 'come on then.'

He massaged her from head to foot, his erection never failing at any point. By the time she had her hands inside his loosened jeans it was too much and felt sure if it got any harder it was going to come right off. Weeks of soft fumbling were over, being laid back and patient now was just not an option, that self control had gone, the gloves were off. However it was going to go down, he had to go all the way. He placed his hand round hers and tightened the grip ten fold.

'Doesn't it hurt that tight?' she asked quietly and he shook his head.

'Like that?' he nodded.

'You're bad for me.'

He didn't respond to that, it was although he had lapsed into a transfixed state as his head half disappeared under a pillow he just murmured things faintly like 'don't stop... a little faster... don't stop' until his back arched and he took a deep breath and she felt something happen and looked downward. She noted that he suddenly seemed to dissolve further into the duvet with a wide smile like a circus clown as he drifted into a cosy coma, he felt wonderful, perfect, better than he had ever felt in his life.

'Mmm,' she muttered looking at the slightly warm off white gunk that seemed to have gone everywhere except on him. She toyed with her right hand looking at the stuff clinging to it while she dug her left hand into her pocket to retrieve a hanky.

She happily then slid herself next to him once again placing her head onto his chest and an arm around his waist and enjoyed her Mr Mellow stroking her hair softly for the rest of the afternoon.

Monday, May 1 (May Day Bank Holiday)

'There's an off-license,' Jay said with enthusiasm.

'Oh yeah,' Adrian responded.

'We can't walk past and not get anything,' said Jay stopping.

'Yeah I guess you're right.'

They entered the premises and found themselves browsing the shelves in thought.

'I'll get this gin and we can mix it with some orange or something when we get in there,' said Jay holding the bottle up for Adrian's approval.

At the student union, just before the band came on, Adrian produced a bottle of vodka. It had been a neat steal, Jay hadn't even realised that Adrian had slipped it into his pocket. They bought a glass of orange each, both swirling it in a pint glass they began mixing it with their alcohol stash. Jay only knew a few Big Country songs but with Trac out he figured it was better than the option of staying in, that did not rate very high on the entertainment chart. The idea for the night was simple, drink as fast as possible and be ready to pogo like mad.

The music was loud and aggressive, totally live and piercing the room. The drummer began first, then the sound of guitars tinkled. Then the audience's outrage came as the music burst into life. They were prepared to jump until there was no jumping, not even standing left in their legs. Jay's face flushed, his body injected with a sudden shot of adrenaline gave him the strength to make his way closer to the front of the crowd.

Unstoppable they leapt into the air with all the energy in their bodies for fifty minutes without pause for breath. After a medley of the most lively tracks the band were into their final encore. The final song started into a rushing, crashing sound straightaway, faster and faster then dropped to nothing. The audience went crazy, shouting and yelling for more, slamming their feet and hammering their fists in the air. The band paused briefly, their exhaustion obvious to all made a superhuman effort and noise swept again as they hammered home their final number. The two of them were buzzing inside, fury in their eyes, powering over the heads of surging screaming fans. Jay yelled something and then left further towards the front ploughing through the people crammed to the stage. He took a few more photos and pushed his body to its limit. The band said goodnight and he retreated as the hall lights slowly came on. Worn out they came out the union building and a feeling of abandonment came down on them. Slightly disorientated, drenched in perspiration, ears ringing and extremely thirsty Jay had his camera clutched in his hand, another moment of student life had been captured for life.

The next few days at college they spent in the library, peeling the metal security strips from the books and placing them on unsuspecting people. When the alarm bell sounded they cracked up in chuckles. They had plenty of work to be getting on with but, as usual, when they didn't feel creative they became restless. They actually found the smallest book and placed it in Dave's art box and watched him with amusement as he tried to talk his way out of it. He put his hand to his forehead with disbelief. He murmured at the lady behind the desk 'Awwgh'.

Jay took further pleasure by standing next to Dave, curious as to whether he would finger him out as the culprit, but Dave being a true mate took it on the chin and babbled a feeble excuse out. Back in the classroom amongst several expletives he called them a pair of dossers which they always took as a compliment. With the fun over, their thoughts turned to food and the contents of Dave's packed lunch.

'You got your pack up today Dave?' asked Jay.

'Yeah I have, why?'

'I'm starving.'

'Me too,' said Adrian.

Dave began sifting through his packed lunch, deciding what sandwich to start on first and what to give up.

By two o'clock the famous three had bunked off to the cinema. Night-times were kept open for parties and general piss ups. They were still banned from staying at Iffley House halls of residence due to the devastation caused to property, noise pollution, ill respect for the other residence, a series of firework fights and a serious incident involving Jay and a fire extinguisher. They had no place to crash out anymore and since missed quite a number of nights out at the union. The plus side for Jay was he could spend more and more time with Trac, who was currently receiving a bit of a cold shoulder. He had gone all funny with her after suffering phone call where all she went on about was Johnny and his sexual habits. She was sixteen and wanted to learn that was all, but it hit a raw nerve and it got his back up. He turned the tables on her, she didn't like that one bit and it had been a cruel way to make a point and he felt slightly guilty about that, it made her realise what she had done but resented the over rub. Unfortunately he was in one of his awkward moods, whatever she said he disagreed with and whatever her opinions were he was of the opposite. The main reason for his mood was the fact he had to get a part time job to fuel his nights out since leaving the bar. He worked out his maintenance allowance paid by his dad, it was just not nearly enough. He had an interview at Wilkinson's hardware store in town for two nights a week, five until ten, recommended by Adrian who got a job at a different branch. Ten hours a week and it won't interfere with his Friday and Saturday nights.

He got the job and was to start on Monday the eighth. It seemed like the only excitement to look forward to in life was the up and coming house party, he still had his fifty percent proof vodka on standby. House parties were the best kind of party he thought, a friend of Trac's obviously had not thought things through, you don't have house parties you just go to them, but he was not about to offer advice on that front for the fear of cancellation.

Thursday, May 4

The road stretched ahead painfully empty, he'd spent another easy going day at college and a relaxed evening with Trac. He was high with excitement, he glanced in his rear view mirror then to his right mirror, there was a noticeable lack of traffic. He continued to glance in the mirrors, a few more times as he slowly put his right foot on the accelerator. Eighty eight miles an hour and The Beast began to shudder sending a mild vibration along his arms, he kept his foot to the floor determined to make a ton before slowing down. Reaching his target he gave out a howl before easing off the gas and applied some pressure to the brakes. As he entered Narborough village a smile still split his face. He was elated, naturally high this had to be his summer, he was having the time of his life.

Friday, May 5

He stepped out of The Beast and took in the early evening air. It was cool and breezy, the ground was damp, it had been raining and helped the smell of fresh cut grass fill his nose. The sun was still out but failed to really show itself. May was a good month he thought as he wandered up the drive to Tracs house. Inside it was only a few minutes before he was walking back down her drive shaking his head in disappointment and waving his hands in the air with a sense of disbelief. She followed him outside onto the drive and began to walk alongside him.

'I don't care,' he snarled. 'Look if he brings a porno round here I'll go.' She turned to him for an explanation, 'you're serious aren't you,' she said calmly.

'You're damn right I'm serious. I don't want you watching stuff like that.'

'So you've never watched one before?'

'No, I'm not saying that,' and gave her an uneasy shrug. 'You don't... we don't need to watch stuff like that.'

'I thought you would like it.'

'I don't want to... you go and get off on it.'

'I didn't say I wanted to get off on it, I thought it would be fun.'

'Look I'm not bothered and I'm not forcing my opinion on you. It's just how I feel right now.'

'Okay then I'm sorry I didn't think you would react like this.'

'Honestly, you go ahead and watch it if you want. I guess I'm just in the romance.'

'I'm sorry.'

'Don't be. I guess I look at stuff like that, the *Sunday Sport* and that. I just don't want us to relate to stuff like that right now. I want to feel the intensity... feel the emotion.'

'If it's tasteful and sensual is that alright then is it?' she said running her hands up the arch of his back.

'Yeah I guess so. Porn films are just cold and false. What we have right now is special. We are at the start of our sexual relationship and that's exciting. We don't need to watch that stuff.'

'I'm sorry I never really thought about it,' she said softly and reached out for him. 'Go easy on me.'

He let out a sigh and put his hands into his pockets wondering as to whether he had been too much of a martyr, or gone too far in leading to a romantic movie moment to make him more worthy than he otherwise might have been.

'You understand what I'm saying though don't you?' he muttered.

'Yeah I do,' she agreed.

They had walked the length of Back Lane and found a country fence to lean upon.

'I'm sorry,' he said, 'I was just as fascinated by sex and that when I was your age. I was even involved in a stealing and selling porno mags racket at school,' and he gave her a confused look.

'I love you,' she said softy and hugged him.

'Maybe I want you to stay pure... I don't know.'

He picked her up off the ground and began to swing her around.

'You're amazing,' she said, 'you're gorgeous I don't deserve you.'

'Yeah, well I am pretty amazing,' he smirked.

She chuckled at his modesty and they set off back to the house.

Saturday, May 6

Laying on his bed, with his pale blue shirt rolled up at the sleeves, Jay was drawing with his music on loudly when Trac appeared at his doorway.

'Hi,' she said peering over at him with a blissful smile.

'Hi,' he smiled.

'What are you drawing?'

'Nothing much. I'm just doodling a cartoon,' and put his sketch pad down.

'Looks good, what's it for.'

'The New Inn is doing a Treasure Hunt so it's for a poster and maybe a flyer.'

'Are they paying you in beer?'

Jay returned the smile as he moved into kiss her. 'It has been mentioned.'
Trac warmed to his embrace and thumbed at the collar of his shirt.

'Unusual to see you in light blue.'

'Yeah well this is my painting shirt, bit scruffy I know but Mum refuses to put it in the washing machine.'

'So what have you painted?'

He stood and turned down the music and rubbed at his chin. 'Nothing,' he mumbled. 'I lost all motivation for that.'

Trac watched him pass her back and forth a number of times sighing and still rubbing at his chin occasionally as he did so. When he had been deeply unresponsive to her for some time she closed the magazine she had started reading and flung it to the floor, stopping him in his tracks.

'What's up with you?' she snapped.

He peered at her for a moment as if he was not sure whether to answer or not.

'Nothing,' he muttered casually.

'Yes there is,' she said.

'I'm bored,' he moaned.

'Don't you want to watch the film.'

'I've seen it,' he babbled.

'What's that?' Trac asked pointing to the album lying on his desk.

'What's it look like.'

'An Elvis album... you're listening to Elvis now?'

'Yeah,' he nodded positively.

'Really?'

'No, I just thought I'd pretend.'

'You've bought this?'

'No it belongs to a friend of my mum's. The thing was I was trying to find a specific song I remember from one of his movies and it's been bugging me.'

'You watch Elvis movies?'

'Yeah used to,' he said, 'hasn't everybody?'

'So is it on here?'

'No, but I did find that there's some pretty good stuff on there.'

'I'm thinking about getting The Cure's new album? I was really looking forward to it coming out ages ago, but now I'm not into them as much,'

'You won't want to go and see them on tour then?'

She gave a shrug that said she wasn't bothered.

'Maybe you could tape the album off someone?'

'Yeah, I suppose I could.'

He leaned into her and replied, 'I fancy doing something?'

She pulled back and frowned at him and he suddenly said, 'not it' defensively.

'I mean... maybe something.'

Her face returned to an expressionless gaze and it didn't offer him any help.

'Erm... doesn't matter,' he smiled and his eyes wandered the room until they set on an unopened bottle of Jim Beam.

'Right,' he said. 'I've got an idea okay. I'll blindfold you and you've got to guess each object that I've got through your other senses touch, smell and taste.'

She frowned at him again not knowing whether to trust his intentions but she sensed a genuine feeling of warmth oozing from him.

As he whispered, 'take your top off.' It was almost as if she were captivated if only for a few seconds.

'If you're a clever girl,' he continued, 'and guess correctly then you get two hundred kisses anywhere you want them.'

'All over,' she replied softly lifting her top over her head.

'Sure, if that's what you want,' he said as he slid a hand between her legs firmly.

'Oh I don't know about that,' she smirked.

He pulled from his drawer a thin black scarf and softly knotted it at the back of her head.

'Is that too tight?' he whispered.

'No it's fine,' came her reply.

'Lay back.'

He unhooked her bra and felt the joy of being able to take in her form without making her feel uncomfortable with his gaze. He began to massage her shoulders and ignored the stirring in his jeans that her breasts had started.

'What do you want out of life?' he asked.

'Not really given it much thought... just want to leave school. You?'

'Me?'

'Yeah. You're the one that's so active all the time, dancing from one thing to the next. I want to know what's going on in that head of yours.'

'Why?'

'Maybe I will understand you more?'

'No great mystery,' he replied. 'I suppose love, freedom... experience.'

'I like that.'

He leaned across to his desk and picked up his first object.

'What's this then?' and he ran it across her stomach and between her breasts.

'Err that feels weird, err I don't know?'

'A rubber,' he said disappointed that she failed, 'that was easy as well.'

He unlatched the catch to his art box and wet a paint brush in his mouth and began to paint on her chest.

'That's wet,' her face pulled expressions of puzzlement. 'This is hard,' she said innocently and it made him smirk.

'Look,' he chuckled, 'if you don't get at least one right that's it.'

She was not doing well he thought as he reached up for the Jim Beam. Carefully unscrewing the top so as not to give it away, he noticed that her nipples were erect now and it pleased him, he was more than happy to sit and stare at her for the next few hours or so but he knew she wouldn't allow that and only think him even more strange than before. He poured some of the whiskey onto her stomach and into her belly button and then over her breasts.

'Now this should be real easy.'

He ran a firm finger down her body and watched the whiskey trickle away with fascination. She wiggled and squirmed as some of the whiskey disappeared down her sides and felt ticklish as well as cold. He wiped a little onto her mouth and the tip of her tongue appeared and ran across her lips slowly.

'That's vodka?... no, no whiskey... it's whiskey!'

'Okay but I told you it was easy.'

She whipped the scarf from her eyes and kissed him quickly and said, 'kiss me all over,' positively.

'Well I won't argue with that. Now I've got two reasons to enjoy it.'

'And if I wasn't covered in whiskey?'

'I'd still enjoy it,' he smiled. 'I've just got an added bonus haven't I.'

He took a swig from the bottle then passed it to her. 'I'm really glad you're here.'

Trac took a draw of whiskey and choked a little after swallowing a small amount. 'I'm sorry,' she coughed, 'I'm not used to drinking.'

He continued to smile, 'try a bit more... just a bit.'

She took another sip and this time it seemed to go down a little easier.

'You're just trying to get me drunk,' she said.

He just chuckled at that statement and went to retrieve the bottle, but she confidently pulled it away from him and took yet another shot.

'Ohh,' he smirked as he leaned into her. 'I like you being a bad girl,' he said in a hushed tone, as his close presence forced her downward onto the bed. Happy to be immersed in her he began kissing her stomach first, counting lightly as he went, one, two, three, four, five, six...

Monday, May 8

For the first few hours, Jay enjoyed doing something physical for a change. The work, for anyone with half a brain was quite well paid. He had to go down to the basement, load his trolley and return to stock the shelves and tonight he worked on the screws and locks aisle. At half past seven he had a break in the small office at the back of the store with the rest of the staff, all of them women in their thirties to forties nattering about how rubbish their fellas were at everything. He yawned a couple of times and realised that on top of a day at college this made for a long day. By nine forty all his work had been done and the last twenty minutes felt more like hours going by. He sat on his trolley toying with a small aluminium door lock in his hands, thinking how it might be an ideal thing to fit to his bedroom door to stop his mum or sister wandering in on him and Trac in a compromising position.

Wednesday, May 10

They were walking back from the college union building along Epinal Way, the three of them getting ready to make an early exit home to avoid listening to a drawn out talk on TV advertising. They already had a fairly dull day, except for a few moments of fun Adrian achieved by repositioning the human skeleton into holding a cup of tea and reading the *Sunday Sport* at one end of the room, while Paul at the other end was more interested in dissecting the fish with his scalpel and HB pencil, before swiftly moving onto pulling the legs off the crab one by one. Otherwise it would have been pure silence, except for the sound of pencils scratching the surface of paper. Jay joined in trying to lift his fellow classmates from the depths of boredom too by bringing a large shrimp to life, bouncing it round the table with full sound effects accompanying it. He seemed totally animated by his own entertainment, while everyone else around the table looked at him with puzzled expressions on their faces. The tutor stood behind him with her arms folded shaking her head and Dave muttered, 'he ain't all there is he?'

'Get my art box Jay,' said Adrian.
'Where are you going?'
'I'm going to get a can of pop.'
'I thought you said you had no money?'
Adrian just smiled and jogged off in the direction of the common room.
'How does he do that?' asked Jay turning sharply to Dave.
Dave shrugged in response, 'do what?'
'Tell them he's put money in that machine when he hasn't.'
'I don't know,' shrugged Dave again as they made their way up the flight of steps to the classroom.
Jay strolled up to his desk and immediately began packing up his markers into his art box. Staring at his layout pad, he wasn't impressed with what he had done so far. He spun round and grabbed Adrian's art box and wandered over to Dave who was leaning over his sketch pad rubbing at it frantically.
'That's not bad for you,' he said.
Dave blew the rubber bits off his sheet of cartridge paper and muttered, 'yeah, apart from Adrian keeps drawing cocks all over my work.'
With that Jay chuckled and patted him on the back, 'he draws them on mine too.'
Undeterred by the letter he had in his pocket from the NatWest Bank, kindly informing him that he was £57.15p overdrawn without arrangement,

he saw an opportunity to get off into town an get The Cult T-shirt he'd spied in HMV.

'I'm going now,' he kept whispering over his shoulder at Adrian looking over at the door to the corridor.

'You up for a beer in town then?'

'No, I'm going to shoot straight off to see Trac.'

'Nice cold pint of lager?'

He pondered for a moment or two and replied, 'as tempting as that is I've got to drop The Beast off at my dad's at some point, it's got to have some work done on the gear box, so for the next week or so I'll be struggling to get over to see her.'

'Well the offer's there if you change your mind.'

It was an escape of sorts leaving the college as they played lookout for each other until they were a good two to three hundred yards clear of the college premises.

'Shall we nip for a quick beer in the Griffin Inn?' suggested Adrian.

'Nope.'

'Oh come on,' urged Adrian, 'let's get some fucking beers down us.'

Jay shook his head 'No, no.'

'Just a couple.'

'No, because we know what a few pints will lead to,' he smiled. He was already looking forward to his entire committed evening of music, low lighting, kissing and maybe if he was lucky something more.

5. Under the influence

Gazing about himself, Jay found that the small train station seemed quite empty, at least on his side of the platform. The alarm sounded and the barriers dropped to the level crossing. He sat chewing gum looking furtively up and down the track to see which way the train was coming. He rubbed his hands gleefully as a train travelled southbound towards him from Leicester. As it pulled to a halt the pressure sound of the carriage doors hissed as they opened slowly and his mate appeared, overnight bag slung over his shoulder with the biggest grin he had seen since the Cove night, his drinking buddy had arrived.

'Will there be many girls there?'

'Adrian mate, it's going to be one massive drunken orgy.'

'Brilliant,' Adrian said excitedly clutching his Mates condom. 'This is just about out of date.'

'Look, don't put yourself under pressure... you probably won't, but you might meet someone.'

'You got the vodka still?'

'Course I have, it's been waiting for this.'

'Let's do it,' responded Adrian in a highly inflected voice.

Hearing the muffled sound of music pumping away along with girls screaming and laughing, they glanced at each other, grinned and headed for the front door armed with four bottles of Guinness, a bottle of fifty percent proof blue label Smirnoff, half a bottle of red label Smirnoff and a bottle of Rosie's lime cordial.

'Trac, Trac, Jay's here!' screamed two girls as they ran away from him. He turned to Adrian, 'all of a sudden I'm so popular.'

As is usual in these types of parties the centre of activity was located in the kitchen, so they headed there first. As they entered a group of girls gave out a loud scream. Trac stood with a drink in hand, wearing snug fit jeans and a black shirt with the ends tied in a knot showing a little of her tummy.

'Umm, I'm surrounded by all these beautiful girls,' and he gave her a teasing grin as he approached her. 'Only joking,' he said hoping to restore her radiant expression.

'You just behave yourself,' she said firmly.

'Looks like the party has started,' he said in an easy tone. Taking her by the arm he guided her as he moved further into the room surveying the layout and noting that no-one was entirely sober as he went.

'Yeah we've all been here ages.'

Elevating himself to be the life and soul of the party he jeered, 'it's safe to say that the guests of honour have arrived to try and crank this party up.'

'Whatever,' Trac replied flippantly and took a sip of her drink.

'Who's this?' asked Jay looking at the girl hovering next to her.

'This is my mate Michelle, it's her party,' she said beaming a very wide drunken smile as Michelle gave him a subtle wave of her hand to say hello.

'You're pissed aren't you Trac.'

'No.'

'I think you are. Your eyes are slow, your cheeks flushed and,' he put his finger in the air. 'You seem to have lost your sense of balance.'

'Okay,' she said in a tone that meant, 'enough.'

'You do look cute though,' and she smiled up at him. 'That's my girl,' he chuckled as he gave her a friendly tug of her left cheek.

'Oh stop it you,' she replied and squeezed his bum firmly before slowly moving her hand round to the front. It was amazing what a few drinks had done to her he thought.

'Where can I drink this then?' he asked holding up his assortment of booze.

'Well,' she paused, pulling on his black shirt and giving him a kiss. 'All the music seems to be in here.'

Adrian surveyed the room and found the ideal spot. 'Just here will do Jay,' he said positively.

The ceremony was about to start and Adrian had the honour of opening the vodka.

'Jay, what are you having first?'

'Give me a Guinness and pour me a vodka and lime... Trac is there ice?'

'Yeah, hang on.'

With a drink in each hand and Trac before him, it was immediately perfect.

'Give me another kiss,' she demanded.

He obliged and sat her down onto his lap, she sparked up a cigarette and poured herself out a large vodka and lime.

'You smell great,' he whispered, as he rested his chin on her shoulder. 'White Musk?'

'Yeah,' came her soft reply.

'I've brought my camera with me,' he smiled.

'Oh great,' she replied kissing his cheek. 'We tried to find one earlier.'

'I've got a black and white film as well as colour.'

'Cool.'

'Trac,' murmured Jay. 'I don't suppose by any chance you would know where the drinks cabinet is, just in case we run out.'

'No, I don't,' she replied abruptly. 'You've got enough anyway.'

'How much have you got?'

'I've got a bottle of vodka hidden in the microwave.'

He was impressed and overjoyed to find her playing the kindred spirit. He nuzzled his face into her hair and neck, planting a soft kiss. Someone changed the music and increased the volume further as a bunch of girls burst into song sounding dreadful.

'So have you got your tights on Jay?' shouted Michelle.

He had suggested to Trac in confidence that he was going to wear a pair of tights underneath his jeans and do a striptease for a laugh.

'Yeah I got them on,' he sneered,

'Oh my God,' exclaimed Trac. 'I thought you were joking.'

He smirked with a slight shake of his head and gave them a quick flash. A huge scream went up willing him on further. 'Later... later,' he said as he waved them away.

The kitchen was full of empty bottles, glasses, cans, and the vodka was vanishing rapidly. A large group of girls in the far corner of the room carried on wailing to the music and began to dance. The first swallow of neat fifty percent Smirnoff tasted strong, it burned Jay's throat and made his eyes water, but in no time at all his body felt warm and his limbs loose, soon to be followed by a happy state of confusion. The camera blinked randomly, he had become a master at reloading a new film whilst drunk, even doing so while a couple were shagging failed to phase him, he just nodded and said, 'alright' to the girl who was sitting on top of a lad he didn't recognise. 'I won't be a sec.'

Growing ever more rowdy as they drank, Jay's dancing had started to become more of a stagger. He slurred something along the lines of 'I'm going to have a look round,' and rambled off.

Stopping occasionally he stood swaying slightly while making small talk to complete strangers until he got bored and promptly removed himself away from such unfamiliar company. He opened a door to see Trac laying next to a lad, too close for his liking, his mouth dropped as she looked up at him. He pulled a face of disappointment and pulled the door to. Twenty minutes and counting Trac couldn't find him. Adrian was busy trying his best to unzip some girl's jeans, so he wasn't very communicative in helping her locate him. After darting from room to room with no luck she finally settled herself at the kitchen table with a puzzled and concerned expression as she drew a series of longer sips from her glass of vodka. Suddenly Jay burst into the kitchen, he had less than half a bottle of vodka in his hand, he'd crashed through the door roaring drunk, making a hell of a noise and was laughing to himself as he fell among the dancers who scattered in all directions. He got to his knees and tried to dance at that level, Adrian came charging into the room, unsuccessful at ripping the girl's jeans off but in time to help Jay to his feet.

'Where have you been?' he slurred as he poured a generous slug of vodka down his throat.

'Trying to get off with some girl,' babbled Adrian. 'One minute she was dead keen the next minute she took off, ran out the room pulling her jeans up!'

Jay chuckled patting him on the back, 'have you got beer all down your front?'

'No,' replied Adrian somewhat confused.

He wafted a finger at him as he swayed, 'I think you'll find you have,' he grinned as he shook a can of beer and proceeded to open it allowing its contents to spurt all over himself and Adrian, they exploded with laughter.

'Need to put some good music on,' roared Jay and produced a tape from his pocket. Trac weaved her way through the crowd and huddled herself up to him as he fumbled with the stereo. Smiling she prodded him a few times and he realised she was very drunk, playfully so.

'I'm sorry,' she slurred. 'I wasn't getting off with that lad.'

'It's alright,' he replied lightly. 'I trust you.'

'But your face,' she whined. 'You looked upset.'

'Maybe... only for a second.'

Trac smiled and gave him a grateful kiss.

'How the fucking hell does this thing work.'

'What are you putting on?'

'I don't mind Transvision Vamp. I even think it's cute hearing a bunch of girls screaming, "Baby I don't care',' but three times on the trot. Time for some Wonder Stuff,' he winked.

'Well try pressing play,' smiled Trac pushing the right button for him.

He gave her a frown as he turned up the volume, the song, 'A Wish Away' kicked into life forging their friendship to camaraderie, they burst into song at the same time. Adrian jumped onto the kitchen table, Trac onto a chair and Jay pogoed up and down between the two of them in a highly motivated frenzy as they all sang along.

Jay had dropped his trousers to a big cheer which drowned the music out and turned into a chant. There he stood vodka in his hand, resting on his hip as if it was a bottle of beer, jeans round his ankles, black shirt undone, Cult T-shirt, wide black tie with large red spots he'd acquired and a pair of tights on while Trac stood with a hand clasped over her mouth.

'Oh my God,' she said half amused and half shocked.

He pulled up his jeans, poured the last glass of vodka from the bottle and upturned it in triumph and staggered into Adrian jeering loudly, loving every note that came from the speakers.

'Now the vodka's gone we need to find more booze,' whispered Jay into Adrian's ear.

'Yeah it's only just gone eleven.'

'Where's Trac's vodka then?' he moaned, disappointed to see the microwave empty.

'She took it,' mumbled Adrian.

'She can't drink all that, it's a half bottle,' and carried on searching frantically.

'Jackpot,' he jeered. 'Grab a load of this.'

From behind a mound of cereal packets he found a half bottle of Cinzano, a quarter bottle of port and a full bottle of Harvey's Bristol Cream. First off was the bottle of Cinzano, pouring an unfeasibly large glass each, he handed the second glass to Adrian who put out his hand so effortlessly that the glass fell from his hand and contents ran down the back of the portable TV.

'Oh shit!'

'It might be okay,' said Jay adjusting his tie.

He studied the TV set and pressed the on switch slowly. To their delight a huge glow and a fizzing noise sounded before it made a bang and a puff of smoke rose from the back of the set.

Jay pushed out his bottom lip, 'maybe not then.'

And Adrian gave an unconcerned shrug.

'Hey you,' said Jay grabbing at a shoulder of the person to his right. 'Do you know Johnny... Err short, not quite a midget... about so high,' he demonstrated a level with his hand. 'Blondish hair.'

'Yeah.'

'Can you go and give him this.'

'Okay,' said the lad looking puzzled.

'Jay, you're giving booze away?' blurted Adrian, concerned his mate was losing his mind.

'Don't worry about it... it's... it's not strong enough and tastes fucking awful.'

Adrian's bladder slowly let him know it was time to go to the loo, finding it in a drunken haze was difficult and eventually impossible, so he ended up relieving himself in the lounge all over the back of the sofa, as another drunken soul, looking very ill, staggered past and advised him to be sick in the freezer. On his journey back to the kitchen a crowd was forming in the hallway. Trac was flat on her back, Adrian half staggered and half ran back to the kitchen.

'Jay, Jay,' he yelled at the top of his voice.

Jay pulled the neck of a port bottle from his mouth, 'what?' he snapped. 'Couldn't you see I was in full tilt then,' and reloaded with more port.

'Trac's unconscious.'

A mouthful of port spurted from his lips across the table. Slamming the bottle down he leapt to his feet, ran out of the room and then ran back again. He grabbed the port, took a swig, and then looked at the bottle in disgust and noticed nothing seemed to have much taste anymore. He pushed himself through the sea of people like a shark. Trac was lying helplessly on the floor. Bending down he put his hand on her head. 'Are you alright?' he asked in a soft tone.

'Yeah,' she mumbled faintly. 'I just feel a bit dizzy.'

'Are you sure?'

'Umm,' she tried a nod.

He studied her lovable red face carefully and said, 'you shouldn't drink so much.'

'Says you,' she muttered.

'I'm used to it though,' he whispered. 'Come on, let's get you up.'

He looked around at the crowd which seemed to have got bigger.

'I just need to eat something,' she said woozily and gave a yawn.

'You had me worried,' he said lifting her upward.

'Now you know how I feel all the time.'

'Sure... You just need to drink loads of water and eat plenty of bread.'

They both stumbled slowly back to the kitchen. Trac sat still and began to eat at the dry bread he had given her while he was eating a banana suggestively miming out rude things with the piece of fruit to the small group of her friends that sat giggling at the display.

'Your Jay's mad in't he?'

'He is when he's drunk,' smiled Trac.

There was no escaping the blatant fact that booze was a driving force behind Jay and his persona. The first time he and Trac had ever spoke was at an all night bonfire party in eighty seven. He had a bottle of wine and two glasses in hand and staggered about offering wine to any attractive girl that seemed unattached, he even had a packet of sparklers that went down a treat. Halfway through the night when the last sparkler had gone and the wine bottle lay empty on the grass he decided to climb a tree, strangely without goading from his mates. He eventually fell out, luckily landing in the middle of a mound of haystacks. Opening up his eyes when he came to, he looked up and fixed them onto a small face peeping over a hay bale.

'Are you okay?' smiled the face with some concern.

'Yeah,' he smiled back lazily. 'I'm... I'm okay,' and he brushed the straw from his hair.

'You are?'

'Trac... I'm going out with Russell.'

'Oh yeah... lucky him,' he replied and she smiled back.

Jay had gone on another search for booze, he found a can on the floor in the hallway. Annoyed that it was bitter, he shook the can violently and released the ring pull. He laughed out loud as the frothy beer jetted out everywhere, splashing a brown stain down the wallpaper. 'Oh dear,' he murmured and began to rub at it with the sleeve of his shirt. The drunken antics carried on for two or more hours until finally a fight broke out and the neighbours' complaints about the noise and threats to call the police began to defuse the atmosphere. The last two beer cans popped open and for a while Jay and Adrian sat on the landing talking. All you could hear was their muffled voices and occasional soft chuckles amongst cans, bottles, various broken items, toilet rolls that had been thrown like confetti, and a few snores. Everyone had finally crashed out and lay in disarray around the room. With no more booze to be had, they managed to reach a semi comatose uncommunicative state. It was time to search for somewhere comfortable to sleep, an armchair, sofa, bed or the floor.

'Don't you think... hic... we should... go... hic...'

'Adrian, I thought you might have pulled by now. Looks like you'll have to sleep on your own.'

'I feel... I feel a bit... a bit sick.'

Michelle appeared from nowhere and stood glaring at Adrian with her hands on her hips.

'Don't worry... I... I don't care what anyone says,' he stammered. 'I'm... I'm a gentleman...' he belched. 'I'm... I'm... not going to throw up in this house... I'm... going outside to throw up because... because I respect your house.'

Jay let Adrian wander off and began his charms on Michelle hoping she would give up the key to the one door that was still left locked, the master bedroom. Whether it was his persuasive nature or tiredness having worn her down she gave him the key. While Adrian made the most of sleeping awkwardly in the dog basket, hunched over it in his navy sleeping bag. Jay found Trac at the bottom of the stairs looking worse for wear and helped her to her feet.

'You okay?'

'I'm just tired,' she muttered.

She wandered up the stairs unaided feeling her way in the half dark. He followed studying her bum as it wiggled up the stairs. Transfixed by its curvature at eye level, sexual thoughts flashed in his head randomly, but just as quickly discharged for wanted sleep. As they opened the door he managed to pull a crafty gleam at her. Locking the door behind them he leant against the wall, his arms folded, with a mischievous grin. She read him like an open book, but he could not maintain any energy, his eyes felt too heavy as if under water. He switched the side light on as Trac collapsed onto the bed. It was silent, no music, no screaming, no talking... nothing.

'Arrh look at the bed Trac. A four poster... it's magic.'

She lay moaning with tiredness as he helped her to undress, occasionally giggling softly. By the time she was half naked he was worn out.

'You don't snore do you?' he asked as he turned the light out.

'Noooo,' and she shook her head for added effect.

He found it satisfying in the intimacy of the darkened room, discovering what he thought of this and that and finding out as he explored her, lightly stroking a hand over her body and fumbling between her legs lethargically.

They soon fell asleep curled up together. He let out the occasional groan as his stomach turned and shooting pains shot down his arms. As it dissipated he drifted into a deep sleep, it felt close to heaven, dreaming that it was his house, his wife and an endless drinks cabinet.

The dream was shattered as a large thudding noise came from outside the room.

'Awgh, Awww,' whimpered Jay as his body slowly came out of its coma. 'What was I drinking last night?'

He opened his eyes and the sunlight attacked them immediately. He took a few deep breaths and heaved himself back into a position that was comfortable. He glanced to his left side, Trac was asleep, head buried deep into the pillow and the duvet up over her shoulders. She looked peaceful, he didn't want to wake her but the constant voice followed with a persistent tapping woke her.

She moaned distantly, 'who's that?' as she turned over.

'Morning Jay,' he said sarcastically.

'Morning,' she mumbled and turned back and gave him a hug.

'Jay, Jay,' came Adrian's faint cries.

He effortlessly slumped out of the edge of the bed, and hit the floor with a thud.

'Awgh,' he yelped. 'For fuck's sake, hang on.'

Stretching out an arm to the small cupboard next to the bed he pulled himself up, undid the catch on the door and dived back into the warmth. Adrian wandered to the far end of the room, to the window and sat on the ledge.

'Awgh, fucking hell,' he said looking across at the bed.

The light was still attacking Jay's eyes. 'Pull the curtains to would you.'

Adrian yanked the curtains open further and Jay ducked underneath the duvet deeper, moaning as he went.

'Last night,' continued Adrian.

'Sorry mate, I don't remember much about last night at the moment,' came Jay's muffled response.

'Trac,' he said. 'Michelle is going mad.'

Trac's face began to peer over the covers and then she finally made an appearance and sat up with the duvet pulled tightly up to cover her breasts.

'What time is it?' she asked.

'Don't care,' mumbled Jay.

'It's half ten,' said Adrian.

'Half ten,' he roared and buried his head in the pillow. 'More sleep,' came his muffled cries as he buried himself further, happy hiding under the covers, his hangover was slightly less painful in the dark.

'What's up with Michelle then?' Trac asked rubbing at her eyes.

'She's going ape shit, there's been a table broken for a start.'

She turned to Jay and nudge him. 'That was you?' she said.

'Me?' he cried! 'No way, I was sitting on it then you jumped on my lap and it broke.'

'It wasn't me,' she harked.

'Okay, then I like to believe that maybe it didn't really happen.'

'Anyway,' Adrian began, 'there's more to it than that. There's soup everywhere, toothpaste, beer, piss, shit, it's all just a mess down there, Michelle is going spare.'

'Well what did she expect?... It was a party,' he chuckled.

A second knock at the door and in shuffled Michelle, looking hungover and more than a little distressed.

'The house is a mess,' she said regretfully.

'Oh dear,' Trac replied softly.

'There's...'

Trac interrupted, 'I know Adrian's kindly filled us in.'

Michelle bowed her head and began to walk back out of the room, she then turned just before she got to the door and said, 'oh and someone's pissed on the video.'

Jay broke out in hysterics, he buried himself yet deeper into the bed laughing, he couldn't face Michelle, it would have been too cruel to laugh in her face. Trac kicked him and pinched him for his rudeness.

'Oww,' he yelped.

He emerged as he heard the door shut and grinned at Adrian.

'I can't wait till the photos come out.'

'Yeah,' laughed Adrian.

'I'm sure they'll be quite incriminating,' said Trac and gave a frown.

'Probably,' mused Jay.

They all looked at one another and began to smile.

Sunday, May 14

Sunday TV was crap thought Jay, the only thing worth watching was the sixties series, *Lost in Space*. So he gathered up a bunch of his records and was sat cross-legged beneath Trac's stereo, ready for a recording session. Trac knew he would be up and down like a yo-yo asking her opinion of a particular record, so she made cups of tea and positioned herself comfortably on her bed with some homework.

The night before he and Adrian had been to see Then Jerico in concert. They had recognised a few faces from the house party and was telling Trac about it all when she interrupted.

'You could have taken me.'

'You should of said, we might have got a ticket outside.'

She shrugged, placing her folder down, opting to pull out a box from under her bed. She began sifting through it, letters, photos and strange objects. Dust particles danced before her as Jay watched her lovingly. The way she acted and moved about made him smile, it was almost as if he cherished every facial expression she pulled.

'Don't stare at me,' she said plainly.

'I'm not.'

'You are,' she mumbled. 'You're giving me a complex,' and she hurled a cushion at him. He threw the cushion back and walked over to the other side of the room waiting for the current song to finish.

'I've got a picture of me and Shelley here.'

'Let's have a look then,' he replied keenly.

She passed it over to him, his eyes fixed on the two of them in T-shirts, short skirts, trainers and holding tennis rackets with Trac showing off her tanned legs next to Shelley's pale white skin.

'Look at your brown legs,' he smirked.

'That's when I came back from America.'

'I like the short skirts too.'

'You perv.'

'Yeah,' he nodded handing the photo back to her. 'I wouldn't mind a copy of that photo.'

She mumbled again, 'why?'

'So when I'm really old, that's if I live that long,' and gave a shrug. 'I can look back on it and think, those are two girls who were best mates and I fell in love with them both.'

'Have you wrote to her?'

'I wrote a letter but I haven't sent it... not sure I should?'

Trac gave a half hearted smile and quickly put the photo away. She didn't like discussing Shelley anymore, sure that he still had feelings for her.

Her mum called for dinner and his heart raced a little as he sat at the table. If only there was some alcohol on the table, he knew then he would feel more like himself. With a beer in hand to soften his senses it would give him the edge he liked.

'Have you got any tomato ketchup,' he smiled. 'Please?'

They all seemed to stop at the same time and glare at him which made him feel even more uncomfortable.

'Err, it doesn't matter,' he jabbered quickly.

'Yes we have some,' said her mum.

He smiled at Trac helplessly. She squinted at him and he frowned back apologetically as she fetched it from the cupboard.

'You don't have tomato ketchup on Sunday dinner,' she whispered as she placed the bottle next to his plate.

'Sorry, I'm a ketchup fiend... love the stuff,' he said and poured a large blob onto his plate.

From here on the meal didn't go badly at all. He let a few peas slip off his plate but that was about it. He made a conscious effort to limit his conversation to simple yes or no answers, her father didn't even have an expression on his face that said 'hurt my daughter and I will kill you in one swift move.'

With the meal over he skipped back to her room.

'I hope I didn't embarrass you. I'm just no good at that sort of thing.'

'No, you were just being yourself Jay,' she replied as she joined him by the window.

'Okay, well at least I've made the effort and some impression.'

He smiled, shrugged a little and continued to sift through his records.

Monday, May 15

Jay had been uncontrollably excited at developing the first half a dozen or so black and white photos of the house party. He found it fascinating to watch the white paper fade as an image of a moment in time slowly appeared before him. It confirmed everything and revealed more of the drunk and debauched night. By now though, he had reached the point where he was almost slumped over the developing tray, holding the plastic tongs lethargically, he was worn down by inhaling too much of the fumes. He wondered how well Trac's exam was going or had gone, but the mild headache had swiftly turned into a migraine and thoughts were no longer a viable option. He refused to let up on the task in hand, all the photos had to be developed there and then and he would not consider the possibility of backing down to another day. By the time he had finished he found the college strangely abandoned. Pale, drawn and feeling light-headed he made his way outside and sat on a low wall, appreciating the clean air and allowing his eyes to readjust to the daylight. From this point on he was nothing more than a zombie operating in auto pilot. He returned home to find a letter from college that read;

BTEC Higher National Diploma Course in Design (Graphic Design)

With reference to your application for admission to the above course which has been received here as your second choice college, I am writing to inform you that the form has now been sent to the alternative second choice college that you nominated. I am sorry that we were unable to interview you on this occasion

He could moan about it, but he figured under the circumstance given his history it had not been the wisest decision to try and stay on at Loughborough in the first place. He scrawled across the letter in black felt pen; *in other words FUCK OFF!*

Wednesday, May 17

Early morning sitting on a bench by the clock tower Jay and Adrian whooped with laughter brought about from the sets of colour photos of the party he'd had developed at Klick photo point.

'Let's not go to college,' he suggested. 'We could go back to my house and draw up some cartoons for the album.'

Adrian picked up his art box and said, 'let's go,' without a second thought.

Anything amusing they remembered that had not been caught on film got illustrated; the house, booze, Marmite, Jay and Trac in the four poster bed, all bound together complete with Adrian's unused condom.

Trac was very impressed by the album, 'it really captures everything.'

'Yeah I'm pleased with it.'

'I'm not too sure about the cartoon of us in bed at the back but it's good.'

'Nothing happened.'

'I know that... still it was nice to have your body next to mine and I wish we did more.'

'Hmm, but someone was too drunk.'

'Like you had the energy.'

'Yeah, remember,' he nodded raising a finger in the air.

She pondered momentarily before nodding back in agreement. 'Anyway,' she continued, 'the pic of you mooning with the vodka bottle between the cheeks of your bum is not the most attractive shot.'

He gave a chuckle. 'The one of me upturning it and jeering that it's empty is great, and the one in black and white with you behind me holding my hands.'

'Hmm, only I didn't know you were holding the banana as if it was your...'

'My what?'

'You know!'

And he just smirked and gave a light shrug.

A number of photos revealed how drunk Trac was, one in particular had her leaning against the wall eating bread and looking very worse for wear. He could tell by her expression she felt uncomfortable about it.

'Not too happy with that one,' she said softly.

'You're joking aren't you,' he said positively. 'That's the best one. I've stuck a copy of that up on my wall next to my Red Stripe poster.'

Her eyes narrowed as she studied his face, 'why?'

'That picture on its own tells you everything.'

'Hmm, not convinced,' she said flatly. 'Can I borrow it though, to show Johnny.'

'Yeah, I just need to do a couple more cartoons for it. Why don't you show it to Michelle.'

'No, I don't think she would appreciate it somehow. It's horrible having to say to her I don't know who splattered soup up the window or covered the toilet in toothpaste... and chucked Cinzano over the TV.'

'Hey let's not get into the detail,' he replied calmly as he flipped through the pages. 'Who's that?' he said pointing.

'You should know, you've got your arm round her.'

'Who is it? It's one of your mates isn't it?'

'Her name's Claire,' said Trac huffing a little and folding her arms.

'What's up with you?'

'She was asking me about you and wanted to know if she got a Cult album which one would be the best one to get.'

'That's tough,' he said rubbing at his chin. 'I mean I'm really into 'Sonic Temple' but that's only because it's new. 'The Manor Sessions' are good and well the 'Electric' albums got great singles on it,' he pondered momentarily. ''Love' is a bit old now but when I first heard it, it was like all the music I was listening to before that was just passing time.'

'Don't you dare wind me up,' she said whilst glaring at him.

'What?' he said innocently.

'She told me you had a chat with her about it... apparently you said you would record some for her.'

'Did I?' he smiled teasingly. 'Oh yeah that's right I did,' he nodded. 'Still it beats all this Stock, Aitken and Waterman bollocks.'

He continued to wind her up about spending a lot of time with her that night. Trac got more than a little bit upset, especially when she saw a photo of Emma just getting off the toilet, a full frontal shot of her private parts and noticed his belt undone in the background of the picture. He shrugged and lifted his arm up in a way that gestured 'I can't remember anything about it.'

'Yeah right!'

'I might have got my cock out... I'm not sure... you'll have to ask her.' Feeling vulnerable, his behaviour didn't help matters in the slightest but he continued to dismiss its implications with casual ease.

'Claire wouldn't go out with you anyway,' she dismissed in a disgruntled manner.

'Yeah she would,' he chuckled.

'No, she wouldn't, you're not her type.'

'Okay give us her phone number and I'll ring then.'

'You wouldn't dare.'

'Yeah I would,' he replied with enthusiasm.

She grabbed her address book and gave him the number, even fetched the portable phone from the hall and thrust it at him.

'Okay,' he said trying to hold back a smirk that was breaking at the corners of his mouth. He began to dial without hesitation. She felt sure he would hang up at the last minute but when he didn't she sat arms folded glaring at him.

'Hi, is that Claire?... yeah it's Jason here... Trac's boyfriend, we met at Michelle's party.'

He grinned over at Trac's sullen expression, he was loving every second.

'Well I was just wondering if you wanted to go out sometime?... Right yeah, I am still seeing Trac but I really fancy you... Okay... well it's just a question of whether you fancy me or not... so you do?' he went to grin over at Trac again but by the look on her face he realised he had gone too far, she had gone past the annoyed stage and had the look of tears being imminent.

'I've got to go, maybe it's best another time then... bye,' he put the phone down and dare not crack a smile, even though the urge to was so intense.

'You sod,' she said snatching the phone from him.

'You dared me,' he shrugged again as if it wasn't his fault.

'Why did you do it to me?'

'So how does it feel to be out of control?' he said in a soft tone that irritated her.

Her emotions were running. She stood and moved to the other side of the room in silence, then turned to leave the room, but he caught her in the doorway.

'Hey... I'm sorry,' he whispered.

'Well you ought to be.'

'I just thought we were playing that's all.'

She looked at him coldly or tried to but he caught her glare. There was something about his eyes he knew he could use more wisely, and was glad she read his sincerity. Her anger was already melting away, she just couldn't stay mad at him, that was the thing.

'You've got to trust me,' he whispered.

'How can I when you do this.'

'If you trusted me you'd know I was teasing you.'

In a effort to lighten the tone, he needed her to be back on side, to stop the guilt that had begun to envelope him. He clicked his fingers a couple of times and started to sing, 'Suspicious Minds' in the best impersonation of Elvis he could manage. Reaching out his arms towards her, he tried to get her to follow his lead in dancing. Firmly rooted to the spot, he managed to sway her from left to right as he hugged her tightly.

'You're daft you are.'

He squeezed at her bum gently, apologised with a whisper, and kissed at her neck several times before pulling back to engage her eyes. 'I really am sorry,' he said. 'I went too far.'

She clapped a hand over his mouth. 'Shut up,' she said. 'You do go on.' She sniffed a little bit and wiped at her nose, as his lips nuzzled her ear further. She was softening and warming to him by the minute.

'Just don't do it again.'

'You've got a beautiful nose,' he said and kissed it.

'It's me who's been silly,' she said. 'I'm just feeling sensitive today.'

'I know I can be a pain,' he smiled. 'But you still love me don't you?'

'Umm... but I sometimes wonder why?'

'If you say it you have to mean it.'

She studied his eyes, they looked clear, even serious. 'I know that...' she replied. 'With other lads it was just... just a word and no real meaning.'

'And now?'

'Feels good,' she smiled as his hand slipped into the rim of her jeans. 'Like a warm rush through me... I feel close to you,' and she kissed him.

Happy that they had made up and the doubt had passed he chirped, 'have you got any felt pens?'

'Why?'

'I thought I might draw a couple more cartoons.' he responded casually as he walked over to the stereo to change the CD.

'Open that cupboard there, there's a furry pencil case with loads in.'

He pulled open the cupboard and unzipped the case and picked out a black fibre tip pen, but then put it down again in favour of a pencil. Clasping his tongue between his teeth, he carefully began to draw a cartoon. He started with the eyes and nose and followed with a wide smiling mouth.

'Maybe I'll draw you,' he murmured.

From here on all his concentration was devoted to turning a blank piece of paper into something special. Trac pulled stupid faces behind his back, but with little response she returned to some homework.

Thursday, May 18

Jay frantically painted a pamphlet cover for *Healthy Eating*. It was a two week design project, only he had started it that morning. By lunchtime he hated it, the fish just didn't look right. Adrian managed to finish his with a cartoon and went home while Dave sat there alongside him getting nowhere fast. He pinned his sheet of paper up against the wall and sat studying it, waiting for an idea to pop into his head. When nothing happened he grinned, 'that's crap,' and huffed feeling defeated by his lack of creation.

'No question about it... it's crap,' he said.

He stuck with his original idea for a while until Dave leant over to have a look and burst out laughing.

'Fucking hell,' he laughed. 'That's a bit shit for you.'

'As long as I get a pass I'm not bothered,' defended Jay.

'No chance,' roared Dave in continuing laughter.

'Well, let's have a look at yours then Dave.'

'What?' his laughter suddenly cut short.

'Exactly cos you haven't done it.'

Dave had as usual spent hours collecting reference but had not actually done anything with it. Ruth, the tutor for the day, came swiftly over to collect the work, she looked over his shoulder, plenty of confidence he thought biting at his bottom lip.

'Nearly finished,' he smiled at her. 'I'm quite proud of that.'

He actually made himself sound genuine. He continued to sing his own praises until the point where he managed to convince himself that it really wasn't that bad.

'I don't think it's quite completed yet do you?' she said bluntly.

'Oh yeah,' he agreed still trying to charm her with enthusiasm. 'Just minor touch ups,' he grinned.

Ruth laid a pile of collected work on the desk and Jay slipped his into the middle and left without her catching him. His thoughts immediately turned to Trac as he trundled down the corridor. After his dinner that evening he phoned her up and she was on her way over. He had a shower and got changed quickly, put some music on and studied the two tickets he held in his hands, *Deacon Blue in concert at De Montfort Hall*. He'd bought them a while ago, in a moment of wishful thinking, back when they were just friends and it made him smile now that they were to go as a couple. An overall feeling of wellbeing washed over him.

Jay moved to the bar with ease. 'What would you like to drink?' he asked softly.

'I don't mind, half a lager,' she suggested.

'Are you sure? I'll get you anything you want.'

'Whiskey and ginger,' she chirped.

'Okay,' he smiled. 'Whiskey and ginger it is.'

'Oh by the way, my sister said the cartoon you did does look like me.'

'Course it does.'

The barmaid approached and he placed his order. 'Whiskey and ginger and one whiskey and ice.'

Smiling, he handed her the drink and they moved into the main crowd of people quite near to the front of the stage.

'On occasions I do like to be romantic.'

'I know,' she smiled back at him.

'You look beautiful, smell gorgeous too,' he said lightly as he gave her a hug.

'Thanks, you're not bad yourself.'

He put his arm round her waist, pulled her close to his side and awaited the band to hit the stage. The opening number 'Circus Lights' began to seep and then pulsate around the room, energising the crowd. The atmosphere lifted ten fold and their excitement rose. He felt an overwhelming emotional sense of happiness, the highest peak in their growing relationship. He felt too lucky and wondered for a second what he had done to deserve such a defining moment. All of a sudden it was as though anything was possible with the littlest of effort.

As the songs poured out and the crowd became mightier, like a strong current it swept them violently from side to side.

'Shall we go and find our seats?' he shouted and she nodded in reply.

Towards the end of the night they hugged each other in a slow dance. He came behind her and pulled her back to his chest, occasionally kissing her neck and cheek lightly. He sang the words so softly, it was all he could do to demonstrate his euphoric state of mind.

'I love you,' he whispered.

She turned and looked into his eyes and he smiled back adorably. It was perfect timing he had been really attentive, she felt very special indeed.

'Do you really?'

He whispered, 'sure I do, I love you like crazy.'

The band swept through its encore and they left arm-in-arm, poster in hand, so fixed to each other that you couldn't even see the join.

Friday, May 19

Jay rushed out at quarter past eight, he dashed to the door and burst out, half in his leather jacket, his art box in one hand and a piece of toast in his mouth, but he soon got organised by the time he got to the end of the drive.

The racket Adrian was making in the classroom had nothing to do with graphic design but had everything to do with winding Dave up. Adrian had exaggerated Dave's nose ten fold in his cartoon portrait and wasn't sure if he'd gone too far when Jay snatched it from his desk laughing.

'It's brilliant,' he hooted. 'Let's go and copy loads of them.'

The two of them slipped from corridor to corridor intermittently sticking up the cartoon of Dave, that is until the wiry frame of Mr Jackson, the head of the department, stood proudly in front of them, expressionless.

'Have you been putting these up?' and held a copy up in front of them.

'Er no,' replied Jay swiftly pushing the copies further behind his back. Mr Jackson glared at them momentarily, 'I've got my eye on you two,' he said, smiled reluctantly and walked on.

'He must be in a good mood,' noted Adrian. 'It's obvious it's us.'

'What difference does it make. He knows, and he knows that we know he knows.'

'Shit. I knew it,' Adrian's face looked panic stricken, 'he's going to kick us out.'

'Don't panic he's probably looking forward to us leaving is all. Besides we haven't done nothing but make a few photocopies without paying for them.' Adrian let out a long breath of air from his lungs as he leaned into the wall.

'It's not exactly coursework is it?'

Jay patted him on the back lightly. 'You need to chill out more.'

Dave came back from the toilet with a scrunched up piece of paper in his hand looking more than a little annoyed. 'My nose isn't that big,' he roared assessing the cartoon of himself on the crumpled bit of paper before tearing it in two.

'Dave,' chuckled Jay. 'It's more like you than you are!'

Dave smiled reluctantly and returned to his desk where his anger soon returned when he found half of his equipment missing from his art box.

'Jay have you had my pencil?'

'Er, no Dave,' he replied and nudged Adrian and smiled as he tried to reference the colour of Dave's face with one of his markers, as the blood rising stress spread about his face.

'Fucking... fucking,' he babbled.

'Calm down,' Jay said softly as he started to feel guilty. 'We've got plenty of time for all the final project work.'

'Suppose,' he muttered back, as he looked around the other tables scratching at his head looking confused as if he was now considering the possibility he may have mislaid some of his kit.

The afternoon seemed to last forever and not being able to see the lads or Trac in the evening made things worse. Working at the hardware store was a pain, switching his Thursday for the Friday was worth it though. As he stacked the shelves the concert was the only thing that still glued a smile to his face and gave him an enchanted persona.

Saturday, May 20 - 21

Jay tucked his jumper into his jeans, the air inside the warehouse was closed and used, best suited for a greenhouse. Having to work two nights on the trot pissed him off all the more and Saturday after a Friday! What was he doing?

He was waiting impatiently for the next explosion of activity on the drinking front but nothing seemed to be on the horizon and it wasn't far from reaching total disappointment. On the plus side, at least Trac had taken the day off work. He looked at the naff aluminium clock on the wall and decided to have a little rest before heaving a large box of ant killer onto his trolley.

'Fucking hell,' he mumbled to himself, wiping his brow with the back of his hand. He heard the phone ring as he loaded the box onto the trolley and pushed it onto the shop floor.

'Jay,' shouted a voice.

'Yeah.'

'The phone, it's for you.'

'Okay, I won't be a second.'

He left the trolley in the appropriate aisle and jogged down to the phone wondering who it could be, no-one phoned him at work?

'Hello.'

'Jay?'

'Yeah.'

'It's Adrian, guess what?'

'What?'

'I've got a bottle of schnapps and a bottle of Scotch.'

'Let's get hammered.'

Suddenly he was beginning to get excited, the adrenaline pumped through him like a drug.

'I'll meet you out of work,' Adrian said. 'Ten o'clock.'

'Right I'll see you in a bit.'

He replaced the phone and felt like skipping on the spot. He clapped his hands together and rubbed them tightly, looking up at the clock, only twenty five minutes to go, so pleased the day wasn't going to pass him by so dull and adventureless as he thought.

He stood waiting for Adrian, anxiously looking right then left along the street. It was ten minutes before he emerged from around the corner.

'DDDDDEEEEE,' he roared as he marched up with a plastic carrier bag in hand, it was clinking delightfully. He took the bottles out swiftly for Jay's approval.

'Three quarters of a bottle of schnapps,' he said. 'And a little Scotch.'

'That's okay,' chirped Jay. 'I've got a full bottle of Jim Beam at home, so we might as well go back to my place. Yeah?'

'Sure. Why not.'

The two of them sat in Jay's bedroom around a small wooden table he'd brought up from the lounge. Two bottles of Guinness, schnapps, Jim Beam, a near empty bottle of Jack Daniel's and a small bottle of Bells. Jay was just in the process of polishing off the Jack Daniel's when Adrian began mixing schnapps and Coke into his bowl-like glass. Jay loaded a black and white film for his camera and chose to consume Guinness next in an attempt to line his stomach before moving onto neat Jim Beam. He preferred it neat, mixing it only distorted its true taste. The first few glasses always had a great kick to it, but once he was on the road to being pie-eyed, it slipped down like water.

Reaching the first stage of drunkenness, they discussed everything under the sun, ideas, music, girls, design and parties while listening to tunes that seemed to infuse their souls and uniquely amalgamated their friendship further.

With Adrian close to finishing his schnapps and half a bottle of whiskey gone, Jay pulled a black jumper over his T-shirt and picked up his jacket.

'Let's go,' he babbled.

Adrian's flushed and relaxed aura was momentarily startled by his abrupt approach to making a move. Bolting upright, it was as though some outside force was prizing him out into the night. Jay eased his way down his drive draining a slug from his bottle, pausing for a moment before nodding slightly to himself. He lurched to the right and proceeded to stagger in the direction of the alleyway without communicating his thoughts to Adrian. Once out onto the main road that runs through the village he could hear music coming from the Four Seasons Hotel and allowed it to draw him in, with Adrian merely keeping in tow.

'Can we get a drink in there?'

'Yeah,' spluttered Jay. 'I'm sure we can.'

He plundered straight through the door past reception and headed for the bar. Adrian took the responsibility of hiding their bottles of booze outside and stood in the reception slightly incoherent to the situation. Jay spotted a buffet table and stood comfortably, glass in hand, pondering the selection of triangular sandwiches on display, then quickly began to ram as many into his mouth as he could.

'You can't do that Jay, it's someone's private party?' chuckled Adrian with a slur.

'Good food,' came his muffled reply and proceeded to ram another ham salad sandwich into his mouth. The schnapps had really kicked in and Adrian began to get a little out of control. When he failed to find the toilet he urinated all over the reception desk. With that and last orders already called they decided to leave, Adrian first followed by Jay with a fire extinguisher spraying wildly as he stumbled.

'Jay, what is it about you and fire extinguishers?'

'To a drunk person like me...' he chuckled erratically. 'It's... it's a real safe form of firework.'

'Where are we off now?'

'We could walk to my old man's house,' Jay suggested.

Off they went in a blind stagger, at least in the right direction. Bottle of booze in one hand and a rounded glass full to the brim in the other, the goal for the evening had been forged.

Two miles down the road they began to sing some of their favourite songs, slightly out of tune but laughing and bumping into each other happily. Their lyrics became rather more bizarre as they made them up to the tune they had now firmly lodged in the only working part of their brains.

'God's got big arms and he does fings like that cos he's great and he's up there. In the sky the stars the clouds and moon and he is there.'

Jay chipped in, 'I can't walk any further, cos my legs are really knackered, and the whiskey is running out, oh I am pissed up.'

Adrian chuckled and patted his pal on the back, 'how much further?'

'Miles,' smiled Jay followed by, 'I got to go for a slash,' and veered off to his right.

He stood in a field swaying back and forth when Adrian spotted something in the darkness moving.

'What's that?' he said curiously looking blindly ahead.

'What?' yelled Jay back across at him. 'Shit' he felt something brush passed his arse. 'Shit!' he yelped again. 'What the fuck was that?'

'SHEEP!' shouted Adrian.

'A sheep?'

'Yeah.'

He joined in with the laughter as his hands left his cock in search of his camera. The poor animal turned and fled as Jay snapped a picture and in the pitch black the flash was blinding, he slipped and dropped to the floor landing on his bum with a splat. 'Bollocks,' he cursed further and made his way back towards the road.

'Can we get over there for a short cut?' shouted Adrian.

'No... No, it's nothing but a field of sheep out there,' he waved Adrian away as he reeled back towards him and began to wrestle himself over the fence.

'Shit,' he spluttered.

'What's up?' chuckled Adrian.

'I'm stuck in the fucking fence now.'

'Are you alright?'

'No... I... I think I've broken my neck.'

Jay heard more than one sheep move at speed and decided to rip himself away from the fence as quickly as possible. He managed to stumble to his feet and hobbled for a second or two. Adrian finished his Schnapps and hurled the bottle up in the air and awaited its smash in the middle of the road. The glass glinted in the light from the nearby street lamp and captured his attention for some time, while further up the road and round the corner Jay paused to swig some more bourbon, his words now quite eligible he uttered something to the effect that they were nearly there and his jeans were covered in sheep shit.

They carried on staggering up the road stumbling into people's front lawns, until Jay tripped on a low fence. There they struggled, Jay on the floor and Adrian trying his best to drag him to his feet when a police car flickered its electric blue lights and pulled up alongside them.

'Fucking hell,' mumbled Adrian pulling at Jay's jacket with more effort. He got to his feet and they stood propping each other up glaring at the flashing blue light that sparkled around the darkness of the wet isolated street. The first police officer stepped out followed shortly by another from the far side of the car.

'Good evening officer,' spluttered Jay.

'Right then lads what's going on here?' came the reply, firm and direct.

'Err... nothing,' gurgled Jay with whiskey bubbling out of his mouth and dripping off his chin. 'We're just... just drunk.' Finding some life and energy from somewhere he jolted upright. 'Or is there a law against it?' he spat and gave an inane grin, hoping now that he had not had too much booze that it was going to impair his razor sharp wit.

The second police officer's voice was deeper and forceful. 'Turn your pockets out lads,' he said.

Jay lurched forward. 'Pardon?' he replied putting on what was a pathetic attempt at a shocked tone of voice.

'Turn them out,' said the voice louder this time.

He thrust his hands into his pockets and turned out an assortment of stuff much to Adrian's amusement, he found his friend wonderful entertainment.

'What is this?'

'Just... just gloves. I... I got them from the petrol station back... back there,' he slurred. 'They were free.'

The officer looked at the disposable gloves, a small stubby pencil, a squashed Black Jack, some blue tack, 10p and a small piece of wood in Jay's hands and pulled a bemused face.

'And this?' he asked picking up this small piece of wood.

'That's err,' confused for a second he waited for a spark to ignite in his brain. 'It's err... a Sparkle lollipop stick. Look,' he pointed to the joke engraved in the small piece of wood. 'What's a crocodiles favourite game?'

'Alright, in the car. I want your names and addresses.'

'What for?' Adrian asked.

'Routine check,' grunted the first policeman.

'SNAP!' shouted Jay at the top of his voice startling the nearest police officer who grabbed him forcibly by the scruff of the neck making him wheeze. From this position he could only manage a strangled squawk, 'alright... alright... it's... it's...' He hiccupped a couple of times once the officer eased his grip, '...it's the answer to the joke... snap,' he said quietly trying to point feebly at the stick in his right hand.

'What have you been drinking to get yourselves into a state like this?"

'Whiskey.'

'Isn't it a bit late at night for that?'

Neither of them responded they just looked at each other blankly.

'Do you know we could arrest you for public drunkenness.'

'We... we are not disturbing anyone.'

At three o'clock they stood putting their items back into their pockets kneeling on the pavement. As the police car turned round they both waved them off lethargically. When the car was out of sight, Jay sprawled out across the grass verge, Jim Beam resting on his chest, stopping momentarily before rambling further up the road. In thirty minutes or so they found the final road towards Leire, it was quiet, pitch black, cold and haunting.

'Are you going in the right direction?' asked Adrian.

'Yeah,' he replied nodding positively.

Not realising how out of control they really were, Jay found a farmhouse car which seemed a warm place to crash out. He discovered the car was unlocked with the keys in the ignition.

'Adrian, it's got the keys in it.'

'What about finger prints?'

Jay pulled out the disposable gloves he had acquired from the petrol station and slipped them onto his hands without a word.

'Come on Jay, leave it,' he replied but it was drowned out by the firing up of the vehicle.

Not being in the league of the professional car thief, Jay sat revving the engine as his hands grappled for the gear stick, smashing it back and forth between the gears. Finally finding reverse, yet forgetting to release the hand brake, he was doing everything possible to attract unwelcomed attention. Suddenly he sped the car backwards onto the road and shunted it forward thirty or so yards, leant over and opened the passenger door and shouted out into the darkness, 'get in!'

Appearing from the pitch black Adrian slipped into the passenger seat with relative ease 'let's go,' he uttered.

'Hold the whiskey,' said Jay thrusting the bottle into his chest sharply.

Adrian swiftly grabbed the bottle from Jay who in turn slammed his foot on the accelerator and pulled off down the dark road.

'Where are the lights?' cried Adrian. Panicking he started pressing buttons and pulling at any levers his hands found. Eventually he leant across and grabbed something, twisted it, and on came the lights. The car, half off the road, was manoeuvred back onto tarmac. Ahead the road twisted and turned sharply. Jay sat nuzzled up to the window screen squinting out trying to identify the road from the grass.

'The corner,' shrieked Adrian.

Jay spun the steering wheel round to the right as fast as he could, not realising he was on top of one of the sharpest bends. The road was too wet and the car began to slide crashing through an assortment of traffic cones.

'Fucking hell,' shouted Jay as the car began to tip and rolled over into a large excavated trench. The noise pierced the night, followed by a deadly silence.

'Shit,' grunted Jay moving feebly. 'Let's get out of here... and quick.'

Adrian didn't respond and Jay nudged him. 'Adrian... Adrian... are you alright?'

'I'm... I'm okay,' he mumbled, but he looked dazed. 'You?'

'Yeah. Let's get out of here... now,' and pulled at his coat. 'Come on.'

Marching off through a field full of corn, in no clear direction, Jay suddenly stopped. 'Shit,' he cried swaying on the spot.

'What?'

'You got the whiskey?'

'No.'

'I gave you the whiskey...'

'I know... but I haven't got it.'

'It's... it's in the car, I'll... I'll have to go back.'

'Leave it Jay.'

It was too late, he had left his presence. He blundered his way back to the car. His arms flailed around in the darkness desperately. He leaned further through the driver's window cursing as he made feeble grabs inside blindly until he made contact with a familiar shape. Great, he thought as the bottle was still intact.

They finally made their way down to Jubilee Walk, it seemed the ideal spot to both crash out and hide out of sight.

'We can rest here,' said Jay panting.

They sat at the bench underneath the bridge. They both fell asleep momentarily, but it was only a matter of minutes before Jay woke.

'There's somebody there!' he babbled.

'There's not,' mumbled Adrian half asleep.

'There's fucking is,' Jay continued with a genuine frightened voice.

He had either dreamt it, seen a large animal that had upset him or was just simply mistaking a tree for the bogeyman. Adrian went to investigate with the Jim Beam bottle held as a defensive weapon.

'Let's just go,' suggested Jay.

'Yeah, you're right, this place is starting to give me the creeps.'

They trudged slowly up the beaten path. Weakened, tired, slightly cold and dizzy, they avoided talking as it seemed to take too much effort. It was now about half past four in the morning, walking all night they began to feel the strain in their legs and eyes. As dawn started to break they were walking across a field towards a farm with their heads bowed to the ground. Jay kept a hand still tight around the bottle and occasionally looked up and appreciated the glow the sunrise made. He couldn't help but wonder what had happened and what was going to happen, he didn't even know where they were. Strangely he felt it was as though he had done this before, walked across a field, this field with Adrian. He mentioned the crazy feeling of de ja vu to him but he just nodded and trundled onwards.

Out on the road, surveying the area, the view struck Jay. A low hanging early summer mist held in the dips and hollows of the sweeping landscape.

'Inspired to paint,' Jay said mildly.

Adrian stopped and took in the view, 'maybe an abstract interpretation, you know shapes and blocks of colour.'

'It's like you don't just look at the view like that do you.'

Adrian agreed, 'it's about feel.'

Before Jay could follow up this line of intellectual chat, Adrian had trundled off.

'Let's have a rest, ' he called after him as he leant on a fence, spread his arms out across it and looked up to the sun hoping it would warm his face.

'Come on,' Adrian grumbled and beckoned him with his hand. 'Let's keep moving.'

'Mate, leave me here to die,' he wheezed with a smile.

They rested for a while but Adrian was furtive and began to walk off. Jay ground his teeth and leapt off the fence onto his feet.

'Hang about,' he called after him.

'I reckon we should go this way,' Adrian pointed.

'I don't know, it doesn't feel right.'

'We're bound to come to a main road sooner or later.'

'Let's toss a coin,' he suggested and Adrian nodded with agreement, he liked the sound of that, it had that unpredictable fate appeal to it.

He patted his pockets until he found a ten pence piece. Grinning a weak grin, he paused to build up tension before he flipped the coin. For Adrian his impatience made it painful but uttered the word. 'Heads.'

'Tales mate. Let's head for those trees over there,' and nodded to the opposite direction. Adrian kicked a stone and squinted up at the horizon. 'Alright,' he replied.

The two of them crossed another field and enjoyed the sun rising and the intake of damp air that was both refreshing and exhilarating. Jay felt strangely back to nature still enjoying the countryside view he held, its quietness and simplicity appealed. They entered a belt of trees and came out onto a gravel walk way.

'Ouch,' cried Jay.

'What's up,' yawned Adrian.

'It's that stinger,' Jay looked down exasperated. 'The bastard's bit me' Adrian chuckled, 'you got any money Jay?'

'Only 10p.'

'No, like real money for say a taxi.'

'No, but I'll give Trac a call in an hour.'

'Can't you leave that till later.'

'I can't, I need a dose of sanity in my life. Besides she lives out this way, if we find a street name she might be able to give us some directions.'

'Okay, that's if and when we find a village.'

Time continued to move slowly. They finally came to a small country village with a pub and very little else.

Adrian craned his neck round. 'What's the name of this place?'

'I don't know I didn't see a sign anywhere. There must be one somewhere, let's keep moving.'

A phone box stood like a phallic symbol at the side of the road. Adrian sat down on a low wall while he phoned Trac. He dialled and heard the engaged tone. Cursing, he slammed the phone down, waiting a moment before re-dialling. This time he got through, his voice soft and expressionless, he asked to speak to her. Thank God her sister answered the phone he thought and took a swig at the remaining drops of whiskey at the base of the bottle.

'Hello,' came a slow weak voice.

'Erm it's Jay, I've had a bit of an accident.'

'Oh, no what?'

He explained quickly trying his best to sound sorrowful, hoping for just an ounce of empathy.

'I don't believe you sometimes,' she griped.

'I'll come round and see you when I get home.'

'How far away are you?'

'I don't know, I mean I'm not sure where we are. I reckon it's about nine miles home something like that.'

'I really don't believe you.'

'It won't take long once I get a sense of direction.'

The phone line was silent for a moment then came a sigh. 'Go on then give me some idea of where you are and I'll see if I can help.'

After a further trek of some ten miles they arrived at Narborough at around ten thirty, still cold, tired and hungry. They sat at the bottom of the stairs and appreciated the comfort with adequate smiles of relief.

'We must have been walking in circles,' said Jay shaking his head.

His mum came from the top of the stairs strangely followed by his dad and he looked bewildered.

'I didn't know you stayed the night Adrian,' smiled his mum and they disappeared into the kitchen.

Adrian frowned and then gave a puzzled shrug. With a feeling of urgency to depart again Jay smiled when he spied the keys to The Beast on the window sill.

'Listen,' he said excitedly. 'I reckon we should take a look. You know, check out the car to see if it's still there. I'll have a quick chat with Trac, by that time my mum and dad will have gone out so we can come back here, have a shower and some kip followed by Marmite on toast and,' he paused. 'I'll give you a lift home.'

Adrian smiled lazily, 'sounds good to me.'

'Let's go before any questions get asked.'

As they slowly drove past the scene where they believed the car had embedded itself half inside a trench, there was nothing. Had it really been an illusion, a dream?

With confusion Jay rubbed at his head, 'where is it?' he exclaimed.

'We best not slow down too much.'

'I can't understand it,' he shook his head with disbelief.

He pulled up onto Trac's drive then wandered up to the front door and pressed the bell, still looking a wall of confusion.

In the first few months of their relationship his sometimes erratic behaviour had excited her. His unruly nature and extraordinary drinking habits enthralled her and made him somehow more appealing, he knew that, only with this event he had plainly gone too far.

She answered the door and looked at him with a calm, mocking expression. He was sure she saw through him. What have you done? was clearly stencilled in capital letters across her face. What was she going to say? He told himself he needed some serious charm for this one.

'You idiot,' she said dully.

He put his finger to her lips, 'shhh!' He frowned at her and gave a slight nod that suggested she be calm. The last thing he wanted was a confrontation at the front door and someone, namely her mother, overhearing.

'It's alright,' she mumbled. 'No ones in.'

Oh dear he thought as they moved into her room. 'I... er-'

'Am an idiot,' she repeated with more anger. 'You could have been killed.' The more snappy her attitude, the more she could control the conversation. He wanted to cover his ears already, looking back towards the door he thought about leaving.

'Hey,' he said softly. 'I'm still here in one piece.'

She stood firm in her peach dressing-gown looking at his face, scouring for scratches or any bruising.

'You're not indestructible Jay.'

'I know,' he whispered.

'You're okay then?'

'A few bruises and I ache a bit is all.'

'You've got to look after yourself Jay.'

'I'm fine, really,' he smiled pathetically playing the vulnerable boy, showing her the small scratches and bump to the side of his head.

'How did you do that?'

He gave her a dismissive shrug. 'Don't know... I probably did it on the steering wheel.'

'You tit!'

'I'm sorry. You're right I am an idiot,' he confessed hopelessly. 'I don't know about tit,' he tried a light smile and she gave him a stern look.

'It's not funny Jay.'

He thought maybe humour was not the right technique and pulled another sorrowful expression at her. She cleared her throat abruptly and continued in a tone that was tougher than ever.

'Don't look at me for support, you've brought this on yourself... what about the police?'

'Look, I didn't know what I was doing. I was drunk.'

'Is that the best excuse you can come up with?'

He brushed that off with, 'suppose.'

'You're unbelievable.'

'I just drank so far down the bottle in such a short space of time and the next thing I knew I was totally out of it.'

'Hmm, lessons to be learnt from that.'

'Okay, okay look at my face... don't I look innocent.'

'No,' she shook her head plainly. 'Guilty as charged.'

He gave a tired smirk. 'Oh, I'm a hunted man.'

'See, you just think this is funny,' she slammed. 'Don't play this down Jay.'

'I know... I know,' he admitted holding up his hands.

This was a serious case of damage limitation and humour definitely wasn't going to work on this occasion, she wasn't giving him an inch. He pulled her close and gave her a short firm hug, cupped her face with his left hand and rubbed her cheek lightly with his thumb. He avoided acknowledging he'd been thoughtless, irresponsible and selfish.

'You look more worried than me,' he whispered. 'To me it just feels like a dream. Won't you just calm down a little or you'll get me going as well,' he said sullenly. 'Don't you think I've thought about it. I've been walking all night. I've had no sleep and I just came round for a hug.'

'A hug isn't going to solve everything Jay. You get up to stuff like this and you have to face the consequences.'

'I know what you're saying and I know you're right. I made a mistake and all I'm trying to do is to stay positive is all.'

'Don't give me those stupid cow eyes.'

'I just really need a hug right now, that's all,' he looked to the ground, hurt in his eyes.

'Oh, you,' she said softly but still denied him a smile. 'What am I going to do with you eh?' and gave him a hug.

He didn't care if he had a hangover, this was what he was waiting for, what he needed. She was like a protective blanket from the harsh realities and he wanted to hug long enough to fill his body with a heavy dose of youthful spirit and optimism. He smelt of stale alcohol and felt as though he could fall asleep any second. Trac pushed him away and he slumped onto her bed. His body remained motionless only his eyes appeared alive.

'So what happened exactly?'

'I can't really remember much.'

'You must remember something?'

'I'm... I'm a little muddled... I'm not exactly sure where to begin,' and gave a feeble shrug of his shoulders. 'All I know is my legs are killing me and my head aches.'

'Haven't you got changed yet?'

'Look, I only stepped in the house half an hour ago and I shot straight round here to see if the car was there.'

'And was it?'

'No,' he replied rubbing at his tired eyes.

'Do you want a cup of tea?'

'Yeah. I mean no, I better go.'

'There's some in the pot, you sure?'

'Go on then I'll have a quick cup,' he smiled.

'Where's Adrian?' she asked calmly.

'In The Beast.'

'Oh right.'

'Don't worry he's got the stereo on, he'll be fine for a few more minutes.'
She went off to fetch the tea and he lay back on the bed and closed his eyes.
He felt safe in her bed, and at present would quite happily stay there for
eternity undiscovered if that was at all possible.

'Here you go,' she said waking him.

'Thanks,' he said in a low tone, taking the cup he appreciated the warmth
it gave to his hands. He smiled to himself thinking about how his night had
made him appreciate something that seemed to go relatively unnoticed in
everyday life.

'What are you smiling at?'

'Nothing,' he replied and peered over to the plate she was holding.

'I've made you some peanut butter on toast.'
The smile dropped as if it had come unpinned by guilt. 'You spoil me,' he
said softly as he took the plate.

'I know I do, God knows why?'
She could see the softness in his eyes that let her know how grateful he was.

'I'm the one who makes you crazy.'

'Yeah you do,' she frowned. 'And I seem to look after you.'

'Maybe I need you looking after me.'
Watching him lovingly sip at the thick dark tea, lost in thought, she found
herself asking him how he'd managed to pinch it so easily.

'It had the keys in it,' he said calmly and gave a small shrug of his
shoulders.

'That was a bit stupid of them.'

'Exactly. That's what I thought, it deserved to get nicked.'
Her face turned slightly stern again.

'Err...' he stuttered. 'You're right it didn't justify me stealing it.'
She frowned once again and took a sip of her own tea. 'You know to be
honest,' she said. 'I've always wanted to steal a car.'

'The tom boy in you eh?'
She smiled. 'Where did you crash it?'

'Not far from where we took it. Just down the road here.'

'How much had you drank?'

'A lot.'

'How much is that?' she insisted.

'Put it this way you know that bottle of Jim Beam.'

'Yeah.'

'It's gone.'

'I'm not surprised you crashed,' she tutted and shook her head disapprovingly. 'You could go to prison if you get caught.'

'I can't do the time,' replied Jay looking worried at the thought. 'I'd hate being closed in, and you know I've got a nice arse... I'll end up getting bummed.'

Trac raised a natural smile to that comment but quickly disguised it by bringing her cup to her mouth.

'Besides,' he continued. 'They've got the wrong kind of bars in those places.'

'Don't get smart,' she replied strongly.

He gulped at his tea. 'I'm not going to get caught for this. I can't,' he said firmly. 'I'm on a roll, everything's going my way.'

'Could be the thing to stop you in your tracks.'

'Don't say that,' he whined.

'If you can't do the time, don't do the crime,' she smiled.

He gave her a confused look.

'And how is Adrian taking all this?'

'I don't think it's sunk in yet.'

'You shouldn't drink bottles of whiskey should you. And you shouldn't even be driving now, alcohol will be still in your system.'

He folded his arms, sighed, rubbed at his left eye and then poised his hand to his mouth for a moment or two, as he pondered on the fact that he had crossed the line of what was acceptable behaviour. 'I'm not building up a particularly flattering portrait of myself am I?'

'And who's fault is that? I'm seriously staring to get worried about you two when you get together.'

'Shit, Adrian,' he sat up. 'I'm sorry babe,' he smiled sweetly. 'I'm going to have to go.'

She took the empty tea mug from his lap. 'Okay.'

He pulled a face, his bottom lip curled down and he fluttered his eyes at her. 'Still love me?' he asked moving in for a kiss.

She looked at him doubtfully. 'You stink of booze and you're still drunk,' she said under her breath. 'Go home and sleep it off.'

'Does that mean you don't love me?' he asked again, eyes now hurting from the strain of being awake.

This time she allowed herself to smile. 'You big kid,' she responded. 'Go on I'll see you later.'

'I love you,' he said and gave her a soft kiss on the lips.

'Yeah. And I love you too damn much.'

Monday, May 22

'Look,' said Adrian, 'I can't find my train pass anywhere!'

'Fucking hell,' said Dave with a concerned expression about his face.

'Stop panicking, just cos you've lost it doesn't mean you dropped it in the car,' said Jay shaking his head.

'Where else could it be then. I haven't seen it since then.'

'It'll turn up, just... just calm down.'

'You two had better start getting a story worked out,' alerted Dave.

'Yeah Jay, Dave's right, we've got to think of something... think...' he muttered in between pacing back and forth.

'Just relax a minute. We'll sort it out.'

'How?... I mean we could tell the truth and explain that we're sorry.' Jay grabbed at his arm to stop him from pacing, 'are you fucking mad or what? We can't do that, that's just not an option. To be fair I don't know what the problem is, I know what we did was wrong but it's just a car, a lump of metal, no-one is dead.'

'Jay you can't measure everything against that.'

'Why not?'

Both Adrian and Dave gave him a lost look that made him ease back onto his desk. A serious expression spread across his face before his eyes, 'okay, okay, if it makes you boys happy, just... just give me ten minutes alright.'

Jay, who had shown no sign of panic whatsoever for the past thirty minutes, narrowed his eyes and bowed his head as he sank into his chair, biting on his right thumb looking confused. He remained in this mode for approximately four to five minutes as he attempted to justify his reckless actions, he started to tap the top of his art box until a glimmer of a plan took shape.

'Right,' he said abruptly, ready to outline his proposal. 'This is what's going to happen...'

Adrian's eyebrows raised and his forehead crumpled, as if he was looking hopeful and in need of some kind of resolution to the crisis in hand.

'Okay, you were pissed right?'

'Very.'

'Exactly... Now you got in a real bad way okay, I mean you collapsed right?'

'Right,' Adrian agreed.

'He was being sick,' suggested Dave.

'No... No, he was really out cold. I couldn't get a sound or any movement from him. I mean he weren't breathing properly Dave.'

Jay paused again, it was almost as if they could see his brain ticking away as they studied his face.

'So I had to do something right?'

Adrian and Dave nodded as if his positivity had won them over, already captivated by his infusing plan.

'I decided it was too risky to leave you in the middle of nowhere to get help, so I knocked on the farm but there was no answer. At this point I'm panicking right, and I just happen to try the car door and it opened. I figured I could drive you to my dad's, call an ambulance and then take the car straight back no problems. I mean it's wrong to take the car but I'm stuck between a rock and a hard place and your safety was my main concern, so what else was I supposed to do?'

'What about crashing it?'

'Well you sort of lurched across at me as I came to the corner and I lost control of the vehicle. Afterwards I got you out the car, you seemed more with it by the minute so we got out of there.'

'Jay, you're still going to get done for it.'

'Yeah but at least this way you were unconscious and in the clear. I can hold my hands up say sorry, yes I took the car but I thought you were in real trouble.'

'I don't know,' said Adrian rubbing at his chin.

'What about you Dave?'

'I think it's pretty good.'

'Look, I know I'll still get into trouble but at least if it goes down this way they may go easier on me.'

'Do you think they'll believe you?'

'Hey, it's got to work better than the truth.'

'Okay,' nodded Adrian and patted him on the shoulder.

'Just remember, when it went pear shaped you were out of it.'

'Yeah I got it.'

'Now, forget about it.'

Jay turned back to his desk and went over it a few more times in his head. By the third time he could swear blind that he was telling the truth without an ounce of doubt in his mind, a formidable skill he had learnt growing up.

Adrian found his train pass later that evening in his jeans that had been through the wash and informed Jay as soon as possible.

'We're okay,' he said gleefully down the phone.

'I guess so, but just in case we're not, stick to the plan.'

6. As only the young can be

Jay contemplated the benefits of getting his mouth round the edge of a pint glass against the increasing hysteria that was beginning to shroud the final project and plans for the exhibition of everyone's better works. His head said 'no' but his mouth was wanting.

'Oi!' came a roar and he jumped from his thoughts. It was Dave, Jay turned to see him coming down the stairs.

'What are you doing?' he asked.

'Dave, why do you always think I'm up to something.'

Dave frowned, shrugged and sipped at his can of Tango. 'Maybe because you usually are.'

Mr Jackson wanted to see him along with his work. He knew he had pushed his luck a little too far; work handed in late, absences and an overall poor attitude were being pulled into question. Mr Jackson then appeared from his office two thirds of the way down the corridor.

'Five minutes,' he said glaring at him.

'What's going on Jay?' questioned Dave.

'Okay, okay, me and Adrian have got to show him our portfolios that's all.'

'Oh,' nodded Dave, 'big trouble... going to get thrown off the course.'

'I'm not going to get thrown out,' he grinned. 'Dave you need to be a bit more positive.'

The tall thin shape appeared again in the frame of the doorway and beckoned him in without a word. Leaning back in his chair, Mr Jackson sat biting at the end of a pencil. Jay figured he was simply doing nothing but a flawed attempt at making him panic, giving him the opportunity to collect his thoughts. He tried not to smirk, or be too cheeky, just hold on to the positivity but not be too cock sure either. He began to chat his way through his work and Mr Jackson allowed his performance without a single comment. When he finally reached the end of his speech, summing everything up, the wiry figure leaned upon him and in a casual voice said, 'well it's quite a reputation you've got yourself, isn't it?'

'I don't understand,' Jay replied innocently.

'You and Adrian that is.'

'What makes you think that?'

'Well,' he shuffled in his chair clearly agitated by confrontation. 'I've had several reports from your tutors and looking at your absences I am inclined to believe what they say.'

Jay didn't reply, he waited for him to continue but he didn't.

'I... er don't know what to say,' he smiled. 'I mean I am here most of the time, sometimes I arrive a little late, usually because of the train, and they don't mark me here.'

Spindly fingers began to turn the plastic sleeves of his portfolio in a slow mechanical manner, occasionally checking some paperwork, concluding that he wasn't behind at all. He shook his head slightly and gave an almost defeated smile before clearing his throat.

'You're pushing your luck,' he said strongly.

'No,' Jay bluffed. 'It's not right me being sat here like this.'

Running a finger around the collar of his shirt and adjusting his tie slightly, Mr Jackson glared at him murderously. Jay leant forward from his chair, 'I do quite a lot of work at home,' he said in a lighter tone and frowned innocently, 'everything is there.'

'Umm,' pondered Mr Jackson whilst rubbing at his small narrow chin. 'I've also been hearing about your outside activities.'

Jay didn't want to go down this route of enquiry so simply said nothing, raised an eyebrow and tapped his thumb on the desk to emphasise the silence.

Now twirling the pencil in his hand, Mr Jackson scowled as though he was trying to figure this young man out.

'I am not at all happy with what I hear.'

'Well, if what you hear were true, as you've said, these are outside activities and not the college's concern.'

'The college has to uphold a moral standing in the community and that is my concern.'

'I don't understand, you're like giving me a hard time over hearsay.'

Mr Jackson folded his arms and leant back in his chair as his eyes narrowed. 'Okay,' he replied resignedly. 'You step out of line again and I'll have no alternative but ask you to leave the course.'

Jay stood up shaking his head in pretend disbelief, 'but the course is about to finish?'

'Exactly, you'll be on probation so keep your head down and work. You have talent don't waste it by being drunk.'

He zipped up his portfolio and shut the door behind him quietly. Adrian came jogging up the corridor with his folder, 'how did it go?' he panted.

'Where have you been? He's waiting to see you.'

'Just tell us quick. What did he say?'

He put a hand on Adrian's shoulder, 'we're in deep shit mate,' and walked off as a voice bellowed from behind the office door.

Half an hour later Jay followed behind Adrian into the classroom, trying to hold his fake sullen face, one glance into Adrian's eyes and he would surely crack up and the charade would be over.

Dave and Andy came hurtling towards them from the far side of the room with bewildered expressions, as they took in the pair's sunken body language and bowed heads.

'So what happened?' babbled Dave.

Adrian made no response and remained blank faced as he began to pick up his things off his desk and load them into his art box.

'Ahh no, you're joking,' cried Dave putting both hands to his forehead.

'We're fucked,' said Jay giving his best acting grunt.

'Fuck!' gasped Andy.

'Yeah,' nodded Adrian and followed that with a mumbled, 'fuck.'

Jay, struggling to hold his sullen expression, decided he was better suited to portraying anger, booting the nearest chair and swearing as he did so.

'I can't believe it,' said Dave looking really lost for words.

Jay had got into the role of being hard done by but Adrian couldn't contain the pretence anymore and slowly split into a grin.

'Arrrh you bastards,' roared Dave holding his forehead again, this time thankful that he had been wound up.

'So you're both okay?' Andy asked.

'Yeah,' replied Adrian. 'But it is more or less a final warning though.'

'Serious stuff,' added Jay.

Adrian turned to him, 'I guess we'll just have to tow the line and keep our heads down.'

'What?' he replied with disbelief. 'You're joking aren't you?'

'We can't afford to cause any more grief.'

'True, but you've got to be yourself... free to do what you want to do. I mean what is this probation bollocks anyway?'

'I just don't want to get kicked off.'

'He ain't going to kick anybody out.'

'Jay, we've only got about a month left,' Adrian whined.

'I know, indulge me...' he said as he squeezed Adrian's shoulder. 'It'll look bad on the college and the course records for a start. It's just not going to happen... carry on as normal.'

'That's just it, your kind of normal isn't normal.'

'You worry too much,' said Jay coldly.

'He'll chuck us out!'

His face looked a strained vision of thought and confusion until he gave up and said, 'oh, who gives a fuck... I'm not about to stop enjoying myself. If he's out to get us, he will one way or another. So we might as well have a good time while we can. I say fuck it, it's way too close to the exhibition.'

'You're crazy, he's serious this time.'

'Look, I'm not going to worry about him breathing down my neck and I am not going to waste my last days of college when we should be having more fun than ever.'

Adrian rubbed at his chin, 'I don't know Jay.'

'Come on... trust me, I know what I'm doing,' and he smiled widely, eyes dilating as he placed a comforting arm around his shoulder. 'Now let's go and get a beer.'

Jay had admitted to having shooting pains in his chest and arms after the house party, agreeing that it was quite possibly drink related, and in addition to that there was the night of the walk that had been forgiven but not forgotten. This now made it easier for Trac to relay her concerns about his alcoholic binges.

Defensively he responded. 'I don't get like that very often.'

'Maybe not, but you always have a few too many, and once you're safe I still worry.'

'You shouldn't worry,' he replied.

'You say that but I do. I care about you.'

Jay pressed his lips tightly together, it wasn't easy to respond to that and she pounced on his delay.

'I can't stand to watch what you're doing to yourself,' she continued forcefully. 'I just hate seeing you in pain, you hurting yourself hurts me too.'

Jay ran both hands into the sides of his hair and replied, 'don't blow this up into something.'

'Okay, maybe I'm blowing everything out of proportion but it scares me to think of what could happen. Half your symptoms now could be connected with alcohol.'

He puffed his cheeks slightly and his eyes rolled. He felt himself getting hot and struggled to reply again.

'Please see my point,' she persisted. 'I love you and by loving you I share your feelings... listen to me, I share your feelings and emotions one of which happens to be pain.'

'I know... I just.... I don't know.'

'If you won't cut down for yourself then please do it for me.'

He had been fearing this suggestion. Pondering for a moment he replied, 'maybe you could quit smoking?' Which took her a little by surprise, and before she could throw it back in his face he offered, 'we could do it together... as a team.'

It was Trac's turn to pause and he thought it was the leverage he needed to end the conversation but she looked him dead in the eyes in only a few seconds. 'Okay,' she said firmly.

It wasn't the answer he was expecting and began to feel lost in the thread of conversation. Before he had a chance to sink into a mood or be distant. Trac squeezed his arm and lightened the tone by saying, 'if you give up drinking you'd probably find out what you're really like.'

He couldn't help but think there was a certain amount of truth to that and gave her a half smile. He liked being drunk and if he wasn't? Well he was hungover and if he wasn't either of those he was thinking about getting drunk. To be honest with himself, he craved that more than sex, which for a guy was far from normal, wasn't it?

The Cult didn't seem to have the same positive effect on his mum as it did for him and three songs into 'Sonic Temple' was too much for her to take.

'Turn that bloody music down,' came a yell.

He appeared from his room rubbing his hair, looking annoyed and poised to be stubborn.

'What are you doing with this?' she howled picking up a can of mousse. 'You're supposed to put this on after you've washed your hair, it's a conditioner.'

'Who says?' he retaliated.

'The label.'

'Where?'

'There,' she pointed.

'Anyway I shampooed my hair yesterday.'

The argument would have continued but he wasn't in the mood. He put on his black shirt and left irritated. On searching his pockets he pulled out a crumpled up five pound note. Glancing at the clock on the landing he was in good time to meet Trac at her house, she was usually home from school about now. Stuffing the five pound note back into his pocket he decided to buy some flowers.

'What the!' He stopped The Beast suddenly. 'Oh shit,' he mumbled rubbing his brow. Stepping out he could see a black crow in the middle of the road. He studied it for a moment or two noticing no obvious signs of injury so he picked it up.

'Ahh, you idiot,' he said to the lame crow. 'Just fly right out into my window screen. I bet you've bust your wing,' he whispered softly.

He took the crow carefully in his hands and wrapped it in a rag and placed it in the open glove compartment of The Beast, talking to it as he set off once again.

'You'll be alright mate,' he said pulling off.

'So what you been up to then apart from the odd bit of flying and eating worms?'

He came to another abrupt halt outside a florists in the village.

'Now you wait here. I'll be back in a minute.'

He smiled sweetly at the lady behind the florist counter and began glancing about the shop, not sure what to get.

'Can I help you sir?' she asked politely.

'Er, yeah I'm looking for a bunch of flowers... about a fivers worth,' he said pulling out a note.

The lady motioned him to the far corner of the shop. 'There you go,' she smiled, 'Carnations.'

'Yeah I like those.' He took in their scent, pondered for a second or two as he glanced around at the other flowers.

'Yep I'll have those,' he said positively.

'Done something wrong have we?'

'Eh?' he quizzed. 'Oh I see, no... no I'm buying them for my girlfriend,' he smiled shyly. 'No reason, just thought I'd give her a bit of a surprise.'

He watched the forty-ish mum looking lady work her nimble fingers between the stalks of the flowers and pink wrapping paper and wondered what her life was like or had been like so far. Had she been pretty like Trac when she was young? He studied the wrinkles unsuccessfully hidden by make up and wondered if she had aged as nature had intended, or was there hard times that had prematurely aged her?

'There you go,' smiled the lady

'Thanks,' he replied snapping from his thoughts, 'thanks a lot,' and gave her a smile back.

As he jumped back into The Beast the crow still glared at him and wasn't moving much at all. He drove carefully all the way to Leire keeping his eye on the crow. As he pulled up outside her house he sat nursing the crow as Trac appeared, school bag over her shoulder, a smile split her face when she saw The Beast.

'Hiya,' she peeped.

'Hi, got you some flowers,' he said as he passed them through the window.

'Arrh, what's happened.'

The crow's head collapsed slowly.

'It's snuffed it now. Must have had internal injuries,' he said inspecting his wings.

'What did you do?'

'Nothing it just flew into me. I didn't know what to do... I didn't want a cat to have it.'

He stepped out of The Beast and began to walk to a hedgerow.

'I'll just pop him over there. I'll be back in a minute.'

'Okay,' she smiled and sniffed at the flowers as she waltzed up the driveway.

He placed the crow gently inside the hedge and jogged up behind her.

'That's a shame that,' he said.

'Poor thing,' replied Trac.

He stood at the kitchen sink, washed his hands and then groomed his hair with wax.

'I was going to say your hair looks funny.'

'Yeah I didn't have time to do it, Mum was giving us loads of grief.'

He ran the wax through his hair and produced his usual style.

'I wouldn't mind some of that wax.'

'Nah,' he said shaking his head a little. 'Your hair looks great as it is. I only use this stuff cos my hair's so thin.'

She put the flowers in water and thanked him again with a kiss.

'What have you been up to then?'

'Not a lot.'

'I've got some freelance work.'

'Oh yeah?'

'Yeah, just some cartoons for a guy who's a clown.'

'How did you get that.'

'I just put a card in the post office. I'm going round to see him on Saturday.'

'That's good,' she smiled. 'Beats stacking shelves.'

'Yeah, I did a live project at college for the clowns Bozo and Zizi, so I've had a bit of a play this morning. I think I can reuse most of it.'

'Isn't that cheating?'

'No,' he shook his head firmly. 'It's using this,' and he tapped his head.

'I suppose.'

'The only thing is the guy is thinking of calling himself Terry Turnip which is a bit crap.'

'Tommy Turnip would be better.'

'I like that... that's good, I'll use that,' and gave her a pleasing smile.

'Does this mean you're going to take me out?'

'Sure, tomorrow?'

'Cool,' she said and clapped her hands in delight. 'Cheese toastie?'

'Cheers,' he smiled sliding into one of the dining room chairs. 'I'm starving.'

He tapped his fingers on the table surface as he watched her move about the kitchen preparing food, a role in which he had yet to witness and although it was one of life's everyday routines he couldn't help but appreciate the moment.

'Nick's thinking of taking his motorbike test,' he said.

'I'd love a bike,' she replied. 'Only Mum wouldn't let me.'

'You been on one before?'

'Oh yeah, once I had a go on the park and fell off.' She licked some butter off her fingers and continued. 'The police were there I got really told off, Dad went crazy.'

'Naughty girl.'

Trac ate the majority of the sandwiches and they lay side by side on her bed. Ten minutes or more of heavy petting and squeezes of her bum, she smiled and asked him if he had any sexual fantasies? It raised a smirk, he liked her in this mood, curious and open to being taught or amused.

'Why do you want to know?' he whispered and stretched out his arms and gave out a slight yawn.

'I am your girlfriend,' she said.

'And?'

'And we were just talking about them at school.'

'In the magazine is it?'

'Yeah, but I'm interested,' she gave a shrug, 'that's all.'

'Well,' he said tapping the CD case in his hands. 'First I'd like a huge king size four poster bed like the one we slept in at the house party. With you in one arm and Shelley in the other and a bottle of chilled vodka close by.'

He expected her to pull a sullen expression at the mention of Shelley, but instead she didn't, her mood remained upbeat and unfazed, she just said 'carry on.'

'Well one of you will have woolly tights on, yeah Shelley will cos I want to see your feet.'

'What about stockings?'

'Yeah nice idea, like it,' he nodded. 'Definitely, you could be in them to start with.'

'Not satisfied with just me then?'

'Oh we are talking fantasy here,' he defended. 'What about you?'

'No. I've never really thought about it.'

'Umm,' he frowned at her.

'Anyway I'm learning all kinds of stuff like that from you, maybe later I'll have some kind of fantasy.'

'Maybe I could dress up as a fireman.'

She shook her head at him. 'It's a good job Shelley is the other side of the world. I don't want to share you with anybody. You're mine, all mine,' she whispered.

'Hey,' he smiled expansively, 'you're my girl.'

She looked at him doubtfully and then gave a shrug that gestured 'oh well I don't care anyway.'

He smiled faintly. 'Look you just need to show me you trust me,' he said as he lifted from the bed.

She didn't flinch when he outlined his proposal; to turn her back to him and allow herself to fall. She just stared at him, unblinking, for several seconds then moved her hands from her hips, tilted her head slightly and said, 'okay.'

He smirked and motioned her towards him, she moved slightly and then hesitated for a moment.

'You can say no.'

She moved towards him again and replied, 'does it look like I'm saying no dummy?'

His face creased into an easy smile. 'Okay,' he said and steered her slowly round so that she faced away from him.

He leant forward, a hand moved her hair from her ear and he whispered, 'no peeking.'

'You are going to catch me?'

'Ready whenever you are.'

A few moments of silence, a couple of deeper breaths than normal and she let herself go and landed in his arms. Eyes closed, she hugged at him tightly as if in relief and it made him chuckle. As if he had been rewarded, he cupped her face in his hands and kissed her firmly, 'I love you.'

Friday, May 26

Jay was parked out in front of the school, waiting with The Cult playing on the stereo. Hot and humid, he was leaning on the driver's side of The Beast sucking at an ice lolly, trying to ease off the heat. He'd had a fairly constructive day talking about jobs and making a better effort to design a CV, so he was feeling pleased with himself for putting in the effort. The minute she saw him she jogged over.

'Let's have a lick,' she smiled.

He scrunched his face up as if to say 'no way.'

'Well, you're here to give me a lift at least?'

Trac peered out the window at the passing hedgerows, pleased that he'd given up the last of his lolly.

'I like this one,' she said and turned the volume up a few notches. 'Wake up time for freedom'.'

Jay nodded, that's good he thought. However the same could not be said for her choice in TV programme, as she demanded he made the tea while she layed on the sofa in front of the TV.

'Old Dallas repeats are on in a minute,' she chirped.

His face contorted only slightly as he felt a sarcastic mood or bout of stubbornness begin to take hold of him.

'You don't watch that do you?' he exclaimed.

'Yeah!'

'It's crap,' he roared.

'No, it's not.'

He mimicked her voice, 'no, it's not,' and it didn't go down well.

'Oh bog off,' she moaned.

He made a face at her. 'I'm not sitting here watching that shit,' he said incredulously and he turned the TV off.

'You don't have to,' and she turned it back on.

'It's awful,' he smirked trying not to get cheesed off. 'I hated it when it came out, it's even worse now.'

'No it's not,' she said shaking her head and sticking her tongue out at him.

'Say Dallas is shit,' he hissed.

'No.'

'Go on say it!'

'No.'

'If you don't say it I'm going,' he said flatly.

'Go on then.'

'I mean it,' he said.

'I'm not stopping you,' she gave a relaxed shrug.

'Right,' he grunted jumping up and slapping his thighs.

Pulling on his boots he began to mumble, 'okay fine. Just let me go then I'm not bothered.'

He stormed out the front door and leapt into The Beast. He sat revving the engine as loud as possible before slamming it into reverse. He sped off the drive with a screech. She stood watching from her lounge window, cupping her mug of tea. He peeled away down the street, braking he slammed it back into reverse and sped backwards. He halted again, looked up out the passenger side window, and gave her the V sign and then drove off again immediately cursing himself as he went. He knew it was stupid, but the fact was it had gone beyond the programme and simply became a battle of wills, both too stubborn for their own good. Trac was so damn head strong sometimes he thought, as he pulled up next to the village phone box.

'Hello,' came her soft voice.

'It's me,' he said quietly into the receiver.

'I know it's you.'

'Do you want me to come back?'

'Of course I do silly.'

'You'll have to fetch me.'

She tutted. 'Where are you?'

'Round the corner.'

She exhaled loud enough for him to hear, 'hold on then.'

He got into The Beast regretting his pointless outburst. I suppose Dallas is not that bad he thought reaching over and unlocking the door as her presence was nearing.

'I'm sorry,' he said. 'I've been stupid haven't I?' and leant over to give her a kiss.

She agreed with him and went to spark up a cigarette.

'Cutting down?'

'I've only had... okay,' she nodded slowly and put it back.

'Fancy a drive?'

'Yeah okay.'

He saw the evening out in The Bell with Rob, Nick and other stragglers. Slumped in chairs on the wrong side of midnight, he could pass the blame off on peer pressure as he drank yet another glass of booze too many, talking about nothing in particular and jeering jointly at anything that could increase the male bonding process.

Saturday, May 27

Terry Turnip sat in a faded blue armchair, worn at the arm rests. Leaning in at his TV with the remote control he was cackling and hooting at his own performance on amateur video. Jay looked at the guy's black mopped hair, thick black rimmed glasses, stubble, baggy white T-shirt with tracky bottoms and worse still white socks in sandals. He never felt less creative or inspired in his life.

'Watch this bit... it's brilliant,' he boasted excitedly.

Jay nodded, smiled feebly and leaned further in to watch this clown in action.

'What about Tommy?'

'Huh?' he muttered not taking his eyes from the screen.

'You know, I think as you've just started out and your name isn't Terry you could change it to maybe Tommy?'

'Tommy?'

'Yeah it's... well more friendly.'

'More friendly?'

'Yeah, don't you think?'

'Eh up love,' he called out and his wife appeared at the kitchen doorway. 'What do you think of Tommy instead of Terry?'

His wife nodded lightly, 'Tommy... Tommy,' she said while tapping at her mouth as she did so. 'What about Tom?'

A loud snap of fingers and he pointed the remote at her and cried, 'Tom!' and proceeded to point the remote at Jay. 'Write it down.... write it down,' he repeated excitedly. 'Cheers love... put the tea on.'

'Tom's good,' nodded Jay. 'We could use Tom-Foolery as a slogan.'

'Brilliant!' he replied gleefully.

'Great.'

Jay noted down his new name without any hint of being obnoxious, although the urge was brimming within. He wrote down Tom Turnip's list of skills; magic, street organ, face painting, stilt walking, comedy juggling, mix and mingle and balloon modelling. He recommended a card, an A5 flyer and perhaps an A4 cartoon of his face that the kids could colour in.

'Maybe just tap your contact details along the bottom of it,' he said shutting his sketch pad hoping to make a move.

'Love it,' he jeered. 'Here take this,' he beamed passing him the tape.

'I don't-'

'Take it.... take it.'

'Really... I-'

'Just don't tape over it or I'll set the wife on you.'

'Right,' replied Jay. 'Okay.'

'Leave it with you,' beamed Tom.

Sunday, May 28

Events began with bacon sandwiches. The smell was the first thing that hit him in the morning. He sat straight up in bed, his nose quivering.

'Someone's cooking bacon,' he uttered to himself.

His sister? He pulled on a pair of jeans and a T-shirt and went downstairs.

'You're not having any. Cook your own,' she moaned instantly.

He looked at the two remaining raw rashers on the side, even contemplated eating them there and then. Instead he waited and cooked them until crisp and folded over the slightly stale end crust of bread. It cured his hunger pain successfully.

'Jay, Tracey's on the phone.'

He wiped tomato sauce from the edge of his mouth and picked up the receiver. 'Hello'.

'I take it you're up then.'

'Yeah,' he replied positively.

'Good night?'

'Yeah it was alright. We had a lock in at the New Inn then went across to Rob's flat.'

'Nothing exciting happened then?'

'No, I didn't get silly.'

'Mmm, I suppose you're worse with Adrian.'

He didn't respond to that so she asked him if he had a hangover.

'Nope feel great. I didn't drink much at all,' he replied.

'Good.'

'Anyway what about you? Did you and Maria get legless.'

'No, not really. I was well behaved too.'

'Glad to hear it, we don't want you getting a reputation.'

She chuckled to that, 'so is it okay if I come over now?'

'Yeah I'll come and fetch you, give me twenty minutes.'

'It's okay, my sister's going out your way and said she'll drop me off.'

'Cool,' he replied with a delighted grin. 'I'll see you in a bit then.'

'Good o,' she chirped.

He was dancing around his room singing and looking completely daft in the process. Waggling his bum in Trac's direction normally set her off laughing but she was not looking his way and continued to read her book thoughtfully. When ideas began to spark in his head he felt he was not wasting his time acting the fool. He told her that ideas floated around in the air and it was just a case of waiting until one struck him.

'Come and dance with me then,' he jeered. 'I'm sure I'll design the best farming leaflet ever.'

'No,' she responded in a stroppy tone.

'Come on, it's good to be stupid once and a while.'

She gave it her best shot but she simply was not in the mood.

'I thought we agreed to study for at least an hour,' she complained as she slumped back down onto his bed.

'I am working,' he replied.

'Jay this is not the way to work, I've got to read this.'

He took the book from her. '*Romeo and Juliet*. I know the story but I can't help you, I did *The Winter's Tale*.' He rubbed at his chin, took a firm standing position and in a deep voice said, '*the self same sun that shines upon his court...*' he smirked and wafted a hand at her, 'and lots of other stuff I can't remember.'

She gave him a funny look, waiting for him to explain.

'It's the only bit I remember,' he said, 'because it means, or I think it means, that everybody is equal and I think that's kind of cool don't you?'

Her expression still hadn't changed and he found himself backing down from his routine, that Sundays equalled music, movies, tea and smooching.

'Yeah okay, you're right,' he said passing the book back to her. 'Some quiet study time, then whatever,' and gave her a slight shrug.

An hour later he was extended out across the carpet, as the blandness of the paper surrounding him seemed to drain him of life. Once his head hit the floor and soft moans of total boredom began to emanate from his vocal cords, Trac looked down from his bed and nudged him gently with her foot.

'You okay?'

'Don't know,' he groaned back at her feebly.

'I'm nearly done and then I'm all yours.'

'All mine?' he frowned.

'Within reason... yes,' she nodded and returned to the book with ease. While he lay there his thoughts were rejecting ideas and being replaced by a series of sexual images, as if she was a seraph being sent to tease him, taking him in, taking him over.

He crawled along the floor towards her, onto the bed from her calves to her shoulders and she turned onto her back to face him. She kissed his gleeful expression and then slipped away from under him.

'Just before you get carried away,' she said picking her bag up and beginning to return her things to it. 'I need a cup of tea.'

He squinted at her, not sure what to say or do to that, and found himself biting on his lip.

'It will help me unwind,' she continued.

'Sure,' he replied faintly and gave a slight nod of his head cunningly.

Trac leant on the kitchen, table both hands laced around her mug of tea. She looked confused as she watched him float about the room, eyes still narrow like he was up to something but she didn't know what. Once he began to hum a tune to himself from behind a cupboard door she placed her cup onto the table and approached him.

'What are you up to?'

She heard a faint chuckle and his head appeared with a glint of mischief in his eyes.

She went to step back from him but he was too quick and blocked her exit.

'What have you got?'

'Now... this is very tasty,' he smirked holding up a small plastic squeezable bottle of caramel ice cream toping.

Still trapped she began to shake her head at him as the realisation of his intentions unfolded.

'No,' she said arching away from him. 'Don't you dare.'

He shrugged at her again, as if he debunked the idea that he had in covering her with it. He grinned further as he began to squeeze the bottle and before her hands could raise upwards to defend herself, the caramel had made its way out onto her chin, neck and top half of her chest where her top gaped open.

She squealed and flapped her hands at him. 'Look, it's on my top.'

He chuckled, 'stick your tongue out.'

'Look,' she said pulling at her top to show him.

He ignored her and he repeated softly, 'stick your tongue out.'

By his third faint request she found herself obeying his command. As he squeezed the bottle again and released a mound of thick sticky liquid onto her tongue, his eyes looked wild.

He took her by the hand sharply, 'let's go back upstairs' he whispered and by his eyes she knew what he had in mind.

'Your sister's in.'

'Is she?'

'Yeah,' Trac nodded.

'I'll lock my door.'

'You're terrible.'

'I know.'

Monday, May 29 (Spring Bank Holiday)

Unable to believe his luck he had thrashed Trac at the game Battle Ships four times on the trot and was revelling in his glory.

'You cheat,' she moaned.

'I don't cheat,' he harked.

'I bet,' she said giving him a disconcerting frown.

'Careful,' he grinned, 'your face might stay like that.'

'Ha, ha,' she said and stuck her tongue out at him.

'I can't wait till I have kids,' he smiled, 'so I can grow up all over again.'

'Yeah I think you'll make a good dad one day.'

'Maybe,' he said toying with one of the ships.

'Shall we get something to eat?' she asked sighing a little.

'Yeah, okay. I can see you can't face losing again.'

She tilted her head and made a groan hoping he would take it as a sign not to carry on teasing her over losing. 'I'll get some money off Mum,' she sighed, 'and we can get a Pot Noodle each.'

Just as he was a Marmite on toast fiend, she was a Pot Noodle addict. He nodded and rose to his feet as she wiggled her feet into her shoes. When she reached the drive she turned to make sure he was following her. She heard the front door being pulled shut and he trotted into view clutching his keys.

He lurked behind the shelf of vodka and he reached up to toy with a bottle.

'Jay?' Trac asked pointlessly. 'What are you buying?'

He avoided her eyes, putting the bottle back his gaze dropped quickly.

'Nothing,' he said, 'just looking at the different brands that's all.'

He dug his hands into his pockets and trundled off up the aisle.

'Chicken and mushroom flavour?'

'Yeah alright, whatever,' he mumbled.

He watched her closely in the kitchen. He noted that she was very much like her mother. He felt very proud of her for a moment and gave her a warming hug as she peeled the foil lids from the Golden Wonder Pot Noodles.

'What do you want?' she mumbled.

'Nothing,' he smiled. 'I just want to give my little baby a hug.'

The evening was spent in each others arms, listening to music, content and warm, with only soft mumbled conversation. By midnight they both began to drift to sleep, when her father's voice bellowed outside her door.

'Come on now Tracey!'

His eyes opened. Blinking he said in a low voice, 'my hint to go home.'

He stretched out his arms for a few seconds then pulled himself upright, 'How come you said your last boyfriend stayed till all hours.'

'He did. Dad's just being a pain.'

Jay rolled over in bed and pushed out his lower lip, 'they just don't like me' he said dully.

'Yes they do,' she said quickly and reached out to squeeze his shoulder apologetically.

He grumbled lightly as he eased himself off the bed and laced up his boots.

'I guess I'll see you tomorrow.'

Her reply was a squeeze of his hand.

He gave her a long firm kiss to the lips and made his way down the drive to The Beast. Just as his mind was on booze, Trac's he felt sure was on a cigarette.

Adrian had given him a disbelieving glance when he told him about his new found abstinence.

'You won't last.'

'You're right, what am I going to do... stay in?'

'Exactly,' smiled Adrian opening out his arms as if to say 'there you go.'

'I'd be boring sober wouldn't I?'

'Yeah, definitely.'

'Okay, so I just cut down.'

Adrian gave him a look of disappointment. Shaking his head he said, 'don't do this to yourself.'

'Maybe,' Jay continued, 'I could cut down on spirits... during the week... a little?'

Adrian still had the same blank expression that made him laugh. He finally broke into a wide smile and shook his head three or four times. 'It's not going to happen is it?'

'Nope!'

Slowly he had to confess that he loved booze too much, and quitting wasn't an option he was going to achieve anytime soon. Sure discretion could be his shield, but he didn't want to be caught up in all the thinking, plotting and covering up, only to get caught out. Besides that kind of thing would make Trac crazy. He figured he just needed to be honest with her as he had with himself.

The moment she tasted alcohol on his lips almost came as a relief to him, even though he initially denied its presence in a jovial manner.

'Somebody's been drinking,' came softly from her mouth.

His thoughts replied, '...and somebody plans to drink some more,' but he chose to remain silent and looked away from her slightly.

'Jay, why?'

'It suits me too well,' he blurted.

'You can at least try.'

'I have been.'

'Jay, it's not even been a week.'

'I know but... you're still smoking.'

'I've cut down.'

His posture deflated slightly and he uttered, 'Trac, I'm no good at anything else. I'm the best at this.'

She mumbled something in reply under her breath, eyes fixed on her tea.

'I entertain my mates. I get them in a good mood.'

She huffed, 'Jay you just get them pissed.'

'I do, and they know I do. Don't ask me to give that up. I mean how else am I going to get rid of all my energy?'

'You could start by doing something more constructive.'

He yawned loudly. Put his hands onto his hips and stared at the wall in frustration shaking his head slightly.

'You're just a piss artist that's all.'

'No,' he said solidly, 'I'm *the piss artist!*'

How could he possibly give that title up? Truth was, he had worked hard for it.

'Where does that leave me in your priorities then? I guess I'm number three behind drink and The Beast.'

'I don't think you're that high up, you forgot my music,' he smirked to lighten the tone but her expression remained blank.

'Okay, you're number one, it's just that right now I need this as well.'

'Why?'

'I just need you to let me be me. Let me do what I want to do, right or wrong. I've got plenty of time ahead of me to be serious.'

Relieved at being honest, he knew it wasn't going to be too long before he was a public disgrace, securing his number one spot as the best party animal, hell-raising piss artist to be proud of, if only due to the fact he was never going to gain the number one slot doing anything else among his friends and peers. By now, his antics had made great gossip and speculation, notoriety was good. He was enjoyed by people he had never even met and it only served to fuel his commitment to it. He figured it was like the closest he would ever get to being famous.

Wednesday, May 31

He wasn't sure how well Trac was taking his quick retraction from not drinking, he thought maybe it was just the house party and the unfolding events he'd involved her in with the night of the walk? He remained aloof on all matters booze related, took time in which to make her feel more than priority number three and allowed that small sensible side of him to surface and shine for a while and it worked. She responded warmly rewarding him with a letter starting with his likening to a drug, *You make me feel so high I can't explain the feeling.* Flipping then to concern over her thoughts in him writing to Shelley, *It's up to you whether you choose to write to Shelley. I'm just worried that your feelings will come out in the letter and everything will brew up again. I don't want to share you with anyone. I suppose I'm doing another 'Blow everything out of proportion' act, as per usual but I can't help it, I can't stand the thought of losing you.* She made him smile further with, *Mum asked me how I got that creamy caramel stuff down myself! Personally I think I lied myself out of it quite well, looking very innocent and saying, 'I don't know.'* She rounded the letter off with *I hope that things can stay like this for a very long time, if forever.* He appreciated the effort she had gone to in creating a little red heart for every time she used the word love. His day had been a little slack in the way of fun and had almost started to get fed up about that but now he felt more than buoyant again.

Thursday, June 1

Jay was leaning against the clock tower, not too concerned over the £78.15 overdraft slip he twirled in his hand as Tom Turnip had paid up and his pockets were loaded with a whole bunch of crisp ten pound notes. He took a moment or two just to watch Trac perch on the edge of the bench in front of Tie Rack. He smiled to himself, he had been hankering after something real to do all morning, so easily did boredom set in when he was mooching about his bedroom. Trac glanced at her watch a second time as he approached her, he raised a smile again as he broke into a few faster and wider strides.

'Hi,' he said when he got within ear shot.

She looked round and up at him in one swift motion, her eyes looking lost for a moment until they rested firmly on him.

'Hi,' she replied softly.

'You okay?'

'Yeah just ignore me,' she muttered as she rose from the bench.

'How long for?'

She tilted her head and sighed at him, so he squeezed her bum and kissed her cheek.

'No school then?'

'No, well I could have gone but Claire and Michelle said they were going to stay at home and study, and I didn't fancy tagging onto anybody else's company for the day.'

'And what about you studying at home?'

'I'm getting fed up with it at the moment. It's all too much.'

'I know what you mean, it would be so much easier if they spaced exams out a bit more.'

'I wish.'

'So does this mean you've more or less finished now, apart from your last few exams.'

She nodded with a smile, looped her arm into his and they began to walk.

'I don't want to stop you from studying though,' he said.

'You're not, I'm just not in the mood to, so it would be a complete waste of time to force myself, I wouldn't take anything in. What about you? You're not missing anything important at college then?'

'No, not really. Everything is about my final exhibition and that's weeks away.'

She hugged closer, face snuggled into his neck. 'So does this mean I've got you for the rest of the day?'

'Err... well I was going to go up the New Inn with Nick and that 'cos there's a football meeting,' he muttered and noted the rising expression of disappointment about to flood her face. 'But I don't play anyway do I?'

'No.'

'I guess they can manage to down plenty of pints without me,' and with that said she hugged closer to him.

'So... what shall we do then?'

'Well I want to get a pack of C90 tapes,' and gave a shrug. 'You?'

She gave a shrug back. 'Don't know?'

'No CDs you want?'

She shook her head.

'Batdance?'

Her frown turned inward, as far as she was concerned, it was the worse thing Prince had ever done and he was currently far from being forgiven for it.

'No way,' she snapped.

'Okay,' he smirked, 'fair enough.'

She emitted a sigh and in a calm soft tone said, 'I do need to find my building society.'

'What do you mean find?'

'It's just a savings account Mum and Dad set up for me so I've never really used it. I think there's one towards the train station'.

'Okay, how about we find this bank of yours, take all the money out and run off to London?'

Her face scrunched up slightly and he chuckled further.

'Okay, plan B. We go and pick up my wages and have a pizza and pinball session?'

She smiled positively, 'yep I'm up for pizza and I'm definitely getting a little hooked on pinball.'

Jumping and bouncing up and down on his bed to some music, he was pretending to play the guitar when in walked Trac with two mugs of tea. He immediately fell to the bed and turned the music down.

'I was just, you know I was...' he paused and then left it at that.

She smiled. 'You wally,' she said.

He gave her a shrug that said 'yeah you're right,' and took his tea from her placing it down on the window sill.

'Are you going to drag yourself to college tomorrow then?'

'Probably not,' they said at the same time and it made him chuckle. 'Am I becoming that predictable?'

'Sometimes,' she smiled.

'You know I'm on top of my workload.'

'Yes but you still have to be there.'

'It's okay... really,' he sighed. 'I can do some stuff at home if it will make you happy.'

'Yes it will and I could get the bus from school to here and save you picking me up if you want?'

'Yeah alright,' and gave a slight nod. 'Do you know what?' he asked rubbing at his belly. 'I'm hungry.'

'No way.'

'Yeah,' he nodded. 'I think I'll have to do some bacon sarnies.'

'You're so healthy.'

'So you don't want one then?'

'No,' she smiled. 'I didn't say that.'

As the night sky began to darken, softer music was chosen. The light from the muted TV, used alongside his road work light, gave a cosy ambiance to his room. They moved from their fully clothed lying position on top of the duvet, to underneath semi-clothed. As he began to get excited by her hand that she swept along the length of his body he did the same back and she whispered, 'I can't.'

'Why?' he mumbled.

'Time of the month.'

He raised his eyebrows at her and said, 'okay.'

'That's probably why I was so moody this morning.'

He smiled, 'really I didn't notice.'

'I always feel really bad the first day.'

'You must think I'm always trying to attack you.'

'No,' she smiled. 'If I don't like something I'll tell you,' and she slipped her hand between his legs.

'I wish I wasn't on though,' she said followed with a yawn.

'It will happen.'

She nodded and rested her head onto his shoulder.

'We can always try something else,' he shrugged lightly.

'Like what?'

'You know,' he gave a nod, but her face looked even more puzzled.

He rubbed at his forehead for a moment trying to think of an easy way in which to describe what he had in mind.

She smirked, 'are you alright?'

'Yeah I err...' he reached down to the floor to where his jeans lay, nearly falling out of the bed trying to retrieve his lollipop he got with his receipt at Pizzaland.

Trac chuckled, 'what are you doing?'

He made himself comfortable in the bed again and held the round lolly in both hands which laced together on his chest, eyes closed enjoying the rhythm she was perfecting down below. She had to give him a nudge to bring him back to life.

'What's that for then?' she asked.

He opened his eyes, 'oh,' he said following with a grin as he unwrapped the clear plastic from the lolly. Eyes narrowing he placed it into his mouth and like the banana at the house party simulated fellatio until he saw recognition in her eyes.

'I haven't... I don't know,' she gave a slight shrug, 'how.'

'First time for everything,' he smiled and placed the lolly into her mouth, watching her tongue move round the lime green glazed sugar teasingly.

'Just do what you're doing now and you'll be fine.'

'Mmm, let me see,' she smiled. 'Practice makes perfect right.'

'When it comes to this, it most definitely does,' and he rolled his eyes.

'Okay,' she said, evidently happy that she didn't feel worried or apprehensive about whether it will go alright. 'I'll see what I can do.'

As he sunk further back into his bed he smiled wider as she disappeared under the duvet.

Friday, June 2

Trac brushed her hand through his hair, he was flat out on his bed in his clothes sleeping lightly. As he began to wake she smiled broadly, 'Is he a baby then?' she whispered placing a letter on his pillow.

He grunted and then rubbed at his eyes.

'This doesn't look like working at home to me.'

He lifted his head, yawned and gave her a lazy smile as he stretched each of his limbs out one at a time.

'Look at you slobbering all over your pillow.'

He yawned and pawed at the envelope, 'another letter?'

'I don't suppose I'll get one back anytime soon.'

He sat up, gave her a shrug and yawned further before raising his arms towards the ceiling.

'So what have you been up to?'

'Nothing really, I was asleep. Before that I had some music on.'

'No mention of a drink then.'

He rolled onto his back, 'no not yet, but then it's still early,' he chuckled. 'Anyway, I'm feeling particularly horny so I'm going to beat you into submission and ravish you.'

'Oh really!'

'No,' he chuckled. 'Cup of tea?'

She gave a tut, 'sure, but don't I get a kiss first.'

Putting on a posh voice he said, 'yes why not darling,' and lifted her hand and placed a soft kiss onto it.

'Thank you,' she said with a bemused look.

'Shall we go then?' he asked and he put out his arm and she looped her left arm in his.

Saturday, June 3

Jay sat slumped in the centre of Rob's flat. It was quite clear from his expressionless face and lifeless disposition, that he was functioning in drunk mode. His right hand rested on the neck of a vodka bottle, the only effort and concentration needed was to guide it to his mouth. While he swallowed, his eyes closed, he wasn't all that far from passing out. Nick sat glued to the TV set, Red Lambrusco in hand, slagging every channel off, 'what the fuck is this?' he jabbered. Rob lay haphazardly in his favourite armchair, squinting at the picture in front of him. 'I don't know,' he mumbled and let his head fall back.

Jay snapped his fingers weakly, 'it's... it's what's his name... Telly Savalis... Kojac isn't it.'

All three of them had drunk to such an extent that communication was becoming difficult. Jay caught his reflection in the mirror and watched himself for a full minute in puzzled worry. Rob began to fall asleep while Nick continued to glare at the TV as if he was amidst an argument with it.

'I think it's Columbo,' slurred Nick raising a finger to the blurring screen.

'What's that?' laughed Jay drunkenly.

'I said I think it's Columbo. Look he's got a long beige coat on.'

'Nah, Columbo's got hair and a funny eye.'

'He's got hair.'

'Has he?' he chuckled and took a swig of vodka before he crawled up to the screen. 'Oh yeah so he has,' he gurgled and laughed some more.

Once Rob began to snore, Jay and Nick both knew he was out for the night. Jay took an unfeasibly large gulp of vodka before stumbling to his feet. Shaking slightly he slurred, 'shall we go?'

Nick took his time, he steadied himself against the sofa as he eased to his feet and spluttered, 'yeah.'

They bundled their way out and rambled off. Nick found himself trailing along behind Jay trying to catch his barely audible mutterings.

'Hold up Jay... where we going?'

'Back to mine... watch some *Monty Python,*' he nodded enthusiastically, spilling vodka as he went.

So wound up in conversation and fast becoming physically drained by the exertion it needed to get home, the lip of a curb caught him out. As he flailed towards a lamppost in a desperate attempt to break his fall, the vodka didn't make it, it left his hand and smashed on the pavement.

'I don't believe it,' he winced.

He dropped to the ground, distraught as he felt about the cold ground picking up pieces of glass.

'That... that was nearly half a bottle.'

He continued to crawl about the floor, it was hopeless.

'Leave it Jay. It's... it's gone, babbled Nick. 'Forget it.'

He reluctantly got to his feet holding what was left of the bottle's label in his hands. 'It's going to take me six months to get over this.'

They trundled onwards and he took solace in silence until he reached his front door. For some time he fumbled with his key, becoming agitated at his lack of ability. Just as he jammed it into the slot, it opened and his mum was stood there in front of him with a blank expression.

'I don't believe it,' he roared. 'I just dropped a fucking bottle of vodka.' Leaning forward Nick gave a tired shrug and followed in behind him without a word.

'Where's that gin?' he muttered under his breath.

He'd spotted it in the drinks cabinet the other day. His mum did her best to distract him but he was blinkered. Bursting into the front room, he glanced at the smartly dressed couple sitting poised on the edge of the sofa.

'Alright,' he slurred, opening the cabinet.

'Where's that gin?' he continued, becoming more incensed by finding nothing but soft drinks and glassware.

'Jay, Adrian phoned,' said his mum calmly.

He withdrew from the cabinet in a state of confusion and dialled the number his mum had jotted down next to the phone. A party atmosphere at the other end muffled out pretty much whatever Adrian was shouting. He figured his pal was having a good time and replaced the receiver and looked lost for a moment.

'Look at your hands, they're bleeding,' said his mum.

'It's nothing,' he replied turning over his hands and watching a flow of blood trickle towards his wrist, 'it's not that bad.'

Tired he lumbered his way up the stairs to his room, each step was hard work. Not sure as to whether *Monty Python* was really going to lift his mood as the loss of alcohol had so cruelly shaken him from his good humour.

Sunday, June 4

Jay opened his eyes and saw the TV crackling. Squinting around, there was no sign of Nick, but he was pleased to be in the comfort of his bedroom. It was good to wake up somewhere familiar for a change he thought as he undressed slightly before falling back into his cosy coma.

At about eleven thirty, with an overstretched arm and torso, he pawed at his jeans determined to slip them on without leaving his pit. He managed eventually, sat up and studied the small cuts on his hands. He registered the demise of the bottle he was carrying, as well as an acute sense of guilt as he thought of Trac. Placing a weary hand deep into a pocket he found a few solitary coins, no more than twenty pence he guessed. He rambled off into the bathroom, his head throbbing. He washed the coagulated blood from his hands and drank long and deeply from the tap. He soaked his hair in cold water, flicking it back with his left hand. He nodded amiably to the waxy reflection in the mirror and relieved his bladder. Downstairs in the kitchen he searched for food like a bewildered animal. Grabbing at a carton of fresh orange juice, a box of eggs and some paracetamol he wondered if he could come up with the ultimate hangover cure. Cracking two eggs into a pint glass he stirred in the orange juice slowly. If his stomach could hold it down, this had to be one of the best ways in which to put back some of the nutrients alcohol had so cruelly robbed his body of. Rubbing his hands together as he geared himself up he muttered, 'this is going to work.'

Wednesday, June 7

It was hot again, the sun blazing down. He opened a window for some air before attempting to tidy the mess in his room. Many photographs of his nights out were dispersed across his bed. Trac picked one up and stared at it then looked up as he spoke.

'I was going to stick those down in an album.'

He began collecting them up. 'I'll do it later,' he smiled. 'What do you think of this one,' he said, and handed her a picture.

He waited anxiously for her to cast her verdict. It was a photo of him on Rob's sofa half in darkness being poured a vodka and having a large grin.

She smiled, 'have you actually got any photos of yourself without a drink?'

'You've got that black and white one of me and I'm not holding a drink.'

'Mmm, that will be the one were you're leaning on the bar at the Cove I believe.'

'Well...' he raised a smile, 'I guess there's not many.'

Friday, June 9

He sank his teeth into the soft skin of Trac's stomach then made a large rasping sound that tickled and made her squirm and giggle out loud. He grinned to himself and trailed his tongue slowly up her body and between her breasts where he rested his chin and stared at her with soft eyes.

'Do you ever think of me touching you?' he whispered.

'Mmm.' Her eyes rolled a little and looked above then back to study his face. 'Sometimes I imagine you holding me.'

'You like me touching you?'

'Yes,' she whispered.

'You have the experience. I should be asking you.'

'I've no complaints,' he chuckled and she gave him a friendly punch on the arm as he rolled off the bed to put some music on, before returning quickly to her side.

'What do you like best then?'

She placed her finger on his mouth.

'My tongue.'

She nodded and said, 'it's softer than your hands,' and she gave a shy smile.

'I like this song,' she mumbled as she buried herself further into his arms, "Stand By Me', Ben E King,' he said and began to sing along to it softly.

'Can't you whistle instead,' she joked.

'No, but I do have a desire to soak you in vodka and lime and make love to you slowly all night.'

'It'd be very sticky.'

He teased a hand through her hair and gazed at her intently, 'I'm very lucky to have found you.'

'Why?'

'Because,' he smiled and bowed his head before looking back to her. 'You're beautiful. You're going to turn into a very beautiful woman.'

'Thank you,' she said, 'and is that why you love me?'

'Partly. The way you kiss me and the way your legs move round me, pulling me in close and how your hair falls on my face... it all excites me. You make me happy.'

'Flattery will get you everywhere.'

'Well I haven't finished. You're honest, caring and dependable. I guess some of the qualities I like even though I haven't got them myself. I love you even when you're stubborn.'

'I'm not as stubborn as you.'

'You help me feel so confident, I can do anything I want.'

'You have that ability but there's nothing you want to do other than get drunk.'

'But you love me right?'

'Yeah.'

'Show me how much?'

Trac held her hands about three foot apart. 'About this much.'

He chuckled. 'Oh come on,' he said and out stretched his arms as far as he possible could. 'This much.'

'If I had something on one of these fingers,' she smirked as she wiggled them at him.

Still holding his arms out he pulled a stupid face at her.

'Okay, okay,' she said. 'That much.'

Sunday, June 11

It was a fine day, mild with the sun shining and the air smelt good. Jay had a surge of pleasure, a feeling of well-being as he enticed Trac into the spare bedroom at his dad's house with a flicker of his eyes and a straightforward approach.

'Fancy going to bed then?' he smiled playfully.

'I'm not tired,' she smiled.

He groaned pathetically. 'You like teasing me don't you.'

'Yep,' she laughed.

Rolling his eyes craftily at her he said, 'we can just go and explore each other. We don't have to... you know do it or anything.'

'Okay,' she smiled and put her hand out.

'I want us totally naked,' he mused, 'no hiding in the dark. I want to see all of you.'

When they lay naked next to each other in bed, they just looked at one another in silence, it was a strange feeling of not having at least some darkness in which to hide. He began to hum, no particular tune just hummed and she smiled. He pulled the duvet up and rolled on top of her. Grinning expansively he disappeared under the covers and began to kiss her lightly all over, carefully and skilfully. Slowly she began to relax herself more and more, she closed her eyes and swallowed loudly as he pushed her knees apart gently. He started to hum the sound track to *Lost in Space*, her eyes shot open and she looked under the covers.

'What are you doing?'

He smiled up at her and continued. Trac lay fists clenched eyes shut, a little tense but still enjoying every second of how it felt and responded by arching her back. He stroked her body lightly and lingered at length around the curve of her buttocks until he decided it was his turn. Although his body was a little skinny, he still had attractive forms and shapes. She always said that she loved his back and his neck. She nervously rubbed round and round on the smooth surface of his stomach. Encouraged by him, she ran her index finger down the scar on his stomach, down further to pinch and rub his thighs. She did not take her eyes off 'Him,' 'Him' being his cock. Her eyes seemed mesmerised, his breathing became shallow. She looked at his face, it was a mask of pleasure, no embarrassment or shyness evident, just pure pleasure. His eyelids almost closed but she could see he was watching her face intently as she slowly massaged 'Him'. He made faint moans so she knew how he liked it and that whatever she was doing was right. She began to perspire and breathe deeper letting him know she was enjoying what she was doing. Fascinated by it all she was starting to let herself go. As she pummelled and rubbed his body, she made no attempt to ease his discomfort in wanting to cum. She found herself slowly winding her hands round and round his belly, circling down and down towards his tight curly hairs, rubbing her hands up from his knee to his inner thighs in smooth slides. She looked at his face again, his eyes squeezed shut, his lower lip gripped between his teeth, his jaw clenched. She was making it very difficult for him, but she showed no remorse. In fact she looked like she was enjoying herself, having a feeling of power, power to control his body, she could do anything she wanted and he'd be powerless to refuse.

As her hands slid over 'Him' he let out a whimper, his feet moved and his knees jerked, she continued to rub intimately up and down the length of his cock and round his thighs. His hips kept raising up as if to say here just here... please! She obliged, kissing and working up her speed and tightness of grip depending on how his body or expression reacted. His breathing became deeper and quicker. His body began to jolt slightly and she increased her wrist speed until his body began to tense violently. Watching his climax she smiled with success.

'It shoots quite far doesn't it,' she said.

'Oh,' he mumbled quietly feeling a little embarrassed at his loss of control.

'Look you've even got some over here. I am impressed.'

She sounded enthusiastic so he kissed her forehead, cheek and mouth and then ran a finger down her nose to her lips. He whispered, 'I can't wait to see what else turns you on.'

With her hair all messed up she looked natural, wild even.

'Maybe we could go a little further next time,' she whispered.

They lay hugging in the spoon position.

'This is nice,' she muttered.

As he roused he whispered, 'I'd love to wake up with you like this every morning.'

Pillow talk soon turned to sleep.

For the next few days they floated through a sort of hazy dream. The days and nights were filled with passion and an insatiable desire for each other. They forgot the rest of the world and were never more than an inch apart from each other getting closer, happy to use their energies between the sheets. Life seemed so amazingly simple.

7. Love nest

If he ever was going to smoke, now would be a good time for a cigarette. Half a packet of Fruit Pastilles would have to suffice, but as he popped them one after the other into his mouth, the pack was soon reduced to a torn mess of paper and foil in the palm of his hand. He rubbed his face and began to bite on his thumb... was he expecting to walk straight into a job? He gave himself a shrug, the interview hadn't gone that bad, over qualified now, that did confuse him.

Looking down at the white shirt, blue tie, blue chinos and the black shoes he was wearing he increasingly felt uncomfortable. Smart was something he was not used to, in fact the tie was borrowed from his dad and the chinos belonged to Nick, so they were way too long. If he was honest he knew the style was baggy but his skinny legs seemed totally lost in the material. He vented a lengthy sigh, placed his portfolio onto the back seat of The Beast and decided the best thing would be to go and see Trac, she'd cheer him up, if not fill him with tea and biscuits.

'Don't lick me,' demanded Trac pulling away from him.

'Why?'

'Because you know I don't like it!'

'Alright I'll give you a love bite instead,' he teased.

'Don't you dare. I'll never speak to you again.'

'Is that a promise?' he grinned and began to kiss her neck. She twitched a little just in case he began to suck at her soft skin.

'Just cos you've had a bad day.'

'Not so bad, I didn't really want the job anyway.'

'Why did you apply for it?'

'Forget about it. Anyway, have you missed me?' he asked cheerfully.

'No,' she said jokingly,

'Fine. Okay,' he muttered and pulled away from her.

'Don't go all huffy on me. I was only kidding.'

She pulled him back and rested a hand on his thigh which sent an immediate impulse to his brain, movement down below began to start. He smiled and warmed to her once again as she ran a teasing hand over his crotch and kissed him with force. She pulled away sharply and glanced down to her hand, then back up to meet his eyes.

'Do you reckon all men are about the same size?' she said curiously.

He gave her a puzzled look for a moment or two until his brain came from his groin back to his head.

'Err, I don't know, probably,' and gave a slight shrug.

'It's just that... '

'What?' he frowned.

'Well we were talking about it that's all.'

'Oh yeah, I get it,' he nodded his head.

'Get what?' she responded with an innocent look.

'I knew it,' he pointed at her and held his lips tightly together.

'Knew what?'

'You girls are just as bad.'

'What do you mean?' she asked softly.

'Well you all moan about how blokes are only interested in sex, but you lot are just as bad if not worse.'

'We didn't say we wanted sex.'

'No?' he smiled. 'Just talk about it then!'

She looked down at her lap. 'Sort of.'

This was obviously difficult for her, she was struggling to find the appropriate words. She gave a chuckle, 'it's really funny,' she said, 'Claire and Michelle are the worst, it's not me.'

'Oh yeah,' he smirked.

'Claire said she gets really bored while she plays with her boyfriend and sits there and wonders what she's missing on TV, or thinks about her homework.'

'Oh charming,' he muttered, his body tensing by the second.

'I don't do that with you,' she said defensively 'I do get arm ache though... sometimes.'

'I hope you don't talk about me.'

'No, I told you, it's Claire and Michelle.'

He started to relax. 'Alright then.'

'Well there is one thing.'

'And what's that?' he asked and followed it with a long sigh.

'About different sizes.'

'Yes,' he said with impatience beginning to set in his tone.

'Well we sort of made this chart.'

'What do you mean sort of? How can you sort of make one?'

She shied away from him and made no reply.

'You want to know how big I am don't you!'

She nodded slowly with an innocent expression. He rubbed at his temple and thought about whether to oblige or not.

'What's the biggest so far?' he asked.

'About five and a half inches.'

'Blimey,' he snapped.

'That's when at attention,' she said confidently.

'Oh right,' he nodded beginning to calm again.

He thought of asking her for a ruler so he could self measure and if he did not have a clear advantage he could refuse the information. He couldn't do that he thought because then she would know he was smaller... he could lie? No there must be guidelines against self measuring. He tried to visualise the last time he saw his cock erect and judge if it was an embarrassing size or not. Oh shit he thought, I'm getting a complex now.

'Hello!' Trac said nudging him and freeing him from his thoughts.

'What?' he moaned, annoyed that his day dreaming had been rudely interrupted.

'Still here then?' she smiled.

'Yeah, I was just thinking.'

'Well?'

'Erm, what if it's not big enough.'

'You mean you've never measured it?'

'Never felt the need to do that.'

'You've not read *Adrian Mole*?'

'Umm penned by a woman, and of course she would know all about it,' he uttered sarcastically.

'I don't know what you're worried about, it looks big to me.'

He was stalling while he had a chance to feel about, trying to gage the size. As it firmed up he became more confident by the second. He took a deep breath, 'go on then before I change my mind,' he said and unbuckled, unbuttoned and pulled his jeans down and lay back with a smile while she went to retrieve a ruler from her school bag.

'I can't find one,' she said looking up from her bag with a confused expression.

'I finally agree to do this and you can't find a ruler.'

'Alright hold on,' she said and looked under her bed.

'It's going down now,' he said.

'Here... here I've got one.'

She jumped back onto her bed with a wide smile of excitement.

'Six and a half inches,' she said, 'I'm impressed, you're the winner,' and she patted his cock lightly. 'You can put him away now.'

He held his cock upright. 'I think if you play with it for a bit it'll get bigger,' he growled.

'Now you're showing off,' she said frowning at him.

He returned it to his boxers and pulled up his jeans reluctantly with a sigh as she floated towards her stereo.

'Don't put that on it's crap,' he griped spying her every move.

'Well I like it.'

'And I hate it!'

She simply stuck her tongue out and played it anyway. He mumbled something to himself then sighed again loudly.

'I'm going home then,' he grumbled sitting up.

'You can be a right sod sometimes if you don't get your own way.'

'A sod,' he pondered. 'Sincere outstanding drinker.'

'Yes that as well.'

'I'm just restless.'

'Well think of something to do.'

He gave her a mischievous grin.

'No,' she said firmly. 'Mum and Dad are in.'

He mumbled again and followed it with yet another drawn out sigh.

Thursday, June 15

Jay stood outside the Very Bizarre shop on Silver Street. He had Elvis' 'King Creole' album tucked under his left arm and a *Jail House Rock* poster from the market under the other as he put on his new chrome watch. Once on he gave his wrist a few turns and briefly admired his purchase before trundling down the road towards the hardware store. Regardless of the fact that he had a somewhat easy day so far he was feeling a bit reluctant to put in a few hours of his labour. Still, he thought hearing the distant rattling of change in his pockets, he could see his day off later in the local pub with a pint or two.

Friday, June 16

The afternoon drawing class with Ruth was dull compared to the sunshine outside but it was getting increasingly difficult to come up with decent excuses. Adrian's latest excuse was the dentist and while he did a great acting performance most of the time it was never helped by Jay, Dave and Andy coughing and uttering, 'bullshit,' or 'bollocks,' at the same time. Jay decided to make his excuse so outrageous that it could only be the truth. He had developed his current idea while sipping on his beer earlier.

'I've got to bury next door's cat,' he said positively.

'Pardon?' asked Ruth squinting at him.

Taking in what he had said seemed to take a few moments as she tried to detect a lying expression about his face.

'Why?' she suddenly snapped almost making him jump on the spot.

'Er... well because it's dead,' he said flatly.

'No, no,' Ruth shook her head, 'why do you have to bury it?'

'Well the old lady lives on her own,' he began to use his hands to help communicate this very difficult lie. 'I basically found it and so she asked me if I'd bury it for her,' he gave a shrug, 'and I said yeah.'

'Can't you do it this evening?'

'No, not really,' he said and caused her to frown at him. 'Look,' he continued looking positively genuine. 'I can't leave it any longer. I know I should've done it straight away. The thing is I've told her now that I buried it on the edge of her rockery, but it's still in a bin liner in the shed and it's starting to smell a bit.' He gave a desperate shrug, 'you know I feel kind of guilty when she's out there talking to it.'

Ruth gave him a discomforted look. 'Alright, alright,' she jabbered waving her hand at him flippantly, 'go.'

She turned to the rest of the class. 'Now has anybody seen Adrian? I know I saw him today.'

Jay coughed lightly to get her attention, 'er.. he left about ten minutes ago,' he said and offered her a weak smile.

'And where has he gone? Not the dentist again?'

'Well he... he... er... told me to tell you that he's gone to a funeral.'

'The cat's?' she droned.

'That's good,' he chuckled softly. 'But no,' he shook his head quickly.

Her words began spilling over him, he wasn't listening anymore, he had switched off. He just wanted to be on his way to meet up with Adrian some way down the road.

'What did you say?' asked Adrian impatiently.

'I told her I had to bury a cat.'

'She believed you!'

He splayed open his arms, 'here I am.'

'Nice one.'

'I said you'd left for a funeral.'

'What happened to my dentist excuse.'

'She made a comment about it before I had chance so, I just thought funeral.'

'God who can I say died now.'

'Your Auntie?' Jay suggested.

'I've had four or was it five pass away already, I tell you I'm losing count.'

'So you had lots of Aunties. Or it could be someone else?'

'I've got it,' he said swiftly, 'Uncle Frank died.'

'Yeah that sounds good... well it doesn't if you really have got an Uncle Frank.'

'What if she checks it out?'

'Well it's your own fault, you should try and be a bit more creative with your excuses. I mean you are supposed to be creative.'

'What like a cat?'

'Well it worked didn't it?'

'I admire your confidence.'

Saturday, June 17

At seven minutes and counting, Jay was wedged in a fern tree, alone and nursing a bumped head and aching thighs. Fucking stinks in here, he thought sucking on a swollen lip. Squinting through the gaps between the leaves and branches he wondered if the distant swearing was still the annoyed taxi driver?

Under the fluorescent lights of the chip shop on High Street, the scars and craters of the young guy's face in Jay's state assumed lunar proportions. It was beginning to put him off his garlic mayonnaise cheese burger when someone in the group had announced rather than suggest that they should all run from the taxi. It came as a bit of a surprise to Jay that no-one objected to this plan, it came as even more of a surprise when he became the last man sitting in the cab watching the tail end of his mates disperse in different directions. The few seconds delay had not worked to his advantage when the angry Asian cab driver began to lose it. Swearing in English, amongst rants in his own language, led to only one thing... an overwhelming desire to run, and fast.

He rubbed at his thighs as he recalled the moment of impact, he struck the metal fence at full speed. 'Why did the stupid alleyway, have a stupid zig-zag fence anyway?' On top of the pain, he still had over a mile to walk back as well.

Sunday, June 18

Bright eyed and bushy tailed Jay was feeling surprisingly good. Spending time with Trac filled him with joy, he felt full of himself, she simply washed his hangovers away. At his dad's house he impatiently stared out of the window watching the corner of the street, waiting to see her appear. Her familiar figure waltzed around the corner, taking quick but small steps. He smiled and jogged to the front door.

'Hi, how are you babe?' he beamed a big smile.

She lifted her bag off her shoulders and looked at him 'okay, I suppose,' she mumbled.

'Missed you.'

She returned his smile and they hugged.

'I've missed you too,' she whispered with a sigh, 'I'm just getting out of a bad mood.'

He held her in his arms for a moment or two before leading her through into the lounge. Elvis Presley was playing on the stereo, he picked up the album cover and twirled it around in the palms of his hands.

'Presley,' he said. 'The King.'

He placed the record sleeve on top of the stereo and then pulled a sip of Guinness from a can. He offered it to her and she took it in her hand and sat down taking a few sips. He was in one of his modest moods which made her laugh, he could cheer her up so easily. He kissed her in his familiar pattern and slowly moved down her neck and onto her ears sending a shudder through her body. She responded very quickly and allowed him to unbutton her top and remove her shirt. She wasn't wearing a bra and her small pert breasts rose to his touch.

'Corr,' he mused and she tried to cover herself.

'What's wrong?' he asked.

'They're too small.'

'No they're not, they're just right.'

'I'm cold.'

'Under the covers will keep you warm,' he suggested.

'You're going to man-handle me then?'

He smiled a little at the thought of it and put out his hand, 'maybe.'

He lay her softly onto the bed, they fumbled, excited and scared. They rolled under the covers kissing and tickling each other. He flung off his jeans and began to wiggle his hips, kissing and squeezing her breast slightly, and slipping down her knickers.

'What's down here then?' he whispered with excitement.

'I don't know,' came her soft reply.

'Trac?'

'Yeah,' she looked down at him.

'Shall we do it?'

'Okay,' she said.

'We can stop any time. Just say stop and I'll stop.'

'Okay,' she smiled nervously.

He sat up and picked his jeans up off the floor and rummaged through his pockets. Retrieving a small packet of Durex featherlite condoms, he held one aloft, showing her proudly and waited for her approval.

'Good,' she smiled a little more at ease.

'I can never get these bloody things on,' he mumbled wrestling with the condom. 'Relax,' he kept saying in a soft voice, 'Flow with it.'

She felt stiff as a board to start off with but step by step he relaxed her until he was inside her and she was laughing. It was so funny they were actually doing it, up and down went his bum in the half dark, everything seemed fumbled and awkward, making more than slightly shy of movie perfection. Afterwards they sat on opposite ends of the bed looking at each other. He broke the silence with a sneeze.

'God I always do that afterwards,' he said, and Trac smiled at that.

He bent down to the bed, supporting his head with his hand he began to play with her small feet that aroused the most intense feelings in him.

'Was it okay then?' he asked softly.

'Yeah,' she replied coyly. She was smiling avidly. 'Do you love me then?' she asked.

'Erm,' he pondered teasingly and she nudged him with her left foot and pulled a face. 'I hate you,' he said in a loving tone.

She knew he found it hard to say when prompted, and accepted that the tone in his voice meant the opposite of what he actually said, but she gave him another prompting nudge anyway.

'You're cute,' he said leaning over to hug her. 'Of course I love you,' and he nuzzled his face into her neck, 'I wish we could stay like this forever.'

'I so want to lose myself in you,' she replied softly.

Trac was quiet and collected but for the big smile that welded itself to her face and she marked the occasion with a black star on her calendar. On the way home in The Beast Jay sang along to Elvis exhilarated, so full of love, so full of energy.

Monday, June 19

'I'll leave you two here while I go and get some beers,' Jay said, grabbing at his keys.

'Oh? Okay I'll put some music on then,' Trac answered.

'Adrian?'

'Right yeah,' he smiled. 'Claire this is Trac, Trac this is Claire.'

'Come on then,' demanded Jay impatiently. 'Let's go.'

They drove down the winding country roads to the village shop. Inside there was so much to choose from, Smirnoff, Jim Beam, Guinness, all classics thought Jay as he picked up a six pack of Foster's and moved to the counter.

'These will do,' looking for confirmation from Adrian. 'Six should be enough. 'My old man's got some of that fifty percent vodka.'

'You'll have to show me your dad's bedroom,' beamed Adrian.

'Now come on, beer first, sex later.'

After filling The Beast up with petrol, they drove slowly back. Trying to drive and drink a can of beer at the same time took a certain skill which he had just about managed to master before emptying the contents down his throat and hurling the can onto the back seat.

They found Trac and Claire still in the kitchen chatting away.

'Where's my tea then?' Jay asked sharply dropping the Foster's on the sideboard.

'You've got beer,' she replied hastily.

He shook one of the cans and opened it in her direction and then claimed it was an accident. He began to grin as he watched her pick up a beer and begin shaking it quite violently before releasing it all over him and she started laughing. Adrian took a couple of cans and Claire's hand.

'We'll leave you two to your foreplay,' he smiled and went in search of a bedroom.

Jay retreated to the lounge where Trac was sat cross-legged on the floor.

'Look at me,' he chuckled still wiping beer from his face. 'I'm soaked.'

She looked up and pulled at her hair. 'Well I've got to wash my hair now.'

'You do look very... and I mean very sexy with wet hair.'

'Well, it's all sticky and horrible.'

'Arrh poor you,' he teased.

'Oh bog off fat head.'

'You and lager, a perfect mix,' he said opening his arms out.

'I thought that was vodka?'

'Come on let's go to bed.'

She glared at him at first before giving him that look she always pulled when sex was mentioned, it began to illuminate her face and he recognised it and beamed back at her.

'Come on girl,' he chuckled.

'I see Adrian doesn't waste any time,' she said as they passed the bedroom door.

The small musty spare room felt like a private and secret place. He unbuttoned his black shirt slowly, watching her all the time. When she was naked he walked round the bed and held her, kissing her lightly. He then gave her his usual smile before laying her softly onto the bed. He had a sparkle of fun in his eyes and slipped off to the kitchen and fetched a can of whipped cream out of the refrigerator. Holding it behind his back he returned to the bedroom looking gleeful. She was sat up, the quilt just covering her breasts, she was looking at him curiously. She jarred her head from side to side to get a look at what he was hiding.

'What have you got?'

He moved closer to the bed and produced the can.

'Oh no,' she said. 'You're not squirting that on me again.'

'Oh come on, why not. It was fun last time.'

'Alright but nothing else.'

He smiled lazily, then dived under the duvet singing to himself happily, moving like a shark through water.

'Dink dink dink a ding dink dink dink a ding ding.'

She could hear him humming away with delight his usual array of tunes.

'What's this then?' he growled playfully.

Shaking her head at him she whispered, 'you're mad,' before letting go of the quilt.

He carried on singing and being silly, he prodded and kissed her belly button, before disappearing further down.

'Where are you going now?' she chuckled.

'Look at that bum,' he shouted grasping it firmly with both hands, 'coorr!'

He turned her over and began kissing her back, 'you smell gorgeous.'

The next minute he was at the bottom of the bed clinging to her thigh refusing to let go and began kissing it quite passionately. She lifted the covers up and looking down at him, he looked like a small boy up to no good, an expression of wild excitement flaring in his eyes.

'What are you doing?' came a soft yet confused sigh.

'Nothing,' he said. 'I'm just in love with this leg.' He smiled to himself,

'I could lay like this for hours.'

'What about the rest of me.'

'No,' came his muffled reply, 'not interested, I just want the leg.'

'You're bonkers,' she said and shook her leg frantically until he let go and eased himself on top of her.

'Does my little baby want to do it then?' he whispered.

'Yes,' she demanded, thrusting her pelvis to him.

She took a sharp breath. He was inside her. They rolled around, wiggling, thrusting, kissing, breathing heavily, the odd sighs and grasping of bottoms, until it was all over and he lay naked exhausted on top of her. She could feel 'Him' pulsating inside her. He tensed his muscles and made his cock move and she smiled lazily, and closed the walls of her vagina in tightly and he chuckled.

'See I can do that as well,' she said smiling.

The two of them lay there staring at the ceiling.

'Was it okay?' she whispered.

He turned to her and kissed her. 'Yep,' he said happily and pulled her closer to him.

'Mmm, sexy pants?' she said and squeezed his bum.

'Sexy pants?' he laughed.

'Yep,' she smiled and hugged him tightly.

They lay there for a good twenty minutes before he decided to make everyone a cup of tea. He slipped on his jeans and crept very carefully out the bedroom and burst in on Adrian and Claire.

'Arrh no... Jay! You bastard,' roared Adrian as he tried to scratch about for the bed covers.

'Sorry mate,' he chuckled, 'I was just wondering if you would like a foursome?' They looked at him bewildered. 'No?... Okay, I can live with that, cup of tea then maybe?'

Their faces dropped from shock to relief, 'yeah tea.'

As he re-entered back into the spare room Trac was propped up in bed smiling, she loved being waitered upon.

'There you go,' he smiled.

'Thank you,' she promptly replied.

'You don't have to drink it, it's lemon tea. It's all that was left,' and gave a shrug. 'It tastes a bit funny to me, but it's not as bad as what you make.' She went to fling a pillow at him but he was too quick. Pouncing he grabbed at her sides and began to squeeze with his fingers.

'Don't,' she wailed in between fits of laughter. 'Don't.'

Collapsing next to her he panted deeply, 'I suppose we'd better get up.'

'Yeah, in a minute,' she replied still writhing from being over tickled.

'I was thinking,' he said, 'we could get a video out tonight.'

'What? Now let me guess. *Friday the Thirteenth*?' she said sarcastically.

'Erm could be an idea,' he chuckled.

He gave her another hug before heading to the lounge to change the music on the stereo. She managed to get out of bed and put her clothes back on even though she could have stayed there quite happily all day. As she walked into the lounge she said, 'they seem to be having fun.'

He nodded, 'yeah, sounds like it,' he replied. 'Want some chocolate?'

Trac reached for a chocolate. 'Just one,' she said. 'If I eat chocolate I come out in spots immediately,' and popped it into her mouth.

'Oh great, confuse me... that's usually when it's the time of the month. Now I won't know whether it is or whether you've been eating chocolate?' She put her hands on her hips. 'I'm sorry,' she smirked, 'but it's tough luck.' The noise from his dad's bedroom had risen drastically in the last three minutes making the two of them smile. Trying to retain a conversation was difficult as they could hear Adrian laughing and Claire screaming. Then silence broke after a huge thud.

'Shit!' came a yell.

'Oh no, what was that?'

Jay rose to his feet as Adrian came into the front room.

'Sorry mate,' he said. 'I think the bed's broke.'

'What do you mean broke?'

'Erm broke as in knackered. I think you'd better have a look.'

Jay shot into the room ignoring Claire who stood there blank faced holding her clothes to her body. Trac found it amusing as she held her cup of tea and leant on the door frame watching as Adrian continued to apologise profusely.

'It's one of the legs,' Jay said. 'It's split in half.'

'Can you mend it?' asked Adrian desperately.

'Yeah I reckon. I could maybe glue it or something.'

'Are you sure, it's wood.'

'I can wrap some tape round it,' he said, holding part of it in his hands.

'What about the other legs?' said Trac.

Adrian studying the bed said, 'they seem okay.'

'Can you replace it?'

'No,' grunted Jay lifting the bed slightly. 'Never get one the same... no time for that anyway.'

'Jay,' said Adrian in a slight whisper.

'Yeah,' he looked up from the broken leg.

'There's something else.'

'What?'

He pulled back the sheets, 'Claire's made a bit of a stain.'

'Oh great,' he said putting a hand to his forehead.

'It wasn't me. It was Claire.'

Poor Claire was still standing at the back of the room clutching her clothes with her blank but now slightly sorrowful expression.

'Claire,' said Jay, 'don't worry about it,' and with that she crouched down and began to dress.

Jay smiled as he studied Trac's concerned face, knowing that she didn't want him to turn round to catch any part of Claire's naked body. As his smile widened and his eyes glinted, Trac then knew, he knew what she was thinking as he continued to loosen the remaining part of the leg from the bed. When it came free they all wandered into the kitchen and Jay became less panic stricken when he found some wood glue and tape in one of the drawers. In between fixing it they all lifted the bed up.

'Hold on,' said Jay, 'I've forgotten the tape,' and he darted off.

While he stood taping up the bed leg in the kitchen he heard a car engine and looked up.

'Fucking hell!' he cried at the top of his voice. 'It's my dad!' and dashed back to the bedroom.

'What are we going to do?' babbled Adrian nervously.

'Lift the bed,' said Jay calmly.

'But what are we going to do? babbled Adrian again.

'Everyone act cool,' continued Jay and firmly repeated, 'pick up the bed. Trac go into the lounge and keep watch.'

They lifted the bed and he quickly twisted the leg in place and they all ran and stumbled into the lounge.

'He's gone,' said Trac coolly.

Jay gave a puzzled look. 'Has he?' and glared out the front window and furtively looked left and right scouring the street.

'Are you sure it was your dad?'

'Trac, after eighteen and a half years I think I know what my dad looks like.'

'Yeah, but he was with some young looking woman.'

He rubbed his chin in thought. 'Yes,' he said softly still trying to think at the same time. 'That's why he didn't come in. He was with his girlfriend. She's at least half his age.'

'So,' said Adrian, still confused.

'Let's not get into that.'

'That was a bit of luck,' Claire chipped in.

'All I need to do now is leave a note saying me and you,' he looked at Trac, 'came round to tape some-'

'I don't think that bed's going to hold you know,' interrupted Adrian as he paced back and forth.

All four of them went back to the bedroom again. Jay sat on the bed carefully, it squeaked and wobbled a little.

'We're just going to have to leave it and hope the glue sets and makes it stronger.'

'But when he sits down it will break,' said Trac.

'Yeah,' he chuckled, 'In which case he'll think he's done it.'

'He won't with tape round the leg he'll put two and two together and think me and you. You know, in his bed, especially if you leave a note,' mumbled Trac.

'I've got to leave a note, he must have seen more than one person in the house.'

Jay frantically began making a dummy list of Elvis songs and crossed some out to make it look as if they had been taped. He left it on the kitchen work top with a note;

Dad, In the middle of recording some Elvis with Trac, finish tomorrow, am going home now.

'Everywhere's tidy Jay,' mumbled Adrian feeling guilty about the bed.

'I think we'd better go,' said Claire.

'Yeah,' smiled Jay. 'I think you're right.'

The following day he returned to check the bed and found it propped up with National Geographic books, he just grinned to himself, 'oh well.'

Tuesday, June 20

Jay and Trac's time together had worked out nicely, his last college project deadline was Wednesday and she had offered her services to him most of the day. This broke the back of what needed doing, but it was now looking as though it would have to roll into the next day.

'What time has it got to be in?'

'I don't know,' he shrugged.

'Well if you come over tomorrow,' she said, 'we can spend the day finishing it off.'

'You've helped me enough today already.'

'I don't mind, I enjoyed it. We could always drive out to Loughborough and hand it in.'

'Yeah but if I get caught handing it in late I'll be in deep shit,' said Jay.

'You can't carry on you'll be too tired to do a good job.'

'Yeah, you're right.'

'What time does everyone go home?'

'About five,' he replied. ' If I nip in the building about six I could slip it in the pile with everyone else's.'

'There you go then,' she smiled confidently. 'Your work's good, they can't fail you.'

He bit the end of his pencil, he didn't know whether he deserved to pass really. Then again he agreed with her, his work was good enough and he was putting the effort in, albeit somewhat late.

He arrived at Trac's house in good time, art box and portfolio in hand. She had woke in a good mood and was looking forward to helping him and sat upright on the edge of her bed waiting for instruction.

'Okay first things first, radio one.'

'Set.'

'Tea?'

'In the pot,' she smiled.

'Magic. Right. Here,' he passed her a green pencil, 'what you've got to do,' he said, 'is trace each individual letter perfectly to make the block of type like this,' he showed her an example.

'How difficult is it?'

'It's tricky and tedious that's what makes it hard. If you get pissed off with it just let me know. Oh and one other thing, it's got to be bang on.'

'Okay, I'll take my time,' she smiled and they set to work.

By lunchtime his stomach began to groan and Trac mused, 'it's trying to tell me something.'

'Think so,' he replied softly.

'I'll go and make some toasted cheese sandwiches.'

He gave her a thankful smile, 'cheers.'

He stood rubbing his brow and picked up the work that she had done.

'How did I do?'

'It's good, you did good,' and kissed her forehead.

'How much more have you got to do?' she asked sitting on the bed. He squatted on the floor and shuffled the papers, then crawled towards her holding a scalpel.

'I've just got to cut it up, stick it together and mount a couple of boards that's all.'

He held the new scalpel blade up to show to her. 'These are dead sharp you know,' and ran it gently across her knee.

'Oh I'm bleeding now,' she smudged the small cut with her finger then licked it.

'Did you feel it?'

'No.'

He cut his palm and pushed it to her knee, 'we can be blood brothers now... souls bonded forever.'

'Yeah right!' she murmured sarcastically.

'Really,' he responded.

'Don't get carried away.'

They ate then Trac did some sunbathing, she wanted to get bronze as soon as possible, while Jay finished the artwork off. At three o'clock they were both sat on cushions on the grass and talking mostly about people she had never heard of. He had been immobile for about half an hour before he got agitated by the heat and began to fidget before sitting up.

'Let's crawl into your nice soft bed and cut off the world for a bit,' he said. Trac brought a hand up to cover the sun from her eyes. 'Okay,' she said lightly and put out her other hand for him to take.

He by-passed the head's office and took the back stairway up to the classroom. The only person to see him was the thin strange looking commissioner. Final project under his arm he sneaked into the tutor's office and located the work. As planned he placed his designs into the middle of the pile and breathed a sigh of relief.

Trac sat waiting in The Beast patiently. He appeared and flagged her over.

'I thought I'd show you round,' he chirped.

'What if someone sees you.'

'It's alright, the work's in the office now.'

'Oh good,' she said, 'I had a terrible feeling you'd find the door locked.'

'No, the cleaners have to go through the building first.'

He gave her a brief tour of his classroom and the common room, bringing a bit more background to all the different stories he had told her about his day-to-day life.

'God there's steps everywhere.'

'Yeah, it's a big place.'

'It's a lot closer to a school than I thought.'

'Yeah it is, except you never really mix with any other classes like you do at school, a shame really as you don't get to meet as many people.'

'So is that it now, you've finished?'

'Yeah basically. All I've got to do is remount a few pieces of work for the exhibition.'

'When's that?'

'Twenty-sixth.'

'Not long then.'

'Nope... not long now.'

8. Happy fish

Things had really started to happen for Jay. Trac seemed more than her usual self, so joyful which made him feel even happier too. For her, being with him was not only sexually educational and exciting but he had opened her up to a whole new way of thinking, a different slant on life. She had experienced so many new things, a bad influence in many ways, but that's what made it all the more interesting. Life, it seemed, was beginning to move very much in the fast lane.

It was a bright and breeze-free summer day and the two of them locked themselves away in his room, more material to their desires. Jay was trying his best not to cum until the end of the tape they were listening to, but as the final song by Prince played out he couldn't hold back any longer.
Trac lay smiling, glistening with perspiration.

'Wooo!' she beamed a smile, 'you're terrible for me. We're always doing it.'
He grinned at her and fell to her side exhausted, 'so you don't want to do it again?'
She gave him a mischievous look. 'Yeah,' she nodded and rolled on top of him.

The fair came to Enderby once a year for a few days. It was not the best of fairs but it was something different. Jay hurtled round the leisure centre car park in The Beast.

'Park just there,' Nick pointed.
Trac leaned over, 'can you lend me some money?' she asked looking at him sweetly.

'Sure.'
'Thanks,' she smiled and squeezed his arm.
'Are you going on the dodgems Jay?' asked Guigs as he tried to clamber out the back of The Beast. He was as tall as Nick, much wider and probably the most laid back person he knew.

'Might do,' he replied casually as he stuck his hands into his pockets.
Nick walked ahead and Trac looped her arm into Jay's and Guigs held his girlfriend's hand as they all rambled up the lane to the fair. Trac was getting excited and impatient, all Jay could see was things moving up and down and round and round at speed, he wasn't so keen on those kind of rides, even just looking at them turned his stomach.

'I'm not going on any twisty turny things,' he said deeply.
He bought some candyfloss which was devoured by just about everyone except him. He leant on the wooden frame of the hook-a-duck stall looking at his wooden stick with only a few whispers of floss left, slight disappointment

on his face.

'I'll be back in a minute,' said Trac.

Jay nodded lightly, not really registering what she said and nibbled at the remaining floss while Nick contemplated about whether to go on the dodgems or not.

'It's not as good as it used to be,' mumbled Nick.

'It is, it's just you're not eight years old anymore.'

'I suppose.'

Trac came running back. 'Have you got 50p?' she asked placing her hand out. He stuck a hand into his jeans and pulled out some change.

'Thanks,' she said and ran off.

Trac and a school friend she bumped into were in a cage, a huge swing. The lads found it fun watching them try to push it right over in a complete circle but they just didn't quite have the strength to generate enough momentum.

'I'm starving,' said Nick walking off to get a hotdog, a king size one with loads of ketchup and onions. Trac, red faced and panting for breath came skipping up to him.

'Did you enjoy that?'

'Yep,' she panted. 'It's really difficult.'

'You nearly did it.'

'Have you been on anything yet?'

'No, I was thinking about having a go on the rifle range.'

Nick strolled back over clutching his hotdog. Looking at his watch he muttered, 'are we going up the pub for a drink or what?'

'Yeah, I'll be with you in a sec. I just want to see if I can win something on the rifle range.'

'I'll fetch The Beast for you when I've eaten this.'

'Okay,' replied Jay and handed him the keys, 'be careful.'

Jay lined up with the sights, two targets down and Trac clapped her hands and gave a little jump.

'Oh it's dead easy this,' he said.

'You only need one more and it's a win.'

'I think I'll make it a bit more difficult and close my eyes.'

'No don't, you'll lose.'

'No I won't.'

He heard the target click then opened his eyes wide and grinned at her.

'You fluke,' she howled. 'I don't believe you.'

'That's one win,' called the scruffy looking fairground chap. 'Anything on the lower shelf there,' he said pointing and fanning his hand across an array of useless objects.

'Erm, I don't know, I'll have... no... no... erm.'

'Have another go, get a chance at a better prize.'

'Err...'

'What about that fish?' Trac pointed.

'Where?'

'There at the end. That yellow one on its own.'

There was a small plastic fish, brilliant yellow and shaped like a Carp, attached to a lightly rusted chain. It was hanging there on its own, almost out of sight, as if it had been forgotten. He immediately became attracted to it.

'Can I have that key ring,' he murmured, his eyes still fixed upon it.

'Which one, the fish?'

'Yeah,'

The fairground chap passed it to him and moved onto the next punter without a word or change of facial expression. Jay ran his thumb along the surface of the small plastic fish and felt the roughness of the scales, and in that moment fully appreciated how great everything was. He held it up in both palms of his hands, it seemed to glow before him and he became instantly besotted with its presence.

'Arrh look at it... it's fucking brilliant,' he grinned at her. 'Oh it's just going to have to go in The Beast.'

He passed it to her and she dangled it about a bit and then passed it back.

'What did you win?' asked Nick.

'A yellow fish, look at it, it's ace.'

Nick just laughed and moved over to let him into the driver's seat. Everyone clambered in one after another. When they were all comfy, Jay made a ceremony of mounting The Yellow Fish. He turned down the music and attached it to the inside mirror, replacing the miniature Smirnoff bottle hanging by string. He smiled for a split second, turned the music back up and put his foot hard on the accelerator and snaked off up the road to the pub.

At eleven fifteen Trac was sat on the edge of his bed. He stood tall next to the stereo. 'What time have you got to be home?' he asked softly.

'About twelve. Why?'

'Er nothing,' he smiled but he could feel the enormous sexual tension in the air. It was simple without words, he wanted her and she wanted him. He looked into her eyes smiling he shrugged a little and said, 'do you fancy a quick one?'

Eyes glinting she replied, 'yes.'

Friday, June 23

Trac continued to carefully mark each time they made love with a black star on her calendar, which pleased him no end, that is until he spotted one on an old calendar. He automatically assumed she had slept with another lad she had failed to tell him about and became annoyed that she had seemingly lied to him and couldn't stop himself from slipping into a moody silence. He drove her to his house, and only ninety seconds later she was being driven back at speed. He drove without speaking only huffing loudly without looking at her. Trac pursed her lips, turned and stared out of the window as if in thought about what she had said or done? There was a quiet depth and dimension to the silence and Jay couldn't concentrate, it seemed to grow and grow. She returned a stern glare as he made further grunting noises as he got more and more worked up.

'Don't be nasty to me, you always do that if you're not happy about something.'

He responded with a grunt that could not be entirely defined as an individual word but spoke volumes.

'Slow down,' she screamed. 'What's the matter?'

With an angry gesture he accelerated The Beast furiously.

'Jay,' she said as she moved uncomfortably about her seat, 'what's up?'

'Nothing,' he grunted irritated by her tone.

She paused for a moment then asked him again. He slowed The Beast down feeling deflated by his mood and babbled, 'you lied to me. I trusted you. Believed you.'

'What do you mean by that?'

'You had a black star on that other calendar.'

She sat in thought and then said, 'that was just a note I made for his birthday.' The sincerity with which she said that reduced him to feeling more than a little stupid. He took a deep breath and even though his voice was back to normal he was gripping the steering wheel so hard that his knuckles were white, now angry with himself.

'Don't you believe me?'

He gave an uncomfortable shrug, 'I guess so. I'm...' he slowed The Beast right down and held her hand. 'I just felt... I don't know... I'm... sorry,' he followed his apology with a forced smile, 'forgive me.'

'Of course I do,' she said plainly. 'You should have told me straight away what was bothering you.'

He shrugged again and squeezed her hand assuring her of his apology. When they arrived back she made him a warm drink.

'We're out of tea so I made some hot chocolate.'

'No. I don't want any,' he muttered.

'Come on it's-'

He cut her off in mid speech. 'I am sure it's very nice, but I'm still in a mood.' She made a face, then brightened, 'forget about it.'

'It's not that on my mind.'

He drank some of the chocolate to please her and sat thinking about college and whether he would pass or not. His attendance days and academic growth had not been impressive. He needed mothering, he needed her to tell him everything was going to be alright, even if it wasn't. She put the radio on, classical music seeped out of the speakers and, as bizarre as he found it, it helped. He began to feel calm, things will work out he said to himself with a slight curve upwards of his mouth.

'Are you okay?' Trac asked.

'Yeah,' he replied. 'I just need to figure things out, build myself up a bit.'

'Positive thinking?'

'Yeah,' he agreed and took another sip of hot chocolate. 'Actually,' he continued, 'this isn't bad at all.'

At seven o'clock the desire to get drunk had began to tick away at him, he pictured the barmaid placing down a pint onto the beer towel in front of him and felt that impatience he always got over the first pint.

'I'm off now,' he chirped.

'Why don't you stay?' Trac said keenly.

'I'll see you tomorrow.'

'Stay, we can curl up together. Mum and Dad are going out tonight.'

He watched her for a moment, she looked quite beautiful, but there was no room for indecisiveness, the decision had been made, he could already taste his first sip and the happy drunk glow that he would feel about an hour later.

'What night is it tonight?' Jay said matter-of-factly. 'It's Friday night right. I don't expect you to understand, I mean we can be together anytime.'

'I'm working tomorrow.'

'I'll meet you for lunch,' he offered, and gave her a loose shrug of his left shoulder.

She sighed softly, 'okay,' she said. 'I guess you won't be happy until you've slipped into unconsciousness.'

'Nope,' he replied, lifting his arms up to gesture 'sorry, I love you but I got to go.'

Saturday, June 24

Jay stood commanding Trac's stereo, she only allowed this behaviour due to the amount of ever growing CDs he kept appearing with for her to keep looking after. He filtered his way along and slid out a Prince album and noted a small piece of blue lined paper. Holding it flat against the CD with his back to her he opened it and a smile spread over his face. Under the heading *Jay* she had written:

- *Makes me laugh*
- *Drinks too much*
- *Can't keep his hands off me*
- *Has a long scar on his tummy*
- *Sleeps on his front*
- *Loves music... is a bad singer*
- *Loves Marmite... Err!!*
- *Loves me... Yipeee!*

Trac asked him if he was putting anything on and it made him jump slightly.

'Yeah... sure,' he replied happily folding the paper through his fingers and placing it back with the CD.

'I got a letter today from Shelley,' she mooted.

He glanced over at her said nothing and turned back to the stereo.

'Don't you want to read it?' she asked.

He said nothing, just shook his head slightly.

'Are you sure?'

'I'm sure,' he whispered.

'She's sent a photo too,' and she passed it towards him. He glanced at it but didn't take it from her hand and again said nothing and returned to his music.

'She did say that she's happy for us.'

He picked up the 'Sonic Temple' CD smiled at her in order to let her know he was pleased with that.

'So,' he said, 'you decided if you like The Cult or not yet?'

Sunday, June 25

Monday was D-day, whatever work he put out was what he was going to be graded on so most of Sunday Jay and Trac spent time sorting out his art folders. Cross-legged on the floor they both pondered over his concepts, illustrations and artwork spread out across the lounge with his nanna peering inquisitively at what they were doing. Jay found it a joy to have her staying over for a few days while his mum was away. The great thing about Nanna, he thought, was the perfection of unconditional love. The only time she'd ever disclosed her disapproval to his mum concerned a twenty minute window one Christmas, during the last stages of childhood, in which he farted loudly, approximately nine or ten times. Nanna only tutted a little and wiggled a bit in her chair and it amused him. That was all part of the magic of grandparents he smiled, they're the only ones to fall for something as simple as a whoopee cushion! In Nanna's eyes he could do no wrong and it was good to have such unwavering support in his camp for a while, with the additional bonus of having a perfectly ironed shirt and being fed and supplied with all the tea they could drink.

Scattered out in every direction from his cross-legged position in the middle of the room, he gave out his simple instructions regarding each piece of artwork.

'Bin,' he'd yell and Trac would scrunch it up and place it into a bin liner. 'Keep,' and she'd place the work neatly to the side.

She was so selfless in helping him. He appreciated her interest in his work. She actually made him feel proud about certain pieces he was unsure of and boosted his confidence more on the others he did like.

Monday, June 26

Monday at college he got more of an idea of what he wanted. He remounted a number of pieces and made a logo of his initials from white polystyrene and black paint. He spent hours beavering away with so much dedication and perfection that he surprised himself. He left early, around three, and bought The Cult's new single 'Edie (Ciao Baby)' on 12 inch from the Left Legged Pineapple, a well deserved treat as he made his way down to the railway station.

Tuesday, June 27

'This is way too early, it's not even seven o'clock,' grumbled Jay as he found a soft back chair and eased into it using his art box as a foot stool, looking as if he could easily fall asleep. Despite this Adrian was in an active mood, he rattled the locked double doors to the small hall in frustration.

'I don't understand,' he said. 'Why lock the door? There's nothing in there but exhibition stands.'

With his eyes closed and feeling relaxed Jay smiled as he heard Adrian mutter something and disappear.

Five minutes or so later he returned and plonked himself down next to Jay and scratched at the stubble coming through under his chin.

'Can't find the caretaker,' he mumbled, 'but I found yesterday's *Sun*.'

Jay yawned and stretched out his arms as he sat up. He rubbed at his eyes and took in the headline of the newspaper on Adrian's lap, yet more front page news about Britain's youngsters going crazy at some acid party.

'I bet that was a mad event,' commented Adrian.

Jay nodded and stretched further. 'I reckon it will take me a couple of hours to get set up. I did loads of stuff yesterday.'

'Me too, I think we should treat ourselves over at the union bar when we've done.'

A couple of clatters and a whirring sound came drifting down the corridor and Adrian's ears pricked up.

'Is that the bloke buffing the floor?' he muttered.

Jay gave a shrug, he wasn't really bothered, he was comfortable and that was enough. Adrian leapt to his feet, 'it is,' he said and squeaked his way down the corridor once more. Moments later a pair of squeaking feet could be heard returning, along with a set of jangling keys. A large man appeared who seemed to be panting.

'You lads are keen,' he said, then sniffed and wiped at his nose.

'He's opening up for us,' smiled Adrian bouncing behind him in high spirits. The overweight figure scratched at his groin as he approached the doors with Adrian pointing at his builders arse with a huge grin.

'You want to get yourself a belt mate,' mumbled Jay, but the guy just tugged at the rim of his trousers a couple of times in between struggling to open the doors.

Adrian picked up his artwork and equipment swiftly while Jay seemed to drag himself along the floor as he shuffled to his designated stand and placed his work down onto the table.

'Right,' he said to himself. 'That pile on there is my preliminary work and this is my display work.'

Slowly the other students arrived and by ten o'clock all was completed.

'I'm quite surprised at your work, it's good,' said Dave.

'What do you mean surprised?' exclaimed Jay.

'Well you're hardly ever at college, and when you are you never seem to be doing any work.'

'Well it's all there Dave,' he grinned triumphantly, baring his teeth in self satisfaction. 'That's what you call talent.'

Their abandoned classroom looked nothing more than a mess, paper still littered the tables, chairs and floor. Artwork had been stripped from the walls and the whole place just felt like it had no soul to it anymore.

'Well that's two years of college down the drain,' roared Jay slapping Adrian on the back.

'I'm knackered,' he replied. 'Not used to getting up so early.'

'Let's go into town, it's too hot in here,' murmured Jay still shuffling about not being able to settle.

'Yeah alright,' agreed Adrian.

As Trac struggled with his belt and the button fly of his jeans he was chuckling lightly to himself. Not one to give up she raised herself up from the bed with determination in her eyes. She finally wrestled them free without any assitance, only to be dazzled by a pair of kid's red rimmed, multi-coloured Y-fronts.

'Oh my god,' she gasped. 'Where have they come from?'

'Poundstretcher,' he replied and chuckled further. 'One hundred percent polyester... do you like them?'

'They look a bit tight,' she said with a little laugh.

'They are.'

'Comfortable?'

'Do you know what, there even more uncomfortable if you happen to have a hard on.'

'Which you do.'

'Sexy pants?'

'Nooo. I think they need to come off.'

No point in arguing with that he thought as he slipped his hands behind his head.

'You just lay back and enjoy yourself.'

He didn't respond to that, just continued to smile appreciatively. For some reason or another he felt harder than normal and looking down at his cock being tended to, it looked bigger too. He closed his eyes and sunk his head back into his pillow and felt strangely proud all round.

'I had a really boring day at school,' she informed him. 'Nothing exciting seems to happen anymore. Everyone's stressed about how their exams went.' A few moments passed and she said, 'I've still got some maths revision to do... I'll have to do it later tonight.'

She then asked him if he was any good at algebra and he didn't respond. He heard her give a light chuckle and opened his eyes slightly to see her light smile making him aware of how amusing she found these one way conversations. More often than not tuned into his own channel. She knew he'd never respond to any of her questions properly, especially while he was being tended to. At the very most he would make positive groans from time to time which brought a wider smile to her face as it was her that was training him to do it. If he failed to answer a direct question she simply stopped wanking him and only continued if he made some positive acknowledgement. His fear of her stopping once she had started kept her amused for the time needed to relieve him.

Her chatting about homework and maths brought about his own memories of school. He didn't have a lot of time for maths, besides which, his teacher was a right old battle axe, in fact, so too had been his form tutor. He smiled when an image of escaped stick insects came to mind. His tutor had snapped at him over something trivial and he swore revenge. That afternoon before going home he had adjusted the lid to their cage. The following day was something to treasure as he sat and watched her panic as she desperately tried to rally the rest of his classmates to help locate and rescue the poor things.

At that moment he felt a pinch on his thigh.

'Oi, Mr Floppy.'

He opened his eyes and glanced down to see Trac smiling and waving his limp dick at him. Amused he replied, 'it's your fault, talking about maths.'

'Don't blame me, I've already got arm ache.'

He thought about reaching for her breasts only he had no energy, but just the thought revived him and it soon pointed northward once again.

She brought him to his moment of bliss and saw her satisfied with his triumphant smile before his sudden decline into wanted sleep.

'You've plebbed everywhere,' she said in a mild way.

He thought it was a different way in which to describe it but he was too mellow to communicate with her. She let him be, knowing by now that if she tried to revive him straight away all he would do is whimper and utter the words, 'leave me,' followed by, 'I'm all relaxed now,' in a soft aloof tone or at least something along those lines.

He smiled, then he was inside her for the third time. It felt warm and tight around him and she gasped deeply. Clutching, kissing, caressing they rolled around the bed without a struggle or effort. It was so simple, they just fused together so easily. They moved positions slowly, her on top, him on top. At the climax he grabbed her bottom tightly, and in the afterglow he lay beside her on his stomach, there they slept comfortably. He felt they both rose together in a kind of spiritual communion. He adored the afterglow.

Being blasé and elevated further by his growing high spirits he said, 'you look fine Trac... you look great, now let's go,' as he tightened his belt.

28th - 30th June. The Great Hall Loughborough College of Art and Design. BTEC National Diploma in Graphic Design - Private viewing cheese and wine 7-9pm.

Trac sat in the front of The Beast moving the cans and bottles littering the footwell and placing them onto the back seat along with his ever-growing collection.

'Don't you ever clean this car out?'

'Hey, it's The Beast and I like it like this, it's... it's got character.'

'No, it just shows you drink too much.'

'Can you lend us a fiver for petrol?'

'You mean give you a fiver.'

He pulled a face suggesting she was moaning too much. She sighed and pulled her bag up from her feet onto her lap.

'Here,' she said passing him a note.

'Thanks,' he gave a smile and checked the traffic in the inside mirror at the same time.

'Where are you picking Adrian up from?'

'Town, back of Mc Donald's.'

There they sat patiently for a couple of minutes before Adrian emerged with two milkshakes.

'He looks smart,' said Trac.

Jay looked down at his dress code and sneered. He felt solid in his baseball boots, 501s and black shirt. Adrian jumped into the front as Trac slipped into the back of The Beast.

'I thought you had to wear trousers and that?' he said at once noting Jay in his usual attire.

'No-one said anything to me,' replied Jay and gave an unconcerned shrug.

'Here I got you a milkshake.'

'Cheers.'

'Oh yeah Dave phoned me up,' he began, 'he wanted to know who wrote *massive bulging lallies* across a piece of his work.'

Jay grinned and slurped at his milkshake.

'What are bulging lallies?' asked Trac innocently.

Jay choked for a second, spitting milkshake over the steering wheel.

'Erm... they're...' he took her hand and placed them between his legs.

'Oh,' she said looking slightly embarrassed.

He drove into the college car park kicking up gravel momentarily before yanking on the handbrake and parking abruptly. 'Let's go,' he hooted as he turned the engine off and leapt out rubbing his hands together excitedly. Adrian adjusted his tie while Jay undid another of his shirt buttons and felt Trac slip in beside him.

'Look at you,' he said. 'You do look great.'

He put his hands in his pockets and, looping her left arm in his right, they moved forward together. Once inside they helped themselves to food and wine. Jay was pleased that the idea of cheese was dropped in favour of strawberries and cream. Jay managed four helpings within the first twenty minutes of being there.

'Strawberries, don't you just love strawberries,' he muttered at Trac in response to her asking him to slow down. 'I love strawberries.'

'I know you do but-'

'That's it,' he said abruptly, scooping his final spoonful. 'If I have anymore I'm going to be sick.' He reached for his wine.

Trac stood over his portfolio and he began to talk about his work, one hand moving freely, the other holding his glass of wine. She took his hand and gave it a squeeze of approval and said how proud she was.

'Yeah, I am quite chuffed with that,' he said patting his work.

'Jay,' cried Dave.

'Yeah.'

'What do you think of my exhibition?'

He strolled over to Dave and began to laugh.

'It's a joke isn't it Dave?'

'Oh come on what do you think?'

'Well I think it's absolutely rubbish,' he jibbed. 'I think you've completely wasted the last two years.'

Dave's face looked a vale of worry. 'It's not that bad is it?' he said desperately.

'I'm sorry Dave,' he nodded, 'but it is pretty bad.'

Dave folded his arms in insult just as Adrian came over to put in his two penneth worth.

'Dave, your exhibition is hilarious.'

'Oh fuck off you lot,' he moaned and stormed off.

Jay turned to Trac and kissed her forehead.

'You two are a bit mean to him.'

'Don't worry about Dave, he can give as good as he gets,' said Jay placing his arm around her. 'You know what, I'm quite enjoying this, showing my work.'

'You like showing things,' she growled and moved a light hand across the front of his jeans.

'And why not, that's about the best part of my body,' he smiled. 'Anyway that's a private exhibition for you only.'

'Jay come here,' called Adrian. 'Wouldn't it be funny if someone spilt some wine on his work,' and pointed over at the competitive display that sat alongside his own.

Jay simply spilt some wine without much thought and replied, 'no,' casually. He then panicked as he realised he had spilt a little too much, just edging the joke towards the serious. He quickly used the sleeve of his shirt to mop it up, the wine was taking effect.

'Best not have anymore,' he muttered placing the glass down and flapping the wet sleeve of his shirt.

'Why not?' asked Adrian.

'Not with Trac, I'm driving,' he muttered just as she wandered up quietly behind him.

'I got you another glass of wine.'

'I'm okay, you have it.'

'I've already got one.'

'Have a few,' he smiled. 'Get a little drunk.'

She took a large sip which began to flush her face, 'I feel light headed already,' she said placing her empty glass down and pulling the second one closer to her chest.

'Good,' he replied before mooting sarcastically how nice it was of his parents to show up. Trac squeezed at his arm to remind him that she was there for him even it they were not. He gave her a thankful expression, looked at the time and patted his pocket for his keys. 'Might as well call it a day,' he sighed and looked across at Adrian. 'You ready?'

'Yeah,' came his reply.

It felt good to be out in the fresh air, he had suddenly switched off and was no longer interested in the exhibition.

'I couldn't stay in there any longer, too many mums and dads everywhere,' said Adrian.

'Yeah,' replied Jay and gave Trac a lost look.

'Dave's mum and dad were there,' smiled Adrian.

'Yeah, I saw them.'

'You got any booze in The Beast?'

'I don't know,' he replied in an amusing tone.

'Yes he has,' said Trac. 'There's some vodka, it was on the back seat but the way you drive it's probably on the floor by now.'

The three of them jumped back into The Beast. Jay studied Adrian in the rear view mirror as he groped around the floor until he retrieved the vodka.

'You need to have a clean up in here mate.'

He looked at Trac, shook his head as he started the engine, 'there's nothing wrong with a bit of litter.'

He could hear vodka sloshing against the pint sized bottle as Adrian brought it to his lips and glanced to the mirror once again.

'Watch where you're going, you,' said Trac nudging him.

He then felt the shock of cold glass as Adrian pressed the bottle against the side of his neck.

'You want some?'

Friday, June 30

It was hot and boring. The lads at college all sat in the middle of the room playing with their lunch. A small food fight burst into life then died out just as quickly as it started.

'Oh, look at my jacket,' cried Adrian wiping tomato off it reluctantly while Jay chuckled to himself.

'It wasn't funny Jay.'

'I thought it was,' and carried on chuckling.

Longing for something to happen they became more and more restless, Adrian sat wafting air into empty crisp packets and then popping them while Jay was skulking up and down the room banging past chairs and tables, sighing as loudly as possible, and making little effort to tidy up. He bent down and picked up a brown tube off the floor, it was once carefully sculpted by him and Adrian to become 'Dave's Rocket', it hung from the ceiling among other models and stupid mobile constructions they had made during the year. He didn't know about any of the others but he knew he and Adrian had spent more effort and time on things like that during their time at college than the work. So much fun and humour was in those things, it was true memorabilia, but now it was all over.

'Adrian have you seen this?' he held up the flattened cardboard tube.

'Ahh, fucking hell. Who knackered that?'

He took the remains and held it for a moment like it was treasure before he slowly sat it on the desk in front on himself, glaring at it in thought. 'Some fucker's ripped nearly all the posters down I did for the Iffley bop.'

'Well it did say, *Cum in your Pants!* in big letters,' chuckled Dave.

'This is still floating about,' smiled Jay passing a sex pamphlet and Adrian's spirits rose as he stood flicking through it.

'I hate waiting around here,' winged Dave, lifting his head from his hands. 'Should be out there sunbathing or something.'

'Fuck this,' snapped Adrian. 'I'm going to find out what the score is.'

Moments later Adrian scooted up to the two of them, he doubled over with his hands resting in his knees.

'Jeez,' he panted. 'I'm so unfit.'

'What's happening?' asked Jay impatiently.

'The moderator... he... he wants to see me and you Jay.'

'Fuck.'

'You'll be alright,' Dave laughed.

'When?'

'In about an hour, after lunch.'

Jay looked to the ground for a moment biting at his thumb, 'I'm going to sit in The Beast for a bit, listen to some music.'

He picked up the keys and the two of them followed. Dave struggled to slot himself into the back seat and uttered, 'I'm way too big to sit in the back.'

'Come on,' replied Adrian and gave his bum a shove.

Dave jumped forward and squashed his face into the thin grey and white material, 'fuck,' came his muffled voice.

'You okay Dave?' chuckled Jay squinting into the rear view mirror.

'I tell you what,' replied Dave as he retrieved the battered can of Asda lager that was digging into his backside, 'this car truly represents your lifestyle.'

He smiled, 'you can have that if you want Dave.'

Jay repeatedly tapped at the steering wheel, not to any music as he normally did, but more with impatience and anxiety which was beginning to rub off on Adrian.

'Are you going to stop that?' he asked.

'Stop what?'

'Tapping?'

'I'm just worked up is all,' he gave a sigh. 'I can't believe it's our last day. What are we going to do? I mean, why have we got to see this bloke.'

'The guy just wants to see us and as long as we don't balls up a quick ten minute chat with him we'll be okay,' and pulled out Jay's black plastic cassette holder from the glove box and studied each tape.

'The Wonder Stuff,' he said.

'Yeah, stick it in.'

'Oh shit,' he mumbled rubbing his palms against his thighs as he entered the hallway, not really registering the, 'go for it Jay,' or 'good luck,' his mates called behind him. The round-faced moderator held a clipboard to his chest and put out a hand to greet him once he got within two metres of him.

'Hi,' he beamed. 'Jason isn't it.'

'Yeah,' he nodded. 'Yeah that's right,' and took the guy's hand and shook it.

'So if you'd like to talk me through your work.'

Jay held his chin and let his eyes wander over his work for a moment or two, trying not to listen to the part of his brain that was yelling 'what are you going to say... what are you going to say' repeatedly. He swayed on the spot and opened his mouth. What came out was quite good he thought so he continued, and before he had the chance to take in some air, the moderator was engrossed in him, nodding away and jotting things down. He was winning him over.

He was just beginning to thrive on the situation when the guy looked at his watch. 'Look at that, we've ran over. I think you have the right approach and your work is of a merit to distinction level. However your discipline and attendance records are an important part of any work. I will therefore have to reduce your grading to a pass with merit.'

That'll do for me thought Jay as the relief spread throughout his body. The round-faced guy in the tweed suit put out a hand again and this time Jay snatched it. Exhilarated with over-confidence it made the moderator flinch.

'Thanks... thanks a lot,' he said shaking his hand firmly.

Jay picked his art box up off his desk and went out into the corridor where he dropped the contents of his wooden locker into a carrier bag, taking all of a minute. He held the padlock in his hand for a moment and realised this was it. Loughborough College had come to an end, he was done. Strange, he felt nothing, neither happiness or sadness. Closing the door to the locker for the last time he then took time to look around and soak up anything he had not bothered to notice in the last two years. Everyone had passed and from now on, his time was his own. All that was left was the final party, The Iffley Bop!

9. One too many

The blurring shapes moved past Jay in slow motion, he couldn't register where he was. He had tagged along with Daz, a heavy set Simon Le Bon lookalike who regularly frequented The Bell. He sat casually at the nightclub bar, eyes fixed on Jay standing in the middle of the dance-floor with a large vodka and lime staring back with a dazed grin. Quite clearly Jay was celebrating, an ideal opportunity to get completely paralytic. Although he rated the Studio as one of the worst clubs in Leicester, the venue didn't seem to bother him when they were offering free entry and discount vodka sponsored by Smirnoff. Besides, once he'd drank a reasonable quoter of booze, he found it relatively easy to have fun anywhere.

As he emptied his glass he slowly made his way to the bar, Daz was still positioned on a stool there with a pint of lager in hand.

'Daz,' he roared, 'Daz mate.'

'Yeah,' he chuckled.

'W... w... watch... watch this,' he grinned. 'Can I have a neat vodka and some fresh lime on the side please,' and he turned and winked at Daz.
The barmaid placed his drink and a small plate of cut fruit in front of him. He picked a wedge of lime, bit into it, and reaching for the glass grinned at Daz once more and knocked the liquor back following it with another bite of lime.

'Can I have another?' he babbled with a slight slur and wiped at his mouth. Daz sat and watched him get through eight vodkas consecutively until he looked terrible and fell slightly. Grappling at a cocktail mixer for support was pointless, he simply took it with him on his way down to the floor.

'I... I... I fell over,' he giggled drunkenly as he struggled upwards. 'Isn't that funny!'

The cocktail mixer was in bits. He tried to fix it by simply pushing it together with a puzzled face while the barmaid looked at him impatiently. Realising he couldn't get his brain to function sufficiently enough to replace it correctly he passed it over to her.

'It's... it's... a gonna,' he muttered and followed it with a shrug that gestured 'I did try'.

'Jay, you're going to be dead before you're twenty,' said Daz as he aided him onto a stool and helped him pay for his drinks.

'I need another one,' smiled Jay wearily.

'You're a crazy drunk,' roared Daz as he put his arm around him.
Jay grinned back, 'it's not easy,' he mumbled, 'anyone can... can be...' he paused, '...be sober. It... it takes a special talent to be a drunk.' He raised a glass, knocked the contents back and slurred, 'it... it takes endurance.'

'What are you going to do now you've finished college?'

'Get pissed every night,' and they united in a drunken roar.

'You know what?'

'What's that?'

'I see people like... who have no sex, no booze, no drugs and I just think... life's about this isn't it... fun, try everything, over indulge in something you like... take chances.'

His friend patted him on the back, 'perhaps they just don't need any of that stuff.'

With that Jay just waved him away and turned to face the bar and glared at all the brightly lit bottles and sparkling glasses. He was content with his current position in life, the only problem he had to face was change. By the end of the night his loaned tie was undone, his shirt was hanging out with most of the buttons missing and a small rip across the neck. He was supporting himself against a pillar, hazy yet somewhat enjoying his own company.

Daz drummed into him that it was time to go, and after a short outburst of staggering in circles shouting, 'more vodka!' he gave in.

In the commotion he ripped down an arched poster of the Smirnoff logo from the wall and refused to surrender it, he figured he had drank enough of the stuff that evening, it was his right. Daz could only envisage a drunken wrestle in trying to retrieve it, he refused to waste an ounce more of his energy and backed down. Jay rolled it up carefully, stuffed it into his pocket and veered towards the exit sign.

'Come on then let's go,' he babbled as Daz followed his lead.

'You enjoy yourself Jay?'

'Absolutely fantastic,' he slurred, 'I think I'm going to vomit!'

Saturday, July 1st

At twelve noon when the *Chart Show* started Jay lay in bed, hands laced behind his head, happily nursing his injuries, recalling the various states of intoxication he went through. He was wondering if the hair of the dog that bit you really worked as the best solution to a hangover when he heard his mum enquiring loudly whether the idle, useless lay-about that she had had the honour of mothering was thinking of taking to his bed permanently now college had finished, and if so would she be required to take his meals up and generally wait upon him. This speech rumbled on for some time, so he had plenty of time to get dressed, wax his hair and burst into the lounge with a performing stance.

'I'm going up town to buy an Elvis record,' he jeered with a mixture of obstinacy and excitement. He pulled on his leather jacket, picked up the keys to The Beast and left via the back door singing. His mum watched him in puzzlement and a kind of curiosity, shook her head and continued to read the TV guide.

He searched through a few Elvis records, found 'Elvis is back' and pulled out a scrumpled up five pound note and some loose change.

'Four ninety nine,' he mumbled to himself squinting at the money in his hand, not sure whether to part with it or not.

He decided to replace it, see Trac for lunch and have a think.

The two of them sat in the Lewis' restaurant. He told her his drunken exploits of how Rob's birthday had morphed into him ending up on his Smirnoff promo adventure. She occasionally smiled, it wasn't so much the events of his night but more in the way with which he presented the tale, he put himself into character, it amused her to a tee.

'So,' she announced, 'are you going to wait for me to finish work?'

He glanced at his watch and replied, 'I think so. I might give Adrian a ring, see if he will come out for a couple of hours,' and slurped his tea in thought.

'You're so refined,' she mused.

His eyes flickered so she could tell he was in thought, 'but you love me right?'

'Yeah, and I'm an idiot,' she said. 'Well I suppose I'd better get back to work, worse luck.'

She kissed him on the cheek and gave him a little wave as she went. He reluctantly dug his hands in his pockets and stood on the spot for a while looking at his NatWest cash card, thinking about what to do and how much he may have increased his overdraft whilst under the influence.

Once the mysterious properties of a sweet cup of tea had began to work its magic, Trac began to put a bad day behind her. As she stood leaning back on the kitchen worktop, sipping at the cup, her stomach gurgling away she said, 'what are you making me to eat then?'

He smiled and got some cheese and tomato pizzas from the freezer, grated some extra cheese on top and placed them into the oven with chips.

While the food was cooking, they sat cuddling on the sofa and let the TV wash over them.

'Mum, Dad and my sister are flying out to Lanzerotte on Thursday.'

'You're not going then?'

'I thought about it, but two weeks with the parents is something I can't cope with, so I fly out the following week to meet them.'

'That's good.'

'Yeah, flying out on the thirteenth when you hate flying.'

'You're not superstitious are you?'

He gave a slight shrug that said 'not sure.'

'You'll be fine.'

'Yeah,' he replied and gave her a squeeze. 'There's always the duty free.'

She tutted, 'is that what you're going to do all summer?'

'It is my favourite pastime... and all time hobby.'

She raised a slight smile at his humourous statement. Grinning back, he eased himself from her and went to serve dinner, thinking now only about getting a new bottle of vodka for the Iffley Bop. He could just see all those coloured bottles that the off-license was holding for him right now. The familiar clanking, the sound of the clicking top as it was being twisted off a fresh bottle.

The fridge light illuminated his face, he turned and asked if she would like a Guinness.

Trac studied his room for any changes and noticed his newly acquired Smirnoff poster tacked to the top of his built in wardrobe.

'So that's from last night I take it?'

'Yeah,' he nodded positively, 'souvenir' he commented. 'I'm going to put these frames up too,' and pointed to two large empty glass clip frames left over from his exhibition.

'What are you going to put in them, some of your work?'

'No, I thought I'd just start filling it with some of the best photos from parties and that,' he replied as he passed her an envelope. 'I wrote you a letter.' She enquired as to whether he was drunk when he wrote it? and he replied, 'nah, I was sober... ish.'

'It's a rare one then.'

'Yeah,' he replied mildly.

'Is it alright if I take a shower?' she asked.

'Sure as long as I can undress you,' he smiled briefly trying to camouflage his excitement.

'We can't do anything, it's that time of the month,' and she disappeared into the bathroom. He was half asleep when she entered back into the room. She switched the TV on, dried her hair and allowed him to brush it.

'Shall we watch a film?' he suggested.

'Yeah alright.'

To a tuneless hum he shuffled through his video collection. An hour later he complained about his eyesight. Trac informed him his eyesight was perfect and that it was his mind that was gone. He simply frowned at her.

'Say something sexy,' he said.

'Nooo.'

'Oh come on.'

She shook her head.

'Okay,' he chuckled. 'Say really big penis.'

Trac's face scrunched up slightly and it made him laugh. 'I'm not saying that,' she said rigidly.

'Say something sexy then.'

She gave no reply so he repeated himself as he began to undress her, his eyes seemed to glaze over.

'How is she then?' he growled kissing her stomach followed by making a rasping sound.

'No we can't,' she blinked, her face flexing with restraint.

'It's not my fault, I never used to be like this before I met you,' he said as he began to squeeze her bottom tightly. 'I'm sorry if I'm turning into a bit of an animal but you're just too sexy to cope with.'

'So I'm the only one?'

'Yep there's only one.'

'Because I put up with everything.'

'Like what?'

She glared at him and he responded, 'alright we won't go into that now.' and made a second louder rasp on her stomach and made his way up to her breasts.

'Smooth, firm and perfectly rounded,' he mumbled. 'Come on let's do it.'

'Fine if you want blood all over the sheets.'

'I know,' he said, 'hold on.'

He positioned two towels on top of the duvet. 'There.'

'Okay,' she said, and gave a slight nod of her head.

He rolled onto his front asking her to scratch his back as he stretched out.

'I haven't got any nails,' she sighed.

'Oh go on,' he insisted.

She gave him a massage and kept tugging at his jeans until he helped her remove them and pulled her to him. His lips burning on her shoulder, she was aroused. He pressed against her feeling the springiness of her body, it was as though they were wrestling. His arms were thin but muscular and quick, strapping her to him. Her breasts pushed into his chest, soft, pointed and gleaming. He locked his mouth to hers, searching for her tongue. His head began to swim with half fused thoughts as he eased his way down her body and attempted to pull her knickers off with his teeth.

'Jay,' she whispered and pulled away from him slightly but he insisted they came off.

He twirled his finger round the string of her tampon and began to pull slowly.

'You don't have to do that.'

'No, it's alright I want to.'

'I'm not sure if we can,' she whispered, her body becoming increasingly hot. She closed her eyes, her control was slipping as he placed the tampon to the side and he reached for the Durex with a natural carefree ease. The dome of the rubber squashed by the packet popped out to his touch. Kissing her stomach he slowly made his way back up to her mouth. Wild horses couldn't drag him away, the desire, the lust was too strong. She wrapped her legs around him. The sudden warmth seeping into his whole body with a sense of relief ran through his head. Smooth rhythm, slow and then quicker, interrupted by a fast hasty motion and then back to slow and smooth again. He wanted to last for hours but his body ached to release as soon as possible to flush out the tension within him.

He made love to her a couple of times until he admitted he was worn out and sat up, flushed and breathless. He was blissfully happy that they had become more and more intimate with each other's bodies over the last month. He wanted to be at one with her body and offered, and then tried his best to insert a fresh tampon. Fumbling away it reminded him of trying to get his house key into the front door after too much booze... hopeless. After a few minutes and with no luck he let her take control and yet he felt somehow defeated at the lack of achievement.

'I don't believe I'm doing this in front of you,' she mumbled.

'I want to share everything with you,' he said softly and kissed her knee. He slipped her back into her black underwear and they lay comfortably listening to music. He half fell asleep and she nudged him from time to time to make sure he was not going to abandon her totally. Minute by minute he recharged his energy, inched out of bed and pulled on his leather jacket. He felt a bulk in his pocket, it was his camera and she allowed him to take a few shots of her half naked.

'I love taking pictures of you,' he smiled coyly. 'My muse.'
Trac didn't say anything just smiled. He drifted away and returned with tea to find her asleep. He noted a small amount of light from the angle lamp highlighted her curves and threw a jet black shadow along the room behind her. Arms folded he leant himself against the door frame and appreciated the naked body on the bed, she looked natural and beautiful. He placed her mug down on his desk and drew open the curtains slightly as he eased himself onto the edge of the bed. He watched the trees move in the wind and enjoyed the warmth his mug made in his hands, it was nothing less than a pure fulfilling glow he was feeling. Once he had finished his tea he drew the curtains back and switched the light off.

'Trac, Trac,' he whispered massaging her shoulders. Her eyes opened partially with registration. 'I love you,' he whispered.

'Thank you,' she murmured, 'I love you too.'
He slipped her under the covers and joined her. He lay staring at the ceiling in thought. 'I remember my last school piss up,' he said smirking, 'I had some cheap lager and Pernod at a party in Shearsby. I woke up in a ditch half a mile away from the party, apparently I tried to walk home.'

'How did you get home?'

'Frankie made this lad who had a car come and find me,' he smiled. 'In those days I could get pissed on a fiver.'

'Pernod's quite nice.'

'I can't drink it now, even the smell of the stuff turns my stomach. I drank too much of it neat on Rob's seventeenth birthday. I couldn't stop being sick.'

He pondered on the past and smiled to himself. 'School used to be a great laugh.'

'I hate school,' she mumbled. 'It's boring,' and gave a yawn. 'I'm hoping it gets better in the sixth form.'

'The thing about school is you've got loads of mates from all over the place. Then when you leave you lose touch with them. It's a shame really.'

'You know Jay, you have a bad habit of staying attached to people.'

'Maybe,' he replied. 'I just don't know what I'm going to do now?'

'Well you've got your last college piss up. Just don't wander off and end up in a ditch somewhere. Then you can start thinking about what you're going to do.'

'I suppose I'll still try and get into another college,' and gave a shrug.

'Haven't you heard anything from Derby?'

'Nothing.'

'You should give them a ring.'

'Yeah you might be right.'

'What happens if you don't get in there?'

'My application goes into a pool with all the colleges that haven't got enough students. Just means I could end up miles away.' He nestled close to her and began to drift to sleep, still feeling the fulfilment.

At eleven she ran her fingers through his hair. 'I'm going to have to go home,' she whispered.

Reluctantly and clumsily he got out of bed, slipped on his jeans and pulled open the curtains so that the room was lit by the street lamp. She watched him carefully, pulling his white shirt on, he left the buttons undone and sat back down on the bed and gazed at her. They eyed one another hesitantly.

'You're not going home until I'm through with you,' he smiled. 'Dance with me.'

It seemed such an odd thing to do, but as he asked her again, she threw the hair back from her eyes, eyes which were sparkling with fun and put out her hand for him to take.

'I don't want to go,' she whispered as she sunk her head into his shoulders.

He looked into her radiant face and whispered, 'stay then,' and she responded with a peck on his cheek. 'Phone your mum,' he continued, 'tell her you'll be back in the morning.'

She pondered for a moment or two biting on her lip. 'Okay, I'll see what she says.'

Sunday, July 2

The outside world had gone, she felt warm and protected. At eight am Jay knew the clanking of the washing machine and hoover sounds that brought him from his sleep were the sounds of his mum's protest against Trac stopping over. He didn't have to be wide awake to understand what was happening.

'Your mum's up and about early,' mumbled Trac, as she rolled over closer to him and tried her best to sink her head under the covers away from the noise.

'What's up sexy pants?' she asked, running a hand across his chest.

'Mum, that's what,' he yawned

She followed his yawn with her own and began stretching out and rubbing her face into the pillow. When the hoover rasped, then banged repeatedly at his door, he lost his calm and flung the duvet back.

'For fuck's sake,' he muttered as he pulled on his jeans.

He opened his door sharply and glared at his mum. She returned the glare and for a moment or two there seemed to be a stand off right there on the landing. He began to sneer but stopped himself midway through and decided to play things a little different. He clapped his hands and began rubbing them together and smiled positively. 'Trac do you want some breakfast?'

'Please,' came her muffled reply.

'Right, bacon it is,' he said cheerfully and made his way past his mum smiling at the thunder in her eyes.

He returned armed with a tray of tea, toast and crispy bacon. Trac sat up in bed with an excited smile.

'You're spoilt, you are,' he said as he perched himself on the edge of the bed.

She stuck her tongue out at him and picked up a piece of toast.

'It's nice waking up together,' she said.

'Yeah,' he responded and took a sip of tea.

'Wish we could do it everyday.'

'You wouldn't get breakfast in bed everyday.'

'It's a bit of a tight squeeze in a single bed though,' she said.

'How about Saturday nights then?'

'Yeah, okay.'

'We just have to put up with my mum being grumpy.'

'Oh god,' she said putting a hand to her mouth, 'is it cos I stopped over?'

'Yeah,' he nodded and half smiled at her reaction. 'That's what all the noise was about, that was her subtle way of letting me know she's pissed at me.'

'I won't be able to face her now.'

He chuckled, 'you won't have to, I can keep you in my room all day.'

'Jay,' she sighed. 'I don't want to upset your mum.'

'Look, she's more than likely pissed off at me for not asking rather than you stopping.'

'You think?'

'Yep,' he nodded. 'Just means you're going to have to stick to me like glue.'

'Why?'

'Because, now I'm in for the standard lecture.'

'I thought that one was about the money you owe her?'

He raised a finger up at her and smirked. 'You're right, it's the second lecture, that I treat this house like a hotel. Anyway, while you're around she won't say a word.'

'Well, when I'm gone and you do get a hard time you can look at your diary.'

'Why,' he asked as he chewed on a rasher of bacon.

'Because I've filled in yesterday for you,' and she passed it to him.

Saw Trac, had an amazing evening xx was written in pencil. He smiled at her, 'well at least I can rub it out,' he smirked and she nudged him with her foot.

Sundays passed slowly and Jay liked them like that he thought, as he pulled The Beast up alongside Broughton Astley newsagents.

'Ice lollies,' he said as he jumped out from The Beast almost before it had stopped and darted into the shop. Trac, still containing the warm glow of waking up next to her man, had given him a stream of compliments, including how great he was looking. He'd studied himself for a second or two, he was his usual self? Maybe there was something warming and reassuring about him in his black shirt?

He appeared back in the driving seat alongside her with a big grin. 'Which flavour, orange or lemonade?' he asked slightly pushing the orange towards her.

'Orange,' she said and took it from him.

As The Beast came out of the bend from Broughton Astley a small red car, in front, pulled out to turn right. Caused by a lack of experience, or just plain poor judgement on the driver's part perhaps, an oncoming vehicle drove over the brow of the hill at speed. By the time Jay had requested Trac to change the music over he scrunched up his face as he bare witness to the events unfold before him. Remarkably the red car stopped and the oncoming car swerved across the other side of the road. It veered back too sharply, and a huge screech was followed by an eerie thud.

Jay bowed his head and muttered, 'fuck' before he pulled The Beast up onto the grass verge and got out.

'Stay there,' he said to Trac sombrely.

He approached the guys in the car first and said, 'move your car to the side of the road' to the pale looking driver. He looked to his left to see the other car overturned and embedded into a large ditch. He glanced around to see if there was anybody else to help but there was no-one. He looked over at Trac who was standing a few metres away from him, biting on her thumb looking anxious. He gave her a slight shrug, 'looks like it's me then,' he said plainly.

As he jumped down into the ditch the driver's door swung open and a transparent looking lady with blood in her hair and shock transfixed in her eyes looked at him feebly.

'You okay love?' he asked softly.

'I can smell petrol,' she replied nervously.

He looked around at his feet and could smell it too, yet it did nothing to faze him. The lady began to move to free herself frantically, breathing somewhat erratically.

'I'm not sure you should move just yet.'

The lady dropped a foot then the other into the ditch. He ebbed closer and put an arm round her.

'Sure you're okay to move?' he asked again.

'Yes,' she muttered as he helped her up out of the ditch.

Trac was still biting at her thumb as she took a step forward. Jay put up a hand to halt her as he saw a guy hurtle towards him from across the road.

'I've called an ambulance,' he blurted. 'I tell you we're always having accidents here.'

Jay looked up at him and nodded vaguely, pleased to let this guy with previous experience take over. He wandered over to Trac and sat down at the edge of the kerb chewing on a piece of long grass as two police cars accompanied by an ambulance arrived. Trac sat next to him leaning on his shoulder.

'You okay Jay?'

'Yeah I'm just glad it wasn't... you know worse.'

'Is she okay?'

'Think so, she's cut her head badly but...' he gave a light shrug.

One of the officers came over to him once the doors of the ambulance had been closed.

'You two see what happened?'

Jay squinted up and replied, 'yeah more or less.'

'Do you mind coming down to Lutterworth station to give us a statement?'

He looked at Trac then back up at the officer, 'I guess so.'

An hour later the two of them took a leisurely stroll down Jubilee Walk, they found it the best place to leave the day behind.

'I was impressed by you,' she whispered bringing her head against his chest.

'Yeah well,' he murmured.

'It was kind of weird though.'

'Why's that?'

'I don't know. I think it was because you were all calm and cool.'

'I just reacted didn't I.'

'It's just that I've never seen you all serious before... I don't know, it was just nice.'

'Yeah a rare moment I must admit.'

'We better get back, we're late for tea.'

He smiled and they turned and headed back down the track joined at the hip.

Monday, July 3

Jay woke the next morning feeling strangely rested. He soon found the reason for this, it was half past eleven. It was time for the last farewell session and he intended to party hard and get hopelessly drunk. Simon, the only resident of Iffley, a stern upright guy, had suggested they should meet at lunchtime so they could have a day's chatting and slow drinking. It must have been about one when Jay pulled up in The Beast at 186 Ashby Road, Loughborough and took a moment or two to take in Iffley House.

'Alright Jase?' came a voice from his left

He turned to see Dave walking towards him with a smile. 'How's it going big D?' he asked.

'Yeah,' replied Dave, 'not bad. They're all round the back.'

'Good,' he replied as he grabbed his stash of booze.

He sat feeling slightly distant, yet rightfully individual in a black T-shirt and cut off jeans amongst everyone else in flowered shirts and brightly coloured shorts.

'How come Adrian's not with you?'

He gave Dave a shrug that said 'I don't know' and took a gulp of beer.

'Maybe we should phone him,' muttered Dave as he checked his watch.

'I suppose.'

'I'd better get myself something to drink too,' said Dave, 'coming?'

Wandering up and down the drinks aisle at Sainsbury's, Dave studied the assortment of bottles reading out loud the alcohol percentages.

'I think I'll get a small bottle of Thunderbird wine,' he said rubbing at his chin.

Jay shook his head and Dave replaced the bottle back onto the shelf and carried on browsing. He paused looking for some kind of sign from Jay, yet his face remained expressionless.

'Trying not to get pissed?' jeered Jay. 'Get some vodka down you.'

'Yeah,' he nodded. 'Yeah alright I will,' and picked up the smallest bottle.

'Come on Dave,' said Jay picking up a larger bottle. 'To get really pissed you need a big bottle,' and passed it to him.

'No... not sure... what about half a bottle,' he replied beginning to look worried by the quantity.

'Okay,' Jay grinned, 'as long as you get the Thunderbird too.'

'I'll need something to mix it with.'

'It's alright, I've got some lime.'

Jay studied Dave reading the back of his bottles as they made their way to the checkout. He remembered how he was the protector of the Iffley gang and had proved himself on the night a spate of booze theft from an unattended bar provoked the bouncers at Tubes nightclub. As Dave launched himself into action with a number of spectacular martial arts manoeuvres, high kicks and roars, he defended his drunken buddies with ease, he was to them a true superhero in action.

'What you smirking at Jay?'

'Nothing mate,' he chuckled and patted him on the shoulder.

At Iffley they sat around the garden in the beige and green chairs dragged from the lounge. Jay finished his beers then stuck two straws in the top of his vodka bottle and began. The fun and games consisted of football and a full scale water fight, Simon had not only built a huge barbecue out of bricks but a waterslide down a long length of clear plastic which was immense fun all round once the beer had began to kick in. Jay started to go through the motions of getting drunk from sucking up streams of vodka, soon he would be ready for all kinds of mischief. Adrian finally turned up and, with not a milligram of alcohol in his bloodstream. Jay endeavoured to cover himself from head to foot in tomato ketchup and sun cream in protest to his pal's lack of commitment to the bottle. Dave followed suit and poured the contents of his beer bottle over his head and laughed out loud as he did so. Adrian was quick to defend himself, 'it's only seven o'clock and you lot are pissed already.'

'Of course we are,' jeered Jay, 'we're out our fucking heads.'

At eight thirty, and with more than half of the vodka consumed, Jay somehow had got tangled up and was incoherently wrestling with a chair. When he gave up the struggle he began to choke on the springs until he was close to passing out. Paul spotted him spluttering, and pulled the thick rope-like spring from his neck while Simon tried to seize a moment in which to snatch away his remaining vodka.

'Come on Jay, you've had too much.'

'No,' he spat. 'I haven't had nearly enough,' he said holding the vodka bottle by its neck tightly to his chest.

'Alright. Just calm down for a bit.'

'What for?' grunted Jay, slouching to the ground.

'Because you're getting out of hand and you've upset the landlady.'

'When?' he retaliated.

'Twenty minutes ago,' he replied looking confused.

'Never.'

'You did.'

'I haven't done anything,' he protested with a slur trying now to get back onto his knees and shaking his head in denial.

'Jay you told her to fuck off.'

He smirked. 'Oh, that old battle axe,' he jeered. 'I thought she was the stripper.'

'For fuck's sake Jay, she's in her sixties.'

'Really...' he chuckled at his own wit. 'I bet she'd give a good blow job, especially if she took her teeth out.'

Simon looked blankly at him, not sharing in his spiteful humour, so Jay gave him a shrug that said 'okay I'll calm down' and proceeded to crawl off on his hands and knees. Walking, it seemed, posed too much of a challenge. Dave, also in a poor state, had drank plenty of beer, wine and polished of most of his vodka and was flat on his back. With a drunken smile glued to his face, and a bottle in his hand, he was immune to everything.

An hour of relative calmness, in which more than half the people were not even slightly merry, gave Jay a further feeling of being on the outside without his drinking buddy by his side. What annoyed him further was the relative strangers that appeared and boasted at how much they had drank, the place just seemed incredibly dull without his partner in crime. Vodka had got a hold of him now as he sat on his own swaying lightly and studying the pond for signs of fish. As he leaned in closer to the murky water, only registering his reflection, he slipped falling head first, conscious only in holding the vodka bottle aloft. Flapping about and grappling his way to the edge, he made it halfway out and blacked out. Simon, on the brink of losing his patience, now saw the opportunity to snatch the bottle away from him while he lay there sprawled out in an unconscious heap face down like a cardboard cut out.

From the foetal position he began to stir, a splutter then a cough, he had come out of his short hibernation. 'Where's my fucking vodka?' he blurted, and no-one replied. 'Bastards,' he spat before passing out again.

'Come on, we can't leave him like that,' said Paul.

'Yes we can,' grunted Simon sipping at a beer. 'Do you know as well as all that vodka the twat's drank, Dave gave him half a bottle of milk of magnesium.'

Paul pulled a confused face. 'Why?'

'Because he's fucking nuts that's why!'

'He'll do anything when he's pissed.'

'Exactly!' and pulled a puzzled face as they dragged him closer to the fire in an attempt to dry his clothes and to at least stop him from going blue.

When the fire died down and he'd not stirred for a while, they got a little worried and dragged him off to the kitchen and put his head under the cold tap. After a few minutes he became conscious enough to speak with a slur.

'Jay, give me your T-shirt. I'll get it dry for you and you can wear one of mine until then.'

'Cheers Simon,' came a babbled reply.

Adrian stood watching the whole thing, still sober. There was a girl on the premises and his sexual intentions had stolen him away.

He stared at Jay's back with wonder at a number of scratches it had, 'how'd you get them?'

'Eh? Jay grunted.

'Your back.'

He glanced over his shoulder and just mumbled, 'Trac.'

'Anyway I got to get back,' he said. 'Ding ding dink.'

'Sure,' he replied in a dry tone.

Simon had built the fire back up, Jay moved close, he had calmed down a little now that tiredness was setting in, disappointed that this was not turning out to be the biggest and best party ever. The past days at Iffley had been far superior, too much fun had led to complaints and its demise. He smiled as he remembered Adrian's unashamed nob exposure, a girl caught him urinating over the communal ironing board and went berserk, hitting him with any object she could grab hold of whilst he had stood, disorientated in just a T-shirt, giggling at all the misbehaviour. He had encouraged it and thrived on it, it had all seemed like perfectly normal behaviour... fun and frolics. Now only Dave was his kindred spirit, even though he was still out cold on the floor, but at least he was naked.

Adrian had invited the fashion girls over for some food, and as they all queued along looking at Dave in his birthday suit, Adrian remarked how much better this exhibition was compared to his end of year show. Rekindling some energy, Jay found his vodka, sucked on it like a dummy until it had gone and ineptly wandered off to another party by junction 23 of the M1. It took him a while to get there but with Dave out cold, and Adrian still failing in his drinking duties, it seem the best option. His spirits began to lift when he heard music getting louder and louder as he plodded on feeling sure he had made the right decision. The journey seemed to have taken him longer than predicted but the fresh air and walk had made him feel a little more sober so that was an unforeseen bonus seeing as how the night was still young. Once inside he headed for the bar and bumped into Dave's girlfriend, which turned out to be another bonus. She brought him several drinks until he divulged the state Dave was in.

'I'll get us a taxi down there,' she said anxiously.

'No way,' he said. 'It took me ages to walk here.'

'Come on Jay. Come with me.'

'No, I like this party, it's got life. No-one's down there and there's no booze left either.'

'Come on Jay please. I'll buy you another drink.'

'What now?' he grinned pushing the empty short glass towards her and she picked it up.

'What do you want?'

'Vodka... double.'

'As long as we leave soon.'

'Sure,' he replied.

On his return to Iffley his legs felt like lead and he struggled to keep his eyes open, he'd had way too much. He got the blame for the state Dave was in and he had no Adrian next to him to take at least fifty percent of the blame. Feeling ever woozy and pie-eyed, he folded up once more wishing Trac was with him, to spoon him, to love him, hug him and keep him warm.

Tuesday, July 4

'Jay get up... Jay.'

'Awww, my head's killing me,' he swiped his left arm out. 'Leave us,' he uttered.

Looking worse for wear he took his time to come round. His eyes looked red and stayed squinted for a good ten minutes.

'Rough night eh?' asked Adrian.

'I still feel pissed,' he replied wearily.

'Here's some water and the kettle's on.'

He reached out his weary arm to take the glass. 'Cheers mate,' he mumbled, and sat drinking the water like a child holding it with two hands so he wouldn't spill a drop. He looked across at Dave's inert body and wondered if he was going to feel the same.

'How's he?'

'He'll be alright. I'll wake him up in a minute.'

'So you had a good time with that girl last night?'

'Yep,' Adrian smiled positively.

'Oh, I see.'

'What?' he chuckled innocently.

'You sad bastard making me cups of tea and smiling at me like a cat that's got the cream. Worth it was she?'

'Oh yeah.'

'Did I have a good time... cos right now I can't remember?'

'I'm sure you did.'

He pulled himself together and made it to the bathroom. Staring at the mirror he looked okay, just that he may have wet himself during the night by the looks of things, or someone else had pissed on him, either option was a possibility.

'Shit,' he sighed and wandered back to sit with his fellow sufferer who had now woken to the same feeling. Dropping his head and raising a hand to his brow to obscure himself Dave uttered, 'I need some water.'

'How's your head?'

'Awful,' coughed Dave as he rubbed at his pale and mournful face.

'Jeez, you two look rough,' came a chirpy voice.

'Piss off Simon,' Jay grunted.

'It was a joke.'

'I know, I just didn't think it was funny.'

Adrian switched the TV on and they sat gathering their energy, while Simon began the clean up operation.

'Where's my vodka bottle Simon?'

'It's in the bin,' he called, then popped his head through the kitchen door. 'Don't worry it's all gone.'

Jay picked himself up and rescued the empty bottle from a bin liner looked at the others and mumbled, 'souvenir.'

By two pm he was back to his normal self. Becoming restless, he announced his departure.

'Well lads, looks like this is it. You coming Adrian?'

'Yeah. I'll just get my stuff.'

The crowd of lads stood round The Beast. Jay and Adrian shook their hands, another brief chance to allow the drunken memories of the early days of Iffley to flood in. Jay pictured himself in his baseball jacket doing something daft and smiled wider with every handshake.

'So long then Dave,' he said giving him a friendly punch to the arm and stepped into The Beast and roared it into action. Adrian gave a quick wave of his hand, 'hang on Jay, wait for me,' he called as he scrambled to the passenger side. The Beast sped out of the driveway onto the road and disappeared.

10. Crazy, beautiful

Wednesday, July 5

Jay was on the sofa flipping through Trac's *i-D* magazine and failing to find anything of interest, twenty pages of summer fashion went over his head, but it had to be said that the graphic design was quite inspiring. Trac trooped around him tidying up and trying to locate the TV remote control. Once she had given up she muttered something in a negative tone and he threw the magazine onto the floor. Putting her hands to her hips she said, 'there's only a load of rubbish on anyway.'

He dived at the James Dean covered TV Times and quickly thumbed his way through it.

'*Blockbusters*,' he chirped looking up at her.

'Help me find the remote and you might be able to watch it.'

He fidgeted on the spot for ten or more seconds and retrieved the remote from down behind the back of the sofa and gave a smile. 'There we go.'

'You're not going to start flicking like you did yesterday?'

'No,' he mumbled shaking his head like he didn't understand what she was talking about, or as if it mattered. 'That was only because the *Lone Ranger* was on the other side yesterday.'

He fell further back into the sofa, adjusting the cushion for his head and put his feet up.

'And don't you get too comfy,' she said. 'Mum will be home soon.'

He smirked and gave her a lazy salute.

Thursday, July 6

Jay stood proudly with a drill in hand having just framed and hung his 'Elvis is Back' vinyl LP Cover. The two glass clip picture frames, semi filled with some of the best photos of the year so far, instantly became the favourite feature of his bedroom, it so perfectly complemented his collection of drunken souvenirs that were dotted around. On the downside though, he was not looking forward to being without a vehicle for a while. He had got so used to The Beast being there but it was time for its MOT. He collected his things together and decided to call in on Trac on his way.

'Mum, where's my black shirt?' he shouted.

'It's being washed,' she replied.

He grabbed it out of the tumble dryer and slipped it on.

'It's damp, you can't wear it,' she said in a raised voice.

'It's not damp,' he said positively, 'it needs ironing...'

He started the engine, lined up the music and was off. It soon dawned upon him that the interior state of The Beast was perhaps not the best impression to give the garage and so pulled over and collected everything up into a HMV carrier bag and slung it in the boot.

At the garage the mechanic greeted him as he handed over the keys reluctantly.

'Do a good job,' he said.

The mechanic simply winked and tottered off rattling the keys in one hand, scratching at his backside with the other, whistling out of tune. This caused Jay to frown, bow his head and kick a few stones as he pondered with concern. He made his way down to the pavement and wandered up to Trac's house. He arrived still in a state of mild worry, which was now becoming overshadowed by a certain loss of freedom The Beast offered. He found the front door open so he walked through calling her name.

'Out here,' came a shout from the direction of the garden.

He folded his arms and leaned on the open frame of the patio doors and admired her. 'Getting a tan are we?' he mooted.

'Yep, as you can see I'm really going for it in my summer gear.'

'All black,' he gave a smirk. 'Why don't you go topless?'

'No way,' she shrieked.

'Oh go on,' he continued, 'just for a couple of minutes.'

For some reason he was in a very breast worshipping mood. He pulled his shirt off and joined her on the tartan rug.

'Took The Beast to the garage,' he said, toying with the edge of the rug.

'Where?'

'Down the road here.'

'When will it be ready?'

'A couple of days I reckon,' he said. 'It needs some work, but the old man's paying so I'll be alright.'

'Any news from Derby yet?'

'Yeah, I got a letter. Apparently they've lost my application form.'

'You're joking, how?'

He gave a shrug. 'Don't know they wouldn't say.'

'What now?'

'They just said they will send me a list of colleges that are short of students.'

'Oh right, they don't seem that bothered.'

'Yeah, I told them I was pissed off about it and managed to force an interview out of them.'

'Well that's something.'

'I pressured them into it so I'd be wasting my time going.'

'They may have some advice, and it will be good experience.'

'I guess so,' he muttered not looking too convinced.

She gave a sigh and put a reassuring hand on his knee. 'Do you want something to eat?'

'Yeah, if it's not too much trouble.'

'No. I was going to make myself something anyway. I might as well feed you at the same time.'

She put the radio on and began fixing some food while he sprawled out across the rug still feeling his sense of loss.

'You want a cup of tea as well?'

'Vodka,' he jested.

She appeared with a small glass holding a clear liquid. No it can't be? he thought, it must be water?

'Here you go,' she said. 'Vodka.'

'Oh thanks,' he said and sipped at it, pleased that it was vodka.

He knocked the glass back and swore under his breath as he wandered over to the outside table. He helped himself to her expertly made salad cream and cheese sandwiches.

'You got any of those Animal Bite biscuits?'

'What made you ask that?' she said half smiling and half frowning.

'I just remember when I was a kid I used to eat sandwiches just like these and I'd have chocolate biscuits in the shape of various animals.'

'Right,' she nodded vaguely, 'no we haven't.'

'Oh well,' he smiled, took another large bite out of the sandwich he was holding and made his way into the shade of the kitchen following Trac on into her room.

'Mum and Dad are off to Lanzerotte tomorrow.'

'When do you go?'

'Next week.'

'Does that mean I can stop over every night.'

'Yeah if you want,' he nodded.

'I bet it will be boiling over there.'

'Probably... What's this?' he asked, noting a new addition to her cork notice board.

'An exercise chart.'

'I can see that, but what for? You're perfect.'

'Umm... not quite,' she said. 'It's to get rid of my podgy tummy,' and with that statement she lifted up her top and patted at her stomach.

'But I like your podgy tum,' he sighed. A glint appeared in his eyes then they narrowed slightly. 'Having said that, I do know a great form of exercise,' and he eased closer to her slipping his hands either side of her hips.

'And I bet I can guess what it is.'

'You know what they say... practice makes perfect.'

'So I'm not perfect then?'

'Yeah, you are, I was just a saying it to get you into bed.'

'So you're taking advantage of me then.'

'Of course I am,' he smiled and eased into her further.

He stripped her slowly, pulling off her jeans and her knickers. She smelt gorgeous to him, a mixture of her and the freshly washed underwear, it was heaven. He couldn't stop his heart pounding with heightened desire as the essence of her intensified.

'We should really do this at your place.'

'Why?'

'Someone might come home.'

'Doesn't that make it more exciting?'

Saturday, July 8

Jay did a lot of thinking lying in the bath. He observed the steam swirling upward as he contemplated the previous evening's drunken mishaps, positive points first. Okay, he reflected, Rob could have been sick all over him as opposed to his bedroom floor, the recollection of which made him cringe. He yawned as he made small ripples splash lightly over his chest. What a performance him laying haphazardly, half in a flower bed, half on someone's bowling green-like lawn, while Rob did his best to destroy it. Wham! A huge bolder piercing the owner's perfect turf. Wham! Another struck as Nick slurring persuasions to 'leave it' fell on deaf ears.

'Just... just... one more,' muttered Rob as he grappled with the last and largest stone.

You just can't beat getting blotto mused Jay as he rinsed the shampoo from his hair. He felt great, no hangover at all, and promised to drink wine more often. He searched about the water until he found the bar of soap, now soft and more pliable. He thought about using it, and then fell quickly off the idea as it seemed too much like hard work, he was pretty clean anyway. He dunked his head under the water for a second or two then reached to the floor for a towel, padded his face and wondered how many hours were left before it was time to meet Trac from work, giving him chance to buy another Elvis album and start his Presley mix.

Harmony was broken by the piercing cry of his mum, 'Tracey, your dad's here.'

'Oh shit!' he snapped. 'Quick.'

'What time is it?' she asked.

'Half eleven. I wish you could have stayed.'

She sat up, eyes still squinting, 'so do I.'

He grabbed her and kissed her in a hurried frenzy. 'I love you. Now come on,' he smiled pulling her from the bed. 'You've got to go.'

'Thanks,' she replied quietly.

It took himself seconds to slip his shirt and jeans on. He flung her clothes at her one by one and made for the door.

'I'll go downstairs,' he said.

'Where are my shoes?' she called holding her left hand to her forehead.

He ran down the stairs tucking his shirt as he went.

'Where's Tracey?' asked his mum.

He paused and looked at her father, 'er shoes,' he said quickly.

'Shoes?' repeated his mum.

'Yep' he shrugged at the two of them, 'she can't find her shoes.'

'Have you looked in the lounge?'

'No I've just come down the stairs, didn't you see me?' he joked to no response.

'Right,' he smiled quickly. 'I'll have a look,' and went for the lounge door.

'I've got them,' came a cry from behind him.

He turned back sharply to see Trac wiggling her feet into the black shoes before looking up at him. 'I'll see you tomorrow then?' she said softly.

'Okay.'

'Bye.'

'Bye,' and he shut the door behind her, walked into the kitchen and grabbed a couple of cans of Guinness out the fridge.

'What would her mother and father say if they knew what you two get up to?'

He gave his mum an unconcerned shrug and drifted back upstairs. He watched the TV for a while before putting on his stereo. He could still smell her on his pillow and happily drifted to sleep.

Sunday, July 9

Trac was contented to watch him busy beavering away in the loft. 'I've got a few things to sort out,' he had muttered.

She sat comfortably on the edge of the hatchway, peering around at all the boxes stacked three deep in places and the odd one open with items protruding out the top.

'It's amazing,' she said.

'What's that?'

'You must keep everything.'

'Just about. Problem is I don't know where half my things are.'

'You're not going to be long are you? I'm starving.'

'No, I'll make us some bacon sarnies in a bit.'

'Okay.'

'Here we go,' he chirped picking up a box. 'I think this is it.'

Trac hopped off the edge onto the ladder, made her way down to the landing and into his room as he followed with his box.

'What's in there then?'

He gave her a shrug. 'Stuff.'

'What stuff?'

'Just stuff.'

Kneeling on the bedroom floor he gave a couple of sneezes before sifting through the dust covered box.

'Boxing gloves,' he yelled with delight.

Putting them on quickly, he began to shadow box before turning his attentions to her. Tapping at her nearest shoulder lightly he manoeuvred her slowly into the corner of his room, where she cowered away from him.

'Jay... Jay! Don't... Stop it... You'll bruise me.'

He froze, 'I'm only playing,' he said beginning to smile, tapping the gloves together keenly.

'Well I don't like it, my brother used to do that to me all the time. I hate it.'

He pulled the gloves off, sat back down and rummaged through the box some more.

'Here,' he handed her a tiny bottle.

'What is it?'

'Jasmine oil. Perfume... smells good. Well at least I seem to remember it did at the time.'

'Where's it from.'

'I got it in Tunisia. I've been waiting to give it to someone for ages.'

'Thanks,' she smiled quietly, taking a sniff at the small bottle's contents.

'Right, that will do,' he said picking the box up and placing it back from where it came. 'So dusty up there,' he muttered as he removed his shirt.

'Don't get any ideas,' she smiled.

He smirked back. 'Hey,' he said ejecting the tape from his stereo. 'This is The Beast's new mix.'

'What's on it?'

Pulling a fresh black T-shirt over his head, he span round and said, 'Presley.' He reached for a black felt pen from his art box and wrote *The King!* in his cartoon style of writing along the tape's label.

'What now?'

'Food,' he said. 'I need some fuel too.'

The smell of the bacon lifted into the air and their noses turned to the direction of the frying pan, mouths watering and stomachs groaning.

'Mmm. I'm really hungry now,' she smiled at him softly.

Modestly he replied, 'I must say I'm an expert when it comes to bacon sarnies.'

'Your speciality,' she said.

'Yeah, apart from Marmite on toast that is.'

Her eyes squinted as she sank her teeth into the first sandwich he had mastered.

'Mmm,' she murmured with delight.

'Nice is it?' he asked and she replied with a nod of her head.

With her middle finger she smudged some tomato ketchup from the corner of her mouth. Jay stuffed the second almost complete sandwich into his mouth.

'Pig,' she said nudging him.

He mumbled something and she guessed it was a comment about her, so she marched off into the lounge. He followed her moments later with two cups of tea.

'Here you go.'

She was instantly settled, sunk back into the sofa reading the back of a book.

'What's this about?' she asked politely.

'Oh yeah, I was reading it earlier,' he said sitting down next to her. 'It's my mum's. What you do is work out your love number, mine is nine yours is seven. Then you find the section male nine, female seven, and it's supposed to tell you what your relationship is like.'

He sipped his tea and found the appropriate page for her.

'It says that nine is the greatest of all the love numbers.'

'It would be wouldn't it,' she said in a sarcastic tone.

He blanked her and continued. 'It says I'm trusting, honest, loyal,' he pointed to the text. 'I try to make my partner as happy as possible and is only difficult when he has good reason to be.'

'Interesting, but not sure that it's true.'

'It says both me and you have high levels of ESP,' he said positively. 'We also have unpredictable flashes of pure inspiration.'

'What's this?' she laughed. 'They are completely in tune with one another, a harmonious relationship.'

He responded with a frown.

She squinted at the text then frowned herself. 'Mr nine is romantic, passionate and impulsive.'

'Yeah, I'm inspiring and have a big influence over people.'

She sighed, 'you just want to read all the good stuff about you.'

'Okay,' he snorted and stuck his tongue out at her as he flipped through some of the pages. 'Look... it says you're intelligent, a big thinker, and are really keen to learn.'

'Apparently I'm extremely affectionate too.'

'What else?'

Her finger ran along the copy. 'Our numbers are a great match, and what goes on in the bedroom should be left to the imagination!'

'There you go then, our combination is almost entirely perfect,' he said sipping at his tea.

'Is it?' she questioned.

'That's what it says, besides Virgos and Capricorns get on well don't they?' She nodded positively as he pulled her close and kissed her cheek. 'I can tell you that you're beautiful... and you don't need a book to tell you how great you are.'

Tuesday, July 11

'That was a fucking waste of time,' chuntered Jay as he slotted his portfolio behind the back of The Beast's driver's seat. He remained standing outside, elbows leaning on its black vinyl roof and rubbing at his brow, annoyed that the interview Derby College had just given him was embarrassingly informal on their part, so soul destroying that the only praise he was given was for arriving early.

The curly topped unshaven tutor had said, 'yeah looks like you perhaps need to do another year, say a foundation course or something similar,' whilst slouching against the common room's table tennis table where his portfolio lay. The guy lethargically muttered occasionally and sipped at his coffee from a badly stained cup in between smoking a skinny roll up. Jay had perched on the rim of a small wicker chair trying his best to resist the urge to get up and knee the bloke between the legs.

Trac had waited nearly a full minute before getting out of The Beast and levelling up to him on the opposite side of the roof.

'No good then?' she asked politely.

He shook his head looking extremely displeased. 'Like I said, a complete waste of time.'

'Well let's get out of here,' she suggested and he responded by giving her a half hearted smile.

'Mc Donald's... my treat?' she said encouragingly which managed to raise the corners of his mouth upwards.

'You know, you're right,' he replied positively allowing to be buoyant again. Not wishing to waste anymore time worrying about the loss of his time that could never be replaced with something better. He dropped into the driving seat started the engine and said, 'Big Macs?'

'And strawberry milkshakes too,' said Trac smiling.

'Okay then,' he chirped slapping her thigh, a gesture that said 'thanks for being here.'

'That's okay I've nothing better to do.'

'I've got to get out of these clothes.'

'You do look smart.'

'Don't feel like me though,' he replied slipping on his black shirt. 'That's better... half way there, just need my jeans to feel normal again.'

Jay was leaning against his chest of drawers having changed back into his usual attire fully and was grinning widely.

'What's up with you?' Trac asked.

'Some girl fancies me,' he chuckled.

'Yeah right,' she mooted.

'Really. Look, she has written me a letter...' and he picked up a small folded piece of paper from his desk.

Sizing up what he held in his hand she said, 'let me read it then.'

'No... no... no,' he smirked shaking his finger at her.

She chased him round his room frantically as he carried on laughing with enjoyment. He stood on his bed holding it aloft so she couldn't reach it.

'I'll read it to you,' he chuckled. 'I'll read it.'

'You're a sod sometimes,' she muttered and folded her arms as she sat back down.

He stepped down and took command of the small area of carpet his room offered, rustled the piece of paper in front of himself and gave a slight cough before he began only to be rudely interrupted.

'It's not a speech you're giving,' she snapped.

'Do you want to know what it says?'

She gave him a shrug that said 'not bothered.'

'Well?'

'Get on with it.'

'Okay, here we go. *Hi there again...* again that's strange I don't recall meeting her,' and he pulled a pondering face. 'Must have been during one of my black outs... Anyway,' he gave another cough, '*well I just thought I'd write you this little note when you saw me last night and asked me why I kept smiling and waving at you. It wasn't because I knew you. It was really because I think you're just so devastatingly handsome,*' he looked up and widened his smile and Trac emitted a sigh. '*Although I don't suppose that means much coming from a plain ordinary girl like me. I mean you must be used to girls with model looks eh? Anyway I wrote this little note just to say hello. I hope it's cheered up your day for you? Although knowing my luck it's probably made you really miserable and you're probably thinking oh my God! Please whatever you do don't show this to your girlfriend,*' he chuckled. 'Bit late for that... *and I know you must have one. I mean who could resist your good looks,*' and he chuckled some more.

'She's laying it on a bit thick,' muttered Trac.

He frowned at her for the interruption and continued. '*Well I must go I've been wasting too much of your time as it is. Hope to see you again sometime.* And three kisses.' He smirked further, 'what a lovely girl,' he said. 'Oh and there's a P.S. *If by a chance in a million you haven't got a girlfriend then maybe you'd like to come down to Narborough park tonight around eight o'clock, only if you're desperately bored.*'

'I suppose your head's the size of this room now.'

He looked at his watch and mused, 'I might have to nip out for a bit.'

'Don't you dare,' she exclaimed snatching at the letter.

He objected, 'come on give it here, I'm not really going to go.'

'Devastatingly handsome?' she exhaled deeply.

'Yeah, well.'

'And what's this about seeing her last night,' she quirked an enquiring eyebrow at him.

'I did drive past some blonde girl.'

'Oh yeah?' she mumbled. 'Then what's this about you stopping and asking her about smiling and waving at you?'

'Okay, I did stop for a sec. I thought I must know her from some place.'

'Is she pretty?'

'I wouldn't say no,' he said giving her a cheeky grin and she dug her elbow in his side.

'Do you want your balls to remain attached to your body?'

That didn't sound so good so he pulled away from her.

'I'm just kidding. I'm head over heels with you,' he said quietly.

'Honestly?'

'Honestly,' he said, but it didn't stop his devilish mood. 'Besides you've got half naked blokes all over your bedroom walls.'

'So, that's different.'

'Why is that?'

'Oh, I'm going to make a drink,' she smirked and waved a hand as if to say end of conversation.

Wednesday, July 12

By now Trac's record of black stars littered her calendar and today had four stars so far. She went on to work out that they had made love twenty times in twenty four days.

'Does that sound bad to you?' she asked. He didn't seem to think so, shook his head lightly at her and replied, 'it's completely healthy.'

'It's weird though, from never doing it to doing it almost every day.'

'Suppose.'

'Five more and we can celebrate a quarter of a century.'

'We do spend a lot of time in my room and never seem to be doing much else.'

'We'll have to take up a hobby like Scrabble or something else that's as much fun like chess.'

'Could do,' he mumbled, and branched out with a yawn. 'Maybe we should have some days without it?'

'Umm, that'll be easy,' she said flatly.

'I don't know,' he yawned again.

'Well it's a good job you're off on hols as we'd be lucky to last twelve hours.'

'Hey, speak for yourself,' he smirked. 'I know I could hold out. I'm just not sure you could.'

'Yeah right!' she chuckled sarcastically, before moving in to kiss his neck and nibble at his ear, rearing up his energy levels.

'Maybe we should get out of bed,' she smiled.

'Well if you don't want to,' he exhaled teasingly.

'No... no... I didn't say that.'

He gave a soft chuckle. 'You are worse than me.'

'I know,' she said nudging him. 'To tell the truth I can't help myself, I always seem to end up wanting to jump on you. I don't know what it is... this control, or power you have over me but it's pretty damn strong.'

'Good, because I want to stay right here all night.'

Thursday, July 13 - 19

He made his way through East Midlands airport customs without a problem but boarded the plane with a vain of worry. He sat squeezing the armrest and looking out of the small port hole window at the tarmac runway. He tried to think about Trac in order to suppress his growing nerves, but it wasn't working.

'Are you alright?' asked the old lady next to him.

'Fine. I'm... fine,' he replied hesitantly.

The plane's engine roared into life, his heart shuddered. Those vodkas in the airport lounge had done little to calm him. The pilot mumbled a few words as the plane picked up speed. He clamped his headphones over his ears and pressed play. The stewardess had been through the safety routine with the worse false smile he had ever seen. As he clutched the laminated safety pamphlet, the plane took to the air. Turbulence rattled the plane and his heart quickened. The old lady stared at him and he gave her nothing, his face a pasty blank canvas. Slowly his discomfort eased as the plane settled in flight and the hostess began to move about the cabin smiling, not as false as before and putting his fears at ease. The meal was a little rubbery but welcomed. He had a few more drinks to wash it down and prepared himself for the landing.

The landing wasn't feared as much as the take off, but he held his bottom lip with his top teeth as the plane started its decent. At touchdown he felt relief wash over him, but soon became anxious and agitated at the queue to get off and didn't feel entirely relaxed until his feet touched solid ground.

He sat waiting for his luggage and became increasingly restless and irritated by most of the people surrounding him. He just wanted to push them away from him, grab his bag and go somewhere, anywhere less crowded. He finally retrieved his bag from the conveyor belt and wandered through customs, greeted by his mum, dad and sister. He smiled and pulled off his headphones, glad that finally he was treated to some space, breathable air and the conclusion that he simply hated everything about flying.

'You got here then?' said his mum, constantly unsure he could do anything for himself. 'Was the flight alright?' she continued.

'Yeah, I'm here. I'm not a hologram,' he snapped, 'and the flight was awful.'

'Oh well you're here now.'

They walked out into the heat and he threw his bag into the boot of their crap hire car. The first thing he did when he got to the apartment was to switch on the TV and slump in front of it with a cold beer, at which point his mum began her first stint of nagging.

'Come on outside,' she muttered while hovering over him.

'I'm alright here.'

'Get yourself in the swimming pool, it's lovely.'

So is this beer he thought taking a swig and looking at his dad for support.

'Leave him,' his father bellowed, 'he's alright.'

He was like his dad on holiday, he wasn't keen on the hot weather, it was okay for a day or two but a whole week roasting was not his idea of relaxing, it just made him uncomfortable.

'What's the point spending the money on a holiday just to come out and sit in the sun, burning, getting skin cancer and being irritated by kids?' he uttered.

'I don't know why I bother,' moaned his mum putting her hands on her hips, a sign that she was close to giving up. 'You come all the way out here just to sit in front of the TV.'

'No I came out here to get pissed,' he muttered.

'Pardon?'

'Nothing,' he said and let out a long drawn out sigh that drove her away. He began to slouch, more relaxed in his chair after the third bottle of San Miguel. He came to the conclusion he was a shade person. If he was out in the sun and there was a piece of shade he would be in it. He would attempt to tan himself for a while until he got too hot and bothered, but his whole idea of a holiday was getting up late in the morning and going to bed late at night, and in between was to drink, be merry and have fun.

That evening they had a large meal. Jay chose lobster and his dad was not impressed with the price, which turned from a debate into an argument.

'I just wanted to try something different,' justified Jay. 'I didn't know it was going to be a whole lobster.'

There and then he realised that the family holiday was well and truly over, his flying over to meet them was not just about the duty free or visiting some place different, it was a last ditch attempt at trying to prolong the family holiday too. Time had moved forward and he failed to feel any guilt for not wanting to be with them. They only seemed to tie him down and hold him back. The more he felt that way the more resistant and antisocial he became. By the time these thoughts had cleared from his head and Trac returned there to put a smile on his face and a flutter in his chest, he was sat outside Charles' bar, pushing at an ice filled vodka and lemonade with a straw. It was here that he was introduced to a lad his sister had met. He was in his early to mid twenties and he thought he looked like the kind of guy who sold insurance or worked in a bank, plain and clean looking. Jay took an instant dislike to this lad, he was deemed to be too old to be with a sixteen year old and no-one seemed to be saying anything about that, so he began his own rude and sarcastic campaign, hoping his opinion was noted forthwith. When no-one responded he gave up. His eyes rested on the blackboard behind the bar, happy hour lasted another half an hour.

'Better get another one,' he muttered as he shuffled off.

He was suitably impressed by the large shots of vodka he was receiving from the bar and the night suddenly began to have that drunken magical feel about it as the alcohol filtered through his veins. After five or six of them he wondered down to the main strip to take in the atmosphere, he was stopped on his travels by a tall slim tanned girl in a glittering bikini.

'Would you like to come in here... free tickets,' she smiled.

He gave her a shark's grin, 'no I'm alright,' he said, holding up his hands and waving them slightly.

'Are you on your own?'

He looked round shrugged his shoulders and smiled, 'yeah I am.'

'Where are you off to?'

'Erm, I'm going to the Club Paradise,' and he wandered off smiling, turning in a circle before walking off up the steps towards the club.

It was as though he was in slow motion, as he studied and soaked up the sounds, colours and the people. He paused at the top of the stairs leading to the club, looked back from where he came and realised he had no idea where his hotel was. He rubbed at his forehead for a second slightly confused before giving into the pulsating music and joyful sounds coming from within this so called club of paradise.

Looking across the crowd of people in front of him, he surveyed the dance-floor and studied the flashing lights momentarily before making his way to what seemed to be the right direction to a bar. Once there he thought, so far so good.

Drowning in a sea of people he was missing Trac enormously. The music was not to his taste, so dancing didn't seem much of an option. Desperate to make conversation he attempted communications with a pretty German girl. He soon got fed up of saying 'what?' and being given funny looks. He got a bar stool and propped himself up against the aluminium bar top and drank more vodka, now only accompanied by a couple of ice cubes. He wondered if he would pass out as his head began to spin and his vision became slightly impaired. He smiled wearily at the German girl still next to him and then went reeling out into the fresh air where he felt a little more relaxed. More and more vodka began to kick in, and before he knew it, he was blind drunk. He moved slowly in what he believed to be the direction of his chalet, a drink still in hand, he slipped, fell and bashed badly against a wall.

'Excuse me mate are you okay?' asked a passer-by.

'Yeah,' he spluttered struggling to get steady on his feet.

'Come on you've had too much mate,' smiled the stranger, finding his state amusing.

'I'm alright,' he slurred. 'Get off me,' he spat trying to prise himself away. The more he struggled to do so, the more he felt he was being stopped from doing what he wanted. 'Get the fuck off me,' he snapped at the passer-by who was trying to motion him to sit down and rest.

'You don't look well at all. Let's sit you down.'
Jay threw a violent swing of his shoulders at him and the guy now impatient with his lack of appreciation let him be. He struggled to get himself seated on a wall, but once he did, he rested for five or ten minutes before standing.

'One more for the road,' he mumbled with a dazed smile. He lurched off up the street knocking the rest of his vodka back and placed the empty glass to his right on the four foot white wall that never seemed to end. He staggered a few yards off the main drag before collapsing into a flowerbed. Seconds later he was unconscious.

At four or five in the morning he felt something wet on his face and opened his eyes. He heard voices and squinted upward in disgust at two security men with an over friendly dog which kept on licking at his face. The man with the dog seemed very uptight and the second one dragged him to his feet.

'You can stand now eh?' said the man with a big bushy moustache.

'Yeah,' replied Jay rubbing his face.

'I come two hours ago. I pick you up you just fall down. You not speak your eyes dead. You stupid.'

'Sorry,' he croaked and began frowning and rubbing his eyes trying desperately to bring himself round but he still felt smashed out his head. He had to agree with the bushy moustache, he could at least talk and walk a little better than earlier and he had to be happy with that.

'You not know how to handle drink?'
He shook his head at the guy, that was all he needed a lecture in the early hours of the morning from a foreigner.

'Where you stay eh? This is private hotel you know.'
The two guards began to escort him out and he had no energy with which to retaliate, he just stayed mute, all he could think about as he wandered back was how strange it was that he had seemed to have gone from being sober to blotto without the merry stage of bouncing about shouting and laughing. He spent a good hour finding the right hotel. As he tip toed through the reception doors, stumbling, he fell onto the large plant pot in the hallway, hurling soil everywhere and breaking the silence.

'Shit,' he babbled to himself and followed it with a little giggle as he scrambled to his feet and snuck off quickly.

The morning sun filled the chalet. He found himself on his back, naked apart from his sister's dressing gown. It bemused him that he was in this position as he normally slept on his front and under the sheets, and when he came to fully he realised he wasn't even on his own bed. This didn't alarm him at all, waking up half in a bush had only served him to appreciate a soft mattress all the more. He felt his arms and face hurt and looked down to see various superficial grazes about his body.

'Awwgh fuck,' he groaned slipping the gown off and getting into his own bed. It was too confusing to figure out where his sister was? Or whether he might even be in the wrong apartment? He just hid himself under the sheets and slept.

The whole week he was nagged at and told he was stupid for being so drunk, which only served to fuel him all the more. Time became irrelevant and he liked that a lot. The only constructive thing he could remember was going to the market and buying Trac an enamelled bracelet before running off down an empty ally to be sick. He had not been sick for years and was disappointed in himself for not holding what was left of last night's liquor. The local booze was cheap with large measures, and what was supposed to have been Guinness was something dark and quite vile, yet he drank it all the same. The heat and blinding sun didn't help with the hangovers, it only seemed to make them worse, but he had to keep going.

By the end of the week he was worn out and ached for Trac emotionally and physically. On his last morning he had the mother of all hangovers thanks to a large selection of potent cocktails. His ill-fated plan to drink for free by offering up tasting comments and consume every one on the bar's list had left him feeling nauseous, his tongue thick with gunge and head throbbing with the occasional splitting pain that ran across his temples.

'Where did you disappear to?' came his mum's voice.

'Err don't know?' he grumbled.

Smelling something horrid he looked over the edge of the bed and down at the floor.

His mum suddenly shrieked at him, 'what's all this... sick!'

'It's mainly last night's dinner...' he replied flippantly, 'vodka, maybe some Ouzo in there somewhere,' and turned away from her.

'You've got a problem, you're bloody mental.'

'No, no problem,' he grunted. 'I love it,' he uttered in a more spiteful tone.

'Get it cleaned up.'

Cursing he was on his hands and knees mopping the floor, he had to keep turning away to stop any unwelcome additional bile. He was even more disappointed that he had not held his drink down for the second time. The only excuse he could muster this time was the Ouzo. Similar to Pernod, the one thing he could not consume in great amounts. Mopping vomit up with a hangover made him gag more than half a dozen times and his mum seemed to enjoy how grumpy and pathetic he looked. At this point he actually began to look forward to the flight home. He couldn't wait to feel alive again and be in Trac's arms where he belonged, knowing she somehow had the amazing ability to make him feel a whole lot better.

Thursday, July 20

He rushed up behind Trac catching her around the waist and lifted her effortlessly from the floor and looked at her with immense satisfaction.

'How's my favourite girl been?' he asked excited and invigorated at seeing her. 'Missed me?'

She turned and kissed him, 'yep,' she said cheerfully.

'Well I'm here, tanned and sexy,' and gave her a twirl. 'The one and only, roll out the red carpet.'

'Give me another hug then,' she smiled.

He closed his eyes and breathed in her scent. Mmm he thought as they kissed lightly, bliss. Craving her, he failed to play it cool and suppress his excitement. He forced her into one of the shop's changing facilities and began to kiss her passionately his hands moving about her body with speed and no self control.

'Get off,' she whispered. 'Wait... wait till later.'

He moved his hand down between her thighs and began to squeeze hard through her jeans.

'Get out of there,' she whispered slightly alarmed.

'I want you,' he whispered. 'I want you now.'

'Well you can't,' she said pulling his hands from her.

He kissed her again and this time she could taste something strong, whiskey she guessed .

'Have you been drinking?'

'Only a bit,' he smiled and she looked doubtfully at him. 'To calm me down,' he said quickly. 'You know how I hate flying.'

'So how much booze did you bring back?'

'One bottle.'

'Just one bottle?' she quizzed, staring into his eyes unsure he was telling the truth.

'Yeah just the one. Honestly,' he chuckled. 'Now are you coming round after work or what?'

'Well that depends,' she teased.

'I'll show you my white bum.'

'Mmm,' she gave him a mischievous glint. 'Okay.'

His heart bounced as he recognised that look, 'can you leave early?'

'Nope, but I won't be long, you'll just have to wait.'

'Okay, I'll meet you over here by the door,' he nodded and she smiled and nodded a yes back.

Time had suddenly become relevant again. He tried to keep his lust at bay by shuffling through some of his favourite band's back catalogue in every nearby record store, but it was no use he soon returned, so impatient pacing outside the shop. Finally Trac came jogging out and they hugged in the street. Walking to the car park he couldn't keep his hands off her, walking faster and faster to The Beast. He could feel her sense of urgency and felt more at ease with the fact that she had to contain herself too, the excitement shone in both their eyes.

'I'm glad I'm back,' he beamed. 'I was going out of my head without you.' He glanced about furtively as he crossed the road hoping to see an opportunity in which to pounce on her in The Beast. There were too many people about, he thought sod it! Let's do it right here, right now anyway, but then he knew she wouldn't allow it.

He sparked The Beast into life and sped out of the car park. All the way home his hand kept on slipping from the gear stick to hold Trac's hand and then quickly slipping down between her thighs. Having an erection most of the way home was very uncomfortable. The excitement mounted as they pulled up to his house, they had barely got through the front door when she grabbed at his belt.

'How's my friend in there?' she growled.

'Excited by you.'

They hurried upstairs into his bedroom and stood looking at each other both aware of their desire. He felt naked under his clothes already as if everything he wore was risen slightly to allow a draft of Trac to touch him.

'I've been aching for you,' he whispered, eyes transfixed.

'Me too.'

The whole day had been humid and the sunlight flooded into the house creating a golden glowing haze. He sat back on his bed motioning her towards him much to her delight. Taking both her hands as she sat down, she wiggled a little and played with his hair, looking at him emotionally.

'I feel so warm now you're back,' she smiled.

'Let's do it,' he whispered into her ear.

He started slipping his hands under her low cut top that fell short of reaching her belly button, revelling in the fact that she wasn't wearing a bra. He ran a warm palm up to her collar bone and then down, cupping her small firm breasts. Her nipples reared at his touch and she excitedly pulled her T-shirt up and over her head, letting it drop to the floor. He then unfastened her jeans, she always wore jeans, they suited her he thought, did her figure justice.

'You're terrible,' she murmured, her eyes still shining with excitement. He had dazzled her ever since he had first burst into her life, fell victim to his soft eyes and welcoming smile. He bent forward and kissed her breasts and then her mouth, his voice soft and gentle but full of eagerness.

Conscious of the frenetic thumping in his chest he whispered, 'I love you so fucking much.'

Her skin was pale to his tanned hands as they passed over and around her body, faint perspiration had broken out across the whole of her body.

'Stand up a minute,' he told her.

She stood as he pulled her jeans to the floor she was standing in front of him naked but for her socks and white cotton knickers. He kissed her right knee, that was now constantly bruised as it so often banged against the wall when they made love in his bed.

She whispered, 'you're crazy.'

'And you're beautiful.'

He led her towards the bathroom. 'Sit here,' he said, and pointed to the edge of the bath tub.

He lightly stroked her thigh, momentarily running his hands inward to the warmth between her legs, before stripping swiftly. He twisted the shower on and pointed the spray onto his hand to check its temperature. Standing her up, she seemed in a trance. He removed both her socks and then her knickers and kissed her thighs, struggling to hold back. He soaped her thoroughly, the last of which was a good coating over each of her ankles and feet. This allowed him to watch the lather sliding down the rest of her body especially her legs with ever increasing excitement. She shimmered as he kissed her neck passionately. He could still smell the White Musk perfume she wore, the smell intrigued him, it was not overpowering but faint and elusive which he adored immensely. He controlled his mouth making tiny pressures on her lips and then onto her closed eyes, sucking the water from her chin, which made her chuckle. He pulled her tight to his chest and moved his hands down her back, enjoying her helplessness. Every square inch of his body was just aching to be touched. He moved his face out from the jet of water so that it splashed her body, water running across her face and down her neck.

'That tickles,' she murmured.

He stopped some of the flow with his tongue and took a crafty lick of her nipple, wiping his wet mouth over her breast as the water haphazardly splashed them both.

'How am I doing?' he asked, nuzzling each nipple.

'Mmm, where is he then?' came her voice, as she moved her hand down between his knees and gripped his erect cock tightly, 'he's a bit hard isn't he?'

He made a short gasp as she began to tease him. She touched him with both hands, gently massaging him. Suddenly he lost control, he was charged up. He bent down and buried his head against her knees to force them apart and slid up to her open legs and his mouth became impatient, she let his tongue explore her. He vigorously reared up and shuffled forward holding his cock against her. She lifted her left leg onto the edge of the bath so entry was possible. He smiled coyly and slowly supported himself as he eased within. They locked together, firmly grasping each other desperately.

'I want to be deep inside you,' he said in a hushed tone. 'Until I can't get any deeper, I want to though... I want to be part of you.'

She squirmed with delight as they thrust, pushed and pulled each other in a frantic rhythm. They half stumbled as they slid out of the shower and onto the floor. He held her sodden hair, and he watched her face, she looked extraordinary as she whimpered with pleasure and her lips quivered as she let out faint moans and sighs that all told him that she loved him. Panting heavily, and still pressed together, her arms gripped and pulled on his back, his hands slid down and gripped her bum as he gasped with a thrust that almost pushed her halfway across the floor he shuddered and clenched tightly. She pleaded for him to continue and she moved up and down with her hips, then her pelvis quivered in a frenzy until she slowly relaxed. He collapsed on top of her, panting deeply into her wet ears.

'You animal,' she smirked moving a hand up to cup the back of his head. He turned and smirked back at her gratefully before giving her a kiss.

They lay quiet, too exhausted and emotionally intense to speak, his body still and relaxed on hers. She moaned lightly as she felt him move his weight to make himself more comfortable beside her. He folded her into his arms, dropping a kiss onto her forehead and murmured his love for her once more and she returned the same.

His bed was inviting and he dried her there in sequence; hair, face, neck, shoulders, legs, between them, bottom, back, then feet. He smiled as he began to cover her face and body with fervent kisses. After he sucked her toes lightly he lingered over her breasts a while. He kneaded each in turn, cupping and squeezing them and moving his warm tongue around her nipples. With a light smile she closed her eyes and wound her fingers into his hair. Moving a hand down he pushed a space between her thighs, his finger finding her clitoris, he moved up to kiss her. Nibbling each other's lips, his finger circled her as she gripped him. Her eagerness marked his as she rolled herself on top of him. Holding her thighs wide apart she sat down on him slowly and his breath rasped as she moved. The sound of his moans became more and more emphatic in her ear as he held the duvet tightly. They rolled back and forth thrusting their bodies forcefully, he grabbed her bum sharply again and she collapsed over of him once he came.

'Wooo. I feel a whole lot better now.'

She nuzzled against his neck, 'me too.'

'Happy?' he murmured.

'Very,' came her reply.

They both smiled at each other, wrapped up in bed. He spread out onto his stomach, his right arm supporting his head while his left lay flat and lightly across her breasts smiling a while before they curled up together and slept fulfiled and utterly exhausted.

They were still wrapped up in each other's arms when he awoke, the room was flocked with moonlight. Bewildered for a moment, then remembering, he turned his head and saw her face next to his, he watched her tenderly for a moment then woke her.

She smiled as she stretched out her arms and gave a puzzled look, then hugged him happily. 'I finally sat down and wrote you a letter while you were away,' she chirped.

'Really?' he replied in a aloof tone, as she reached her free hand into what had now become her overnight bag and idly passed it to him.

'It's a good thing,' she murmured. 'When someone's not around, you find all these things you want to say but can't or otherwise forget.'

'I'll read it when you've gone,' he said as he took it from her. 'That way it will be like you're still here.'

'I know you've written me a few,' she mumbled as she nuzzled her face into him. 'But I seemed to have lost one, and you did take one back.'

'Did I?'

'Yes.'

'I don't remember that.'

'You have to be kind to me when you've read it. It's a bit of a slushy one,' she smiled. 'You'd only been parted from me for less than fourteen hours and it already felt like it had been a couple of weeks. I was starting to forget what you look like.'

'I'll have to give you another photo,' he chuckled lightly.

'I missed other stuff too,' she whispered and seemed to shy away from him slightly.

'Like what... tell me.'

'Just what your voice sounds like and how it feels to be close to you.'

'That easy to forget then?'

'No, you know what I mean don't you.'

'Sure.'

'I missed you at night the most. I'd be lying in my bed half asleep and turn over and expect to feel you lying next to me so I can cuddle up to you. All I seemed to get was Penny the Panda, or the dog snoring.' She gave out a small yawn. 'If only we could lay like this forever.'

'Must be true love then.'

'Mmm,' she mumured. 'More than you'll ever know.'

She wrapped her legs around him and hugged with a soft moan before stretching and rubbing her face deep into the pillow. He traced a finger down her cheek and followed the hair that had fallen onto her shoulder then onto her breasts.

He gave out a sigh and said, 'I'd better get you home, it's gone eleven.'

'I'll phone Mum,' she yawned. 'Tell her I'm stopping over.'

'Sure,' he nodded pleased.

She gave him a grateful hug and mumbled softly, 'it's so gorgeous waking up next to someone and being able to give them a kiss and still think I'm so in love with you.'

He smiled happy that squeezing themselves into a single bed for sleep brought them closer still. 'You'd better phone her now before you fall asleep,' he whispered.

'Umm, you're always so damn warm,' she smiled, 'just five more minutes like this'.

Friday, July 21

Jay vented an expressive yawn, glad that his short shift of manual labour was over. On the way home wrestling with The Beast's tape deck took his concentration from the road and a metal fence came towards him at speed. His heart fluttered for a moment or two but once his stomach started groaning the experience had passed. He stopped off at Enderby chip shop for a chicken and mushroom Pukka pie, sometimes it was lovely and sometimes disappointing, but it was fuel to keep him going, and although a small thing, it was somehow worth looking forward to. Once consumed he had enough change and time to make it to The Bell for last orders.

'We're all going to the Motor Cross for the weekend,' jeered Nick raising his beer glass up in the air in splendour at Jay's sober position.

He grinned back, 'oh yeah, it'll be shit without me!'

'I didn't know you were going to be back.'

'Well,' he chuckled, 'you're going to have to fit me in.'

'There's no room in the car.'

'I'll take The Beast,' he said positively and a huge jeer went up. 'What time are you leaving?'

'About five in the morning, after the big fight.'

'Well I best go and get my stuff then.'

There was nothing like being impulsive he thought downing his pint. The Beast growled into life and he pulled away from the car park with Elvis playing.

Saturday, July 22 - 23

Three o'clock in the morning and the Tyson fight had been the result everyone had expected, but knockout 93 seconds into the first round was disappointing, especially given all the media hype beforehand. By five o'clock he was the only one still awake watching some rubbish movie on channel four staring Kurt Russell. He decided to take charge and wake them up, only to receive dull groans and muttered swearing as one by one they surfaced from a semi drunk sleep.

'Good old ham sarnies, can't beat them,' smiled Nick as he sliced the bread.

'You got any crisps?'

'Yeah in the cupboard over there.'

Rob finally rubbed the sleep from his eyes and within his first two cups of tea had quickly reverted to his prior sleep excited mode, 'come on then I'm ready,' he said clapping his hands and grinning.

Nick shook his head at him as he placed the food into a carrier bag. 'Me and Jay will sort the grub then Rob,' he snapped sarcastically and Rob just chuckled lightly in reply.

Nick's brother Carl, a little shorter than him, medium set with dark blonde hair, stood leaning against the door frame looking alert and ready for action. He was around five or six years older than Nick and came across as sensible, or maybe that was just the age difference, but he seemed calm and collected to Jay, happy to let things wash over him and soak up the parts in which he enjoyed.

Carl, Rob and Aidy set off in front, leading the way. After an hour and a half of driving, Jay felt tired, the blinding sun set in the clear blue sky took them by surprise. Even with the windows down it was hot, made worse by The Beast's radiator as it began to overheat. Water bubbled out the top of it, the only thing they could use to mop it up and tie round it was their socks. Nick took over the driving while Jay finished off the last sandwich, which by now was nothing more than dried bread with a slice of rubbery ham. The last of the Coke was warm and flat, and made his teeth feel awful.

As they drove into Bath, Jay was impressed, it was very scenic, the houses, the streets, the flowers and a woman in a short sexy red dress. Rob and Aidy were already signalling her with wolf whistles, she didn't turn around, just carried on wiggling her bum as she walked, she was pretty and she knew it.

'Hell of an arse,' announced Nick.

Jay agreed and flipped over the Elvis tape, yawned, stretched a little and in an effort to bring a bit of life back into his numb bum gave it a squeeze.

At nine o'clock they had arrived at Farley Castle, socks hanging out The Beast's window to dry, a Coke can hanging off the aerial and all holding expressions of relief in getting there. Jay patted the wing of The Beast, thankful it had not let him down. Carl took charge and put the tent up in a matter of minutes, it was very simple in design yet the flowery decoration was giving off a minimal cool seventies style aura, a mixture of orange and brown circles stood out like a sore thumb against the more modern tents that surrounded it.

'What do think of the tent Jay?' laughed Nick.

'It's fantastic,' he mused.

'Do you think we'll all get in there?'

'Yeah,' he nodded positively, doubt had no place on a road trip.

Carl was humming to himself as he smoothed out the ground sheet inside the tent. The opening flap was pushed aside as bags were hurled in, one of them hit Jay in the face as he tried to exit.

'Cheers guys,' he muttered sarcastically.

There was no response. They had trundled off to watch the bike's practice.

The smell and the noise took Jay back to when he used to race and he began to wish he had never given the sport up, it was so much fun and had that hint of danger to it. Carl, also an ex racer, studied the track and found what he believed to be the best spot next to a large jump where the bikes came tearing over at high speed, got airborne giving the riders a chance to do fancy foot work to please the crowd.

'I can't believe how hot it is,' Nick sighed as he ran a hand across his brow.

'Plenty of scantily clad girls,' noted Aidy, less interested in the bikes.

'We'd better load up with some booze hadn't we,' said Jay and they all agreed.

Wandering along the drinks aisle of the local supermarket Jay paused and was thinking about maybe trying something he had never had before.

'I wonder what this Taboo tastes like?' he smiled looking at Rob who promptly opened the lid and, as if performing on stage in a double act, knocked back a mouthful.

'And?' quizzed Jay eager for Rob's verdict.

'Absolutely disgusting.'

Jay got rather excited by his reply as he looked left and right to check the coast was clear before taking a swill for himself.

'You're right,' he smiled. 'It's awful.'

'You two are nothing but common thieves,' smirked Nick.

'That's right mate,' chuckled Rob putting the bottle back on the shelf. Positively encouraged he cracked open a bottle of Newquay Steam lager when the grey-haired spindly Gateway manager spied him from a distance and came hurtling towards them, almost gliding a long the highly polished floor.

'Oi, you stop clowning about or I'll have to ask you to leave the store.'

'Fuck off,' coughed Rob under his breath.

'I hope you're going to pay for that.'

'Pay for what?' mocked Rob.

'That half finished bottle in your hand.'

'What this?' spat Rob holding it up. 'Of course we are.'

And Jay chuckled at that.

The list of items in the shopping trolley was very basic in content:

12 Budwieser
12 Hofmeister
12 Heineken
12 Carling Black Label
12 Tennents Pilsner
2 Brut Pommagne
1 Liebfraumilch
1 (Consumed) Newquay Steam Lager
5 litre bottle of Buxton water.

The young fresh faced checkout girl smiled as she looked at the huge pile of booze being stacked before her. 'You guys havin' a party?' she asked.

'No,' replied Rob sourly and snatched his stash of beer. 'It's a wake.'

There was enough beer for them to get totally drunk but just in case The Beast held in its boot his duty free bottle of vodka, some lime and a few bottles of Guinness. As he made his way through the electric exit doors he caught sight of a payphone and felt a slight sense of guilt pass through him. Trac hadn't a clue where he was and wondered whether it would be best to phone her. The guilt increased as he made his way to The Beast, he grappled with the change in his pockets, 'hang on a sec' he called to the lads, 'just going to phone Trac.' They all gave out a large sigh and hurled abuse at him but he just blanked them.

'Hello' came her voice.

'Hi it's me,' he said.

'Are you coming over to see me?' she asked in an excited tone.

'I'd love to, but I'm in Bath.'

'In the bath?'

'No, in Bath you know the place.'

'What are you doing there?'

'It's the World Motor Cross Championships. I'm just here for a few days.'

'You've only just come back from Lanzerotte.'

'I know, it's just one of those things, I just bumped into the lads and... I didn't plan it.'

'Yeah right!'

'Honestly, you know me I'm sooo easily led.'

'Hmm, more the instigator.'

'Look I'll be back tomorrow night. '

'I was looking forward to seeing you though.'

'We've got the rest of the summer together. Just you and me, we'll have a great time.'

'Okay,' she said and gave a sigh of disappointment.

'I'll come straight over to see you.'

Trac said, 'goodbye,' softly.

He replied, 'sexy,' and hung up the phone.

With the weather still bright and warm it gave rise to a friendly but somewhat discordant game of rounders with a family opposite. As the alcohol filtered away it soon transformed into an erratic game of football and just as swiftly decended into chaos. They got wilder and louder, gurgling and spraying beer at one another accompanied by much raucous cheering and laughter.

Inadvertently drinking such a mixture and amount of alcohol was just one of the problems of that night, they appeared to annoy everyone around them. Jay, not being able stay awake or find an adequate place in the tent, headed for The Beast. He snatched at the tartan blanket laying across the back shelf and wrapped it around himself. He stuck Elvis on and decided he would sleep where he sat, make a bed of the cramped front seat. If any luck was due him he would pass out in record time.

Jay's face was a picture. He had woke ridiculously early due to the noise of the surrounding campers. The impression the door had made on his forehead seemed to hurt slightly too but the handbrake, that had found its way up his bum slightly, had a nice feel to it. A bit confused by that he bolted upright, not to dwell on he thought as he emerged from The Beast slamming the door behind him. He leant against the wing and surveyed the scene in front of him. The ground was awash with litter, beer cans, bottles and burger papers. The remains of an orgy of destruction he thought as he pawed at his aching head and then ruffled his hair. He remembered he'd mixed his drinks again... result: torture. He scrapped at the gunge that had formed on his tongue and wished he had packed a toothbrush. Maybe it might be an idea to keep some provisions in The Beast or simply have purchased more than booze and water from the supermarket. A few moments into relieving his mouth of the awful taste by swilling it with vodka, he finally felt the camper's stares burning on him, sympathetic to his condition they weren't. By way of an apology he suddenly found himself tidying up. A sense of doing something useful seemed to help, yet bending down made his head feel far worse so it wasn't all that long before it stopped being a novelty and started to feel like the chore it so obviously was. Putting on a brave face in regards to his pounding head was a tough call but he managed it and enjoyed waking his mates, allowing them to collectively share feeling awful. To make things worse the bacon frying next door was a bit like Chinese water torture. They made a few murmurs to try and prompt some free grub but Jay had noted a streak of stout on the outside of the guy's tent which clearly meant that wasn't about to happen.

They got through the morning's grid position races but it was a struggle, it did give them enough time to at least feel half alive. The weather was getting hotter by the minute and Jay seemed to have more ice cream round his mouth than in it.

The afternoon saw Dave Thorpe, the English contender, fall off his bike, but come back to take the championship. Pleased with the result they packed up their gear and went home. It had been a great weekend... a great road trip.

11. Play

For Jay a certain amount of boredom had set in, it was one of those long summer days, a do nothing day. He sat pulling a few comic expressions at Trac, making her chuckle in the process. They both sat on the bonnet of The Beast in the sun, eating ice cream and letting the day tick by.

'Eat your own,' she said noticing he occasionally glanced over to see how she was getting on with hers.

'What?' he said with fake innocence, knowing full well she knew what he was up to.

'You've got your own, I've got mine... and I am eating every bit.'
He sneered at her playfulness and she responded to that by sticking her tongue out at him with a rasp.

'The doctor told me to cut my drinking down,' he mumbled. 'He suggested I have a drink at meal times only,'

'That's an idea,' Trac smiled.

'Yeah I suppose so, I've just got to figure out how to have thirty six meals a day,' he smirked as she nudged him disapprovingly.
He moved to his feet and opened The Beast's door and pulled a pair of black sunglasses out of his shirt pocket and got into the driving seat, slipping them on as he started the engine. Trac leapt from the bonnet and he drove off leaving her standing, hands on her hips. He jolted The Beast back into reverse. Smiling he said, 'come on girl.'

'Where are we going then?' she said as she got into the passenger seat.

'Anywhere,' he smiled, 'anywhere you want.'

She sat watching him for a moment in thought. It didn't look as if he was serious about getting work or going back to college. The one thing she did know was that he wasn't ready for a job. A life of doing nothing but driving around in The Beast, drinking vodka and listening to Elvis seemed the plan of the moment.

'Let's go round your house and drink all your old man's scotch!'

'I don't think so,' she said. 'Me and Mum had words about you'

'What about?'

'She just went on about how my ex was a nice boy.'

'Oh, that's a surprise,' he replied laced with sarcasm.

'Then she went on about you.'

'What about me?'

'Just you.'

'And, what did you say?'

'I said I liked you the way you are.'
He suddenly broke into song and accompanied Elvis in his version of the 'If I Can Dream'. She looked out of the window at the passing trees, while

he wondered if she would come out with her usual line, 'can't you whistle instead!'

'Pass me my cash card,' he asked, 'it's in the glove box.'

She looked through the assortment of tapes and muttered something as she did so.

'What's up?'

'You've not got any money in the bank.'

'I can add to my overdraft.'

'You shouldn't do that.'

'I'm a student.'

'Not anymore.'

'I'll get into a college somewhere.'

'When?'

He brushed that off with, 'well I tried didn't I... least I did that.'

'Try harder.'

'Maybe I just want to get fat, do nothing and go nowhere.'

She sighed deeply, he could be hard work when he was in this mood. 'That's the plan is it?' she said following it with another sigh.

He shrugged lightly and carried on tapping the steering wheel to his music lethargically, as if it hadn't registered with him at all.

'So you're going to leave it to the last minute like you do everything.'

'No, I don't.'

'Yeah you do.'

He shrugged again. 'I'll sort it,' he said, 'don't worry about it.'

'Well it's a bit of a risk leaving it day after day.'

'The whole of life is a bit of a risk,' he preached, 'so just give me the cash card.'

'No,' she said unswerving.

'Give me the card or I'll have to slap you and spank your bottom several times,' he mused.

She passed him the card slowly, 'that's not very nice,' she frowned.

'I'll be alright you wait and see. Something's out there calling my name, trust me,' he said in an easy tone.

She looked doubtfully at him, he was a self confessed prat, an incurable piss artist and the worst part about him today was that he was turning everything into a joke. If it wasn't spiteful or just a little crude, he was just plain stupid. In between all of this he managed to drop the odd, 'oo-er!' every time she said something genuine that he could twist into a double entendre, but she found comfort in the fact that at least he was entertaining and life would be fairly flat without him.

'They don't call me Mr Sexy for nothing you know.'

'That's right,' Trac smirked. 'They don't.'

He dropped down his shades and peered over the top at her. 'That's not entirely true,' he grinned lightly. 'I'm very sexy and you know I am.'

'Oh maybe just a bit,' she teased.

He pushed back his shades and laughed.

'Where are we going then?' she asked in a more positive tone this time.

'I am taking you Trac, for a driving lesson.'

'Where?'

'There's a place I know up here.'

She smiled back, she liked the sound of that.

Five or so minutes later he turned The Beast sharply into a large almost derelict looking gravel car park just inside the village of Whetstone and grounded The Beast to an abrupt halt.

'Right,' he said and clapped his hands together with excitement.

'Are you sure this is a good idea?'

'Positive,' he replied as he got out of The Beast and trotted round to the passenger side.

'Go on,' he said smiling and waving a hand for her to move across to the driver's seat. She slid nervously across and sat not quite knowing what to do with her hands, an unsure frown had found her face.

'Now, first check it's in neutral.'

'I think it is?'

Jay waggled the gear stick and said, 'yep fine, now start the engine.'

She looked at him blankly, 'go on you'll be alright.'

She began to fidget about in the seat, 'I can't reach the pedals properly,' she mumbled as she managed to slide the seat forward a little and followed that by double checking the gear stick was in neutral and turned the key.

'That's good,' he smiled. 'Now push in the clutch and move it into first and give it a bit of gas.'

Trac followed his instructions carefully and occasionally glanced across at him for approval.

'You're doing well, now ease out the clutch and increase the gas,' he smirked. 'Just remember, the brake's the middle one.'

The Beast jerked forward about a metre and stalled.

'It's okay,' he said, 'there's plenty of time and plenty of room. Now start again.'

'Neutral first,' she smiled.

'Yeah.'

The Beast sparked into life with the turn of the key and sat ticking over for about twenty or thirty seconds until she felt ready to go. As she eased the clutch in and out, The Beast crept forward, they were on the move.

'Good,' he smiled, 'now put the clutch in and move into second... straight back, all the way.'

'I can't.'

'Sure you can.'

She eased The Beast into gear easily enough, but she began to panic. As they began to move faster and faster her stress levels increased.

'Don't worry, you're doing fine, just stay in second for a bit.'

Trac manoeuvred The Beast around the pot hole ridden car park and once she had made her first full circuit her face began to light up. She was starting to enjoy it.

'I think I'll be better off in a smaller car, this feels really big.'

'Do you want to get up to third?'

'Okay,' she replied with a slightly unsure tone.

'Wait until you come back down that straight flat bit, then when you get near to the end, brake a bit and drop down into second.'

The stern concentrated expression returned to her face. A slight cranking of the gears and a loud rev of the engine and third had been achieved but, with Trac not wanting to go faster, The Beast was showing signs of struggling. At the opposite end of the car park a blue Escort hurtled in and did a hundred and eighty degree handbrake turn.

'Oh shit.'

'Don't panic, just stop. Put your foot on the brake and put the clutch in at the same time.'

The Escort did a wheel spin towards them, kicking up gravel and a cloud of smoke. Trac stabbed at the brake and The Beast stopped abruptly and stalled as the other car flew past them and did another handbrake turn.

'Popular place,' she said.

'Yeah,' he muttered glaring in the direction of the Escort disappointed at the interruption. 'Come on we'll go, you can't concentrate with that other car,' he said. He stepped out and marched back round The Beast as she moved across to her usual spot.

'How did I do?'

'Eh... What?' he replied clearly agitated. 'Sorry. You did great, better than I was when I first drove.'

She smiled happily with a sense of achievement and gave a light clap of her hands.

'Do you want to go anywhere?' he asked as they made their way to the exit.

She gave him a vague shrug as she twizzled a pack of Silk Cut cigarettes in her hand, desperate to have one but trying to abstain for as long as possible.

'We could go to my house but my mum's in nagging mode.'

'Mums are born to nag,' she replied.

He stopped The Beast before pulling out onto the road to rummage through his tapes trying to find one that would inspire him while Trac gave into nicotine.

'You seen The Cult mix?'

'The fucking Cult mix?'

'Yeah that's the one,' he chuckled.

'No, but what about this one?'

'Our mix... don't think so,' he said teasingly and she stuck her tongue out at him.

'Okay, okay I'll put it on.'

She was obviously feeling better after a couple of drags of her cigarette and asked, 'what are we going to do now?'

Jay responded by folding his arms, and leaning back in his seat with a laid back tone said, 'I don't know?'

Tuesday, July 25

He sat in the garden having just started doodling a cartoon of him teaching Trac to drive. It was her driving The Beast, hand changing gear out of shot, with him in the passenger seat with a big grin on his face suggesting her hand was elsewhere. Trac appeared from the side of the house and seemed to looked far better than when he saw her last. As she wandered towards him, he glanced from the striped deckchair lifting his dark shades up a touch.

'Great summer gear,' she smiled. 'You're as bad as me.'

He looked down at his black shirt, cut off jeans and DM boots and gave a slight shrug.

'Don't I get a hello then?'

He gazed back admiring her beauty, which only served to make her uneasy.

'Don't stare at me,' she said and pawed lightly at her hair.

'I'm not staring at you,' he replied innocently.

'Anyway I'm having my hair done later so I will need to be back by four.'

He slowly rose from the deckchair to greet her properly. 'Fine,' he said and gave her a hug.

It was a warm day with a good clean smell of fresh air. She sat down cross-legged on the grass and they chatted about her shopping trip, but it was only to fill a hole in conversation because it was another one of those humid days where you just sat about not wanting to do anything except drink ice water and sigh a lot.

'What are you drawing?'

'Nothing, I only just started.'

'Let me see.'

'Later when it's finished.' And rose to his feet with an idle ease that almost needled her once he said, 'fancy a lager?'

'Is this pretty much how you're going to spend your life?'

He pondered scratching at his chin and began nodding slightly, 'yep.'

'It's not normal Jay,' she said plainly.

He continued to scratch at his chin. 'Who wants to be normal anyway?'

'Well, what are you trying to be?'

'Nothing, I'm not trying to be anything.'

'You can't carry on like this.'

'Tell me you haven't come round here to hassle me about college. I'm relaxing, appreciating the time out.'

'Hmm... not convinced.'

'Look one day I know I'll have to work and be responsible. I just want to avoid it for as long as possible.'

'If you get the right job you'll love work.'

'Even if I did get the ideal job sooner or later it will become mundane, stale and boring.'

'Your mum will make you get a job.'

He shook his head vigorously.

'Then she will kick you out... where are you going to live then?'

'In The Beast.'

'You would as well wouldn't you.'

He gave her a frown and nodded with a smile, liking the idea more and more as he imagined how life would be in The Beast.

'I seriously worry about you.'

'Don't.'

'I can't help it. You just need something to focus on.'

'I'm alright.'

'Are you?'

'What are you saying?'

'Well when you do get bored you just get out of control.'

'I don't though,' he muttered and made a face at her.

'Yes you do.'

He gave her a shrug.

'Jay you know what I'm talking about.'

'I'm eighteen, I'm supposed to be out of control.'

'I'd feel better if you were going to college or trying to get a job.'

'Well I'm not in a rush to join the rat race that's for sure,' he said. 'Once you're in it, get a house and the rest of that material bullshit you're trapped.'

'It doesn't have to be like that.'

'No, but it probably will,' he huffed. 'I mean I might have a great car and a great house one day, but I won't own them, they'll own me cause once you've got them you won't be able to give them up and when that happens bang goes your freedom, you're trapped.'

'So you're saying own nothing and do nothing and you'll have nothing to give up.'

Jay sat forward and massaged the back on his neck. 'I don't know...' he mumbled, 'I just need to be free spirited.'

'Maybe you should be a hippy.'

'Yeah, that's not a bad idea. At the end of the day none of anything really matters does it, we're just visiting, one day we will all be gone... I think I'll grow my hair.'

'Okay, I'm up for that but one day you'll have to work and you've got to give yourself the best chance. And as for long hair, I don't think it will suit you.'

He grumbled and wafted a flippant hand at her. 'I don't want to think about all this right now. Just get pissed and enjoy the summer for as long as possible, besides it's not all bad, occasionally I have been known to watch the odd documentary on the TV just to keep my brain functioning.'

'Really?'

'No,' he chuckled. 'If only I was a real artist and you were my muse. That lifestyle would really suit me.'

'Well you're a proper piss artist,' she said.

'Yeah, I am,' he replied positively and smiled at his favourite compliment. 'Then I guess I'm something.'

'That reminds me, I'm thirsty.'

Still hot and bothered he returned to the garden sipping from a can of Red Stripe. Still sneering, he belched deliberately because he knew it would wind her up.

'Do you have to?' she snapped, annoyed at him. 'You did that deliberately. You need to know what's going on around you and make some kind of a decision.'

'I do know what's going on around me.'

'Half the time you don't, your head's in the clouds.'

He gave out a dismissive sigh. 'Look I'm sorry. I just get a little sidetracked. My mind wanders, I'll get into a college, I promise. Just please don't worry about me,' and he gave her a hug.

'Come on, let's go and put some music on.'

'I'm sorry to have a go at you. I'm not used to having someone to look out for. Sometimes I'm just scared that I'm going to lose you.'

'You'll never lose me,' he said. 'We're bonded, soul mates I reckon.'

'You believe that?'

'Course I do.'

Wednesday, July 26

The moulding of a Grolsh ceramic bottle top into a key ring and disposing of the limp burgundy leather strap from The Beast's keys was far from easy, a cool idea to Jay but when it came to the practical side of attaching the keys, the frustration began. He had cursed half a dozen times or so and was now sucking on his thumb to relieve the pain of pinched skin or split nail he wasn't sure, it just hurt.

'Why don't you let me buy you a new key ring?' Trac chuckled.

He mumbled something back but with his thumb still in his mouth it was hard to figure out what he had said so she just gave him a shrug and carried on looking at the photos and cartoon he had put together from the road trip.

'Looks like you enjoyed yourself.'

'Eh?... Oh yeah, see it's not just fuck all but get drunk this summer.'

'Mmm, looks exactly like it to me, I think the motorbikes were just the excuse.'

He dangled the keys proudly in front of her. 'I told you I'd get there.'

'Oh, is that what you said.'

He gave her a puzzled look and she uttered, 'forget it.'

Once the pain in his thumb had subsided and Trac had finished reading about new man in Cosmo, her new hair did have an effect on him. He sat with his hands laced together on his lap hiding any possible signs of an uprising in his jeans, this was certainly not the behaviour of a new man, a new man had to become erect at the appropriate moment, stay that way for a substantial period of time, give the female an orgasm if not multiple and on top of that show no signs of wanting sleep after release. His first experiences were a case of 'oh my god I'm actually doing it' moving then swiftly on to self satisfaction, to a genuine emotional attachment, when he met Shelley but now at least he had moved a step further and could admit that Trac was the first girl he consciously wanted to actually please. But it all sounded like hard work, things a couple of generations ago must have been so much easier at a time when the female orgasm didn't seem to exist. These days the clitoris seemed to be endlessly talked about. He pondered as to whether to ask her if she'd had a slight orgasm but felt little point in asking as she was clearly in one of her laid back happy go lucky moods where he knew how the conversation would go;

'No' = Him sullen face.

'Don't worry about it.' = Him still with sullen face.

'We've only just started having sex.' = Him showing slight signs of positivity.

'Anyway the more we practice...' = Him beginning to break into a smile.

By now his erection began to feel painful, he felt tension build in the sides of his head and couldn't seem to budge the thoughts of shagging her, God I'll never last long if I start thinking about it now, got to get it out of my head!

'You okay Jay?'

'Yeah,' he croaked. 'Fine.'

'A bloke's got to be a bloke,' he suddenly babbled and she frowned at him wondering where that statement had come from.

He grumbled something else as he began to fidget about and tried to salvage something positive from his love making abilities... energy, yes stamina he did have that, the ability to go again and again and that had to count for something didn't it?

Thursday, July 27

Thursday was highly anticipated. Jay and Adrian were out in The Beast cruising along broad tree-lined avenues, full of new houses with manicured lawns.

'Music maestro please,' roared Jay grinning.

Adrian turned the tape over and The Wonder Stuff blared out of the speakers. They both began to sing along with enthusiasm. Jay took his eyes off the road for a second or two after Adrian had shouted, 'phwooar look at the legs on that!' At which point The Beast mounted the grass verge and the steering wheel slipped from his hands. Losing control he just missed a large sign which read; *Welcome to Cosby Village please drive carefully*.

'Shit,' he yelled, following with laughter once he had gained control. Pulling up to a newsagents with a screech they leapt out, feeling to him like something from an episode of *The Professionals* or *The Sweeney*.

'So, when can we get the fast cars and the walkie talkies?' he joked.

'You watch too much TV,' smirked Adrian.

'Good morning,' he grinned at a passer-by, 'like your shirt,' he smiled widely.

'A couple of lemonade sparkles and a packet of Maltesers?' suggested Adrian.

'Of course,' replied Jay, 'the usual.'

The weather had been relentlessly sunny, the news had said it was the hottest summer since 1976, a hose pipe ban was in full force. He wondered how that could be as they lived on an island? They had driven from village to village via the country lanes, windows down enjoying the sunshine. Summertime was great they had decided, they did what they wanted, running wild and free, racing The Beast, drinking beer, laughing and shouting without a care in the world. They were full of themselves, full of confidence and self esteem. Intemperance was fun, an adventure they only ever saw as play, and they were proud.

They leant on the bonnet of The Beast eating their sweets and appreciating the moment, their freedom. Jay finished his ice lolly looked at the stencilled wooden stick disappointed it had only taken a minute or two to devour before reading the joke... 'What's the biggest ant of all?'

'Elephant,' said Adrian sharply.

'How do you know that?'

'I've got the same joke.'

'That's rubbish that is,' he chuckled as they hopped back into The Beast.

'Where are you taking us now then?'

'Town.'

'Yeah,' Adrian nodded, 'all the girls will be out.'

The closer they got to the town centre the more freedom became eroded by bumper to bumper traffic. The first break Jay saw he hammered The Beast into gear, overtaking a bus and three cars, slipping back just in time from the on coming traffic. Adrian had his hand on his heart and sighed with relief once back on the correct side of the road.

'A bit close that was.'

'Yeah,' said Adrian with a large intake of breath.

'We'll crash one day I tell you.'

Jay sneered, no doubt in his mind that he was unbreakable. He turned the music up to fuel his adrenaline further.

The centre of town was busy as predicted. They wandered as usual from one record shop to another, idly sifting through the assortments of CDs and videos. Adrian bumped into a few people he knew, while Jay stood hands in pockets, occasionally sweeping his right hand through his hair to keep it from his eyes. Mc Donald's then a swift pint before parting company. On his return to The Beast he found a piece of paper stuck to the window screen. He ripped it off and saw it was a parking ticket. He paced backwards and forwards while he read it, 'twelve quid,' he exclaimed. Standing shaking his head in disgust before he shoved it into his back pocket and clambered in. It was his first parking ticket but that somehow didn't make it special.

Friday, July 28

Under Jay's drunken but guided supervision, snake bites went into production and were lined up along the black veneer bar of The Bell Inn.

'Fucking hell Jay,' said Nick. 'I don't know if we should drink them.'

He grinned back, nodded his head slightly and looked beyond him to where Rob was standing for much needed coercion.

'Barmy fluid,' chuckled Rob and clutched the nearest pint and took an enormous gulp from the cloudy mixture and followed it with a belch. That was enough, the marker had been set.

Saturday July 29

Jay lay in the garden with a comfy cushion under his head and a bottle of beer by his side. This is the life he thought, time to wonder what the hell he was going to do, time in which to ponder on his future possibilities and if he was really good enough? It was a quiet day, subject to the sound of birds and the odd drone of a car going by, the blue sky and gentle breeze should have been ideal conditions for such thought processes, if it wasn't for Trac. She just kept popping into his head and it was almost hard work even stressful trying to remove her. She was becoming more of a problem once she was half naked and caused a stirring between his legs which only led in one direction, tension, frustration... headache.

Bolting upright he snatched at the bottle and took a few swigs of beer.

For fuck's sake, he thought. I am but a simple chap... I just want sleep, food, booze and of course sex. And there's nothing, absolutely nothing wrong with that... is there?

'You know what I think? Trac said.
Jay was parading back and forth to the mirror and occasionally squatting then sitting. He could hear Trac whispering to Maria as he twirled a few more times tutting at his reflection, not too sure if they were out of scale with the rest of his body.
'Maria agrees you should try the 501s.'
'Narr, I like these... these are okay.'
'Jay they're baggy.'
'So, I like baggy.'
'Like way too baggy,' she said firmly.
'Why do you sell them then?'
'Everyone is a different size and shape. You're slim and straight, perfect for 501s.'
'I just can't see why they cost so much, even with you getting discount.'
'Why don't you try the 517s they're a slightly looser fit,' suggested Maria.
'Yeah okay,' he nodded.
He stepped along, stopping expressionless, looking up and down checking the fit and awaiting their judgment.
Trac moved her head from side to side, 'see they're a better fit already.'
'Mmm, not sure. They're baggy around the thigh but not at the ankle.'
'Honestly,' said Trac, 'trust me on the 501s.'
He took them from her and went into the changing room. When he appeared both girls smiled, so he shuffled further and Trac went as far as giving him the thumbs up and nudged Maria positively.
'They're okay,' he said softly sticking out his bottom lip slightly and moving his head from side to side as he checked himself out.
'A snug fit,' said Trac.
'Yeah, feels nice on the thigh... bit tight round the knackers.'
Trac puffed out her cheeks and leant into the desk looking every bit as though she was about to give up.
'I bet you don't do that in front of your other customers,' he quipped.
'Jay,' she sighed, 'other customers are easy compared to you.'
Mindful that he'd overstepped himself, he thought it best to show more keenness and engage Maria too. 'What do you think Maria?' he asked with a frown that said 'come on help me out here.'
'Yeah they look good...' she replied politely. 'I guess if you like baggy and these feel too tight round the... maybe the 517s are the way to go.'
He nodded with enthusiasm and Trac stuck her tongue out highlighting her cheekbones and making him chuckle. He slapped his thighs and said,

'Okay, I'm not sure, I'll have to think about it,' and disappeared behind the curtain.

Trac slipped her head through the gap and whispered, 'you're a nightmare.'

'I know,' he agreed. 'It's been ages since I bought jeans and I was never this fussy before.'

'Anyway before you go thanks for last night.'

Pulling up his own jeans he was puzzled, 'last night?'

'Phoning and telling me that you love me.'

'Oh right that,' he replied bending down to pull on his boots.

'They say you tell the truth when you're drunk so maybe I should believe you.'

'True.'

'So, the 501s?'

He smiled and made an 'err' sound before saying, 'I don't know... I like the baggy ones.'

Trac shook her head lightly. 'Anyway, I've got to get back to some real work. I hope you didn't do anything too bad last night and if you did,' she went on, 'which no doubt you will have done. I suppose I'll hear all about it later.'

The front door sounded and his mum called him from the foot of the stairs. He reluctantly got out the bed and dressed. He wandered down and spoke to her briefly. Among the verbal message she relayed to him, he was useless and his father had washed his hands of him, apparently stopping his allowance now he was no longer a student.

He sat staring out of his bedroom window with a bottle of vodka resting on his thigh.

'What's wrong?' asked Trac lightly, concerned by his sudden change in mood.

'What do you think,' he grunted. 'I'm sulking.'

'That's not like you.'

'I like to sulk,' and took a swig from the bottle.

'What did your mum say?'

'Oh, my dad's just stopped my maintenance payments.'

'What have you done?'

'Got born,' he uttered.

'He probably expects you to get a job now. If you go back to college he'll start paying it again.'

'Maybe?'

He stared down into the bottle, then back out the window.

'I'm obviously rubbish.'

'Don't be silly,' she reached out a comforting hand.

He sighed. 'I don't know?' he said. 'My brother's brainy, so is my sister.

I've just been the black sheep of the family, well what's left of it.'

'They're just clever at other things and in other ways. I mean you're creative, you're good with your hands.'

'Yeah not my brain though.'

'You are though,' she said soothingly, 'a lot more than you make out and your heart is in the right place.'

He looked at her and smiled. 'They think I'm probably wasting my time and that I'll get nowhere, there's not a career in it.'

'So prove them wrong.'

He sighed again.

'You're crying,' she whispered softly.

'No I'm not. I've just got something in my eye is all.'

He stared back out of the window lost in thought. She handed him a note written in pencil at the front of his diary. Drawn on it was a clown style cartoon face which she hoped would snap him back into a better frame of mind.

Love you so fucking much, you're gorgeous and you're all mine!
Now do I get a kiss for that?

This time he gave out a prolonged sigh that slowly but surely morphed into a smile. He kissed her as she held him in her arms, halving the emotion with him. Feeling stupid and helpless he stayed there for a long time, stroking and playing with her hair.

Sunday, July 30

'Oh do what you bloody like,' snapped his mum. 'Go and catch flu off her.'

'Whatever,' he muttered.

He jumped into The Beast and sped off down the street, music blaring and the engine growling. It was another beautiful bright day full of summer promise and Trac was ill in bed.

Her parents were out in their front garden leisurely pulling out weeds and planting seedlings as he jerked The Beast to a screeching halt, instantly catching their attention.

'Is she alright then?' he asked as he wandered up the drive twirling his keys in his right hand.

Her father came striding towards him. 'You can't see her,' he said rigidly. 'She's really poorly.'

'What?' he replied astonished by her father's abrupt manner.

'Look, she really is not very well.'

He put his hands on his hips and drooping his head towards the ground, what the..? I'm her boyfriend he thought, confused about what to say or how to handle the situation he struggled to look her father in the eye and found it more comfortable looking back down the drive from where he came. Fortunately at that moment her mum approached the two calmly.

'Oh she'll be pleased to see you,' she smiled looking at her husband then back at Jay. 'I think she's awake now anyway. You'll be alright to see her for a while.'

'Thanks,' and gave a slight nod of agreement.

He peered round Trac's door quietly just to make sure she wasn't asleep. There she was under a mountain of blankets shivering quietly.

'How's my little baby then?' he asked soothingly, gently approaching the bed.

'Ill,' she muttered.

He leant a palm on her forehead to feel her temperature, 'oh too hot,' he smiled before leaning further over to kiss her where his hand had been.

'Thank you,' she said, sinking back into her duvet further.

She looked pale, her hair dark and straggly, her eyes were red as was her poor nose too. She clung to a wet and soggy scrunched up piece of tissue, he took it from her, placed it in the bin and passed her some clean sheets.

'There you go,' he continued to smile.

'Thank you,' she replied although somewhat muffled.

'You don't have to keep thanking me.'

'Okay.'

'So then you're not pretending you're ill to get all this attention?' he said in an authoritative voice and she tried a smile.

'Right then,' he said. 'I'm here to cheer you for a bit.'

He was good at that she informed him. He began by telling her the story of his day so far. It wasn't necessarily amusing, it was just the way he came across, the way he pranced about her room not bothered about looking or sounding daft. Starting off with the line, 'while I was looking particularly attractive this morning,' and completing with an array of impressions of people and then fell to the floor widely grinning at his own modesty. Unfortunately he couldn't go on being silly to such an ill audience.

'Okay,' he panted. 'So you feel like shit eh?'

She gave him a nod with closed eyes and struggled to sit up and make her way to the edge of the bed.

'Do you want anything? A glass of water or something?' he asked positively.

'Yes,' came her weak reply.

As he came back into the room she reached for the cup feebly. As she took it he rolled onto the floor by the side of her bed.

'I'm dying,' he chuckled holding his chest as he began to roll around making stupid wheezing noises.

'What are you doing you nutter?' laughed Trac watching him sprawling at her feet.

He suddenly stopped, laid there without moving until she began nudging him with her foot. As he let out a pathetic moan she began to laugh again, she enjoyed him like this, this was him at his best, managing to pick her up whatever the circumstances.

'You're mad,' she giggled.

He grabbed her left foot, bit it gently but made an aggressive noise like a savage beast and she managed a slight shriek.

'How is it that you can make me laugh when I feel ill or sad?'

He shrugged his shoulders and kissed her firmly. 'No secret, just good chemistry.'

'You'll catch my cold.'

'Probably,' he replied.

She felt happy he was there for her, happy that he didn't care about the cold, only for her. He sat brushing her hair behind her ears for a while before kissing the tip of her nose as she lay back down under the covers. She didn't move for hours until a hand reached out from the covers and feebly clawed at her dressing gown.

'I want to go to the loo,' she demanded, like a little girl who wanted her own way. She moved slowly up and out of the room while he switched the black and white TV set on that her father had brought down from the spare room, holidays and being ill being an exception to the rule. When she reappeared he was idly playing with her teddy bears, except Penny the Panda who got squashed against the wall.

'Hey, leave my panda alone,' she moaned slumping down next to him.

'Sorry I don't like that one,' he said plainly.

She tutted and slipped back under the mountain of covers. Her face looked like a lost puppy. He lay down beside her squeezing her small beige bear close to her cheek with a soft 'weee' sound as he spooned himself around her tightly.

Wednesday, August 2

Trac pushed herself from the window of Tie Rack as she caught sight of Jay marching towards her at a swift pace.

'Hi,' she said positively once he was within ear shot.

'How are you feeling?' he asked, as he gave her bum a light squeeze.

'Good,' she replied.

'Still up for the party tomorrow night?'

'Yeah,' she nodded keenly as she brought the bag she was carrying to his attention.

Jay took it from her and pawed at the material inside, 'jeans,' he smiled as he pulled off his dark shades.

'I hope you like them, or should I say you'd better like them. We decided that the one's you'd chosen were a touch Dodge Mc Rodge. So I did a bit of bargaining and managed to get you the 501s for the same price.'

He pulled a grumpy face that said he still liked the other jeans better, or maybe it was just his stubborness in not wanting to allow the decision made, he mumbled something that she couldn't make out but responded to his mood swiftly.

'I'm sorry I got the 501s,' she said firmly, 'but please make your mind up.' He frowned at her and nodded lightly as if to say 'okay fair enough'.

'Anyway I can always change them even though Maria agreed your bum looked better in them.'

A slightly pleased expression morphed into a frown and the second nod of his head was more positive.

'Okay... thanks,' he said closing the bag up. 'What we up to?'

'I saw this top last week, it's brilliant,' she smiled. 'It's so damn cool.'

'Yeah?' he said in a slightly unsure tone.

'No, seriously I've got to get it. You'll probably hate it though.'

'Oh right,' he grumbled.

'Don't go all huffy on me,' she said. 'Come on,' and put out a hand and marched him off to Miss Selfridge.

'I've got to find something for my holiday too.'

She browsed around while he acted stupid to entertain himself. Putting on a lady's hat and the worst pair of sunglasses he could find and followed her around the store grinning.

'Get away from me,' she chuckled and took a few quick steps from him, but he only increased his footing to match hers so she gave up and put her hands on her hips and said, 'I can't take you anywhere can I?'

'Nope... and,' he smirked. ' I'll do anything for a fiver.'

'Now, just be serious for two seconds okay.'

He gave her a nod of his head.

'Now,' she said. 'Here's that top,' and pulled out a medium from the rack. 'What do you think?'

'Do you want me to try it on?'

'For me stupid.'

'Umm... I don't know,' he said, trying to picture her in it.

'You're-'

'Yes I like it,' he suddenly blurted. 'In fact I love it.'

'At least take the hat off Jay when you try and sound sincere.'

By the end of the day she had finally bought a T-shirt, a hamburger and an ice cream, yet sat on the edge of his bed somehow unfulfilled.

'You're still thinking about that top aren't you,' he said passing her a mug of tea.

'Yeah,' she replied, and gave a sigh.

'Why didn't you get it then?'

'Can't really afford it.'

'I'd have given you the money.'

She responded sarcastically. 'Yeah right. You're already seventy pounds overdrawn.'

'Well it's a little bit more than that now.'

'Well then.'

'Money comes and goes. I'll manage, besides I got my wages.'

'That's not enough though.'

She was right, ten hours work at the hardware store was nothing, it was beer money he thought as he rubbed at his chin. 'Why don't you see if your mum will give you some money.'

She nodded and looked at him blankly.

'Come on girl, brighten up a bit, you should be looking forward to the party,' and gave her a nudge.

'Yeah,' she said positively. 'You're right.'

'You okay to stop over?'

'I hope so. I'll have to clear it with Mum first.'

12. Hazy, lazy, dreamworld

Thursday, August 3

Only two minutes to go thought Jay. With aching shoulders and gritty eyes he lumbered the final few boxes onto the top shelf and wiped his brow. He was glad it was time to freshen up for the party, Wilkinson's didn't have the best of toilets to change in but it was better than nothing. He rummaged through his bag, lined up his beverages and money for the night; a small bottle of gin, a small bottle of vodka, a bottle of extra strong lager and eleven pounds thirty two pence. He clasped his hands and rubbed them together with excitement beginning to fill up his senses. Aftershave, hair wax, 501s, black T-shirt, black jacket and he was set to go. He gave himself a wink of satisfaction, brushed his hands through his hair and took a swallow of lager.

'Not bad at all.'

He finished the lager and left Wilkinson's in an elevated mood of exhilaration and anticipation. He sat on a bench by the clock tower consuming sips of gin until Trac appeared with her friend.

'What's that?' she immediately asked sizing the small bottle held firmly in his hand.

'Gin, and...' he said pulling out the other bottle, 'vodka.'

'Great,' she said sarcastically and folded her arms.

'Look, it's okay, it's just that I haven't got much cash and the drinks in the club are so expensive.' He shrugged at her and continued with his justification speech. 'I've only got eleven quid, I'd never get drunk on that,' he explained and followed it with a shrug that said 'give me some slack.'

He noticed Trac's friend and acknowledged her with a smile. She was slightly taller than Trac with blonde shoulder length hair and quite a chunky build, was that offensive he thought? A swimmer's build then? He decided it was better not to remark on how she looked, the simple smile would suffice.

'Shall we go then?' Trac said more positively as he rose from the bench. He took a few last gulps of the gin and then dumped it in the nearest bin as they began to move towards the club. He noticed Trac was wearing a new top. 'I see you decided to buy the top then?'

She did a little twirl. 'You noticed,' she said smiling at him.

'Yeah,' he said positively, 'it looks nice.'

Her eyes narrowed slightly as she studied his face to detect if there was any ounce of sarcasm or not.

'No it's great, really,' he said quickly.

As they approached the club, he began to feel a rush of adrenaline surge through his chest and limbs, generating a tingling heat that urged him to walk faster and shout when he sighted a crowd of friends.

'DDDDEEEE!'

He disappeared into the mob of lads who cheered and engulfed him. Adrian placed an arm round his shoulders and pulled him close and introduced him to one of his mates.

'So you're Jay,' grinned the lad. 'Then you must be the piss artist.'

'Yeah,' he frowned. 'Among other things, I suppose I am.'

'Adrian tells me you're fucking crazy.'

'Oh yeah?' he replied and stepped back to weigh this person up before he thanked him for what seemed to be admiration. He chose to add to his reputation by producing the vodka and taking a frenzied swig holding the neck of the bottle away from his mouth so some of the alcohol spilt and splashed over his cheeks and down his chin.

'Waaaaheyyyy!' roared Adrian further joined by supporting jeers from the crowd. Jay shook his head violently, like a dog he felt cocky and invigorated.

As the commotion subsided, they filtered into the club in single file. The more people that turned up the more Jay drank, he even went as far as saying 'no' to buying Trac a drink.

'Why not?' she harked.

'Because,' he explained confidently with a bit of a slur, 'if I buy you a drink then that's one less drink for me.'

It did seem selfish of him, but then not altogether surprising. She understood though, or at least tried, knowing what he was like around booze. Meanwhile he placed his jacket behind the bar and purchased a bottle of Grolsh. Trac kept showing glimmers of jealousy as he seemed to flirt with every girl he bumped into. She admired his tactics, a little slimy maybe but funny as well. He was on a roll, in the limelight, socialising with everybody. When he had disappeared for a good half an hour she searched the place high and low. Finally finding him, the only reception she got was a dumb smile and a request for a drink before he fell down a short flight of steps. 'Fu... cking... hell,' trailed off as he went. By the time she got to the bottom of the steps he'd began a playful wrestle with Daz. She threw back her hair and ignored his errant behaviour, 'I guess I'll leave you to it.'

Nick and Rob sat at the top bar drinking lightly and having a more pleasant evening until Jay managed to disrupt that as well. He burst through a door ranting, 'they ain't got any Elvis!'

Unfortunately for Jay, the door had slammed open right into a bouncer's face who took it upon himself to keep a close eye on him. Too much in too little time, he wandered round in a drunken haze, occasionally falling into the wall or somebody for support, his legs beginning to give way. Losing his sense of balance Rob helped him into a seat.

'Here Jay, drink this,' he said.

'What is it?'

'It's Coke. It will make you feel better.'

He grasped the glass and knocked it back in one but his stomach soon began to reject it. Rob knew the one drink he could not handle was Pernod, and what he had just knocked back happened to be a double. Jay's cheeks kept bulging, he was going to be sick, something began to rise up his throat towards his mouth. He leant on the table and began to gulp managing to stem the possibility of filling a glass or hurling vomit across the table.

'Fucking Pernod,' he muttered wiping at his mouth. He upped and left for the bar.

'Need something to get rid of the taste,' he spluttered.

The barman observed him holding onto the wooden panelled bar pulling himself along with ease. It was like he was on the deck of a ship in a rough sea.

'I think you've had enough.'

'No,' he slurred. 'Not... not nearly enough!'

'I don't think you should have another drink.'

'I... want one... okay... I'll have a Coke with it.'

'Why don't you save your money.'

'Look just one vodka and I'll be fine. I'll sit over there with my mates.' He turned and gave Rob and Nick a smile.

'Jay how are you doing? You still got that vodka left?' came a voice to his left.

He turned to see Adrian and Dave looming over him in their bright flowered shirts, Adrian's yellow, Dave's pink. He thought maybe he should follow fashion and get one himself, at least if he was sick down it you wouldn't notice.

'Well Jay?'

'Eh?'

'The vodka?'

'No... no. Sorry mate,' he babbled waving his hand at them. 'I... I drank it ages ago.'

'Have you got the camera?' Dave asked.

'Camera?' it puzzled him for a moment. 'Yeah,' he then nodded feebly. 'Used it all up,' and pulled it out his pocket to show them. 'All gone,' he said, and tried a smile but he was rapidly becoming tired.

Dave looked to Adrian, 'you best go and get Trac, he's well fucked.'

Jay placed an arm around his shoulders, 'Dave... Dave... mate, get me a drink they won't serve me anymore.'

Dave propped him up onto a stool under the stairwell and fetched a drink for him. He said something then laughed to himself, he looked dazed and confused, stripped of his customary poise he stared foggily at Trac. His mouth formed an involuntary smile while his eyes rolled back eerily. He appeared slightly retarded in his current mode, he looked simply helpless.

'I... I'll be back in a minute,' he whispered and slumped off the stool.

She sat down next to Nick and Rob, her night was becoming a worry. The bouncer, now standing by the door again, watched the corner where they sat glaring firmly. They all watched the door like they knew what was coming. It burst open again, Jay chuckled as he fell to the ground and began to crawl towards them moving feebly like a landed fish. The bouncer wasted no time and grabbed him. He only managed a shrug at his friends as he passed their table and Trac shook her head in disbelief. A second bouncer joined the first in hurling him outside onto the pavement.

The cold concrete on his face finally brought him out of an unconscious state. After two or three minutes building up energy he pushed himself to his feet and wandered back inside for his jacket, knocking into a glass collector on his way.

'Sorry,' he shouted holding up his hands as if someone was pointing a revolver at him. 'It's okay,' he said. 'I just... just... came back for my jacket... that's all.'

It wasn't long until closing time, so he huddled up in a shop doorway with Adrian talking about something drunkenly for a while before the rest of his crowd appeared and forced him into a taxi. The female cab driver didn't have any Elvis either which set him off again.

'Why haven't you got any Elvis?'

'Because I haven't.'

'Well I suggest you get some,' he smirked and then gave her a long stare as she ignored him. 'Why haven't you got a seat belt on then?' he continued.

'I don't have to wear one.'

'It's 'cause you're fat isn't it?'

'No.'

'Yes it is. It's 'cause you're too fat,' he mused enjoying the supporting laughter from the back of the cab. Making observations of her black and white spotted dress he chuckled and began prodding the white spots.

'Do you want to get out here?' she said sharply, motioning her hand as if to shoo him away.

He glared out the window for about ten seconds and said, 'no, it's absolutely nowhere near where I live.'

Narborough at last. Trac yawned as they climbed out of the taxi. She settled the cost with her friend and looked down at Jay now sprawled out along the kerb babbling incoherently.

'What are you doing?'

'I misjudged, missjjj... I mean I... miss... miscalculated...' by the time he managed to get a word out he simply forgot what he was trying to say.

He didn't appear to be at all steady on his feet once she helped him up by pulling on an arm and the collar of his jacket. With his deteriorating vision and semi-coherent mutterings, she looked worried that he may give way at any second. Looping her arms around him she supported him the rest of the way. He felt safe in her tight embrace, she was warm and the smell of White Musk comforted him further.

'I love you,' he began to babble with a slight whine. 'I had too much didn't I?'

'Why do you have to go further than anybody else?'

He didn't answer to that and instead muttered, 'I'm not feeling so good Trac.' She helped him inside the house and into his room. Switching off the light he fell in the darkness yelling, 'I think I've gone blind.'

She put the light back on and decided to leave it on and helped him undress. He mumbled, 'I love my bed,' several times as his head sunk into the comfort of his pillow.

Rolling onto his back to allow Trac room to join him, he stared at the Smirnoff poster in front of him. It began to whirl about in a clockwise motion, the letters a good six inches tall jiggled about... was he hallucinating? This failed to worry him, he simply tried his best to reposition the letters and failed.

Trac eased back in bed next to him and held him.

Drunk and dizzy he uttered, 'I'm... I'm sorry,' and with a rare moment that doesn't come often enough, confessed to having maybe had too much. Within seconds he was out cold.

Friday, August 4

Seven hours later he woke in the exact same position and it felt bizarre, he glanced to his right to see Trac supporting her head with her left hand looking at him. He found it amazing that his fingers were still laced together on his chest.

'Sorry babe,' he mumbled. 'I guess I got a little drunk.'

'A little drunk? You call drinking until you collapse a little!'

'Okay I was totally wasted,' he groaned rubbing his forehead. 'Don't give me a hard time, my head feels awful.'

'You were quite amusing actually.'

'Really?' he queried and gave her a frown. 'So what happened?'

'You don't remember,' she yawned. 'Probably a good thing.'

'That bad?'

'Just promise me one thing.'

'What's that?'

'We won't go there again.'

'Promise.'

She yawned and dropped her head back onto the pillow. He carried on rubbing at his head and trying to revive a dry mouth while he pondered on what he may or may not have done.

'Hey,' he said excitedly rising out of his seat almost hitting his head on the luggage rack above.

'Sit down,' Trac whispered as she tugged him back, 'people will think you're weird.'

'Yeah but look,' he said as he began to fidget.

'What? I can't see.'

He allowed her into his reading zone of the *NME*. 'Look,' he pointed. 'The Cult tour dates. We've got to go... We've just got to.'

'There's not many venues is there?'

He shook his head as if to say 'so.'

'I don't think Mum will let me go to London.'

'There's Birmingham, at the NEC, look, on the fifth of November.'

'Umm, I don't know Jay. Maybe next year.'

'They won't be playing next year,' he said beginning to look lost. 'Oh come on,' he mumbled bowing his head.

She ran her fingers through his hair. 'You're totally broke Jay.'

'I'll get the money.'

'Well why don't you go with Adrian?' she suggested and his shoulders began to shrug. 'Maybe they'll release some more dates and come to Leicester?'

'No,' he sighed.

'You've seen them before.'

He lifted up his head. 'That was years ago, they're a bigger band now.'

'Yeah I suppose they are a glamorous stadium rock band.'

'No,' he said scrunching his face up in insult and shaking his head at her vigorously. 'Gothic rock,' he demanded.

'They don't look very gothic anymore.'

'What are you on about?' he said shaking his head again in disbelief.

'They're just a band Jay.'

'What are you doing to me?' he said raising his hands to his temples and feeling the early signs of stress.

'Well, who's the one that plays the guitar?'

'Billy Duffy,' he droned.

'All that lovely blonde wavy hair.'

He turned his attentions back to the *NME* and rustled it flippantly. He shunned her by turning his back to her slightly and began to mumble on about how rubbish he thought the charts were, 'fucking Jive Bunny number one, what's that all about? Look,' he rustled the *NME* again 'Sonia, Bros, Kylie, London Boys all in the top ten. Pants, that's all I can say, better off just listening to Elvis.'

Trac edged across her seat to him and said softly, 'arrh is he upset because he loves The Cult?'

He hunched a little, rustled the paper again and muttered something she didn't quite catch.

'Jay,' she whispered in his ear as she eased the palm of her right hand onto his thigh. 'I know they give you a great deal of pleasure but surely not as much as me?'

He felt a wave of warmth flow through him that had an uplifting effect so he turned back to her slightly. He squinted his eyes at her, as he tried to read her face to see if she was teasing him further or trying to make a genuine amend. His eyes eased open as he turned back into his seat properly. Still unsure as to her position he muttered, 'there's supposed to be something in here about New Order too, but I can't find it?'

She could see frustration bubbling beneath the surface of his face, as he flipped the pages over rapidly.

'I must have gone by it.'

'Do you want me to have a look.'

'I knew I should have got the *Melody Maker*!'

'Then you wouldn't be able to read about The Cult.'

His eyes narrowed at her again. 'Hmm true,' he replied, folded it up and placed it on his lap as the train began to slow down for Narborough.

Sunday, August 6

Everything around him had seemed to have grown, the lush greenness of it had a calming effect on him. He didn't know about Trac, but he loved it down the old railway track.

'I like green,' he said. 'Green's my favourite colour.'

'Yeah I had noticed,' said Trac from behind him.

Dew from the lower foliage brushed against his shins leaving wet lines on his jeans. A few paces on, it became dotted with heavier and longer grass, nettles, brambles entwined with lush leafy bushes creating a tunnel of green where the trail tightened, where undergrowth now brushed your thighs and hips as you ducked and weaved your way through. At times only a few spangles of sunlight filtered down onto the foot path marking spots of different colours. They remained for a moment in that dappled light, kissing. He opened the top two fastened buttons of her shirt without her noticing until she felt his warm hands slowly pushing the fabric aside, one cupping her breast the other moving round to the small of her back.

'I'm getting all wet.'

'Oo-er,' he chuckled.

'Not like that,' she smiled giving him a slight shove. 'It must have rained last night.'

'Looks like it.'

He could see ahead where the path opened to a wider space. 'Let's get up to that clearing,' he smiled enthusiastically.

'I think it's going to rain Jay.'

'Nooo,' he shook his head. 'Look it's a blue sky.'

No sooner had he said that when the sound of rain hitting the trees around them began.

'Oh no,' yelped Trac. 'My hair will go all frizzy.'

'I don't believe it,' he mooted holding out his right hand, palm side upward. 'How cool is that.'

As the speed in which it fell became greater Trac squealed and darted under the nearest tree and huddled close to its trunk while Jay looked up to the sky and allowed the rain to hit his face. 'I love it when it's hot and it rains,' he said with a pleased expression, it was as if something magical was happening.

Trac looked at him and laughed, 'you'll get wet'.

'Come over here,' he said still smiling. He held his arms open as his hair began to flatten by the pellets of rain.

'Jay, you're getting soaked.'

Squinting over at her he wiped at his eyes with his sleeve. 'I don't care... I want to get soaked.'

'You're mad.'

'Don't you see it?'

'All I see is you're getting wet and you've got no change of clothes.'

He wafted a hand at her that said 'okay you do your thing and I'll do mine' and continued to wander down the track towards the next bridge enjoying his soaking to himself. A hundred yards down he heard her break into a squeal as she ran after him from one sheltered spot to another. Once she had made it less than fifty feet from the bridge he was telling her to hurry up.

'Quick come, look at this.'

She made a final push, reached his side and looked up to where he was pointing.

'What am I suppose to be looking at.'

'Ugh... the rainbow.'

'I have seen a rainbow before.'

'Yeah, but you've not seen this one. Look at the colours of it.'

She pottered around him and hummed, 'red and yellow and pink and green, orange and purple and blue,' as she did so.

'That's brilliant.'

'It's just a rainbow,' she said flatly.

'Is it?'

'Yes,' she nodded. 'Why, do you think if we walk to the end of it we'll find a pot of gold?'

She sat up on the fence under the bridge, pulled out a cigarette, fumbled with her lighter and lit it.

'Okay, maybe I'm making a moment out of this... when was the last time you saw one?'

She shrugged at him, 'don't know.'

'And why is that?'

'Because I'm not seven anymore.'

'That's my point... well two points. First point is, this shows us that we take things for granted, and two, that this is... well a miracle of nature.'

'I wouldn't go that far.'

'Okay... two, why when we grow up can we not retain what it's still like to be a kid?'

'Because everything when you're small is new.'

'You know I should write about this... Yeah that's what I should do.'

'Write about a rainbow?'

'No,' he shook his head, 'about how much of a good time I'm having with you, the drink, music, The Beast, the sex... friends. It's... It's like this could be my last great summer.'

Trac took another deep pull on her cigarette, 'that would be interesting.'

'Yeah...' he nodded positively. 'I just... just can't believe how good I feel. It's like there's so much spirit in everything I do.'

He ran a hand through his hair a number of times while he pondered. She watched him carefully and could see his mind ticking away.

'I could get Adrian to do cartoons,' he muttered.

'So would this mean you'll have someone like me in it?'

His eyes narrowed as he studied her. 'Yeah, course,' he answered.

'Cool,' she smiled.

He joined her on the fence, watching and listening to the rain. Once her cigarette got as close to the filter as she liked, she dropped it to the floor and pushed herself off the fence.

'Rainbow's gone,' he sighed.

'Mmm and we're stuck here until it stops raining.'

'Correction,' he said as he jumped down from the fence, 'you're stuck here until it stops raining. Me? I'm already wet.' And he darted off back down the pathway looking gleeful.

'You're not leaving me here,' she called after him.

He turned round and gave her a wave.

'You can't get in my house without me.'

'Oh, I'm sure your mum will let me in and give me a towel.'

She stood under the middle of the bridge, hands on her hips, turning in a circle thinking about what to do. He kissed his hand and then pretended to aim it at her before blowing her the kiss.

'You sod,' she yelled.

He put a hand to his ear, 'what's that?' he shouted back with a wide grin. 'I can't hear you.'

There were two people cramped next to Jay in a Mc Donald's booth. He slurped on his strawberry milkshake, looked at the discarded burger wrappers and felt sure they were about to leave. He looked back across to the queues and saw Adrian coming towards him with a tray in hand. Once he got within two feet of the table the couple got up and left.

'That's better,' said Jay spreading out.

The girl that accompanied Adrian opposite him smiled politely. She was pretty and petite, her hair a nice flow of dark and light brown, but she seemed to apply her make up in three or four layers. It was so thick Jay reckoned it was a mask. She gave him a brief glance noticing he was eye-balling her.

'They could have put their rubbish in the bin,' complained Adrian as he swept it to the side in order to lay down his food in the right place.

'What's that?' Jay muttered being snapped from his thoughts.

'You eaten yours already?'

'Yeah, don't take me long, quick eater.'

The girl counted the change out loud with one hand, while the other shoved chips into her mouth which made Jay smile. He didn't know why but he was confused, they looked poles apart.

'You should've brought Trac along.'

'Yeah, I didn't know you err,' he went to point at the girl like she was some kind of object, then stopped himself. 'She's busy,' he frowned.

'I'm nipping to the loo. Don't eat any of my French fries,' she said and trotted off.

'Adrian?'

'Yeah.'

'Can I say something?'

'Fire away.'

'It's just...'

'What?'

'Doesn't matter,' and took another slurp of his shake. 'Adrian they're chips right?'

'Yeah?'

'She called them French fries.'

'So?'

'That's French.'

'Your point is?'

'We're not in France.'

Adrian gave a shrug, 'you're mental'.

'I'm mental. Remind me again why you fell out with Claire.'

'She didn't like pigeons.'

Jay held his hands in the air, 'and I'm mental?'

'Well you see the thing about pigeons-'

Jay interrupted, 'they're flying rats.'

Adrian pointed a chip at him, 'look mate, let's not me and you fall out over pigeons.'

'Fair enough.'

'Anyway I like the sound of this script you want to write.'

'Yeah I'm going to base it on two piss heads.'

'Us?'

'Yeah, but one starts out a complete drunk and the other gets pulled along into it.'

'I'll write some bits and you can illustrate it.'

'Maybe do a bit next week while Trac's off.'

'Where's she off?'

'Ten days in France.'

'Nice one,' smiled Adrian waving another chip. 'You know what.'

'What?'

'These are French fries you know.'

'Eh?'

'Well you see chips are thick cut fried potato and these are fries because they're thin. The French obviously came up with the thin chip.'

'Okay... okay,' nodded Jay. 'I just don't like the French.'

'Really, or is it the fact that Trac's off there?'

Jay just contorted his face slightly in response.

'Now the best chip, is the British chip,' smiled Adrian. 'Needs to be at least ten millimetres in width.'

'Just forget the chip thing,' he dismissed as he picked up his milkshake.

'She seems to be taking her time?'

'Maybe she's putting some more make up on,' chuckled Jay.

Adrian could react in one of two ways to that, be pissed off or laugh. He was glad to see the corners of Adrian's eyes crease up as he tried his best to chuckle without choking.

'Look I'm going to shoot, see what Trac's up to.'

Adrian gave him a thumbs up and attempted to say something but both of his cheeks were bulging. Jay patted him on the back, 'let me know how it goes with what's her name,' and made his way out to High Street.

Thursday, August 10

Trac gave him a puzzled glance but the expression on his face told her there was no time for questions, no time to worry who else was in the house or to play games. He carefully locked his door and put some music on, he lay her softly onto his bed and began kissing her neck and wiggling his hips. He unbuttoned her jeans and forced them down to her ankles until she obliged and took them off for him. They lay together under the sheets, there for hours they wound in and out of each other.

Friday, August 11

Adrian continually told Jay how much he loved to just sit in town during the summer, idly gazing lustfully at the many young long legged girls who pranced around the town, their breasts bouncing beneath the thinnest of cotton tops. Jay on the other hand didn't pay attention so much, yet he couldn't help wondering whether Trac felt the same thing when she looked at tanned hunky men who so perfectly complemented the long legged girls. As soon as that thought occurred to him he felt uneasy, and so turned his attentions to the boot polish shaped tin of Black Diamond hair wax he had just purchased. It was expensive but he had to try to keep his hair somewhere close to his chosen style, even though it was gaining in length.

He spent the evening entertaining Trac. He darkened the room slightly and put on some loud music. Bored, he began acting as though he was in a nightclub and started chatting her up. Smiling, swaying and bending in time to the music he was holding a shot of vodka in his hand as though it was a piece of sculpture. She sat comfortably on the edge of his bed listening to his banter. He swirled round singing, smiling as he approached her.

'Hi, you alright?' he smirked. 'What's your name then?'

'Trac,' she smiled brightly, joyed to be part of the plot.

'I'm Jay, you going to dance with me?' he flashed his smile again. 'Come on,' he pulled her to her feet. 'You've not got a boyfriend have you? Beacause I'm really attracted to you.'

She loved being part of his little games and fell into his arms willingly.

'I don't know whether I trust you,' she murmured.

'Awwh, poor baby,' he chuckled. 'You don't have to worry I'm loyal. Besides you could have anybody you wanted. You're clever and pretty, all I can be is... mildly interesting?'

She gave him a tight squeeze and he kissed her on her cheek.

'You know the important thing about both sexes is, a man loves the woman he's attracted to and a woman is attracted to the man she loves.'

'What do you mean?'

'Well, if you walked into a club, you're so attractive you'd have men falling at your feet. They wouldn't have to know you or even speak to you, that's the way men work, they are attracted by looks immediately. Whereas women only become more interested after knowing a guy reasonably well.'

'I know what you mean,' she said, 'but you've got charm.'

'What?' he asked looking at her softly.

'You can make girls warm to you, especially when you've had a few drinks and you give them your smile.'

'It's an illusion, drunken confidence that's all,' he smiled. 'I only want you.'

'Okay.'

'Good. Now be careful over in France, I know what French men are like.'

'They're horrible,' she smirked.

'True, but you've got to make sure you eat thick cut chips.'

'Right... okay,' she responded with a puzzled frown.

'I'll miss you.'

Patting him she said, 'you'll just miss shagging me.'

Saturday, August 12

The Bell was quiet for a Saturday until he instigated a round of snake bites and whiskey chasers. By kicking out time at eleven twenty, Jay was half on a stool, half on a table, glass raised into the air jeering and singing a poor rendition of Elvis Presley's 'I can't help falling in love,' with Rob, Nick and Daz in tow. It was less than a minute into their performance and the landlord was beckoning him down, which only served to make them even more of a nuisance.

'Get down,' waved the landlord becoming impatient as Rob hollered at him constantly.

'Come on, you're going to get yourself barred.'

Jay thrust his free hand to his chest, 'me barred?' he roared, 'but I fucking live here,' and a cheer went up that made him feel like a king. 'Sooo,' he continued to roar, 'that's four more whiskeys all round,' as he swept his glass across the crowd generating another cheer.

'Come on just... just get down.'

'Line 'em up bar keep... pour yourself a drink too,' he hissed playfully.

'Right that's it, you're out,' and the landlord leant across the table and grappled at his jeans until he had a firm enough grip to pull him down. 'I don't want to see your face again.'

The conflict made Jay chuckle, 'oh, come off it.'

'Just because you have a few drinks doesn't mean you can come in 'ere and take over my pub.'

'It's just a one off,' he smiled looking slightly dazed.

'No, it's not just this occasion, it's every bloody week. Look you're a great lad when you're sober and a pain in the arse when you're pissed. Now come on, shift it,' and jarred a thumb in the direction of the door. 'And that goes for the lot of you.'

Surrounding friends gave out a loud dull groan.

'Look, I'll sit down here and be quiet,' Jay pointed.

'I know you and your mates spend a lot of money in here, but enough is enough.'

'Come on,' smiled Jay. 'I was only messing,' and he opened out his arms to gesture 'I'm sorry mate.'

The landlord put his hands to his hips and just glared at them all. 'I'm tired of seeing you lot in 'ere... come on, please... just... just bugger off.'

'Hey,' smiled Jay putting his arm round Rob's shoulder, 'you're sorry aren't you Rob?' he said patting at his chest.

'Yeah, I'm really sorry.'

Jay could see the guy lighten up in his eyes and used it as the ideal moment in which to surrender his glass for full advantage. 'You'll see me tomorrow,' and nodded over at the bar.

The landlord took the glass and tried not to let Jay's cheek get the better of him by allowing a smile to rise, and said in an altogether lighter and friendlier tone, 'go on, get some sleep.'

'And you lot,' he pointed. 'I'm not serving any more fucking snake bites.'

They gave out a friendly roar and each patted him on the back as they gave up their glasses and meandered out into the car park.

'Eh Rob, I thought we had a drink problem,' he smirked, 'then I found this,' and he pulled out a small bottle of vodka from his jacket and a cheer went up yet gain.

'Let's get some food,' said Daz rubbing at his growing beer belly.

'Chips and beans,' hailed Nick and they let out another one of their cheers.

'Jay, Jason,' called his mum. 'It's the police.'

Squinting, he looked at the glowing hands of his alarm clock, three twenty am. He was woken up so abruptly he felt nauseous for a moment or two before he eased himself out of bed and hit the floor with a thud. He pulled on his jeans and a T-shirt and walked downstairs.

'What's happening? What are you on about?'

'It's the police.'

'What's the problem?'

'Is that your vehicle in the road?' came a voice from the side of him.

He squinted out into the darkness, not feeling that steady on his feet as he stumbled out onto the drive and saw that The Beast was embedded into a neighbour's van.

'Shit, yeah,' he yawned rubbing at his head.

'I take it you didn't park it like that.'

Jay refused any kind of response other than floating the keys to the officer.

'Here. I can't move it, I've been drinking.'

The officer then proceeded to question as to whether he had been drunk earlier when parking but Jay desperately want to get back to his bed.

'Of course not,' he replied dryly.

The Beast came out of the ordeal with a dented bumper, the other vehicle was an old battered work's van and the bloke who owned it didn't seem to be all that bothered. The police left, leaving him four weeks in which to produce his documents. He could see his mum was not amused, so he smiled at her wearily and said nothing that could instigate a row. He wan^ ^ed back to bed without a word and as his thoughts turned to Trac he felt a little lost, it was as though half of him was missing. It was clear, the week was going to progress with the predictable nights out followed by a day's recovering.

Tuesday, August 15

The hospital corridors were so long that the nurses, doctors and visitors who walked down them had vaguely worried expressions on their faces. From time to time the nurses would break into anxious little runs, suggesting that a patient was on the point of death.

He sat in an uncomfortable orange chair leaning forwards, while the nurse pumped air into the cold dull black band of rubber she had wrapped around his arm. He studied the walls, not quite a tranquil cream, more of an off white yellow on one side and an insipid green on the other.

'That's normal,' said the nurse.

He nodded vaguely as he studied a few of the children's paintings held up by lumps of flattened Blu Tack.

'Have you had any problems?'

'Nope.'

'Eat okay?'

'Yeah I can eat what I like.'

'That's good, it's not always the case. How long ago did you have your operation?'

He considered blurting, 'why don't you read the notes.' But he caught sight of his huge folder on the desk and realised he could hardly blame her for not reading everything about him, so he smiled and replied, 'seventy eight.'

'Quite a while ago now then.'

'Yeah, made a big scar, but I guess they cut the right bit out.'

'Quite unusual to have Chrones at that age.'

'So they told me.'

'Do you still have vitamin B injections?'

'No,' he mumbled. 'Not for years. I only have these check-ups once a year.'

'Well, now that you're eighteen, you won't be assigned to the children's ward anymore, and providing your blood sample is normal then we won't send out another appointment. You'll just need to contact your GP if you have any problems, how does that sound?'

He managed a smile, 'sounds good,' he said. 'Apart from the bit about taking my blood. Maybe we could just miss that bit out?'

She smiled back at him and for the first time he really noticed this person, this middle-aged caring lady attending to him.

'I'm sure you must be used to it by now,' she said softly.

'Doesn't mean I like it though.'

'Well, hopefully this will be your last one.'

Although a small amount of blood was taken, he somehow felt weak and light headed, maybe it was a state of mind, he just hated hospital and no amount of false assertion was going to give rise to real positivity. He looked blankly at the small plaster on his left forearm. Even if this was to be the last time, it brought about no relief, he simply rolled down his sleeve and made his way out.

Wednesday, August 16

A setting sun generated a golden orange sky that soon fell to darkness. Stolichnaya vodka, two small glasses and a small bottle of Russchian, an aromatic mixer, stood proudly. An arm appeared and picked up the bottle of vodka and proceeded to pour two large measures into each of the glasses. Pouring in the Russchian Jay felt a happy sensation. Raising his glass Adrian smiled. Freedom felt wonderful. There they sat, the two of them in an open field, talking and drinking until sunrise.

'Well, here we are then,' Adrian chuckled.

'Yep.'

'It's got a peachy taste to it,' announced Adrian.

'Yeah, tastes good,'replied Jay. 'Are you still seeing what's her name?' Adrian shook his head. 'No, no way.'

'Oh right, that's a real shame,' he mused.

'She stunk.'

'Too much perfume as well as make up?'

'No, down there,' he pointed between his legs.

'Right okay,' cringed Jay. 'Just a little too much information for me.'

'I tell you what right...'

Jay raised a hand to stop him, 'no really, I don't want to know,' he said firmly reaching for the booze. 'More vodka?'

'Most definitely,' Adrian replied and passed his glass over for a refill. 'How's you and Trac then?'

'She's great. Can't wait until she's back.'

'How long now?'

'A week.'

'All that time without sex,' chuckled Adrian.

'Miss her company too,' he paused, 'like telling her the events of the day and stupid stuff like that.'

'True love eh?'

'I feel happy all the time knowing she's with me, like nothing else matters... you know.'

Adrian took a large swallow of his drink, then poured out another helping of vodka and added a slug of the mixer to soften its bite. 'I get bored real quick with the one girl,' he said.

Jay smiled, 'variety that's good.'

'Suppose, it would be nice to have someone special,' he mumbled and took another nip of vodka.

'You'll find someone.'

Long after much of the alcohol had filtered its way through their systems, the night became a little windy and the new Russchian mix ran out by three o'clock, at this stage drinking neat vodka posed no problem. The alcohol, more refined now, moved them to continuous monologues of carefree gibberish as they passed through the coldest and bleakest point of the night, when they began to philosophise and discuss God, the universe and aliens. Fondness of the bottle always came to this for Adrian, somekind of meaning to life Jay guessed.

'Do you reckon he's got a home then?'

'Who?' smiled Jay followed by another pull of vodka.

'God!' slurred Adrian.

'What a big mansion type thing?'

'Yeah.'

'Don't know,' he chuckled, 'probably,' he belched. 'Isn't he... supposed to be om... om... omni present.'

'Omni what?'

He shrugged his shoulders and opened his arms, 'don't know.'

'I do like looking at the stars,' mumbled Adrian.

'There's no real God, it's just in the mind right and it's all science...'

'Yeah,' nodded Adrian feebly. 'Wonder if there's another planet... you know with life?'

'More than likely... but hic... hic... nobody wants to believe it.'

'Would be scary though if we found aliens.'

'Bizarre as it might sound... the one thing... hic... more scary than finding... p... proof of the existence of aliens... would be the discovery that humankind is... is totally alone.'

'That's... that's very worrying... profound, but worrying.'

'So then God is just created in the human mind... is what we're saying?'

'Yeah... it's like humans need that comfort type thing.'

'Like an illusion'

'That's it, we're programmed and... and it's the same with love.'

'So now... hic... hic... you're saying love is an illusion.'

'Yeah that is exactly it... our minds deceive us, love is just designed to make us fuck.'

'Ahh... you're proper doing my head in,' mused Jay and was about ready to give up any sort of communication. He took another long swig of vodka and said, 'if that's true then how come you're happy to fuck anything that moves,' and they both laughed.

With the sun coming up and the last few drops of vodka still going down, the darkness faded in the shades of the morning light. They felt very calm and contented, as the rays of light began to spill through the gaps in the clouds.

'Now... that is impressive,' murmured Jay.

'It's magic init,' smiled Adrian.

'I love being out here in the country, still cold but I feel really relaxed,' and poured the last of the vodka into Adrian's glass.

Their day had quickly turned into night and then back again. At half five they made a pathetic effort to go that involved no actual movement just the verbal idea of it being banded back and forth as it was too much like hard work to take it further than that. Jay was becoming dehydrated to the point of almost being seduced by the animal trough, and had a growing need to lie down somewhere comfortable and warm. It was another hour before they stumped up the energy to get back home.

A hot shower brought him some way close to feeling normal. They moved round leisurely, from the kettle, to slumping onto the sofa and back again with little conversation. Just the sound of sipping tea, while hiding the daylight with shades at all times. They felt clear and collected though, just ready to doze off. Nights like these really cleansed the mind of its emotions and problems, they were either released or solved.

Thursday, August 17

There's not much to decipher from an MOT certificate and an insurance document certificate, but the female police officer behind the dark wooden counter seemed to be making a meal of things and was treating him with what only could be described as disdain. He began tapping his fingers without knowing he was doing so until he received yet another glare from the woman.

'You guys should paint this room yellow or something,' he smiled, 'it's depressing.'

Another glare was followed by a grunted, 'can you sign here?' and a biro was thrust towards him. He signed the book and left the police station shaking his head, glad that he was not on a path towards becoming an officer. Apart from the mask you had to wear for the public one hundred percent of the time, they all seemed to be miserable and surrounded by so much negativity. He could feel it about his person and it made him shudder. Thankfully, 'She Sells Sanctuary' was lined up ready to play, within seconds of it rocking through his veins, all that negativity had been obliterated.

Saturday, August 19

Jay felt himself begin to wake. His back ached so he tried to move into a better position but found his movements restricted. He opened his right eye which brought The Yellow Fish into focus, he was in The Beast. He rubbed his eyes with the hope of waking a little more. He was on his own and the air in The Beast was stale. He managed to turn the window down and let in a gentle breeze of fresh air. He realised at that point he was not wearing his usual attire. He had a large lady's brown fur coat, tights and a flying cap on. No wonder I'm hot he thought. The coat made him itch and while scratching, he wondered whether the fur was fake or not. He tried to convince himself it was fake but failing that he used up all the energy he had wrestling it off. Twenty four cans of Asda lager, four Breakers, four Millers Lights, four Foster's, four Budwiesers, four Castlemain, four bottles of Guinness and vodka had been loaded onto the back seat of The Beast, an image of Nick and Rob in similar ridiculous attire did manage to raise a smile. Insobriety had caused them to find amusement in a pile of old clothes that Nick's mum had put out for a rummage sale. Once dressed they adopted southern accents and set about the local pubs in Enderby, seemingly annoying and irritating everybody else around them with great ease. Jay admitted he found it difficult to quell the urge in provoking people into reacting, whether it be good or bad, particularly when drunk. His anarchic behaviour had risen the three of them to youthful cocky defiance and now vicious merriment. Enderby Conservative Club couldn't comprehend such an intrusion and escorted them out immediately, threatening them with fists. Maybe a statement was being made thought Jay, while he swayed in the middle of the street being entertained by Nick arguing from the bottom of the steps of the club in a dress. The 'f' word was being thrown about loosely, and as voices rose further and a drunken scuffle was ebbing ever closer. Jay felt quite unprepared in his current ensemble and remarked to Rob with a casual slur that he should perhaps do something. Rob responded by sizing up the situation, burping loudly with a smile and calling the nearest guy a shit head. Nick immediately followed Jay in a ruptures bout of mirthless laughter to Rob's juvenile quip which seemed to placate the situation almost instantly.

The next thing that disturbed him was the taste in his mouth, lager always left a layer of thick gunge on his tongue that tasted awful.

'Fucking lager,' he mumbled and tried to scrape at it hopelessly.

He scratched around the footwells of The Beast trying to locate a bottle of water. He knew it was in there somewhere, he used it to top up The Beast's radiator all the time. The taste in his mouth got worse and his headache began to get worse too. His impatience and desperation for finding the bottle of water began to bring about a certain amount of stress. Just as he began to get angry and felt like lashing out he found the bottle and opened it so hastily that water spilled about over his chest.

'Shit!' he snapped.

He took a few swigs and rinsed his mouth out but the water in the bottle didn't taste a whole lot better. It had become discoloured with time, algae had started life in there. He eventually sat up and pulled the tights off and searched in his jeans, hoping he had enough change to get a bottle of Lucozade and some Maltesers, the closest thing he found to a hangover cure apart from the usual sweet tea and mounds of Marmite on toast. To his disappointment his pockets were empty. He wiped the condensation from the window screen and looked out. He was in Enderby, still about a mile or so from home and feeling low he realised he was missing Trac badly. He began the search for his keys like a bewildered animal, desperate to get home to sleep it off until things looked like they may be improving or an aura of well-being could take hold. The thought of his bed comforted him, especially the idea of creating a cocoon with the duvet and slipping into a coma, removing him from society for the rest of the day or even until Trac returned.

Sunday, August 20

Jay, always the one to get consumed by new things he loved, now had Nick in tow with all things Elvis. Rob enjoyed a few of the songs like 'In the Ghetto' and 'Such A Night' but the rest of Elvis he could let wash over him. Like Chinese whispers or simply just plain old gossip, the word had been passed from pillar to post that Elvis, as far as Jay was concerned, was better than ninety percent of the chart music currently on offer. This had prompted Rob's mum to send him a typed letter detailing an Elvis convention in September taking place in Leicester with the suggestion that he visit her friends Pat and Mick, regular Graceland visitors.

Pat and Mick lived in a semi detached house on an estate in the village of Cosby that was an ever-increasing shrine to The King. They sat in separate armchairs and allowed Jay and Nick to huddle on their two seater sofa with delicate white china cups and saucers, holding milky tea resting on their knees while being force fed Battenberg cake and listening to their extreme devotion to Elvis. It was clear that Mick was not quite as obsessed as his wife, but he made an enthusiastic pitch for the rare video footage they had just purchased from the states. He grunted as he knelt to the floor to slot the tape into the machine and grunted again as he struggled to get back up to his seat.

'Look at the lamp,' whispered Nick.
The badly moulded figurine of The King in a white jump suit, microphone in hand and a light-bulb holder sprouting from his head was perhaps the most tacky of the memorabilia that littered the room and made a welcomed chuckle.

The video footage was poor, visually blurred and grainy with muffled sound, the quality was not too dissimilar to a seventies porn movie that had been duplicated and watched thousands of times.

After another hour the two of them began to feel dizzy and claustrophobic.

A third pot of tea had been consumed, their bladders were bursting and the cake reduced to mere crumbs on the Elvis coffee table in front of them, it was a case of get the tickets and make an escape.

Monday, August 21

Jay bounded down the stairs and burst into the kitchen, his sister emerged almost immediately behind him. They disagreed on almost everything, if only to annoy one another, but the one thing they did agree on was Monday's usual; mashed potato, chops and beans. The rest of the week their mum put little effort into cooking or even shopping for that matter. He grabbed the plate that seemed to have the biggest portion, but couldn't help looking at the other two plates wishing for more as he felt his stomach groaning in desperation to be filled. The dog yapped like crazy at the commotion, by the time Jay sat at the table both trouser legs had been snaffled by Sam.

Nothing much was said about the interview he'd had at Berkshire College other than the guy interviewing him liked his portfolio, but seemed more interested in getting places filled than anything constructive or negative about his work. On the plus side, his confidential report from Loughborough had been lost, so he figured he had a better than average chance of getting in. Apart from the distance from Leicester and the idea of leaving Trac, the college itself seemed a bit bland and the setting nothing more than a concrete jungle and not quite as appealing as Nick's plan to go travelling.

'America,' Jay suggested with enthusiasm.

'Can't stand yanks,' muttered Nick shaking his head. 'I tell you where we want to go,' he smiled. 'We want to go to Australia.'

Jay had sat back in his seat more and took a sip at his pint as he remembered all the videos and photos he had poured through with Shelley, the sunshine, the golden beaches, the wildlife, it did look a fantastic place.

'But... but it's the other side of the world.'

'Really?' Nick replied sarcastically. 'You know Tez?'

'Yeah, yeah,' nodded Jay.

'Well I'm going to see one of his mates, get all the info as he's off on a year's working visa.'

'It will still cost a bit though.'

'Yeah, you need about two and a half grand.'

'Fuck, where am I suppose to get that kind of money?'

'Get a job.'

'A job?'

'Yeah a job!'

Jay bit on his thumb in thought, Australia, this is possible... this really is a possibility.

Jay lay in bed waiting for Trac, wondering what time she would surprise him with her return. A phone call later and she was on her way. He stood impatiently by the front door occasionally peering out through the little glass windows. He wanted to be carefree and cool about her return, but he quickly faced facts; two minutes into a kiss and his brain would leave his head and enter his jeans. He smiled when a car pulled up and she appeared from it, hair tied back, bag over her right shoulder, black T-shirt, blue snug fit jeans and lovely tanned arms. He pulled his dressing gown round himself and opened the door with excitable energy. She paused smiling, took a deep breath then stepped inside and let his joy and hospitality envelope her.

'Sight for sore eyes,' he beamed. 'You look great.'

'Thank you.'

'Tea?'

'A hug would be nice,' she said with a shine in her eyes. He embraced her and they kissed.

'Come on,' he said taking her hand in his and led her up the stairs to the seclusion of his room. He slipped back into bed leaving her standing with an unsure expression.

'Please don't ask me to get out of bed,' he said.

She smiled and dropped her bag to the floor. He rubbed his face into his pillow and waited for her to join him.

'My bed is my favourite place to be in the holidays. I sleep off my drinks here. I make love to you here, all my emotions, dreams and fantasies are here,' he smiled at her lazily, in a state of dreamy arousal. Next to the phone on the floor was a list of colleges he had every intention of phoning and with Trac back, the rest of the day could easily take place without moving much at all.

'Come on girl,' he chuckled. 'Join me.'

'You're terrible,' she said, and began to undress.

He was intently stroking and patting his mattress on the space he wished her to fill. He watched her every move, becoming excited as she wiggled out of her jeans.

'Sexy,' he gripped her thigh in a tight clench.

'Ow... you'll bruise me.'

He grappled at her further, pulling her onto the bed. 'Look at that tanned body,' he growled.

'Get off me,' she began to giggle as he tickled her sides.

'Stop. Stop it,' she cried out but he ignored her pleas.

Taking in her scent with each kiss comforted the loss of her for the last ten days, and he felt immensely happy. Her desire was increasing, with his swift hands he circled her tummy then moved down between her thighs.

'She's very wet these days,' he whispered.

'I know, I can't help it.'

Glad to be together again they tickled and played in bed. What were once childhood games had become adult sex games.

'Wooo. I am too knackered for all this,' he joked.

'But you haven't even done anything yet.'

'I feel a bit rusty.'

'I've not been gone that long.'

'Feels like it. Still, you know me, I'm no good until the afternoon.'

'It is the afternoon!'

'Is it?'

'It's quarter past twelve.'

'Oh shit,' he rubbed at his eyes. 'I best phone a few colleges up,' and he snatched at the phone.

'You don't fancy doing it then?'

His eyes glinted, 'yeah,' he said looking furtive. 'Let's do that first,' and replaced the receiver.

He continued to stroke her slowly, trying to prolong the experience but the urge to jump on each other became too intense, lust was taking over. She lay helpless as he moved down her body, pulling off her black underwear and gripping her buttocks with delight.

'And who are you going to satisfy with that?'

'Me,' he mused.

'It's going to fall off one of these days,' she said, and smiled as she pulled him close.

'Wait, I want you naked.'

'I am.'

'No. Necklace off... rings off, everything,' he smiled as he undid the black strap of her watch.

'Why?' she asked as she began to remove her necklace.

'I want the natural you.'

Love making was usually quiet, they had developed that skill due to other people often being in the house. This time there was no-one around and the need was distracting, allowing themselves to let go.

'More slowly,' she murmured, 'more slowly inside me.'

His mind was racing, his head began to spin and his body tingled all over.

'Don't stop,' she whimpered.

His breathing was rapid until he jerked frenziedly for twenty seconds or more. The tension flowed into relaxation as he made a slow collapse to her with relief and satisfaction. Holding his head he rolled next to her onto his back. He was flushed in the face and still breathing heavily.

'Wooo,' he gasped. 'I'm tingling all over... that's weird?'

She lifted herself up on one elbow and smiled at him. 'Was it good?'

'I feel dizzy. Sorry it was a bit quick,' he panted. 'That was unbelievable.'

'Massage,' he said mildly, as he floated down into the covers giving her a lazy smile that was hard to resist.

This is heaven he thought, in love, in bed and having a wonderful rub down by the love of his life, could he get any more relaxed? He returned the favour, massaging her arms, squeezing gently down her thighs, he enjoyed that almost as much. His lips were so soft and gentle as he kissed her face, lightly on her eyebrows, her eyes, her nose across her mouth and cheeks. He sucked at her chin, he did that a lot. He tickled his way over her ears making her wriggle and laugh. She purred like a cat, but not once did his hands or lips go where she now desperately wanted them to go. Up the length of her body from her toes, the soles of her feet, calves, her inner and outer thighs, her buttocks, her fingers, her sides, arms, back, neck, shoulders, head. He smiled as he turned her over and did the same as he travelled his way back down her body, her breasts, tickling her belly button with his tongue until finally he was between her legs, there was no part of her that he missed.

'You're staring at me,' she whispered.

'I'm not. I'm watching you,' he smiled smugly.

'Stand up in front of me.'

'No,' she pulled the covers close.

'Go on, I want to see your body.'

'You can see it.'

'Stand up.'

She shook her head wanting to avoid being the centre of attention.

'I want you to stand in front of me. Just for ten seconds,' and he gave her a friendly nudge.

Knowing full well that he wouldn't let this go, she uttered, 'alright,' and reached across and slipped into his towelling dressing gown. She stood in front of him, the curls of her hair tumbled down all sides, biting her lip as if she were doubting the wisdom of letting him see.

'Ready?' she said tilting her head to one side.

'Yeah,' he nodded eagerly and she opened up.

'Well the hips aren't bad and the legs aren't bad either.'

'I'll sit down.'

'No don't,' he said. 'You're absolutely fucking gorgeous.'

'That's it, that's more than ten seconds.'

'No, more,' he smiled making a conscious mental photograph. 'I need to see all of you.'

Trac gave a tut before slipping the dressing gown off and doing a quick twirl before she hopped back into the bed.

He began to hide his face behind his pillow, peering now and again over the top of it, while her eyes scoured his room for any possible changes, hoping that it might just give her a hint of what he may have been up to for the last ten days.

'What's this? Been studying while I've been away?'

She picked up *The Joy of Sex* book from his window sill.

'I found it in one of the cupboards. It's quite a good read,' he said still peering at her over the pillow.

'So that's why you're good in bed? You know all the little tricks.'

'Well I put the effort in, but all women should come with instruction manuals,' he smirked. 'The only thing I had trouble with is the bloke's got a full beard in it,' he said rubbing his jaw. 'The closest thing I can get to it is a few whiskers on my chin like Shaggy from *Scooby Doo*.'

Trac chuckled, 'I don't think the beard's required Jay.'

'You don't think so?' he grinned.

He noticed she seemed to have an aura of vulnerability about her, had she missed him that much? He pushed the book back onto her, and adopting an affectionate tone mumbled, 'take a closer look you might learn something.' She simply smiled. Immediately upon opening it she looked inquisitive. Happy that it would keep her busy for a while he snatched at his diary.

'Right, colleges,' he smiled, as his attention turned to the list of numbers, and began dialling.

Trac peered over at him from time to time and then returned to the book. This went on for some time and made him smile. Unsubtle tactics began as he felt Trac's finger run slowly up and down the scar on his stomach.

He looked up at her, 'you're not a man until you've got a few scars. Hello is that Sailsbury College.'

He began a conversation and she began to arouse him, she took his cock carefully in her hands, traced her fingers slowly up his hard shaft and rolled it slowly between her palms.

'Thank you,' came a high pitched yelp. He coughed deeply putting his right hand over the mouth piece of the phone and frowned. Trac just smirked back at him.

'The book interesting is it?'

'Oh yes... very.'

She looked at the book and his body in a fascinating way. She kept making funny 'umm and arrh' sounds as he tried to make his way through his list of colleges without much luck or progress.

'What bit are you reading?'

'*Males by him for her*.'

He smiled expansively, his feet began to wiggle and his eyes closed as she toyed with his cock. He always reacted the same way and it amused her enormously.

'So you really are going back to college then?'

'Yeah,' he croaked, 'if I get in anywhere.'

'You're just too idle to get a job that's all.' She gave him a smile, 'I've told you before, you can't spend the rest of your life coasting through college and getting pissed every night.'

'I can try though.'

He felt himself getting harder as she put her mouth to him, and his hands clutched the quilt with delight. She used her tongue to excite him further, teasing him she felt wicked. He moved towards her, his hands stroked her naked breasts and nipples gently, until they stood up firmly. His hands worked softly across her body, his actions no longer gentle and patient but firm and demanding. She pulled him up towards her, sat astride his lap and they grinded together, kissing without control. Reaching to a heated climax, he sunk back into the covers slowly.

'Was that amazing or what?' he muttered as he stretched out trying to resist the urge to sleep.

She snuggled into his embrace, closing her eyes as a thrill of happiness washed over them both. Looking at him intently he returned her gaze with his. They lay face to face, heads supported by a hand so that they mirrored one another, lightly touching each other with their free hand. He did things like describing the outline of her hair against her face, stroking her jaw line and along the stretch of her mouth. She reacted swiftly and held his finger in her teeth with a smile.

'Ouch,' he chuckled, with his mouth raising at the corners. 'I like this position, the light on us... talking and feeling.'

'Me too.'

'Love me then?'

'Mmm,' she said softly as her face squashed into his shoulder, 'too much.'

'I missed you no end.'

She stretched upward, hugging her knees to her chest, she tilted her head slightly to one side and said, 'I've got you a present.'

'Oh yeah, what's that then?'

She leant down, picked her bag up and began sifting through it. 'I got you some aftershave. Oh, and your postcard.'

'Umm, a hand delivered postcard that's original,' he mooted and she just stuck her tongue out at him.

He took it, read the comical joke on the front first before reading the back.

'Complete piss heads eh... so the reps were a lot like me then.'

'Yeah,' she smiled warmly, 'out for a good time.'

'Maybe there's a career in it for me?'

'Mmm.'

'You had a good time then?'

'Yep, but I got injured, look,' she pointed to a scar on her lower back. He smiled at her and she continued, 'I was going to get you some Dunhill but I thought this smelt nice.'

He opened the small box to reveal a bottle of Xeryus aftershave. He flipped the top off and took a sniff.

'Smells nice,' he said, and splashed some onto his neck.

'So have you been behaving yourself?' she asked as she began to revive his cock again.

'Yeah, had a few drinking sessions.'

'I didn't mean that.'

He looked down. 'Oh you mean... yeah right as if.'

She gave him a questioning frown and he quickly responded with, 'hey, you know I've only got eyes for you.'

'Umm, so what trouble did you and Adrian get into?'

'A few sessions... went to see Batman.'

'Any good?'

'Yeah, it was alright. I think all the hype ruined it a bit for me, but Adrian's gone Batman crazy.'

'Nothing I should know about then?'

'No not really... fairly sensible actually,' he replied casually.

She made a sceptical 'hmmm' noise and rolled her eyes.

'Ok-aaay... I did wake up in The Beast in some rather bizarre clothes after a night out with Nick and Rob.'

'What kind of clothes?'

'Err... I had a fur coat on and some lovely white tights,' he chuckled, and told her the events of the night. The absurdity stumped her momentarily as if she pictured him in a fur coat.

'Why though?'

'I had to, I was drunk,' he mused.

'You're daft you are,' she smiled.

She shook her head at his weakness to liquor that so easily sent him astray from normality.

'It was a good night out, I'll show you the photos in a bit,' he said casually as if it was an everyday matter. 'Oh shit,' he suddenly snapped.

'Oh no, what now?'

'I got woke up by the police at about three in the morning.'

She looked at him sternly as if she was checking his honesty.

'The Beast, it had rolled down the road and into the side of a van.'

'You're joking?'

'I'm not winding you up, honestly it happened. I must have forgot to put the handbrake on.'

'You're terrible.'

'Oh come on,' he smirked. 'You're the sensible side of me.'

'So what are you saying... I should be with you all the time?'

He clicked his fingers. 'Yeah, that's exactly what I'm saying.'

'You are unbelievable,' she said shaking her head again. 'Was there much damage?'

'Not really considering how far it went. Just a dented bumper and the bloke said he's not bothered about his van, it's a heap anyway.'

'You're always so jammy aren't you, what's your mum say?'

'Just the usual, can't wait till I leave home. I've no respect... erm... how would you like it if I played Cliff Richard that loud... Oh and I treat my room like it's a bed-sit that kind of stuff.'

'Cliff Richard, that was a bit harsh.'

'Yeah I know. I told her I'd throw the stereo out the window. I was just trying to humour the situation, but it set her off again.'

The conversation withered as he got closer to another climax. His right eye opened and he looked down at the fresh semen on his chest and stomach.

'There's six calories in spunk,' she announced. 'I read it some place.'

'Why don't you try some then?'

Her face crumpled as she wrinkled her nose up and veered away slightly.

'Why not?' he chuckled. 'It won't kill you.'

'You first,' she replied, curiosity beginning to relax her to the idea.

He paused in breath and pondered for a moment or too. 'Erm, okay only if you do it straight after.'

'Alright,' she smiled.

She placed some onto her finger and thrust it to his face.

'Go on then,' she demanded.

He stuck out his tongue slowly not convinced of his offer. He took her finger in his mouth and sucked, she in turn did the same.

'Oh, it's got a strong taste to it, it's a bit salty too.'

His expression still looked contorted but he managed to utter, 'it's supposed to be an aphrodisiac as well... although I can't see it myself.'

'Where's your camera?' she chuckled. 'Your face!'

With that said, he scrunched up his nose further, folded his arms tightly and huffed loudly. She shook her head until her hair was out of the way, wiggled her toes and picked the book back up, still amused at him and eager to learn more; the theory then the practical.

An hour later, and he had been prodded and poked enough, despite some things she did he liked. He retrieved the book from her and demanded it was his turn to read about females. She responded just as eagerly, sex was still a whole new adventure for her and she was learning heaps, her excitement level was high which made it all the more fresh and exciting for him too.

'A lad on the bus back from France said I've got sexy feet.'

'You have,' and he kissed them. 'Are you trying to make me jealous. You should cover these up.'

He pulled her feet together, placed them between his legs and she aroused him with the soles of her feet, using her toes too. He decided it was his turn to tease her, beginning with the slow kissing of her inner thighs.

'Still no orgasm?' he suddenly chirped and popped his head up.

'No,' she whispered looking down at him.

He immediately sat up, folded his arms and huffed loudly.

'Tut,' she moaned. 'Don't go huffy on me. You come very close,' she said. 'It's not you anyway, it's me.'

'Okay,' he sighed.

'I haven't done it a lot have I?'

'Well we need to sort that. You seen some of the positions in this.'

'Mmm.'

'We'll have to try out a few of these,' he chuckled.

Kneeling on the bed and treating her as if she was a prop he studied the book and then her as he inspected different parts of her body. Lifting her legs in the air was a pleasant and exciting experience, he liked to see her bum in full glory. He looked up anal sex in the index and kept looking over at her cunningly. When she asked him which bit he was reading, the welcomed naughtiness of it seem to vanish instantly and that seemed to confuse him somewhat.

'Just a bit about bums,' he smirked. 'I mean you have to try these things.'

'Mmm, I suppose.'

They made love again in various positions, some a struggle that led to impatient muffles. 'Look, you're not doing it right,' to some she said did nothing for her, to positions that needed awesome skill and dexterity. They finally finished in their usual comfy position.

'Wooo,' he said, 'that has worn me out. I'm all done.'

'Don't you dare fall asleep on me.'

'Just five minutes,' he said.

'No. I'm not having that.'

'Oh come on, I'm all empty. I need to recoup.'

'You just can't keep up.'

'Well let's have a shower then.'

'Yeah okay,' she smiled. 'Then food.'

Jay sat up on the kitchen worktop with just his jeans on, eating some of Trac's speciality, peanut butter on toast followed by a can of chilled Guinness to wash it down.

'I don't know. Drinking again.'

His response to that was just to gargle a mouthful as loud as possible. When she pulled him up for it, he rasped his tongue at her and followed it with a chuckle.

'You slob,' she said with a smile.

'I try my best.'

'What shall we do now?'

'I'm going to have to phone some more colleges I guess.'

'What are you going to do if you don't get in any of them?'

He shrugged. 'I've no back up plan. If I don't get in anywhere... I don't know? I don't want to work, maybe I'll go back packing for a few months.'

'You need money for that.'

He shrugged again. The longer the summer went on, the more relevant his future became, to the point where it should have made him anxious but it still bored him to a certain extent.

'Oh, I'm not bothered,' he muttered dropping off the worktop. 'Neither should you be. So let's talk about you instead.'

'You know I'm going to do my A levels,' she replied. 'I get my results Friday and I'm shitting myself as to what they are.'

'They'll be perfect.'

'I'm not so sure, I did fuck about a bit, so I know they're not going to be that good. As long as I'm able to face my mum and dad I'll be fine,' she smiled. 'Anyway no use moaning now.'

'Okay then, so you're sorted.'

'Let's concentrate on you then.'

'Part of me just can't be bothered you know.'

'You just need a push.'

'And you're the one to do it?' he frowned.

'Doesn't it bother you that you've taken my life and turned it inside out, all I seem to think about is you?''

'Isn't that why you love me.'

She gave him her own shrug this time, 'might be.'

'I know I live in my own world... it's just easier that way.'

He took another swig from the can. 'Some things can just happen to you for no reason at all, that can just make you switch off and give in.'

'You're getting all cynical on me.'

'It's just that bad things happen to good people all the time and it's just not fair, at least if you're a bad person or at least someone who never puts their all into something it doesn't matter so much.'

'You've got to think about your future though.'

'I tell you what. You can earn the money and I can well... just breathe creativity.'

'That's really going to earn you a living.'

'Does any of that really matter? It's like... life is so simply we just make it complicated. What matters right now is you,' he smiled.

'I worry about you Jay... that's all.'

'I know you do, but you don't have to keep reminding me.'

'It's nearly the end of August, college starts in two or three weeks.'

He gave out a groan, 'I don't know... maybe I should just get a job?' and looked at Trac vaguely, almost hoping she would take control of the matter and decide for him.

'Jay,' she exhaled, 'when it comes to deciding about college, work and travelling, I'm sorry if I don't seem any help, but it is your choice. Only you can make the decision... what's right for you.'

He groaned again and felt like dropping to the floor as if all the energy had been drained from his body.

'I'd stop worrying at the moment. Wait and see whether you do get into a college first.'

'I have been trying to get in somewhere and to be fair I was making calls but somebody was distracting me,' he frowned at her.

'Okay,' she smiled and clapped her hands. 'Pass me your diary.'

'Why?'

'Come on,' she beckoned it to her with her hands so he passed it to her lethargically.

'Right you read out the colleges that sound good from the pool list and I'll write them down. Then you can ring round in order of preference,' she said positively. He went to salute her again but she was too sharp for him and said, 'don't even think about it.'

He smirked at her, picked up the list and said, 'I'm glad you're back.'

'Me too,' she smiled and they began working their way through the list.

The conversation switched from one topic to another, somewhere in between he took a call from York College with an interview offer and that managed to resolve some of the issues discussed. She was glad he was trying to further his education, she only wished he was doing it for the right reasons and not just as a way of avoiding work for the next couple of years in order to pursue his drinking career.

13. In between days

'Boogaloo,' Jay muttered.

'What?' Trac asked.

'The record shop,' he said with more definition. 'I'm going to the record shop up there,' and pointed.

'Oh you,' she moaned.

'Look, you nip to the bank and I'll meet you outside the shop. Then I can walk you to your bus stop before I go to work.'

'Alright,' she replied.

He smiled and jogged up the road. Town seemed busy for a week day, five o'clock was closing in and five hours of stacking shelves was slowly turning into a torturous affair. He sifted through the vinyl LPs and flipped a coin to make the decision... heads... he bought an Elvis album. Leaning against the shop window empty handed, he thought about flipping the coin for the best of three while he waited for Trac to appear. He glanced up the road to see her running towards him.

'Jay!' she cried.

As she got closer, he pushed his back from the glass ready to greet her hurtling desire to be with him.

'A bloke,' she stammered, 'he just said something.'

'What?' he questioned. He was confused looking at her desperate red face.

'What he wanted to do to me,' she babbled.

'Where the fuck is he?' he shook his head and tried not to get worked up by her distress. He realised quickly that he needed to hide his anger and offer comfort. He moved back to hug her but she backed away from him.

'I'm going,' she mumbled. 'Phone my sister... I'll... see you later.'

With that said, she disappeared down the street, leaving his anger subsiding into disappointment.

At work he moved around the aisles like a zombie until he leant on a shelf and felt like slipping to the floor and staying there until he felt better. He phoned Trac at six thirty and pleaded for some kind of answer.

'I'm sorry,' came her voice. 'I just freaked out and spoilt the whole day... sorry it happened.'

'It wasn't your fault was it,' he replied. 'I've been worried about you ever since.'

'I'm okay, honestly it just scared me. I really don't like things like that and in broad daylight too.'

'Why didn't you let me near you.'

'I don't know, I just felt awful. When I met my sister I just cried it all out. And I had to tell my mum cause she heard us talking.'

'What did she say?'

'She went mad at me, insisting I don't travel back to yours by myself and that I should never walk around on my own in Leicester.'

'Easier said than done.'

'I know she has a point, but it can happen anywhere at anytime, I can't spend the rest of my life paranoid about it.'

'I would've taken the night off work you know.'

'I'm sorry I ran off.'

'I feel bad, I should have ran after you.'

'You can't be there to protect me all the time.'

'I just wish I was though,' he urged.

'You sound more upset than me.'

'I felt angry at first, now I just feel hurt. If someone hurts you, it hurts me too.'

'Can you finish early and come over?'

'Sure, I'll see you about nineish.'

'I love you.'

'Love you back.'

At eight thirty he left Wilkinson's, jumped into The Beast and, roaring it into life, he tore off down the road and broke at least four speed limits before arriving at her house. In an emotional state she welcomed him with a warm smile and a tight embrace that lasted.

Friday, August 25

Jay sat in The Beast on Trac's driveway, the sun in his eyes and a sparkle of dew on the ground, waiting and wondering where she might be. He turned down the music a few notches adjusted his seat to give himself more leg room and began to read her latest letter;

To Jay,

Hello! Wow! you cry, a letter from Trac, to what do you owe the pleasure? Well I'm unsure too. I'm just in a letter writing mood. Yes I do know my writing is messy but it has been a long time since I last picked up a pen. Thank you for a nice welcome home it's nice to receive a big hug and a kiss on my return. I missed not having you there to put up with my moaning and to pick me up in my moments of misery, so I promise I'll never take you for granted ever...

'You got my letter then,' came a voice to his right.

'Hi, yeah I was just...' and placed it back into the top pocket of his black shirt. 'Where have you been?'

'Post box.'

He climbed out The Beast and gave her a soft kiss to the forehead, put his arm around her and walked her up the rest of the driveway.

'So you got your GCSE's then?'

'Nine of them,' she said triumphantly.

'Who's a clever girl then,' he smirked, and gave her a squeeze. 'That's great, I'm pleased for you... I'm proud.'

She was totally absorbed by her results, happily tidying the kitchen, not listening to him yakking away as she floated from one cupboard to the next. He gave up the power of speech and sat at the dining table twizzling a two pence coin and listening to the soft crackle of the radio, when she uttered, 'I'll make us some tea.'

'Any biscuits?'

'Sure,' she smiled. 'Why don't you go to my room and put some music on and I'll bring it through in a sec.'

Slouching onto her bed with the stereo remote he noted that she had been peeling off her wallpaper again hoping her mum would give in and decide to redecorate. He had made a point of enlightening her to the fact that white wallpaper with thin red diagonal lines was so very early eighties. She knew this already and he found it now grated at her all the more. He wrote in small print *I love you* on the wall next to her pillow so she would see it easily.

'What are you going to get me for my birthday then?' he asked as she approached with two cups in hand.

'I don't know yet,' she said passing him his tea.

'What about a nice bottle of vodka?'

'I'm not buying you alcohol,' she responded harshly. 'I thought you were going to cut down?'

'I am,' he replied. 'I'm off the bottles now.'

'Why? Have you found there's more in a crate?'

He lifted the tea to his face and chuckled softly at her joke. 'Maybe you can get me a hip flask.'

'No,' she replied flatly.

'I've seen one. It's stainless steel with a black leather surround and the cool bit is... it's got a safety catch on the lid so you don't lose it when you're half cut.'

She smiled at his enthusiasm for this item and not wishing to dampen his spirit she replied to that with a shrug that said 'we'll see.'

'Well it's going to be low on the present count anyway,' he muttered.

'Why's that?'

'Mum and Dad are getting me a stereo but it's too expensive. I'm having to wait until Christmas now.'

'Oh good.'

'How's that figure?'

'Well, I get to keep all your CDs a while longer.'

'Guess so, brainy,' he smirked and she mooned up at him. 'I take it your mum and dad are proud.'

'I think they expected me to do well, but you're proud of me.'

'Yeah I am... knocked out, really.'

'Good.'

Saturday, August 26

Trac took the day off work and found Jay in high spirits. He wasn't vocally equipped to pose any threat to Pavorotti or The King, but that didn't stop him from treating her to a poor rendition of, 'Release Me'.

'You're in a good mood,' she smiled.

'Yep,' he cried twirling a frying pan in his hand.

'Must have been a good night?'

'Unbelievable,' he smiled broadly.

'Human sacrifice?'

'Just a bit of harmless drunken fun is all.'

He gave a cunning glance which she knew meant one thing; he'd been up to no good.

'What did you do this time?'

'You know, the usual.'

'Hmm,' she murmured with curiosity but he failed to divulge and replied with a smile and a simple shrug.

'While we're on the subject of piss ups, I've got tickets to an Elvis convention on the ninth of September. Me and Nick are going, I wondered if you wanted to come along too?'

'No, I don't think so.'

'Oh, why not? Come on it will be good fun.'

'An Elvis do!'

'Yeah. It'll be a right laugh.'

'Honestly Jay,' and she shook her head at him.

'Oh come on, live a little.'

'And watch you two get drunk and pour beer all over your head, it's cute but I think I'll give it a miss.'

'Okay... bacon?'

'Please,' she chirped leaning over his shoulder.

'Arrh positivity at last,' he said with an element of sarcasm, as he flipped the frying pan about further.

Trac sat cross-legged on the sofa, elbows on her knees and head in her hands. Jay's bottom lip was sticking out further by the second. He toyed with a cotton thread that was hanging loose from the bottom of his curtains continuing his hard done by aura, but Trac wasn't budging.

'Let's just try it,' he moaned. 'See what it feels like without.'

'No.'

'Why?' he persisted.

'Because you'll get carried away.'

'These take the romance out of it,' he complained throwing the empty pack of condoms to the floor.

'I'm too young to go on the pill and I've got to be baby-proof somehow.'

'Okay fine,' he sulked.

'Besides,' she said, 'if you're going off to college we won't be doing it as much.'

He grunted something but she couldn't make out the words. 'Don't wind me up,' she said calmly.

Giving her the silent treatment was his next plan but it didn't last long, it never did with her. He gave her a frown and a shrug of his shoulders, feeling guilty for his mood on the subject, he opened his arms as if to say 'I'm sorry' and mumbled, 'I just want to feel you.'

'Mmm... okay then, but just a few times and then you have to put one on.'

'Might be a problem,' he said looking helplessly at the discarded packet on the floor. 'All out.'

'Looks like a no then,' she said. 'Unless you want to be a dad that is.'

The sexual thoughts cramping their way into his head didn't appreciate the invasive notion of fatherhood. When he failed to respond verbally she asked, 'how many kids do you want?... obviously not now but when you're older... if you ever grow up that is.'

He glared up at her thinking 'what kind of question's that?' and continued toying with the thread of the curtain.

'So how many?' she asked again, putting more energy into her voice, willing him on to give her an answer.

'None,' he sneered, still trying not to equate his sexual thoughts to the realities of procreation. 'I hate the little fuckers,' then broke into a chuckle at the sight of the shocked expression that had transformed her face. 'I'm only joking,' he said. 'It's not something I've thought about. Maybe one of each.'

'And one accident.'

'Yeah, but no more,' he moved closer to her, bringing one of his knees up between hers and through her thighs and began to kiss her neck.

'This is not fair Jay.'

The ideal solution then popped into his head. 'We could use the one from house party photos,' he smiled expansively.

'Use what?'

'Adrian's unused jonny from the house party. I put it in with the photos because he didn't pull did he.'

'Yeah, because it's out of date.'

'It'll be fine... we could have a shower?'

Her eyes lit up and he took her hand. Ten minutes later, music blaring out loudly, water running, they were in the shower. Within half an hour she was tugging at his towel and chasing him around the landing.

'I'm sorry, but no more today,' he laughed.

'Come on.'

'Go away,' he chuckled. 'Okay... okay... it'll cost you.'

Finally he made it back to his bed but for a short sleep only... he insisted.

It was the phone that woke him. When he opened his eyes he found his bedroom bright, the clock read eight thirty pm. Trac was sprawled out on top of the covers fast asleep, her body washed in the remaining sunlight, bold curves that gleaned softly, her perfect form satisfied him. He slipped his hand down and picked up the receiver.

'Hello,' he croaked rubbing at his eyes.

'Jay, it's Nick are you coming down the pub you poof?'

He listened quietly for ten seconds as he wrestled with his conscious.

'I'm with Trac.'

'So bring her with you.'

'Yeah, I might later,' he replied and put the receiver down.

'Who was it?' he heard Trac mumble.

'No-one,' he said and kissed her on the cheek. 'Go back to sleep.'

Sunday, August 27

Jay woke with a parched throat. Trac gave out a whine and pulled the duvet up to her midriff, her breasts looked even more shapely in the light of day. He closed his eyes saying to himself 'she looks so gorgeous first thing in the morning'. Pressing his body to hers he whispered, 'I love you.'

A soft, 'umm,' resonated from her as she began to wake slowly. He kissed her cheek and told her she looked beautiful. She said nothing and rubbed the sleep from her eyes. He sat up and caught his reflection in the mirror at the bottom of his bed, only to see he had hair like Stan Laurel.

'Just think I could've spent the weekend at the Reading Festival,' he yawned. 'Seen The Wonder Stuff, The Mission-'

'And New Order,' she yawned back.

He squinted at her to see if she was being sarcastic or not.

'Well,' she said positively. 'You've had a much better time spending it with me.'

'Never had the money anyway,' he replied flatly.

He leant forward and grabbed one of her feet that was sticking out from under the duvet.

'Sexy feet,' he roared squeezing her foot hard.

She pulled it away quickly under the covers and put her hand on his arm. He thought to himself, I'm going to have to pounce on this splendid looking lady.

Monday, August 28 (Summer Bank Holiday)

It was warm and bright despite the breaks of rain. Leicester town centre was crowded and Trac was waiting in the usual place tapping her fingers in the doorway of Tie Rack. She was wearing a black cotton jacket, tight ripped jeans, and carrying an umbrella. She had a great shape in those jeans, terrific legs he thought, having not given them much of his time recently. She smiled a big warm smile when she saw him. In this weather he was certain Trac would not want to wander around window shopping and therefore knew that within an hour, the several pounds jangling in his pocket would be no more.

'Hi,' she said, 'you look like a drowned rat.'

'I feel like one,' he muttered shaking some rain from his hair. She noted the corners of his mouth rise and asked him what he was smiling at.

'I got into Berkshire College.'

She raised a smile herself and seemed to do a little jump, and that was it; he was right, she was more excited about it than he was.

'Give us a kiss,' she said warming to him.

He opened his jacket and pressed the only dry part of him to her and they kissed. She was in a great mood and any doubts he had of going off to college had to be put to the side, how could he ruin how proud she was of him?

'Are you still going up to York to have a look.'

'Yeah, my mum's taken the day off work and that so...' he shrugged lightly.

'Come on then,' she chirped. 'We should celebrate and have a drink.'

They were laughing when they got into the pub but he felt the sinking feeling again when Trac ordered a whiskey and ginger so he ordered a half of lager to balance the cost.

'My overdraft doesn't make for good reading,' he muttered defensively.

'I'll get these then.'

'No, it's okay,' he said.

He wanted to treat her right which meant drinks, pizza, night clubs and the cinema, or at least right when he was sober.

'As long as you're sure,' she said in a concerned tone.

He avoided a sigh and replied softly, 'yeah I'm sure,' as he picked up the small pathetic amount of lager in a half glass that only offered him two, maybe three gulps.

Tuesday, August 29

Jay had to stay upright for a moment and think. He leant his portfolio against the car and rammed his hands deep into his jean pockets. He began to shuffle his weight from one foot to the other, and was about to start pacing when his mum got out the car.

'What are you doing?' she asked, looking at his puzzled expression.

'Just stretching my legs before the journey home.'

'How did you get on?'

'I got in,' he said with no real tone, certainly not as uplifting as she might have expected.

'Oh that's brilliant,' she said, her face lighting up with a wide smile. 'York is such a nice place as well.'

'It's okay.'

At least someone was happy he thought, he just felt confused, whether it be Berkshire or Yorkshire it meant leaving Trac and that was something he did not want to think about, it only created a sinking feeling in his stomach. Once inside the car and half an hour into the journey he felt increasingly uncomfortable in his seat, wishing he could be in a far more friendlier environment, a place where he could think things out. His mum, as expected, had not stopped going on about it, in fact it was escalating. She had began to make plans already and made him feel increasingly claustrophobic.

'This will mean your dad can't stop paying your maintenance.'

'Right,' he nodded vaguely.

He didn't wish to dampen her good spirit by grunting something negative about the whole thing as he could see it leading to an argument and then a horrible awkward silence the rest of the way. Besides this, she was the happiest she had been for him for a long time, if not forever and maybe even a little proud. So he just nodded occasionally and waited for everything to sink in.

At home she was straight on the phone to his nanna, then his dad, but there her mood began to change rapidly.

'At least he's shown interest... Berkshire and York... Well he will be qualified to be a graphic designer... Yes I know... but he's not interested in... you know he's more creatively minded.'

He made a cup of tea and sunk into the bean bag in front of the TV and wondered what was worse, seeing his mum overjoyed for him about something he was so unsure about, or her defending him on it? Once the word maintenance payments and court had been mentioned, he figured he'd been quickly turned into a pawn in the bigger battle of their ongoing separation and turned the volume up on the TV in an effort to drown it all out.

Wednesday, August 30

He arrived expansively grinning.

'What? What is it?' she looked at him with puzzlement.

'Well I was saving it to tell you... I got in at York.'

'Oh that's great.'

'I suppose I've got to choose now.'

'You should have phoned me.'

'Well I was kind of happy but deflated all at the same time.'

'Why?'

'I'm not so sure about it... they're both miles away.'

'What else are you going to do if you don't go?'

He shook his head. 'I want to go back to college, it's just that there so far away.'

'We'll be fine,' she smiled. 'Which one are you going to accept?'

'York I think.'

York felt like the right choice, although he hadn't based the decision on anything significant.

'You'll soon get used to being there.'

He shrugged vaguely. 'I'm not sure.'

'You'll have a great time.'

'At least I won't be nagged. It's just... you might meet somebody else.'

'So might you.'

He smirked, 'yeah, I suppose I could have two girlfriends on the go.'

'Yeah right!'

'It's not a bad idea,' he teased. 'Think about the sex.'

'Not unless you want to keep what's between your legs attached!'

'Oooo,' he mused.

'You watch it with that damn smile.'

'I'm only messing,' he chuckled. 'I don't want to meet anybody else.'

She smiled, 'well that's okay then.'

'Say you love me'.

'You know I do'.

He pulled a sad face at her, 'don't let me go,' he said.

'I won't,' she repled. 'Besides you might stop wanting me.'

'I'll always want you in my life,' he said calmly. 'You're my best mate.'

She didn't say anything to that, didn't even smile, just stared right into him unblinking for several seconds as a tear sprang into the corner of her eyes. She then jumped to her feet and clapped her hands.

'Hey,' she chirped, 'I'll have to show you the dress I've made. Wait here I'll go and put it on.'

He let her go, to him they were a team, they connected. She made him feel strong. She believed in him and now a move to York suddenly didn't seem so bad anymore. As she entered back into the room, his eyes lit up as he rose from her bed overwhelmed at how great she looked in the long sweeping charcoal black dress.

'Look at you,' he smiled as he eased his way towards her.

'You like it then?'

'Very... very sassy. You look... you look amazing.'

She tilted her head to the side. 'Well you'll have to memorise this image, I don't often wear dresses.'

'Oh babe,' he chuckled, pulling her to him, mischief flickering in his eyes. 'Let's do it now,' he urged.

'I can't, Mum and Dad.'

'Look, just shut the door, draw the curtains and leave the dress on,' he said quietly.

'You're crazy,' she whispered.

'You make me crazy.'

'You're so bad for me.'

'No,' he smiled. 'I'm good for you.'

She pulled an unsure expression as she bit down on her lip.

'Is that a yes I see?'

The answer was a squeeze of his hand as she eased onto the bed and lifted up her bum slightly allowing him to pull her knickers off swiftly.

'Jay?' she whispered.

'Yeah?'

'How did you know I would respond to you the way I have?'

'Because... I see myself in you.'

They walked a third of the way down Jubilee Walk where it opened into a bald spot and scurried halfway up the left hand embankment. It was peaceful and gave them time away from parents and everything else in life. This was perfect he thought walking, talking and playing in each others arms. He sat astride her and began to smirk.

'What are you up to?'

'Me?' he replied, 'nothing.'

'Yes you are, I can tell.'

He laughed as he began to tickle her sides and she wiggled in a frenzy.

'Stop... Stop it,' she screamed.

Her shirt came loose from her jeans, so he pushed his face into her belly and began to make rasping noises.

'I swear you're mad.'

He looked up and smiled. 'You know what, you looked real good in that dress. I don't know why you don't go into fashion.'

She shrugged, 'I'm not sure? Just want to be rich... maybe be an accountant.'

'It's a bit boring though isn't it? I'm not so bothered about money I just want to be happy and do something I enjoy doing.' He looked in a thinking mood and paused momentarily. 'What will you miss about me the most?'

'Being together...' she answered, as she moved him onto his back. 'Seeing you in your black shirt, smiling at me.'

Growling, she bit the top button from his shirt, took it from her mouth and passed it to him, 'here.'

He looked at the small black button resting in the palm of her hand and gave her a frown as he retrieved it. She adjusted his collar slightly and said, 'it looks much better having more buttons undone.'

'Well if you like it that way I guess I can live with that,' and lay back lacing his fingers together on his chest, quite content for the day to run its own course.

After several hours of idle conversation, kissing and snoozing, he leapt to his feet and clapped his hands. 'Right got to go then,' he said as he began to look furtively at his surroundings. Trac gave a yawn and stretched her arms out and found it amusing that he went from one extreme to another, well from being lethargic to being hyperactive anyway, there was never an in between.

Friday, September 1

Jay was nineteen, and that, he realised with a shudder as he slipped into his black shirt and jeans, was the end of being eighteen. So now in the last year of his teens, mature adulthood seemed to want to grab him by the ankles and race him forwards, but all he wanted to do was go the opposite way.

He rang the doorbell and peered through the patterned glass to see Trac reach for the door and unlatch it. He hopped in grinning, resting his hands on her shoulders and gazing down into her eyes he planted one kiss on her lips before plonking himself on the second from bottom step of the stairs. He unlaced his boots while she sipped at her tea, swaying happily.

'Nineteen! Big boy now,' she said.

He looked up and laughed, 'yeah, past my sexual prime now.'

'We'll have to see about that,' she smiled.

Every detail of him finally began to find a place, each piece of information was part of a jigsaw puzzle she was putting together to get the fuller picture.

'I thought your tax ran out yesterday.'

'It has, I'll get a new one soon.'

'You shouldn't be driving without a tax disc.'

'I agree, but I can't afford a new one so there you go,' he muttered as he followed her into her room. He happily put on 'Presley' the all time greatest hits double CD that she'd bought him. He smiled at the note she'd written inside on the back of the booklet; *Love you very much, Trac x*

'Are you okay Jay?' she asked. 'You look a little sad.'

'I don't know... you're the only thing that's made my birthday special, plus I'm getting old,' he complained.

'You're not old.'

'It's just that now I'm going to York, I worry that we'll drift apart.'

'You're coming back to see me at weekends aren't you?'

'Yeah but...'

'We'll be okay.'

'Then why is it that the bigger part of me doesn't want to leave you?'

'I can't ask you to stay.'

'I just always want to be there for you. York seems like a million miles away. I don't want to leave you behind.'

'It's not Australia.'

As he moved to the edge of her bed, he had a veil of worry spread across his face, Shelley... he had been here before.

'You know, you've got to do this,' she said firmly. 'You might love it meeting new people.'

'I'm really happy here and I don't want to meet new people.'

She pulled another present from under the bed and passed it to him. 'Here.'

'What's this?'

'What's it look like.'

'But you already bought me a CD.'

'I spotted this and just had to get it.'

He unwrapped the present, it was obviously an album by the shape. 'Elvis in concert' the two record set from CBS Television with additional songs recorded on tour, June 1977. 'Magic,' he smiled.

'I've listened to it and it's quite good... oh and here's your card.'

He gave a warm smile. 'You spoil me, you do,' he said, and she nodded in agreement. 'Finished at Wilkinson's last night so at least I'll be able to see you a bit more before I leave.'

'Except Saturday night,' she mumbled.

'I bought the tickets for the Elvis convention ages ago, I didn't know it would be my last Saturday... I did ask you to come, you still can if you want. I'll buy you a ticket on the door.'

'No it's alright, I'll see you on Sunday, besides you'll want to get drunk before you go.'

He wasn't going to argue with that statement and bowed his head to study the album.

'So what time are you going?'

'I've only just got here.'

'No, I meant tonight.'

'Erm, I don't know. Whenever.'

'Come off it Jay, it's Friday night, it's your birthday, tradition has it you'll go up the pub with the lads.'

'You don't mind do you?' he asked softly.

'No,' she shook her head. 'I know I have to make these sacrifices.'

He gave her a light hearted smile, then dropped his head to the floor and played with his hands. There was a long pause, she was looking at him in an odd sort of way and then she said in a low voice, 'do you really love me sexy pants?'

He nodded. 'Of course I do.'

'More than?'

'Yes more than Elvis, The Beast and,' he coughed to cover up the word, 'drink.'

She didn't seem to mind, just gave him a friendly punch on the arm.

'The only things I care about is me and you. Just don't go telling anyone.' She smiled widely, 'thank you.'

'So does that mean you'll stay over some nights next week?'

She bit her lip and nodded. 'I'd already thought of that.'

'You're terrible.'

'It's your bad influence.'

Later Jay relived some of the romantic moments of the evening, sure that Trac would be doing the very same and wishing that he had stayed and continued the romantic atmosphere that made him feel so enchanted. A police siren screaming down the road rudely struck him from his daydreaming. He pulled on his black shirt and poured himself a large glass of whiskey, holding it up to his reflection in the mirror, he wished himself happy birthday and knocked it back.

'I'm going to drink like a fish tonight,' he said calmly, and began to button up his shirt.

In less than an hour he was in the New Inn, Enderby, drinking whiskey and having a ball. He spent most of the night making a racket on the piano and singing with only a marginal hint of musical talent. Everyone there was jeering him on and wishing him a happy birthday.

'So now you're off to college. Does this mean you're going to go all twaty on us?' asked Nick slapping him on the back, followed by Rob's delayed jeer.

'I doubt it, seeing as it's me stopping you pair from being twats.'

'You're coming back at weekends right?'

'That's the plan.'

'You better, I can't put up with this muppet on my own,' smiled Nick thumbing at Rob.

By last orders they were all absolutely paralytic as they made there way to Sam and Hung's mobile Chinese, in the heart of the village.

Saturday, September 2

He put the TV on for the *Chart Show* and sunk into the sofa. Bleary eyed with messy hair, crumpled Cult T-shirt and jeans that felt a little too tight around the crotch area, he squeezed the dog's mini black and white football until he leapt from the floor and snaffled it from his mitts. He usually enjoyed his birthdays and had to admit yesterday had been a lot of fun, now the day after seemed harder. Lacing his fingers tightly together on his lap, he didn't feel so good and on top of that he was worrying. He got this from time to time, worrying too much about silly things and fretting about what might or might not happen. Luckily this doubting side had always been overridden by a mega self confidence, verging on cockiness, that came from nowhere and rounded it well with cheeriness that more than made the balance. He kept telling himself that nineteen wasn't old and that going to York was a great idea, and that got him so far. Instead of feeling the most pathetic guy in the world one half of him was now feeling pleased with itself, now all he had to do was to recoup with tea and Marmite and wait until Trac had finished work. Hopefully she would come round and persuade the other half that everything was going to be just fine and flicker bright once more.

Trac fumbled around in her pockets, the soft material giving a moment's protection against the cold. She pulled out a cigarette and shivered as she put it to her lips. Protecting the match with her cupped hand she struck it against the box, blue and orange flames seemingly leaping from her fingers, momentarily distorting the surroundings. She discarded it to the ground as she inhaled deeply and leaned on a low wall, as if the alcohol was about to take her legs away from under her. She happily watched Jay wrestling with the buttons of his jeans. His bladder was full to the point of pain and discomfort.

'Can't you hold it?' she smirked.

'No I can't...' he blurted 'I'm going to piss myself in a minute.'

'Watch your money trickle down the wall.'

A few more muttered swear words were soon forgotten as he gave out a jeer once his cock was free and a streak of pee came bounding out in a perfect arc. Trac lifted her hand cupping it to her mouth, 'Oh my god,' she said softly before she began to giggle on the spot and waft her hands quickly. He thought about turning towards her, but knew the humour would turn immediately into anger if he did, a few more pints and that thought wouldn't have come into it.

'Feel better now?'

'Lots,' he smiled as he swaggered towards her.

She let out a hiccup followed by another then another and said, 'I think you gave me too much to drink,' and followed that with another hiccup.

He chuckled as he put an arm round her. 'You'll be alright,' he said in a mild way, 'I'll get you home.'

Sunday, September 3

Jay and Trac strolled along Jubilee Walk. The sky was bright blue with puffs of white. September shadows lengthened across the grass as the sun had risen up above the trees at the top of the embankment. The pathway bathed in a glory of sunshine, still jewelled with the morning dew. It was going to be another long summer's day. Their hips bumped together as they walked. Jay paused in the middle of the walkway and drew her to his chest. Her cheeks and lips felt cold but her tongue was soft and warm, he broke off for a moment to look intently into her eyes and she smiled up at him and they kissed again. Swaying pleasurably they carried on walking. Trac, a little ahead, was humming slightly in between catching her breath. When they got to the timber fence at the end of the path, he squashed her up against it with a wide smile. She half closed her eyes, his stomach was fluttering and his heart began to race.

'I'll miss you.'

'I'll miss you too.'

'I'll come back every weekend.'

The width of his smile increased momentarily.

'What?' she asked curiously studying his face.

'What?' he chuckled back.

'You're smiling?'

'Yeah?'

'What's funny?'

'Nothing,' he smiled again innocently.

'Oh come on, what is it?'

'I was just thinking that's all.'

'About what?' she asked politely.

He began to behave in a peculiar manner and he could tell that she desperately wanted to know what was on his mind.

'What? tell me!' she demanded.

'Well it's a nice day, I'm feeling horny and I want to make love right now... outside,' and he pulled her close and kissed her passionately.

She broke away smiling, 'you're always feeling horny.'

'It's not my fault, if you didn't excite me so much I wouldn't feel so turned on all the time.'

'We can't do it here,' she said her eyes squinting at him.

'Why not? Just a bit further up there,' he grinned pointing beyond the fence. 'Come on it will be fun,' and gave her a reassuring nudge, 'there's no-one around.'

'It will be different, I'll give you that.'

'Come on then,' he said positively, 'I'll find somewhere comfortable.'

He put his hand out and they climbed over the fence, both slipping and stumbling for a second or two, but they managed to balance each other and push on under the bridge and trees. With a swifter pace they weaved their way through the longer undergrowth allowing the leaves to brush their faces as they steadied themselves upon the narrowing, loose and uneven trail.

'Wait a minute,' she said. 'I hope you've got something.'

His eyes flashed back at her. 'Of course I have silly.'

He found the ideal spot where it opened up and allowed the sunlight in to warm them. There was no-one around for miles, nothing but fields. He flattened a patch of grass and lay down his black shirt. He stood and unbuckled his belt, loosened the buttons of his jeans and she tugged them down his thighs, bringing her lips to him for a short while. His hands moved gently through her hair and she looked a little unsure as he slipped the sleeveless summer top from her shoulders.

'Lay back,' he whispered as he stripped her as quickly and lightly as possible. The long grass was heavy with droplets of water that brushed their bodies, dripping water onto their arms and legs. He kissed and caressed her, not needing to excite her much.

'You've got wet quickly,' he smiled. 'Been thinking about it have we?' She didn't hear him, she had a blank look as he kissed her cheek.

'I'm so in love with you,' he whispered into her ear.

They gave their bodies to each other, filling themselves with high emotions and pleasure. She ran a hand through his hair. Eyes closed, he made a conscious statement, he loved this girl more than anything in his life.

He pulled up onto his knees, idly glancing around to check the coast was clear for some hugging time. Jolting up straight he looked wide-eyed, 'shit!' he blurted.

'What?'

'I don't believe it, someone's coming,' he muttered.

'Oh yeah?' Trac smiled merrily basking in the afterglow and not believing him for a second.

'I'm not joking,' he exclaimed, pulling up his jeans rapidly. The speed in which he was dressing began to worry her, so she sat up and peered over the top of the tall grass, saw a lady walking her dog and immediately panicked.

'Oh my god,' she said flapping her arms in front of her.

'Just get your clothes on,' he said tightly.

She joined him in dressing quickly before jogging off back down the track. Once they had made their escape they couldn't stop laughing.

Wedneday, September 6

Trac sulked, and then sulked some more.

'I can't believe you phoned her.'

'I did say I might...' he babbled.

'You didn't.'

He wondered whether to trust the words that ran from his lips as he thumbed open his shirt.

'Then it wasn't important....' he said, 'besides, it was coming up to her birthday.'

'Now she's writing to you,' Trac replied taking his offer of the letter hesitantly.

Brooding, she sat on the edge of her bed, hands tucked under her bum, Shelley's letter resting on her thighs.

'It's just one letter,' he offered, standing tall now, a full two feet above her. 'Anyway it's just about boring stuff like, how was my holiday and that I'd better make a go of college. She asked after you too.'

Trac looked down to the letter and read, '*Please tell her well done on her exam results*... Wow, big deal.'

'It's nothing... forget about it.'

'She still loves you.'

'No she doesn't... there's no mention of that?'

'Yeah but she still wants to stay in touch.'

'It's just a once in a blue moon thing.'

'What would you do if she came back... what then?'

'The two of you all to myself,' he smirked. 'It'd be like happy hour.'

She shook her head and the urge to be more playful was quickly diminished by her worried expression. He held up his arms, smile curling his lips, 'okay... okay. Bad joke.' He then scratched at the side of his head and said softly, 'she's not coming back, not ever.'

'You don't know that.'

He gave out a long sigh. 'I wish I'd never shown it to you now.'

'So you can keep how you feel a secret.'

'I can't win can I?' he remarked, beginning to lose patience. 'It's not about love.'

Trac looked back down at the letter;

By the way, if (and you'd better) you write to me use the address above, I just don't want to cause trouble between you and Trac, but if you can write I'd love you to!

She read no further and said bluntly, 'what is it about then?' and pushed the letter to the floor.

Jay folded his arms defensively, 'you're taking it wrong,' he replied. 'She's just being friendly... asking if things have changed much here since she left? What's everyone wearing and what sort of music is everyone into? that's all. She's not trying to claim me as hers.'

Trac's eyes glazed over. He wasn't sure if it was just the letter or his reaction to it. He felt bad for snapping and apologised as he reached down to retrieve it.

She whispered, 'please go easy on me,' as he sat down beside her, leaning his body into hers.

'You knew that she might write,' he murmured and she responded with a slight shrug.

'Here take the letter, I don't want it. Weird thing is I'm not interested. Do what you want with it, I don't want her address.'

'It's not that I didn't think she'd write or anything, it's just... now that she has...' she gazed down to her hands and the letter, 'I just didn't know I was going to feel like this.'

'Like what?'

She studied his eyes to see a softness within them and in a tone that proceeded no further than the edge of the bed said, 'like I'm competing with her... Like her shadow will always be there... That her mark on you will always be there.'

14. Drunken joys

The sky was changing every minute, deepening and darkening, the pink changing to red and then purple to grey. Jay had less than a week of home life left before moving up to York and it had slowly started to become a thorn in the side of his relationship with Trac. He had now come full circle and built up enough positivity about the move that he had totally convinced himself it was the right thing to do. Trac however, had started to realise the massive implications of the move, and now wasn't so sure about him going. Although she didn't say as much, he could tell it was beginning to get to her as each day passed.

Adrian still had no plans to further his education, he wanted to break out and use his talent, he had phoned to let Jay know that there was a big student union party at Loughborough. Everyone was going to be there, the whole Iffley gang. It was a chance to say goodbye to everyone before moving on indefinitely. Trac, brooding about his last Saturday night to be spent at an Elvis convention, meant this impulsive urge to just live for the now was being stretched to the limit.

'Oh, do you have to go with Adrian?'

'Yeah everyone's going to be there,' he frowned. 'I've got to go.'

Staring down at her hands, she deflated with a light but lengthy groan.

'Come with us,' he suggested but she remained silent. 'Do you want me to go alone?'

'Jay, I don't want you to go at all,' she pleaded.

'I've got to go... it's my duty.'

A downpour of rain burst from the sky as Jay hopped into The Beast clutching a bottle of vodka. Slamming the door he took off into the night with the usual screech of burning rubber, snaking off up the road.

He sat in The Beast outside Mc Donald's rear entrance, wrapping his coat around himself and leaning his head out the window searching for Adrian who appeared with a handful of food.

'Alright?' he said as he opened the passenger door.

'Yeah,' replied Jay.

'You been waiting long?'

'Nah. Just got here.'

'I got you a burger.'

'Cheers mate,' he smiled.

'You got any drink?'

'Yeah,' smiled Jay pulling the vodka bottle from the back seat.

'You got any?'

'Yep,' and produced a large bottle of vodka.

'Jinx,' they choursed.

'Magic, I'm going to get so wasted tonight,' chuckled Adrian.

'I've done a Wonder Stuff tape for you, it's got loads of the B sides on it.'

'Oh ace, put it on mate, put it on.'

He stuck the tape in and off they went, driving fast, singing loudly and feeling great. Adrian sat swigging vodka and banging his head to the music. They pulled up at the back of the union complex early so they found a dark quiet space and sat drinking.

'Oh, this song's fucking excellent,' jeered Adrian. "A Wish Away' reminds me of the house party.'

Jay thought about the party and wished he could be back there again and relive it all over.

'You alright Jay?'

'Eh?... yeah fine, it's just the vodka. My stomach's not been all that keen on the stuff since Lanzerotte.'

He knocked a shot back, swore and wiped at his mouth, 'quite a bite to it.' Adrian smirked, 'it's good stuff neat.'

'Yeah it certainly does the job alright,' spluttered Jay.

Halfway down the bottle, he felt a little light headed and opened the door.

'Sure you're okay?' asked Adrian.

'Yeah,' he choked. 'Oh dear.'

'What?'

'I've just been a bit sick,' he uttered. 'I'll have to have some more vodka to get rid of the taste,' and he took a shot from the bottle.

'That's not like you?'

'I know, I just seem to have a problem with vodka recently. I'm going to have to switch back to whiskey.'

He stepped out of The Beast and wandered round a while. The cold air awakened him and he began to steadily drink again. Their main topic of conversation was the future, Adrian had it all mapped out, it seemed so clear to him after half a bottle.

'I just want to carry on and see if I can work freelance,' he said.

'Yeah that would be good,' added Jay.

'Problem is, I go for weeks without any work and then I get too busy that I need help.'

'I'll give you a hand.'

'There's not much cash in it either.'

'That's alright, just pay me in scotch,' he smirked and Adrian chuckled.

'It's looking a bit more lively over there, do you reckon we should go in?'

'Yeah... what about the rest of this drink.'

Adrian began to look around The Beast. 'Ain't you got an empty half bottle in here somewhere.'

Jay found a bottle under his seat and began transferring the booze from the larger bottle.

'Hip flask,' he said. 'Us two should be alright after a few beers and this,' and held the bottle up like a trophy.

'Let's go.'

Hearing a roar he recognised Dave turning from the crowd, 'Awwgh no!' he shouted. 'What are you two doing here?'

'Couldn't let a party like this go by,' grinned Jay.

'How's it going then?'

'Alright. I am off to York College,' replied Jay energetically.

'You got in then?'

'Yep... two more years of parties.'

Adrian interrupted by belching loudly before taking a swig from his bottle.

'I'm not going back to college,' he said casually. 'I'm just doing a few cartoons, getting by and getting pissed.'

'I don't believe you two. You're dossers, you really are.'

The two of them staggered about for several hours trying to do normal tasks, like dance and find the toilet but not having much luck with either. Horrendously drunk, Dave couldn't control them. Adrian had reached the point where he knew he could no longer chat a girl up with success, so resorted to being a little rude and mildly offensive. One girl threw a drink over him. Jay could not believe the sheer waste of alcohol. 'If anyone's throwing their drinks away can they throw them at me,' he roared.

The place was full of people Jay no longer recognised, and although his passion to rekindle the Iffley days had never been stronger, the reality was those days had passed, in fact they had never felt so far away. The summer was slipping, friendships slipping, it seemed life was changing, whether he liked it or not. The downturn in his mood had him sat at the end of the bar finishing glasses and babbling offences at Adrian. He so wished he had stayed at home with Trac. He studied his watch but it was already past midnight, so the only solution was to keep on drinking until he couldn't physically drink anymore, at least that would bring the relief of being unburdened of adulthood. The two of them made a final spectacle of staggered dancing which mainly consisted of them sliding and falling about on the dance-floor, trying to use each other as support and getting nowhere fast. The only smile Jay had managed in the last hour was during his wrestle with two bouncers. He slid along the floor as they grappled with him, trying to hold onto any free limb. Once he had seen Adrian being hoisted up by the scruff of the neck and marched off he decided to give up the fight.

Slipping down the embankment, he sprawled out on the grass, looking about in the dark, trying to associate himself with the surroundings. The drink had gotten hold of him now.

'Where the fuck am I?' he groaned holding the remainder of Adrian's vodka.

'They chucked us out the fire exit,' came a splutter.

'Really... how... how ingenious of them,' he babbled as he rose and began to wander about in the darkness.

'What... what time is it?'

'About half one,' mumbled Adrian.

Jay, in need of some food, lurched forward and disappeared with Adrian calling after him. Having hit a low brick wall and tipping over it, he found himself face down in a mix of mud and fallen foliage like a star fish, hand still firmly attached to the small bottle of vodka. Tired and winded he was more than happy to lay still until his lungs reflated. He'd sustained a number of scratches and grazes to his body from the bush he'd travelled through before hitting the dirt. Limbs lifeless he strained his ears to hear muffled music and a distant call, 'Jay... Jay?' His face felt cold and the urge to sing out a response was taken by the weight of his eyelids.

Dave found him and brought him round with a few light slaps to his cheeks. Leaning him against the embankment he spoke softly with genuine concern, 'you okay?'

Jay gave a lazy smile and spluttered, 'it's a good job you know this place better than me Dave.'

The two of them sat there a while. Dave reminisced about some of the drunken times to try and steer him from the antagonism that he had, to a happier mode. Perhaps even slow the increase of what was becoming a step further in self destructive behaviour.

'Yeah,' Jay gave a slight nod. 'I can't believe you pissed on me at the bar in Tubes an... and while... while I was talking to that girl.'

Dave chuckled. 'You pissed on me first earlier outside the pub.'

'Did I?' he replied and followed it with a soft chuckle.

'Yeah you did, so I was only getting you back.'

Jay had done his upmost to invoke the spirit of the Iffley days, consuming a superfluous amount of booze yet was still left wanting.

'We had some fun,' he smiled lightly.

'Yeah we did.'

'I tell you being with Trac, getting drunk and partying with you guys is all I want.'

'Yeah, but things change.'

'I don't want them to.'

'The future just opens up in front of you Jay and you have to just go with it.'

'Haven't you ever thought you've had the... the best moments happen in your life already... and nothing will ever better it?' he blurted as he lurched to his feet. 'Eh Dave?' What if... what if it's never as good again,' and he staggered off in the direction of The Beast.

At day break Jay awoke, his throat parched, 'what's the time?' he asked shaking Adrian. 'I'm well thirsty,' he whined as he began ferreting around The Beast upsetting Adrian's comfortable position. 'So thirsty,' he continued to mutter.

On the floor of the back seat there was a notable increase of Guinness cans, vodka bottles and glasses that he'd acquired from various pubs and clubs he'd loomed out of drink still in hand, but nothing he could find to quench his thirst except the algae water that looked worse than ever.

'You fucking sleep in here enough, I would of thought you'd have a food store in here by now,' complained Adrian leaning forward.

'Bollocks,' moaned Jay. 'It's no good, I'm going to have to drive to a newsagent and get a drink.'

He set off down the road, wiping the window screen as he went, face almost pressed up against the glass. He re-parked The Beast at a very poor angle down a side street a few steps from a shop on the main road. They dined on Maltesers and Lucozade and then opted to further their sleep.

They seemed to wake in better frame of mind second time round. Jay pulled his seat upright and began to wipe the renewed condensation off the window when he realised something was missing. Almost choking on his words or putting too much pressure on a dry throat blurted, 'The Yellow Fish... where's it gone?'

Adrian jarred pretty quick given the awkward position he was in.

'Shit,' he snapped. Eyes widening, 'arrh... we got to find it.'

Jay seemed to grow paler by the second, 'bollocks,' he babbled a number of times as he twisted frantically about in his seat feeling ever more nauseous as he did so.

'We'll find it,' assured Adrian, who kept his eyes fixed on the task in hand. In under a minute he held it a loft between finger and thumb and whistled, 'found it,' with a humourous freed anxiety.

'Thank fuck for that,' exasperated Jay, relieved at locating the mascot.

'I think the chain snapped.'

Adrian sat fiddling with it before passing it on to Jay, who positioned it back to its rightful place at the base of the inside mirror.

Looking at Adrian he grinned. 'I'm as pale as fuck and my hair's a mess. I'm wearing my black shirt that reeks of vodka. My baseball boots are knackered and we're driving around listening to The Wonder Stuff with no insurance and no tax, and on top of all that, we've had fizzy pop and sweets for breakfast! What is my life coming to?'

Adrian chuckled. 'It's a laugh though, and we've still got this for later,' and he held up a bottle of booze that still had an acceptable amount left.

Jay smirked, saluted him and said, 'let's get out of here and get some Marmite on toast.'

'I don't believe it,' complained Jay. 'We'll have no house left.'

'Don't be silly,' replied his mum.

'The house will get smashed up,' he snapped.

'Jason,' explained his mum tersely, 'your sister's friends aren't like yours.'

'I just don't believe it,' he responded and tottered off mumbling as he went, 'you go away for one night and you let her have a party.'

He climbed the stairs shaking his head, thank fuck he had a lock on his door, still that wouldn't stop him.

'You go to house parties, you don't have them!' he informed Trac.

She took his hand and tugged him close. 'Come on, it will be alright,' she smiled. 'We can get a couple of films and I'll stay over.'

'Okay,' he replied. 'Who am I to stop anybody getting drunk.'

'Exactly.'

He drove The Beast up to Nick's house, he wanted him and Rob to pop down at about eleven just in case things got out of hand. Somehow he managed to let Trac out the passenger door and trip over it, making Trac burst into laughter.

'Fucking hell,' he snapped.

'Calm down,' she giggled.

The door had got out of line and now could only be closed by slamming it quite firmly.

'How the fuck has that happened?' moaned Jay.

Trac shrugged slightly.

'The Beast is falling to bits!'

'No it's not, it's fine,' she said calmly.

He put his hands to his hips and huffed loudly. 'I've got a dented bumper, now the door's fucked and the boot's accumulated water from somewhere.'

Trac tried her best not to giggle again, but the more she tried not to, the more she did. He gave her a stern look and enquired exactly what was so funny.

'Nothing,' she replied now wiping tears from the corner of her eyes with the sleeve of her top.

His tone began to mellow and his face lightened to a smile. 'What is it?'

'Just you,' she continued as her cheeks began to redden.

He raised another smile.'What about me?'

'Accumulated,' she babbled and he began to laugh with her. 'You never use words like that!'

She was now using a tissue to dry her eyes. He nodded and agreed that the word was a little out of place for him but was glad that it amused her and managed to snap him from a potential grumpy mood.

It was eight o'clock and he was in fine spirits, even though they disagreed at the video shop as to what film to get. He was determined to watch *Friday*

The Thirteenth Part Six; *Jason Lives* and she was determined to watch *The Lost Boys*, so getting both solved that. They curled up together in bed and began to watch the movies. All was going well until just before eleven when a series of loud bangs detached him from the film.

'Great,' he snapped. 'I'm going to see what's going on.'

Trac grabbed his arm. 'Leave them you'll only upset your sister.'

Someone then knocked on his door and he leapt to his feet again.

'Leave it to me,' and began to pull on his clothes.

Nick and Rob arrived on cue and joined in trying to control things. One lad was making a noise in the garden so Rob tied him up using the washing line cord, but that didn't seem to deter him. Jay respected that, so they loaded him up in The Beast and drove him home.

'Thank you,' said his girlfriend.

'That's okay, I know what it's like to be out your face.'

The lad was carried from The Beast by his dad who certainly was not so understanding. Jay found the whole thing vastly entertaining, it was just a bonus that he'd been of some use.

When he got back, his sister was sat talking to Trac on the stairs.

'Eh Jay,' laughed Rob. 'This lad's ralfing up.'

A pale-looking lad was supporting himself outside the back door against the fence vomiting severely.

'That's it son,' laughed Rob patting the guys back lightly. 'Let it all out.'

'I feel... feel bad,' came a feeble whine.

Jay thrust a small bottle of vodka at him.

'Here, this will make you feel better,' and he gave a sharp grin.

Rob backed him up by saying, 'trust him, he knows what he's on about.'

At one o'clock taxis came and went as his mates escorted them out safely.

'Look come on,' said Rob impatiently trying to push one lad out of the lounge towards the front door.

'I'm finishing my bottle of gin,' slurred the greasy haired lad.

'Go on then,' said Nick.

The lad didn't respond and whimpered something.

'Jay you finish it,' suggested Rob.

Jay accepted the challenge and impatiently snatched the small bottle from the lad's feeble hand and promptly sucked on the fluid with ease. A cheer went up between Nick and Rob which only served to fuel him further, so he downed it in one go like a true hero.

'It's gone mate,' he gurgled, waving the bottle teasingly in front of the lad.

'Arrh. That was my gin.'

'Not anymore,' snapped Jay.

He was unsure whether or not to believe his eyes when he returned to his room to find Trac laying naked on his bed in the orange glow of the Minilite, with the duvet just loose over her legs.

'All over,' he said softly. 'They're all gone.'

'You've finished your horrible big brother routine?'

'Yeah. Even got some gin out of it,' he said, as he changed the tape in the stereo.

'Now there's a surprise.'

'You been waiting for me then?'

'Umm.'

'I thought you were talking to my sister.'

'She went to bed ages ago.'

He slipped off his clothes, her hands moved over his body and pulled him into the warmth of the bed.

He smiled apologetically. 'I'm sorry if I've been a bit moody lately. I don't mean to be, it's just the move to York. I guess I can't bear the thought of us being apart.'

'Hey, I haven't got to worry about you have I?'

'Just spoon me.'

Trac wrapped an arm and leg around him and squeezed him tightly and they slept entwined.

Saturday, September 9

'Come on,' he shouted as he leaned over the bar. 'What do you have to do to get a drink round here?'

Nick stood beside him glaring at the hotel's restaurant. The plastic burgundy chairs and mirrors everywhere projected a sleazy feel that seemed a bizarre setting to have an Elvis convention.

'Fuck,' moaned Jay, his mouth salivating at the thought of his first sip of beer.

The place was deserted, it seemed all the Elvis fans were downstairs viewing rare footage of The King's final performances. A bit morbid thought Jay. When he saw reflective movement he summoned attention by waving a five pound note. A lad appeared and trundled down the length of the empty bar with a wet cloth in his hand.

'Two pints of lager.'

'Draught beer's off,' he replied.

'Two bottles of lager... Budweiser,' he said looking at Nick.

'Yeah I'm okay with a Bud.'

Jay's eyes wandered around the bar area and fell on the optics, he wasn't ready for them yet but he eyed them up all the same. The music of The King lingered upstairs and the gathering of Elvis worshippers increased. As late evening began they wondered down to the basement and collected a large plate of food from the buffet.

'Right, where's the bar then?' he smiled clasping his hands and rubbing them together with excitement.

The basement was small and dingy, the lights became lower as the food was finished and the disco started. They positioned themselves in the corner of the bar and drank. The girl behind the bar recognised him and smiled.

'You used to go out with Sue, didn't you?' she asked.

'Yeah I did,' he replied, giving her a big easy grin.

'Can I have another pint, this one's really flat.'

'Sure,' she smiled.

Jay turned to Nick with a devious expression. He had a plan.

'See that girl, she knows Sue. I've just asked her to get me another pint cos this is flat and I've drank most of it. With a little charm I'll get us some free drinks.'

He turned back to the girl all excited at the prospect of free booze. Picking up his fresh pint he said, 'thanks,' and gave her a boyish smile. He began to ask her what she did and where she was from, overall he flirted with her.

'Can I have a whiskey, a pint of lager and a black Russian... each. Please.' After plenty of smiling and the proposition of a date, she fed them both free drinks. After a while, the two of them pissed, Jay began to get cocky and demanded a bottle of wine.

'Oh go on,' he persisted, 'no-one will notice.'

'Don't do that.'

'Do what?' he replied innocently.

'Smile at me, you've got a very persuasive smile.'

'Well then I'm going to keep smiling.'

Nick seemed to show little interest in wine, he was beginning to look ill. The whiskey had disagreed with him and so did the sausages he kept catching in his mouth, as Jay hurled them across the bar at him.

'I've already given you loads of free drinks,' said the barmaid.

'Okay, fair enough,' said Jay with a tired smirk. 'Just a glass?'

She paused for a moment then replied, 'okay a glass.'

'Perfect,' he cheered. 'And have one for yourself.'

He convinced Nick he would feel a lot better if he made some effort to dance to 'Such a Night' but he went from bad to worse and started to look a pale shade of green. He stopped all movement and closed his eyes, he definitely looked sick. He clasped a hand over his mouth after shouting, 'I'm going to be...' and pulled a face of disgust.

Jay realised that something unpleasant had filled his mouth and followed him as he weaved his way swiftly to the toilet. He watched him empty the contents of his stomach, seeing and smelling the first lot of vomit made this a lot easier. Within a matter of minutes Nick had filled the small basin to the brim. Jay hung himself by his left arm from the loop of the blue toilet towel, swaying and cackling with laughter.

Sunday, September 10

At seven the alarm sounded. He got up and went to the bathroom and stared at himself in the mirror. His hair was untamed and spiked, so wild in fact he convinced himself it was fashionable.

'You look rough,' he said to his reflection noticing some dried blood on his chin.

He sat on the toilet, eyes squinting and rubbing his temples, pulling back the events of the previous night, but for the time being his memory eluded him. He waited for his early morning erection to subside so he could pee freely, and bending over the edge of the bath he lethargically chased a small spider down the plug hole with his sister's hairbrush. It was early alright, but he wanted to spend as much time with Trac as possible.

He had a quick shower, some toasted Mighty White bread with the usual spread of Marmite, washed down with a sweet cup of tea. Feeling more civilised, he opened his curtains slowly and began to search for something to wear. The clothes piled in a large heap, festering in the corner, didn't look a good place to start, besides he was too idle and weak to sort them out. He pulled on his black T-shirt featuring The Wonder Stuff logo in magenta and a fresh pair of jeans, both still damp from being washed, and stuffed the keys to The Beast into his pocket. He sat in the lounge for a while longer, still trying to wake up slowly with the help of another mug of tea, some aspirin and the cartoons on TV.

Some good things had happened before the move to York. He figured all the nights out boozing were a combination of not wanting it to end, forgetting about leaving for York, blocking out fears of loosing Trac and saying to friends, 'cheers to you. I may not see you so much for a while.'

With his head jerking to the music on his personal stereo he rang Trac's doorbell. She appeared and nodded vaguely towards her room. True to his nature he was playing it down, the option of ending it now refused to register at all.

'How did your night of Elvis go?'

With a light chuckle he said, 'really good.'

She sighed, 'I can't believe you're going.'

'I'll be back next weekend,' and gave her a comforting smile.

She brushed her hair away from her eyes. 'Is that for me or for drinking?'

He hugged her. 'Don't be daft. I'll come straight round to see my little baby.'

'Until you meet somebody else.'

'You're my number one girl,' he whispered.

As he ran a hand through the tangled strands of her hair that spilled about her neck and shoulders, he felt a fierce protectiveness towards her. He wanted to keep her here with him, away from the rest of the world, safe in his arms. She smiled slowly and handed him an envelope, a good luck card perfumed with White Musk and a purple box.

'What's this? I wasn't expecting a present.'

'It's just a little something for you to look at when you're alone.'

He pulled a concerned expression so she continued after a little shake of her head, 'I'm hoping it will bring a smile to your face, remind you of how much I care and how much I'll miss you.'

He opened the box and inside was the small beige bear he often played with.

Trac took the bear from the box and smiled, 'it's Wee.'

His soft eyes creased at the corners, he remembered the first time he'd playfully brought the small bear to life, whistling 'weeeee' as he slid him down her thigh.

'I don't know what to say,' he murmured.

She twirled Wee in her hands for a moment and replied, 'you love me.'

'You know I do.'

'I don't want you to go.'

'I've got to go... what else am I going to do?'

'I understand.'

'Besides Mum said if I don't go I've got to find somewhere else to live.'

'That's mean.'

'She's just trying to push me. If I don't like it, I won't stay.'

'I'm sure you'll have the time of your life... but you've got to make a proper go of it.'

'Yeah I will. I want to do better,' he muttered. 'I want to do better for you.'

He unfolded her letter, conscious of his heart picking up beat.

I'm going to miss you so damn much and I'm always going to be here for you, why? cause 'I love you' I love you very much.

He felt himself becoming hot and flustered as his chest pounded stronger.

Good luck and enjoy yourself (but not too much). I'll always be thinking of you and I'll miss my little cuddles. Have fun and look after Wee.

He gave a cough giving his voice a chance.

'It's not fair.'

She replied simply, 'I know.'

As soon as he'd turned eighteen it was like something had clicked inside him, positive it was time to do what he wanted, what he felt. Now he was forced to compromise, his life had taken a turn, society had got its claws into him for the first time and that he detested. Why couldn't things just stay the same, at least a while longer, somehow it all hadn't quite seemed long enough.

The afternoon went too quickly. For the last hour she nestled cosily in his arms and refused to move. He stroked at her hair and tried to make the time linger, happy to talk and be there. He tried his best to appear strong all week until the time came for this final day. When the moment came to leave the blasé attitude had gone for sure as he felt himself buckle. His stuff was all packed and waiting in his room at home. He said nothing as he tapped at his watch, not able to change time or avert the huge emptiness beginning to grow from the pit of his stomach reaching his heart and making it pound harder and faster. Feeling hotter by the second it was almost as if he couldn't breathe.

'I just wish you were coming with me,' he said softly.

Trac nodded lightly. He squashed the small bear back into his box and managed a slight nod back, 'thanks for Wee,' he said faintly, feeling his mouth drying up.

She took a deep breath. 'That's okay,' she said softly. 'Just don't get too drunk.'

It took all his strength and will to get to his feet. 'I'll try,' he answered. The muscles in his face tried their best and produced a near smile.

'Think about me.'

'Every second.'

Tears began welling in her unblinking eyes. As he watched the first few break free and roll down her face, he began to hate himself. He made a conscious decision to remain strong if not for himself then for her. As he framed her face he kissed her apologising rhythmically with a wave of tenderness as his hands moved to stroke her hair while he repeatedly kissed away any tears that fell onto her cheek.

'Hold me tighter.'

She buried her head into his shoulder and tears began to flow freely down her cheeks, 'you've taught me so much.'

'I just happened to be around is all.'

He rolled his eyes three or four times, trying to even out any tears that may be forming of his own.

'Trac, if I don't go now I'm going to start crying and I don't want to do that.'

'Take care of yourself Jay,' she said with affectionate eyes.

'I will.'

'This has been... the best summer I've ever had,' she said softly.

He pulled away from her. 'Whatever happens Trac, we will always have that won't we.'

He stood tall as he slipped on his leather jacket. Arms folded he leaned himself against the door frame. Overwhelmed, tears once again began to spring to the corner of his eyes and made them shine. His lips pressed tight together as his eyes rolled again. He gazed up and down and to the side, anywhere but straight.

'I didn't think it would be as hard as this,' he whispered.

Trac brought a tissue up to her face to stem the flow of tears. 'Love me?'

'I'll always love you,' he whispered and moved to kiss her forehead. He closed his eyes, turned away from her and made for the door. He gave her a wave as he unlocked The Beast. Once sat he started the engine, kissed the palm of his hand, aimed and blew her his final kiss. It was only then that he allowed himself to tear with the realisation that she really wasn't just his girlfriend, she was his pal, his companion, his best friend.

It was nearly six when he entered the railway station. As expected, its general air of tattiness did nothing for his morale. The enormity of what he had chosen weighed more heavily on his mind, effecting the whole of his body. Inhaling deeply and with a fair amount of effort he forced one leg forward, then the other as he descended the steps down to the platform, following on into the waiting room was like walking through syrup. As usual it seemed to be full of cigarette smoke, though the only person smoking was a guy in his mid fifties with grey hair in a dark leather jacket with huge lapels, leaning forward in his seat, muttering and coughing to himself.

He looked at his watch and turned back round, then went out onto the platform. He made his way to the far end and sat down on one of the fold down seats. He placed his two bags of clothes down to his left and his art box and art folder to the right. He let out a prolonged sigh as he wondered what Trac might be up to? Beginning to feel low he anxiously sifted through his jacket hoping to find something of interest to distract him. All he had was a train pass, his NatWest cash card, two hundred pounds and a scrap of paper with the address of where he was going to be staying once he got to York.

The hollow feeling that was rising within took him back to how he felt when he lost Shelley and he began to rub at his forehead, 'you'll be alright,' he told himself over until the announcement came that his train was approaching. This is it, he thought, should he stay or should he go? He stood up from his seat and became agitated as the rumbling noise of the train begin to echo from the tunnel at the other end of the platform. Being confused and indecisive wasn't something he was used to, and therefore only dragged him down to an even lower state of mind. Come on, he thought. What else are you going to do? Right! He picked up his bags, cheeks bulging as if he was weightlifting and took deep breaths as the train trundled the length of the platform, screeching slightly as it slowed. A wave of panic swept over him and he dropped his bags to the floor and had to fight the urge to sit back down and watch the train pull off without him.

'Fuck,' he mumbled Fuck!' Putting his hands to his hips he studied the other people further down pushing their way through the crowd. Many were like himself, young with big bags full of clothes no doubt. One girl looked excited by the whole thing as she kissed her boyfriend goodbye and waved at him, continuing her wave as she made her way down the aisle to a window seat. Hands still on his hips, he slowly began to be surrounded by empty space. There was now only a guy in a dark navy uniform and square hat with a red band marching along the length of the train towards the driver's end, slamming any door that was left open and blowing on his whistle. This really was it, make or break time. Any last minute hope that Trac would suddenly appear running down the steps and ask him to stay were crushed.

'Are you getting on the train?' the guard asked as he paused at the last door

'Life ain't quite like it is in the movies is it?' replied Jay, as he scrambled at his belongings and literally threw them on board along with himself. The door slammed and the guard's whistled sounded, this time longer, the final signal for departure, the point of no return.

He sat there on the floor, leaning into his bags like a wounded animal. As the train's engine began to rev and slowly pull away, loss engulfed him totally. He couldn't face the sight of Leicester disappearing out of view and decided to stay where he was until he had the motivation to move or until his bum got too cold.

After twenty minutes or more he had found a seat and sat with his head leaning against the window, watching the passing countryside with his headphones on, music pouring into his head. He changed connection at Leeds and went through the same emotions and indecision all over again but finally made it to York at just gone eight thirty. As he stepped off the train he held the piece of scrap paper in his teeth and looked around curiously. It had to be said that the station had, for whatever reason, a warmer feel to it, it looked newer and cleaner. He shuffled along the beige marble tiles and out to where a bay of taxis lined up and stood pondering for a moment.

'Where are you going?'
Jay dropped his stuff to the floor and took the piece of paper from his mouth, 'err... here,' he said.

'No problem,' smiled the guy looking at the address. 'It's not far from here, a couple of miles,' he muttered as he bent to pick up his bags.

The house on Burton Stone Lane, like most of the ones surrounding it, was semi detached with a drive and black iron gates. He paid the cab driver and trundled up to the front door, but before he managed to ring the bell, the door opened and a large lady with dark brown curly hair stood in front of him.

'You must be Jason.'
He raised his eyebrows at her. 'Yeah, that's me,' he replied scratching at his head.

'Well,' she bellowed. 'Come in pet.'

He squeezed past her and rested at the base of the stairs.

'Did you have a good journey?'

He felt like telling her the truth and replying, 'no it was fucking awful,' but opted for, 'yeah it was alright,' just to be polite.

'Would you like a cuppa?'

'Eh? oh tea... no I'm okay. A bit tired actually,' he mumbled.

'Right, well here's your key. The room's the first on the left.'

'Thanks.'

'First day tomorrow is it?'

'Yeah it is,' he said looking up the stairs. He gave her a false smile, 'right well... er thanks,' he said and proceeded upwards.

The room seemed spacious enough although there wasn't much in it; a thin dark wooden wardrobe with no hangers, a low single bed with pale blue bed linen, matching the worn thread bare and stained carpet, nastily faded woodchip wallpaper, a side table and a small dirty window with a crack running through the glass allowing a slight breeze of air. He put his things down by the bed and felt desperately stranded. His heart was beating unpleasantly and he felt that he was about to be sick as a horrible cold sensation was shuddering up his spine. He sunk himself down onto the bed and set his small alarm clock. Staring at his bags, he had no urge to unpack except for a few photos of Trac. At around ten thirty he was still gazing at her photo, rotating it in his hands over and over again and day dreaming. He kissed the picture and put Wee onto his pillow, undressed and switched the light off. He climbed into the bed and curled up in the duvet. He felt remarkably lonely once he was on his own. He lay there in the blackness, the sound of his own breathing roaring in his ears, and just hoped he had made the right decision.

15. Split in half

Monday, September 11

The alarm sounded, the hands on the clock pointed to seven thirty, and Jay slowly rose for breakfast. His landlady had prepared cereal, tea, toast and a cooked English breakfast to welcome him, but he had no appetite at all, just a unsettled feeling still within his stomach. He slept badly and forced down what he could, if only to be polite.

He caught a bus and got to the college just before nine. He found a desk in good time and looked about at all the other blank-faced students. The day went by slowly, they introduced each other and some paired off together. The only comforting matter was that they were all in the same boat. The form tutor established a routine week of filling forms and visiting the sights of York. All in all he'd not had a bad first day, but he was glad that it was over. Now all he had to do was to wait for his housemate to turn up and sat wondering whether this guy was going to be a geek or not? All he knew about him was that his name was James.

Tuesday, September 12

Jay went into the living room and rounded up some mugs that looked and smelt like they had been there for some time. He made a cup of tea and tided up his belongings into any available space he could use in the room, before slumping onto the bed and looking at his watch. He couldn't remember time ever passing this slowly. Time... it didn't really fly, not when you wanted it to.

James arrived, a fresh faced seventeen year old, shortish build with a shock of mad curly hair that seemed to have a life all of its own. Jay noticed he would tug at his fringe occasionally like he was nervous or confused, starting off conversations with 'erm... erm...' He had very little in the way of belongings, and therefore lived in a pair of badly faded and fitted Lee jeans, a plain sky blue T-shirt, a black worn biker's jacket and seemed only too happy to survive on tea and biscuits. Jay figured it was best to get to know this lad, in simple terms it was someone else to go out drinking with if no-one fancied it at college. James had a motorcycle so that was okay, his favourite film was *The Great Escape* so that was more than adequate criteria for him to befriend this lad, take him under his wing and teach him a thing or too... well at least get him drunk more often than not.

To Trac,

Guess what I'm listening too? Yep Elvis! I'm feeling a little sad but I'll get used to it. Fucking hell I love you so much, I feel so fucking lonely. My room's alright, it's cosy, and my only friend at the moment is Wee. I've been cuddling him a lot and I hug him in bed thinking of you, thank you. I can't truly say what a comfort that little bear is. I can't wait to see you, hopefully Friday. The lad in the room next door has just moved in, I've just watched a movie with him and he seems okay. I'm going to be so excited when I see you, and I can give you the biggest hug and squeeze ever and kiss you to death.

All my love

Jay xx

Wednesday, September 13

Jay watched the growing crowd of people around the York Minster, unfortunately it looked very unattractive due to the scaffolding down one side while restorations took place. He found the group visits to the museums a bore, so a few of them retired to a nearby pub The Cross Keys. He joined them with the first amount of enthusiasm all day. He drank his first pint in less than two minutes.

'I'll get another round,' he said cheerfully.

He swallowed his second pint almost as quick which appeared to cause a ripple of stares in his direction, but he just shrugged it off. They called him a southerner and said he had a quirky sense of humour. His two hundred pounds wasn't going to last that long and he began to wonder about his student grant, everyone else seemed to have received theirs. A guy he befriended called Anthony, who bared an uncanny resemblance to Dirty Den from *Eastenders*, muttered a more political comment to his predicament, 'it's because we have a woman in power. No wonder things are in such a mess.'

He phoned Trac that evening, his phone manner was surprisingly ineffective, most of his communication abilities were down to his body language and facial expression, studying the person he was addressing was so important that inevitably he struggled to say what he wanted to say with any real emotion. He didn't feel as close to her as he wished; in fact he felt more distant than ever.

'Do you love me?'

'Of course I do,' she said.

'Say it,' he whispered.

'Why?'

He repeated softly and followed it with, 'if you don't I'll quit and come home.'

'Okay... okay I love you.'

'Now pat your head with one hand and jump up and down and say it.'

He managed to smile as she did what he had asked of her. In an attempt to make him feel a bit more wanted and made a rule that he would put the phone down first to make his mind rest easy.

He studied his working timetable that he had drawn out at the back of his diary, Monday graphic design, Tuesday animation and life drawing, Wednesday illustration and drawing visual research, Thursday photography and typography, Friday preparation for print, history of design and computer studies. He doodled underneath home, Trac, shag, mates, drunk and soon moved onto his sketch pad drawing the framework for a cartoon of himself and Nick at the Elvis convention for his photo album.

The only other eventful thing that happened in the week was nearly getting his vital parts blown off whilst urinating up the door of the Penguin book shop on Copper Gate after spending his first night out with his class. Soon after relieving himself it appears there was a bomb attack by an extremist, in a more direct approach than the collective demonstrations held up and down the country, to vent outrage of Penguin's publication of Salman Rushdie's *Satanic Verses*. He had no particular political or religious opinions in general, so his views on the subject matter seemed unimportant. He only felt compelled to give it some sort of thought once everyone seemed amazed by how close he had come to partial demise. What was it, he thought, the pen is mightier than the sword, or in this case the bomb was mightier than the glass and wood of the shop front, then again the book will live on. Immediately bored with this kind of forced thought, it became overwhelmingly apparent that his cock had a narrow escape and that had to be a cause for celebration of the utmost importance. The idea that he could get the seemingly uptight bunch of class mates, especially the girls, to toast a glass of booze to his nob amused him but no-one apart from Anthony, now only known to Jay as Den, and perhaps one or two others with a little goading seemed interested in a pub crawl. He had to settle on the purchase of some Jiffi cocktail flavoured condoms and a bizarre shaped one from the pub toilets that looked quite alien ready for his return to Leicester, maybe there Trac would appreciate his tale.

Friday, September 15

It wasn't long before he was back in his room with Trac in his arms. She tugged tightly on his leather jacket pulling him close and kissed him passionately. Wrapping his arms tightly around her he kissed in his familiar pattern.

'Mmm, you smell great,' she said looking up at him.

His eyes fluttered as he ran a slow finger down the centre of her face and whispered, 'I don't want to ever lose how this feels.'

She warmed to him even more, and noting the wild look in her eyes, he allowed the excitement to rise within. The desire was too much, within moments they were in bed, conversation was minimal as if their bodies needed to say hello to each other too. Once inside her there was no escaping the feelings that flooded in. He loved her more than anything, it was as if she was his life force.

Saturday, September 16

Jay considered going down to The Bell to meet the lads but didn't have the funds to reach a respectable level of drunkenness. Trac offered to take him for a pizza but he felt like he should pay his way and muttered, 'I've got a fiver.'

'Keep it,' she smiled. 'I'll treat you.'

'You don't have to.'

'Come on, before I change my mind,' and she put out a hand.

He tucked his *Melody Maker* under his arm and took her hand in his. While they sat eating pizza he felt like part of a couple, it was a good feeling he decided and wanted to participate in more of the same.

At eight pm the two of them lay naked on his bed. He was quiet and lay there with a smile, while his eyes studied her softly. His eyes glanced away for a second then back to her, he increased the width of his smile and she informed him he was dangerously cute when he wanted to be. He rolled his eyes at her and she returned a charmed expression, happy now they had the whole night. Trac lay reading a book he'd found, *Love without fear,* a guide to sex techniques for every married adult.

'What are you reading that for it's well old?'

She had her nose firmly stuck into it and didn't hear him, or if she did, chose to ignore him, so he lay down beside her and closed his eyes.

'Any good?' he asked after she shut the book.

'There was an interesting story about a headmistress giving two boys a spanking for being naughty and the two boys achieved orgasm, but what they didn't know is that the headmistress had too.'

'Really? My form teacher used to throw blackboard rubbers. One hit me once, on the side of the head, I'm pretty sure I never reached an orgasm but it was so long ago, I can't remember.'

She chuckled, tapped him with the book and called him, 'silly' before suggesting he needed to be more fun, so he rolled onto his front and let her whip him lightly on the backside with his leather belt.

'Does that do anything for you?'

'Well it's nice, but I'm not getting an extremely large kick out of it,' he chuckled.

She sat back down onto the bed and spanked him a couple of more times.

'I don't want to be whipped,' he whispered. 'You're sitting on what I want.'

'Hmm,' she smiled dropping his belt to the floor and stretching out on the bed.

'Just need to be close.'

'You just want to shag me,' she replied faintly, noting his change of expression.

'Not yet,' he smirked. 'Turn over.'

He massaged her back feebly, when she obliged he put in more concentration, giving her bottom a soft pummelling with his fist followed by firm squeezes. He kissed his way down her legs then back again, lightly squeezing at her bum. Emotional longing had quickly been pushed from his mind in favour of sexual mischief that rose without control, putting him into a very kinky mood. He moved further, kissing her lower back to her shoulders before his weight began to bare down on her firmly.

'No,' she said strongly.

'What?' he chuckled softly.

'You're not putting anything up my bum!'

He chuckled at her response, 'I just thought we could try it,' he said nudging his way.

'No get him away,' she giggled slightly. 'Get him out of there. He's not going anywhere near my bum, leave my bum alone,' and rolled over onto her back.

He smiled broadly, 'okay... okay,' and leaned forward pulling the curtain free from the window sill and produced a small box.

'I got this last night out the jonny machine.'

She giggled at the variety of condom shapes silhouetted on the outside of the box.

'Look at number eight.' she laughed. 'Are you putting it on then?'

'No,' he replied. 'It's too thick and horrible.'

'What did you buy it for?'

'I was pissed.'

'Oh come on put it on.'

He wrestled with the thick unlubricated condom. When he was happy that it wasn't going to fit any better he sighed.

'Very attractive.'

'It's about as thick as a bike inner tube.'

'Well, if you don't want to,' she replied jokingly.

'No... no, I didn't say that.'

Sunday, September 17

Trac heard the slam of a car door and hurried to open the front door for him. She saw The Beast and then Jay's familiar figure stroll briskly up the driveway. He hesitated in the wind to brush his hair from his face and approached with a smile.

The candlelight flickered and sparkled in the reflection of her eyes as she sat cross-legged in front of him. She waited eagerly for his response, laid out on her bedroom floor was a picnic; sandwiches, sweets and wine. He squatted down and kissed her brow.

'You didn't have to do all this for me,' he smiled.

'I wanted to,' she said. 'It's a shame we couldn't have it outside.'

'Thanks,' he smiled again picking up some chocolate and slipping off his jacket.

'Well, haven't you noticed anything?'

'What?'

'Look, there's six of everything.'

'There's only five pieces of chocolate.'

'Well there was six.'

'There's not six bottles of wine.' He picked up the bottle and began to pour, 'I bet I could get six glasses out of it though... Six of everything for six months.'

'It's funny, they seem to have flown by,' she smiled widely in reply.

'You know, it was happening for us way before that.'

'Yeah, but you have to have a date to celebrate,' and gave him his anniversary card and hugged herself tightly to his chest. He responded by kissing the top of her head.

'Thanks,' she whispered.

'You don't have to thank me.'

'Well I hope the next six months will be as interesting.'

'Sure it will.'

She whispered, 'tell me how much you missed me again?'

'Heaps,' he said. 'It was dead weird, I dreamt of you every night.'

'Oh yeah?' she said speculatively.

'They weren't all X rated,' he informed her. 'Although I can't quite believe that I had a wet dream. I've never had one before.'

Trac looked away so he couldn't see her smile, but she couldn't contain herself and burst out laughing, shoulders hunched she let go of him and brought her right hand to cover her nose and mouth, she was tickled pink. He folded his arms in insult and he felt his face go hot, was he blushing? Come to think of it, as far as he'd known, he had never blushed, how weird was that he thought putting a hand to his cheeks to double check that they really were as hot as they felt.

'What's so funny?' he mumbled. 'It's only because we had so much sex before I left and then none for ages, I couldn't help it.'

'No it's just when I think of wet dreams I think of guys that are about fifteen.'

He muttered something under his breath and resorted to pushing his bottom lip out as he dropped to her bed with a thud.

'I bet you ache for the real thing,' she teased as she crawled across the floor towards him perversely enjoying his vulnerability.

His lip retracted as she tickled his sides and said, 'I'm just your humping bag aren't I,' in good humour as she felt his hard cock through his jeans.

'Yeah,' he agreed.

Jay used both of his hands to touch and massage her back, regularly bending forward, he kissed her between the shoulders. On occasion he released one hand to the back of her neck, running it up through her hair helping his kisses to be firmer. She started to wiggle her feet, so he gave them some attention without hesitation.

'How's my little piglets then?' he asked softly as he pulled off her thin black cotton socks.

Trac rolled over onto her back allowing him enough access to kiss her toes one by one. She let herself be absorbed by him all too easily. She said days without him were filled with boredom as well as loneliness.

'I remember when I first ever saw you,' he said and took a sip of wine. 'I thought you were a very attractive little thing.'

'When was that?'

'Russell's bonfire party in eighty seven.'

'Oh god yeah... I would have been fourteen.'

'I saw you some time after that in town. I was with Shelley at the bus station, you were all made up, shades on looking attractive but...'

'But what?'

'Pretentious.'

'Well you know I'm not like that.'

'I know but I remember it that way.'

'I want to come to York,' she yawned and stretched slightly.

'That's just the wine talking.'

'Mmm... I'll have to wait another week for your cuddles.'

'Maybe,' Jay began as he loosened the buttons on his shirt, 'I can help with that.'

Trac looked puzzled as he slipped his arms free from the material.

'We can't do anything,' she said faintly.

He smiled at her as he handed her his black shirt and she returned a confused expresion that widened his smile further, 'take it,' he said.

She lifted her left arm and took it from him. Looking flattered and biting at her lip slightly, she scarcely managed a reply. 'I can't take this, it's your favourite.'

He nodded briskly. 'I know,' he remarked, 'but I'll get another one.'

Scrunching the shirt up and holding it to her face she returned a soft smile.

'You're sure?'

Leaning to her and placing both palms of his hands to her knees, he kissed her lightly and said, 'if I can't find a new one I like, then you can give it me back, deal?'

Her eyes locked with his, and looking a lot happier she replied, 'deal.'

York station was dark and gloomy, he felt prematurely aged. Everything about the return back to York had been slow and tiring; the journey to the station, the train journey itself with the possible mis-connection at Leeds. When he finally arrived it was later than expected and reluctanly paid out for a taxi. He played back the weekend over in his mind as he stared out the window at the isolated buildings and other people he didn't recognise, he found it miserable not being known.

Monday, September 18

The only disadvantage he found York College had, apart from being a hundred and twenty miles away from Trac, was the fact that unlike Loughborough it had no student union bar. Sure the place had a pool table, jukebox and somewhere to chat, but he was unable to get a quick drink whenever he fancied. So he left clutching the only thing it was good for, his student discount card and vowed that he would never return, well apart from collecting his new card for his second and last year, that withstanding he remained in York. The nearest pub; The Fox and Roman was a good ten minute walk, so once he had made the trek he liked to spend a good few hours in there wedged next to the tropical fish tank, with a small sketch pad and pencil to thrash out his ideas and concepts. That was the one element he enjoyed about continuing to study graphic design, it was a very self managed environment. Apart from the odd meeting and life drawing, he had the freedom to wander wherever he wanted. As long as his work was of a good standard when completed, and he met the deadline given or had available a good enough reason for being late, it was easy.

Tuesday, September 19

Jay sat on a low wall in Duncombe Place studying the stream of tourists taking photos of one another. One short stocky looking guy had resorted to lying on the ground to get the full height of the Minster in frame, ruined by his goofy looking wife or girlfriend in a red and white stripped jumper bearing her teeth down upon him. It made him smile as they swapped places before wondering off, necks remaining craned upwards to the building as they went. He turned away ready to grumble about his new companion for making him wait so long for food, but before he could do so James was upon him smiling and handing him his newspaper laden with chips.

'These chips look green,' moaned Jay holding one up in better light for inspection.

'I was hoping I was going colour blind,' James mooted looking down at his small mound of light green alien looking chips.

'Well we're not going there again,' smirked Jay.

They tasted alright so they ate them anyway and strolled to Lendal Cellars, the starting point for a pub crawl. As he reached the bar he glanced round, found the place fairly empty and looked at his watch, seven thirty pm, is that early? he thought as he looked around once again... guess it must be.

'Any people from your course here yet?'

'Nope, looks like I'm in pole position.'

'Maybe we should've nipped into the Olde Star for one first?'

'Yeah, that seems like my kind of place,' Jay replied. 'Still we're here now and we can always go there later.'

'Yeah,' James muttered nervously nodding as he pushed a folded five pound note towards him.

'What's that?'

'Erm... erm get me half a lager.'

'Half? Look I'll get a couple of pints and you can get the next ones in,' he said, and he slid the note back to him.

'They won't serve me,' he said quietly.

Jay was about to break into a chuckle and about to say something spitefully funny, but James had a lost look about him that he couldn't bring himself to make the lad feel any worse than he already did.

'Okay, grab a seat over there.'

On approaching the bar for the second time, in walked Den and gave a little jeer as he saw Jay.

'Mine's a pint of bitter,' Den said, before wandering over to the video jukebox.

'Have they got The Cult on there?'

'You're into The Cult?'

'What, you don't like them?' replied Jay confidently.

'Fuck yeah,' Den chuckled. "Sonic Temple's' the best fucking album in years, well since 'Electric'.'

Jay smirked, this was a rare moment, a fan of the most underrated British rock band of all time, it can't be true he thought. Here was a guy who has turned up early for beers, loves design, is into The Cult and looks like Dirty Den, this he thought is the start of a great friendship.

'There we go, 'Edie Ciao Baby',' and pushed a coin into the machine.

Wednesday, September 20

Jay woke at about four am, his neck felt uncomfortable after falling asleep awkwardly against the arm of the sofa. The TV displayed nothing but rolling pages of cefax. He hadn't the strength to switch it off and thought about closing his eyes and spending the rest of the night there, but as he eased to a more comfortable position he noticed the remains of a half eaten kebab on his chest. As he put the effort into placing it onto the coffee table, he felt cold tea soaking into his jeans. At that point thought he might as well tackle the stairs. He lurched out of the front room into the hallway and was confronted by a five foot cardboard cut out of Charles Bronson. He scratched at the side of his head as he tried to recall where he had acquired it from and made his way carefully up the stairs.

Jay's beans were bubbling away when the phone rang, he looked at the clock on the wall only to be diverted when James came through the back door muttering something about his motorbike and looking pissed off.

'Hey James.'

James stared, mute and stiff as a block of concrete.

'Finish this off for us,' continued Jay as he darted into the hallway noting the smell of oil and petrol as he passed him.

'Hello,' he panted down the receiver.

'How's the horniest little devil in the universe?'

'You after Jay?' he teased.

'Oh shit... yeah,' came Trac's surprised voice.

He chuckled down the line and she was quick to call him a sod as he sat on the floor with his back against the wall, phone cord at full stretch.

'What you been up to?'

'Getting mad.'

'Why?'

'I'm sure, no positive, I have Gremlins in my room, either that or my dog is madly in love with you and secretly steels your letters and hides them away to drool over. Of course I could be extremely forgetful.'

'What are you on about,' he replied in an irritable tone.

'Okay, I'm really sorry but I've lost your letter.'

'Oh right, don't matter I can write you another,' he replied softly as he wriggled his toes into the hallway carpet, trying his best to warm his feet after being stood on the cold kitchen floor.

'I know but it was a real 'cutey' one with lots of nice snuggerly bits in,' continued Trac, 'makes me miss you loads and want to give you a big hug, even though you were in a lonely mood when you wrote it.'

'Yeah well I'm freezing now and...' he shouted, 'starving,' loud enough for James to hear.

'Okay don't shout,' came Trac's quiet voice.

'No... not... don't matter.'

He was immediately flanked by James who dropped the plate on the telephone table with a clatter of cutlery. Jay put a hand over the mouth piece and said, 'you couldn't grate some cheese?'

James brought his cigarette to his mouth, stuck his middle finger up and before Jay had a chance to mouth, 'fuck you then,' he had disappeared into the front room.

'What are you doing?'

'Just having my dinner... beans on toast.'

'Again? Jay you can't live on beans.'

He tucked the receiver under his chin and took the plate. 'You know a nice steak and mound of chips next to them would be great but what can I do?'

'Okay point made. What you doing later?'

'I don't know... James is on about getting a video, so nothing exciting,' and scooped some beans up with a piece of toast.

'Sounds good to me, all I have as a comfort in this lonely old life is a black shirt which I snuggle up to at night.'
In between munching away he managed a sarcastic 'arrh' sound.

'It still smells of you, poo wee,' she chuckled.

'Cheers,' came another muffled reply. 'I'll take it back then.'

'Not really, it smells gorgeous... anyway us hard workers have to crack on with some homework.'

'Okay.'

'Miss me?'

'You know I do,' he replied meekly. 'I just feel out of place here.'

'It'll get better.'

'Yeah maybe, I'll see you Friday.'

'Can't wait, love you loads.'

'Me too... bye.'

Thursday, September 21

Time to move on? No looking back? Hmm... he wasn't convinced, more worried about the fact that he didn't have the buzz inside to want to get drunk and that struck him as odd. He came to the decision that he would go, well he had to, everyone else was and he felt sure the urge would kick in. He would be up and away and be able to turn what could be a dull 'get to know each other' night out into a full scale no holds barred party. He couldn't force it though and certainly couldn't fake it.

He got some cash out of the hole in the wall, increasing his overdraft to new heights and trundled down to Raffles Bar. He got a pint and knocked about half of it back and decided to order another when someone slipped in next to him.

'Hi,' came a voice.

'Hi,' he replied recognising the girl's face.

'You hang about with Anthony.'

'Yeah, it's Jay.'

'That's right, I'm terrible with names.'

'Well it's just one letter, after I in the alphabet.'
She looked as though she took that the wrong way and marched off, but before he could worry about it he was flanked by Den and Jeff, Jeff was average in height and rather plain looking, that is apart from his red nose, he constantly had a cold. A running nose and coughing up phlegm left Jay caught between being disgusted and feeling sorry for him.

'Alright Jase?' said Jeff patting him on the back.

'Yeah not too bad.'

From this point onwards, until heading to a club, the night had gone as predicted apart from the adrenaline buzz he was waiting for still hadn't kicked in. But he kept holding out, hoping that at any given moment the transformation would take place. He continued drinking more and more to aid in fuelling its arrival in someway, but it was failing, he simply wasn't getting into the party.

Friday, September 22

He woke dehydrated, eyes barely open, to find himself skint and recalled visiting the bank in between the bar and the club, and again afterwards for food. He decided not knowing how much he had spent would be okay, and lay instead thinking about the boring predictability of the night. A night that had been built up by everyone had somehow become an anti-climax, a hangover to boot he could deal with, but a party failing to reach that pinnacle of excitement he couldn't. It was clear from the beginning that it was too planned, too hyped, or just too many people he didn't know or care about. He did however enjoy the music, once it had veered from dance into indie. He got passed a joint at some point and inhaled a few good lung-fulls hoping it would be the cure to the evening. All he wanted was to feel fucking fantastic, instead it reminded him of the lift you got from a tequila slammer, but with everything he'd drank so far it just made him dizzy, a fuzzy feeling in his head that made it even more impossible to join in the banter. Euphoria hadn't been reached but a perfect state of escapism and uncaring bliss that took over had carried him independently through the remainder of the night.

Jay was relieved just after seven to be in Leicester, to be home. He washed and changed quickly just in time for Trac's arrival.

'Here she is,' he mooted, 'the most beautiful girl in the world.'

'Are you feeling alright?'

He rolled his eyes at her and they seemed to sparkle. 'I'm not quite sure,' he joked.

With the initial hugging, kissing and catch up chat he was on top form, himself; comfortable, cheerful, energetic.

'I'm glad to be back,' he smiled.

'Bad week?'

'It was okay,' he shrugged as she followed him into the lounge. 'Five days just seem like a life time.'

'Mmm,' she responded.

He frowned, 'yeah, it was a struggle but I'm here now.'

'Is it alright if I stop over tonight?'

He smiled playfully, 'well it looks like you've got your overnight bag.'

'Oh that reminds me,' she said jumping on the spot for a second. 'I've got you a pressie,' and she eased herself onto the sofa, opened her bag and passed him a copy of the week's *NME*.

'Oh brilliant, I was going to get this tomorrow.'

'I saw it had The Cult on the front.'

'And a New Order pull-out as well.' He was delighted. 'I've struck gold,' he said as he jumped into the spot next to her and sat with his legs crossed shuffling through the pages.

'Eh listen to this; *Billy Duffy had one girl in his arms and another between his legs. He was thinking of cars and sunshine when Axl Rose walked onto the couch and slapped the kneeling girl across her back. The girl choked and bit Billy back to reality.*' He gave out a soft chuckle. 'What's she up to then?'

'Umm, I wonder,' replied Trac.

'Hey look The Wonder Stuff's new albums out second of October.'

'I'll look forward to getting that played twenty four seven then.'

'I'm not with you twenty four seven am I?' he muttered and turned another page.

'There's tour dates in here as well, I'll have to phone Adrian tomorrow. I'll get my mum to sort some tickets out for us. Do you want to go?'

Trac appeared genuinely happy to have been asked yet declined the offer with, 'I'm okay. I'll leave you two to it.'

He folded the music paper in half and put it onto the arm rest, 'shall we go down the pub?'

Trac seemed to ponder on that for a moment or two and he wondered if she was about to decline that too, wanting him to herself, not sharing him with his friends or a row of optics behind a bar. She looked at her watch and tapped at it a few times. 'Yeah, we can go for a bit,' she replied with a quiet smile. 'As long as I have you all to myself tomorrow night.'

'Yeah,' he nodded and clapped his hands together.

The usual people were down there, standing in their usual places which pleased him no end, walking into The Bell felt like home. His mates gathered round the far end of the bar by way of habit, or tradition. He was greeted with warming smiles and a loud jeer and grinned approvingly in response, looking forward to the raucous laughter.

'What do you want to drink?' asked Trac.

'You buying then?'

'Yeah.'

'A pint of Guinness.'

He had to admit he missed the lads too. Life was still good back in Leicester, he had changed a good thing for the sake of his future and was beginning to resent the fact that what he was doing wasn't for the here and now, the reality of which was based simply on whether he could afford to gamble his future for her and for his friends? He brushed those thoughts and feelings to the side and hoped it would disappear altogether, and if not at least for the time being.

At ten thirty he drained the last of his beer and slid off his stool. Rob came up behind him and patted him on the back. 'You're not going are you? he jeered.

'Yep, afraid so. You bunch of twats are boring me,' he chuckled and headed for the door with Trac looping an arm in his.

Saturday, September 23

The Secret Jazz Company bar at the top of Leicester's High Street was a relaxing place for a drink on a Saturday afternoon. Adrian had started to frequent the place on a regular basis and arranged to reunite the Loughborough College three at twelve noon for what was supposed to be a quiet drink. Rather predictably, one quick pint led to another then another and by half past three Jay was in a fairly intoxicated state, he'd held his spot at the bar through lunchtime. He'd drank steadily and continually while Adrian and Dave were happy to keep the pace.

At four thirty, unkempt and a little worse for wear, they wandered out onto the street and down into the centre. Dave had the fuel inside him now to visit the sex shop and buy some poppers, soon after which all three of them looked ill, pale faced and red eyed, but in hysterics with dazed smiles. They had reached a very precise, all be it fleeting phase of drug and drunkenness, when it's out of the question to explain the joke, when there's little chance of the laughter subsiding anytime soon. The only downfall from sniffing this tiny jar was that at some point it was going to leave them with awful throbbing headaches.

By six o'clock Jay's head felt just about normal. 'I'm checking out,' he mumbled at his mates.

'Trac?'

'Yeah,' he coughed and gave them an idle wave as he stumbled off.

He cooked pizza and they sat cross-legged, excited as he opened the case to The Cult's 'Love' and 'Electric' videos he'd purchased. Trac knew for the next half an hour or so he was in another zone and communication was on hold. The only thing he blurted was something about Harley Davidsons as he jigged on the spot and pointed at the TV excitedly.

In the glow of the Minilite, Jay eased himself onto his front and sprawled his arms under the pillow, squashing Trac further into the wall as he did so. She coughed politely and he replied with a mumble, 'scratch my back.'

'I've got no nails,' came her reply and he gave her a huffing noise so she massaged his neck.

'Oh, that is superb,' he responded, and let out a soft pleasurable moan.

'It's really funny,' she said.

He knew with that line and the tone with which she said it, she was about to tell a little story or confess to something and it pleased him.

'When I was at this party last week, I told my mate all about me and you and I told her how much I like doing it in the shower.'

'Got a little tipsy did we?' he murmured. 'I love it when you're wet all over.' Bolting upright he said, 'let's have a shower now.'

'We can't, your sister's in.'

'So... come on.'

'No,' she said firmly. 'You'll just have to wait until some other time okay.'

He gave a exaggerated sigh. 'Alright,' he replied reluctantly, and turned over onto his back. She began circling her head so that her long fine hair skimmed and glided over his hips, thighs and stomach. There was a playful smile in her eyes as she began to tease him. Visually it was appealing and it felt fantastic too, he made polite groans, naturally but with professional sincerity, pushing his hips towards her until his aching erection gained attention. She said things like 'Jay, you're terrible.'

He gasped as she took him in her mouth for a brief moment before he slid a hand down between her thighs and began massaging her with his thumb. His mouth pressed against her ear and his erection against her thigh as he moved slowly down, teasing her breasts with his tongue. He blew hard on her stomach making a loud rasp that made her giggle. Sticking his tongue in her belly button she wiggled. Her hips began to buckle as he moved between her. His tongue moving inside her now with expertise as she clutched the duvet with delight. He had been yearning for her all week, penetration brought about relief both physically and emotionally.

Sunday, September 24

Sunday was slow, it was late morning when they woke and the first thought that hit Jay was that he had to go back to York, it felt like such a low blow to his chest. Luckily, the spellbinding effect of Trac's naked body had him swiftly nudging into the side of her leg. She signed deeply and put her hand to her mouth and flashed him a hands-off look before stretching outward.

'I need to get home.'

He sat in The Beast not sure if he was fully awake sifting through his tapes for five or so minutes while Trac brushed her hair and applied some lip balm.

'Right,' she said. 'Are we ready?'

Giving out an over exaggerated yawn he squeezed her thigh and started the engine.

'It's definitely worth a try,' he smiled, holding a small brown bottle in front of her.

She took it from him and slowly unscrewed the lid.

'What's it do?' she asked.

'It makes you giggle,' he smiled. 'Try it.'

As soon as Trac sniffed the contents she sat up abruptly. It didn't seem to make her laugh but she pulled one or two unusual expressions that made him laugh out loud and brought tears to his eyes.

'Oh that's weird,' she muttered.

He put the tiny poppers bottle to the side among her rabble of cosmetics and empty tea mugs.

'You feel okay?'

'Yeah. That was strange,' she said looking confused.

'You should've seen your face,' he chuckled again.

'Shall I have another go?'

'No leave it, you've tried it,' he said softly. 'Oh, you know my shirt,' he continued. 'The black one.'

'Yes.'

'The one with the button bitten off.'

'Yes.'

'Well I kind of need it back.'

'What do you mean kind of? I thought you have a new one?'

'Yeah, but it don't feel right,' he shrugged again. 'I don't know... I'm lost without it, it's like I just don't feel... like me.'

'Okay, but it's a bit creased I've been sleeping with it.'

'No worries, I don't mind looking scruffy.'

She looked a bit deflated as she passed it over to him, so he promptly suggested she took his jacket in exchange.

'Your leather?'

'Yeah, I've got a long coat, I can wear that.'

'What's the catch?'

'Well...' he picked up the jacket and showed her the split that needed stitching under the right arm.

'How did you do that?... No don't tell me.'

'Can you do something with it.'

'Yeah leave it with me,' she smiled, pleased that she had something that had the fresh Jay smell upon it.

Her mum entered into the room with a plastic bottle in hand and her usual stern look which he noticed Trac had inherited from time to time.

'Here you go,' she said. 'Put some of this on.'

'What's that?' he asked curiously.

'Oh, I've got little spots all over my feet.'

'What are you on about?'

She took off her socks, 'look.'

'That's weird,' he said as he helped rub the cream onto the soles of her feet. 'Does it hurt?' he asked.

She looked down at him, 'sometimes, if I do a lot of walking it's a bit sore.'

'Arrgh, poor little baby.'

He stayed for dinner and without rushing pulled away from her house in The Beast, took aim and blew her a kiss.

Tuesday, September 26

'Trac?'

'Mmm?'

'It's me.'

'I know.'

'How's my little baby then?'

'Not too bad. You?'

'Okay I guess.'

'What's up sexy pants?'

'Just feel like I'm stuck here.'

'You just want a shag?'

'Mmm... yeah. What are you wearing?'

'I've got on my black T-shirt, jeans, black socks and knickers... I think they're black.'

'You could've made something sexy up?'

'Is that not sexy enough for you then?'

'Better if you were half naked.'

'I'm standing in the hall Jay, I'm hardly going to be half naked now am I.'

'You could pretend.'

'Oh, well... I've just slipped off my socks real slow and I'm now pulling down my jeans and they're taking my knickers with them, if only you could xxxx me real hard and clench my xxx very tight and...'

'Trac?'

'Yeah?'

'What are the xxx's?'

'I'll have to stop, Mum might hear.'

'You can't do that to me... Go into your room then.'

'Okay hang on.... Oh it's so hot in here... so hot I'm going to have to take off my top, wishing you could lick and nibble my xxxx and play with my... Jay are you laughing?'

'No.'

'So do you like me talking dirty to you?'

'Course I do.'

Silence.

'What are you doing... you're not?'

'I was nearly there then.'

'Really?'

'No, but I'm going to be so horny come Friday and I can't wait to give 'Her' a kiss and a good xxxx.'

'You're a bad boy.'

'Yeah I am. Are you still naked?'

'No, I've just quickly put everything back on so unfortunately you'll have to chuck some cold water on him.'

'Hmm.'

'On Friday I'll let you know what all the x's were.'

'Mmm... still wish I was there to give you a cuddle though.'

'Me too. I have started writing you a letter and wondering what the likelihood of me receiving one back is?'

'Pretty good... better than average.'

'Before the weekend?'

'I guess. How's school been?'

'Rubbish, one of my teachers had a wap at us for talking today. He split us up and gave us an essay to write on... what was it... hang on... here we go... what do you understand by realism in the arts and how important it is and what are its limitations.'

'Sounds boring.'

'Oh and there was me thinking you were going to offer your services at the weekend.'

'Oh I might do... it depends.'

'On what?'

'Whether you've mended my leather jacket.'

'Oh I did that Sunday night, looked cool in it at school.'

'You've been wearing it?'

'Yep.'

'But it's way too big for you.'

'I know it swamps me, but when I get bored in lessons I can wrap it round me and imagine you holding me.'

'Mmm, you know I want it back.'

'Oh... please let me keep it.'

'Nooo.'

'I've got to keep it now, they've all nick-named me the mean biker. I promise to look after 'Him' this weekend.'

'Hmm, okay.'

'You're so weak.'

'Yeah... but I don't care.'

'I've finally started to redecorate my room with the help of Craig.'

'Good. White and red diagonal striped wall paper has become more than a little dated.'

'Well, we peeled off most of it last night.'

'I hope you saved the bit I wrote on.'

'I tried to save it but I just couldn't get it off in one piece.'

'Hey, are you eating... that's cruel.'

'Mmm... these biscuits are yummy...'

'What kind of biscuit?'

'Chocolate Digestive. What did you have for dinner?'

'Nothing yet.'

'You've got to eat Jay.'

'I do, it's called Guinness, a meal in a glass. It's good for you.'

'Seriously.'

'Oh come on you'll start sounding like my mum in a minute.'

'Says you... Oh look my jacket's ripped can you mend it for me.'

'No... yeah... well... you're good with stuff like that.'

'Mmm, a compliment in there somewhere. So what have you been up to at college then?'

'Had to spend the afternoon drawing a naked woman.'

'Was she old and wrinkly?'

'No, she was pretty fit actually.'

There was a pause.

'You git.'

'No, I'm all sweetness and light.'

'How would you like it if I was drawing a hunky bloke... it's not funny Jay.'

'You're over reacting.'

'Saying she's fit sounds the same as you saying she's really nice and you're attracted to her... physically.'

'No... I didn't mean it like that. You asked me if she was wrinkly.'

'...Suppose.'

'I can always switch to drawing something else like a stuffed badger.'

'You don't have to do that.'

'I don't mind, I like badgers.'

'No, stick with your slapper.'

'Professional artist's model.'

'Hmm... I must be too jealous for my own good.'

'I like you being jealous.'

'I just don't like the thought of you looking at anyone else. And just so you know, where you're concerned, anything that's got long blonde hair and is fit poses a threat to me.'

'Sorry babe.'

'Umm... well I have ran out of perfume.'

'Will I be forgiven then?'

'...we'll see.'

'How is York anyway, sunny?'

'Sunny it's not... there's still quite a lot of tourists and that though, I keep getting asked to take photos. Hey, maybe you could come up one weekend instead, you'd love it.'

'Mmm, but I don't think Mum would let me.'

'Think about it... What you up to later?'

'Watch some telly... listen to some of your CDs. I have got some geography and maths homework... boring I know but if I do some tonight and maybe tomorrow, then I'll be all yours come the weekend. How about you?'

'James wants to see *Lethal Weapon II*, so probably end up doing that.'

'Anyway... I'd better go.'

'Okay speak to you Thursday.'

'Good o.'

'I can't blow you a kiss down the phone.'

'Well I'll let you make up for it on Friday.'

'Okay then, bye.'

'Bye.'

'...Are you still there?'

'Yeah.'

'Hang up.'

'You first.'

'No you first.'

Thursday, September 28

Drawing visual research, boring as hell thought Jay sharpening his pencil in an aggressive manner. It was a hopeless lesson, kids at playschool could come up with better works of art. The briefs were so structured that nothing creative was ever achieved. Most of the work actually ended up on the ceiling, the place Jay decided all the worst designs ended up. Den seemed to own most of the ceiling thanks to Jay. He would walk up to his desk and say 'ceiling' before half of his work was finished, but he retaliated much the same if not worse. Vince, the young Status Quo styled rocker, with long straggly blonde hair was probably the worst in the class, but he never joined in such banter, he just came in early to take the previous day's work off the ceiling and try and save it from a bigger disaster. Rich in art it wasn't, all in all they found this day of the week annoying or amusing, either way it was never taken seriously.

They were both sat silent, basking in the warmth of the sun coming through the dining room window. The blue smoke from James's cigarette was spiralling upwards towards the shaft of light, surrounded by a hundred dancing particles of dust and sending Jay into a daydream. The crashing of dustbin lids stirred him from his thoughts as the noise of a hissing cat battle ensued. He smiled as he stretched out his arms to the ceiling and peered out into the garden as he rose from his chair. He packed away his equipment into his art box and placed his freshly doctored *York Minster Bus Travel*

Card on the table.

'So how have you done that then?' asked James.

'Well, the end date is stamped onto the paper, so with a rubber, a black pencil and of course skill, I can tweak the date to get more travel time.'

'Isn't that fraud?'

Jay pondered for a moment rubbing at the small amount of stubble sprouting from his chin, before nodding lightly. 'You know what,' he smiled. 'I think it probably is.'

'Shame you can't do that for your train tickets.'

Jay beamed, 'I'm already working on that.'

'You're joking.'

'Nope, I can't do anything to the ticket but when I get a return ticket I have a month in which to use it... so for the first three weeks all I have to do is not get it stamped, that way when I come back here I just get a one way ticket which is cheaper.'

James's face looked confused and he pulled at his fringe. 'I wish I could think of stuff like that.' Moments later he followed it up with, 'but how do you avoid getting it stamped?'

Jay shrugged, 'hide in the bogs... or better still, loiter round the buffet bar or something, if I get asked there I'll just say it's back at my seat... it's not always going to work but each time it does I'm up.'

James put out his cigarette. 'So if I got one of those bus passes, you could sort it for me when it runs out?'

Jay rubbed his forefinger and thumb together to let James know it would cost him.

'Right,' he said, as he branched out with a yawn. 'I'm hungry.'

James joined him in the kitchen. Leaning onto the worktop by the fridge, he opened it, ignoring the smell of sour milk he reached for a yoghurt. As he spooned the contents of the small pot into his mouth, Jay had began to empty the cupboards in a brooding mood. He muttered as he sifted through trying to find something to fill his belly, 'half the stuff in here is out of date,' he moaned.

'Is it?' James frowned looking about his pot for a date.

'Yeah. Just look at this Pot Noodle, it's out by a whole year.'

'Jase have you absolutely nothing better to do than read the dates on the food packets?'

'I have a sensitive stomach that's all.'

'Yeah?'

'Yeah,' he nodded sharply, 'really.'

'I'm alright living on chips, biscuits and fags.'

'Hey look, some multi-vitamins,' and opened the bottle.

'Jase, you can't eat those. What about your sensitive stomach?'

'Yeah, but these are good for you,' and gave him a thin smile as he popped

two of them into his mouth, washing them down he uttered, 'disgusting.'
James chuckled. 'Is that to counteract the usual abuse you give your body?'

'At least a pint of beer's fresh.'

'It might help if you bought some food, besides they're only best before dates.'

Jay stood shaking his head with disbelief. 'A whole fucking year though,' he moaned as he waved the Pot Noodle at him.

'Chuck it out then,' snapped James.

'No, I'll leave it in there, it might become an antique.'

James nodded vaguely. 'Anyway, did I tell you the landlady's got a couple more students that are looking for a place to stay?'

'Well there's no room here is there?'

'We could share for bit.'

'No chance.'

'She'll drop the rent down by half.'

Jay rubbed at his rubbish bit of stubble again, 'half.'

'Yeah half,' James nodded positively. 'I haven't got much stuff, you go home at the weekends. I'm skint... you're skint, could be an idea?'

'Yeah, but I like my own space.'

'It'll help until your grant gets sorted.'

Jay continued to rub at his chin, this could be a wise move, 'more money for food I suppose.'

'And booze?'

'Since you put it that way. I think it's a great idea, but if Trac ever comes up for a weekend you'll have to sleep on the sofa.'

'No problem, I could always go home anyway.'

'Deal.'

'Cool,' smiled James. 'I'm going across to the shop, do want anything?'

'Yeah, get us a 10p mix,' and flipped a coin at him.

'I think I'm getting addicted to shop lifting,' smiled James as he sparked up a second cigarette, 'what do you think I should do?'

'Well if you can't sort your grant out, maybe you should seriously think about getting one of those long coats like mine with big inside pockets.'

James chuckled, 'you up for going to the Corner House for a drink and a few games of pool later?'

'Yeah,' Jay approved as he tried to get a whole Kit-Kat into his mouth.

Friday, September 29

After snoozing most of the way home Jay gave out a yawn as the train made its screeched halt at Narborough station. As the doors hissed open several people in front of him straggled out onto the platform. He checked the time on his watch and was pleased it had arrived on the dot.

He lumbered his bag over his shoulder and shuffled out. Squinting upward he could see Trac leaning over the rail of the foot bridge. Catching sight of him she waved and called out his name.

He smiled under heavy-lidded eyes, yawned again and was about to burst into a short run but resisted to look cooler, and settled for a brisk pace.

As he got to the foot of the bridge her little feet had already skipped half way down to meet him. She greeted him with a kiss and a light but positive squeeze of his arm, she was chirpy.

'Here,' she said brightly, 'I've got you some chips... although I have eaten most of them.'

Having not really eaten anything but crisps and a Marathon bar he was starving.

'Oh great,' he replied as he put out a hand to take them, whilst trying to hide yet another yawn.

'Tired?'

'Yeah a bit,' he mumbled and scooped some chips into his mouth.

Trac looped her arm through his and they meandered towards his house. When she uttered the words, 'so what do you want to do? He halted and his eyes narrowed as if in thought.

'Maybe,' he said, 'you could show me what all the x's were you so kindly teased me with on the phone?' and smirked ruefully.

She flushed and he wondered if she was about to fumble her words but she just blinked at him for a moment or two then chuckled affectionately, 'mmm, we'll see.'

He gave her a little encouraging nudge and she said, 'oh, okay. That's if you have the energy.'

They walked on and he seemed to perk up almost instantly.

After four rings the answer phone clicked in and Nick's voice came crackling through, 'Jay... are you in or not you gay-'

'Hey,' panted Jay as he snatched at the phone, 'you weren't about to leave the C' word on the answer phone were you?'

'No, I knew you were in, I saw you walking and being all lovey dovey.'

Jay gave out a long sarcastic yawn and eased down onto the last but one of the stairs.

'So are you out tonight then or what?'

Trac handed him a can of Guinness with a stern brow as if she was worried that his inability to say no was going to alter their evening.

'No,' he said quickly. 'I'm busy.'

'Oh come on, Rob's not out either.'

'Looks like you'll have to play with yourself,' he chuckled in response.

'Why don't you just come down with Trac?'

He half smiled, he didn't want Trac to be anywhere beyond lying in his bed. He enjoyed the fact that their evenings rarely varied, the all-inclusiveness of her, the one constant thing in his life that seemed to comfort him.

'I'll be out tomorrow night, yeah.'

'Up town?'

'Yeah okay, where?'

'Sector Five or the Fan Club. Your finances looking better then?'

'No, but you know me. Look I'll meet you in The Bell.'

'Okay, I guess I'll just have go to the New Inn.'

'Wonderful,' Jay sniped. 'Great idea.'

'Fuck you then,' jabbered Nick, 'and I hope you have a shit evening.'
Jay chuckled to that. 'See you,' he replied and took a sip from his can.

'Okay,' Nick replied and proceeded to call him gay and tapped the 'C'
word to the end of it before he disconnected, leaving Jay unable to return a
similar term of endearment. He replaced the phone back onto the corner shelf
as Trac asked if everything was okay. He took another larger gulp from the
can and feeling the minutest amount of alcohol begin to hit his bloodstream
and lift inside his head, he smiled back at her and said, 'fantastic.'

Saturday, September 30

Bundled snugly in his long coat, Jay shuffled silently through the door of
The Bell. He purchased a drink and moved into the corner.

'Alright lads?' he smiled.

'You going up town then?' Nick asked.

'Yep. You?'

'Yeah I reckon so. Rob, you're going ain't you?'

'No,' he growled sarcastically then chuckled, 'yeah I'm going.'

As they all piled into the taxis he was in high spirits, drunk and looking
forward to getting wiped out.

Standing on tip toes he stared across the crowd of people dancing,
searching for Adrian as he took to his watch for reference, the tap on his
shoulder revealed Adrian's big grinning face.

'Are you pissed already or just blind?'

'Blind I think. I got some vodka to help on the pissed front,' he smiled.

'There's no time like the present,' replied Adrian pleased with the
hospitality, 'let's make the usual.'

Swirling some lime in a pint glass he held it up to check its measure.
Without taking his eyes off the glass he trawled his pocket with his right
hand until it settled on a small bottle. He spun the top off with a flick of the
wrist and upturned the contents in one brisk manoeuvre.

'Here we go,' he whispered to himself, filling the glass. 'Magic,' he
smiled and passed the rest to Adrian.

It wasn't too long before his glass was drained and the beer throwing
began. The Wonder Stuff's music blared out and a mass of kids pogoed like
crazy, bumping into one another as though it were a ritual. Jay seemed to

dance in a loose pogo, with reasonable beat, managing to make space around himself to lurch back and forth in an aggressive manner. Adrian joined him, arm in arm shouting out the lyrics and bobbing up and down in a frenzy. As the songs got heavier, they threw themselves about even more with a wilful abandonment, an explosion of pushing and shoving more like a rock concert than a dance-floor ensued. They released all the energy and angst they had and returned to the bar frequently.

Jay stood soaked in beer and sweat, 'bastard,' he grinned pulling at his black shirt. Rob and Nick joined him looking very much in the same state.

'I'm knackered,' laughed Rob.

'You just need some more lager Rob.'

By one o'clock, their level of intoxication had passed the point at which it might have been excused as severe drunkenness. Even Nick and Rob had consumed more than their fair share of beer, but they were drunk enough to be manageable. Jay stood finishing the odd drink off at the bar or pouring it over his head to amuse his friends, being driven by every cheer they gave. It was a crapulent stage in which he laughed raucously at just about anything, even nothing, doubling up in fits of giggles, quickly changing into misjudgement. His head began to spin as he started to wobble and fall apart, but enjoying every minute of it.

Two o'clock had come again. It wasn't a surprise to see Adrian and Nick chatting to girls and Rob still dancing. Jay was half falling down the stairs in a bid for some fresh air.

In the cab on their way home he slumped against Adrian and fell asleep, all he wanted to do now was rest, to drift away and let the day be forgotten. He began to dream about Trac and woke with annoyance as it was time to get out of the taxi. He had no money which came as no surprise to Nick, but pissed him off anyway.

'Fucking hell Jay,' he cried, 'It's like this every fucking time. Next time you can give me your money before you spend it.'

He gave Nick a slight frown before slumping out the car door. Adrian handed Nick all his loose change and gave a shrug. 'Sorry Nick, it's all I got.'

'I hope you've got some money Rob?' asked Nick.

'I gave mine to Jay,' chuckled Rob.

Meanwhile, Jay was trying to unbutton his flies and ended up discharging more urine on himself than the floor.

'Oh shit,' he mumbled feeling the warm sensation of his bodily fluid seeping through his jeans. He leant on the lamp post by the corner of his street with a dazed grin glued to his face. They helped one another to his house, negotiated the stairs quite well, the halfway landing was a big help to Jay after nights out like these. When he finally made it to his bed he was out cold immediately, whilst Adrian made the best use he could of the floor.

Sunday, October 1

Jay groaned as the sharp pain in his neck woke him, he rubbed at it unsuccessfully and reluctantly moved from the bizarre shape in which his body had slept in. He found that he still had his clothes on, including his boots. He then noticed Adrian on the floor curled up, he woke him as he tried to reposition himself more comfortably.

'What time is it?' asked Adrian with a whisper.

'Ten o'clock,' responded Jay with a light chuckle.

'What's funny.'

'It's like the old days, you on the floor rough as fuck.'

Adrian rubbed his face and sat up, 'Put some music on Jay.'

'Adventures?'

'Classic.'

'What you doing this afternoon?'

'Going round to see Trac.'

'Tea and sympathy?'

'Yeah, something like that.'

'You give me a lift back in The Beast.'

'Sure.'

16. Come play with me

Taking full advantage of being accountable only to himself, and feeling slightly off colour, Jay made it half way to college and found himself in a record store buying The Wonder Stuff's new album 'HUP'. He was eager to listen to it, but he didn't have a CD player, and didn't know anyone in York who had one either.

He sat on a picnic bench outside the King's Head, down by the River Ouse, feeling a little down hearted. York dragged at him like a ball and chain around his ankle, he missed Trac, he needed her and certainly didn't want to lose how it felt to be close to her. It wasn't far to the train station to get onboard to Leicester. He sat there confused as he did his best to talk himself into seeing the week out, thinking that if he paced himself perhaps he could remain partially drunk all week? Finishing his pint he felt at his neck, wondering if he was coming down with something or whether it was just his general mood that was bringing him down. He wandered back to his digs and fell back into bed with ease and decided he would stay there for the day.

Tuesday, October 3

Jay was getting bored with the lecture on print production, even though it had moved back from a twilight lesson. Huddled at the very back of the classroom, perched up on the work surface that channelled down one side of the room, he flipped his scalpel in his hands as he studied the *News of the World* Sunday magazine next to him. He noted it with interest as the cover had a photo of Elvis' daughter with her grandchild. Before he knew it, he had cut out the eyes and mouth, rotated them a hundred and eighty degrees and was in the process of sticking them down when he was in stitches of laughter at his own entertainment, wiping tears from his eyes together with Den and Jeff.

'That's brilliant,' babbled Jeff.

'Erm... is something going on back there that I need to know about?' came a call from the front.

When no-one responded the tutor looked at her watch and said, 'okay I think it's time for lunch.'

In the canteen he sat with a hot chocolate, not really listening or taking part in any conversation. He studied a group of girls sitting outside on the steps all dressed in what looked like donkey jackets, tight leggings and DMs. He thought how attracted he was to that, which was kind of odd... or maybe not, it was those woolly tights again.

'I'm going to head back, get stuck into some work.'

'Are you feeling alright Jay?'

He put a hand up to his throat, 'not really,' and off he went.

Hunched over his desk, he spent the rest of the afternoon immersed in a new fashion poster and ticket brief. Being fresh it allowed his thoughts to solidify so that by six thirty, well after everyone else had gone, he had more than a few approaches to the problem.

He yawned a couple of times and rubbed at his eyes as he entered his digs. On the floor was a small blue envelope. He recognised Trac's writing and raised a faint smile as he slouched into the sofa and opened it.

To Jay,

Hello darling, how are you then? I realise you must be a bit shocked to actually receive a letter from me and wonder to what you owe the pleasure. Well I am not sure really, it could be the fact that I love you lots and miss you loads, or it could be that I've tried to do my maths and can't so I'm sulking and thought I might as well write you a letter before you go moody? Or could it be both, I don't know? Anyway, I'm snuggled up in bed with no clothes on my body buried between the pillows and quilt, with just my head and hand emerging from beneath, to write this. I can't wait till Mum and Dad go away, then you can come round and snuggle in with me. Two whole weeks of going mad, doing what the hell I want (coming home at what time I want). When you're home we can do lots of naughty things whenever we want, wherever we want, we can do it as many times as you want in my bed. You can kiss me in all those wonderful places you wanted to in your last letter and I can do all those things you like so much (that make your feet move, your eyes roll and your hands clutch). Well I'd better go before I start getting terrible and say things I shouldn't. I hope this gets to you by Tuesday, just in time for a reply from you before the weekend. Not that I'll see you much, you'll be too wrecked with Adrian, but I don't care, I can take it.

Anyway bye bye, Love you soo, soo, soo much I miss you already.

Trac xx (Your little baby)

He read it a few times, then put his hands behind his head and laid out along the sofa, staring in thought at the combination of light and dark blues on the ceiling before the need for a medicinal kip had taken route.

Wednesday, October 4

From his hiding place under the two duvets and a blanket, Jay woke with a pounding headache and wondered what he'd been drinking. The slow recognition of his sore throat confused him. Then he remembered he wasn't hungover, he was genuinely ill and recalled that he'd fell into bed like a dead man.

Now several thoughts banged through his head in a split second.

He was in York.

Late for college.

Alone.

In need of medicine.

WATER!!

His body twitched as he tried to respond actively to each thought in turn. His eyes half closed, he could see a glass on the bedside table and was dismayed that it was empty.

'Need to get up,' he muttered rubbing at his head as his eyes picked up a trail of clothes along the floor; shirt, socks, jeans, boxers, T-shirt. The idea that he was going to ease out, semi-clothe himself, make himself some toast, self medicate, drink plenty of fluid and lounge deep into the sofa in front of daytime TV was just too much, way too much. He felt like a trapped animal, huddled up and enduring a slow painful death. I should be at home he thought, back in Leicester with his mum and Trac to look after him. The more he began to wish for that and envisage being with Trac, the more he ached for home, now lovesick too he wished he'd never woke.

Thursday, October 5

James stormed through the door and placed two large bottles of wine on the table.

'Magic, how much was that?'

'Let's just say it wasn't expensive and probably tastes awful.'

Not normally a wine drinker Jay pawed at the two bottles.

'Hopefully it will go straight to my head,' he said as the thought began to excite him.

'You're taking the cans of Foster's too?'

'Yeah.'

'What time are we off?'

'Don't know, we want to get there just as it gets going, make a grand entrance, I like them,' he smiled picturing a drunken arrival in his head.

The sound of rain drumming down made the prospect of walking a mile to the party a nightmare.

'We're going to get soaked,' bleated James.

'Don't worry,' said Jay slowly, 'there's a chance it might stop.'

'I don't think so,' James continued to moan as he stood by the front room window, pacing back and forth, occasionally fidgeting with the net curtain and eating into Jay's patience. He tried to dissuade James by not responding, it rarely worked, but it suited him, he didn't require much in the way of communication, just another's presence. He took a swig from a can of beer and rolled it around at the back of his mouth momentarily. With pencil in hand, poised just inches from the sketch pad, he was ready to transfer deep sensation to paper.

'What are you drawing then?'

'Oh fuck,' he griped and rose to his feet. 'Nothing by the looks of things.'

'Why don't we get a taxi?'

'Too expensive,' to which James let out yet another grunt. 'Have you got the money?' continued Jay.

'No'

'Well then.'

'I tell you, we're going to get soaked.'

'Look,' suggested Jay with his face squashed against the front window, we can take a push bike, we'll be there in ten minutes. Besides it's slowing down already.'

Like a flash they were zigzagging up the road, two up on a small push bike, no lights and a bag full of booze trying to avoid the flurry of rain. They could hear the party in full swing as they got closer and dumped the bike in the front garden, bursting in, roaring and spraying beer into the air. A huge 'waheey!' had Jay turn to see Den come charging over to him, pint in hand and spilling a little with his hurried motion. He jeered back in the same way, narrowly missing the oncoming spray of lager.

'Where have you been?'

'Getting ready.'

Den stared at him and frowned, then mumbled something he couldn't hear because the music drowned it.

'Slow down, I can't understand a fucking word you're saying!'

'I don't know what I'm fucking saying.'

'Let's go through there,' he yelled and nodded in the direction of the kitchen.

A few people greeted him as he made his way through and he nodded with a false smile of acknowledgement as he passed them on his way out into the yard.

'You're not pissed yet then?' chuckled Den.

'No. Not yet, I've got a bit of catching up to do,' and he poured himself a pint of wine and stashed his six pack of Foster's lager.

'So where were you yesterday?'

'Ill,' he informed him raising a hand to his throat. 'Still feels bad now.'

'Bullshit!' spat Den.

'No seriously.'

Den gave him a stare of disbelief.

'I am really... honest.'

James leant against the wall sipping at his beer quietly until Den slapped him on the shoulder.

'Alright James?'

'Yeah. Not bad.'

James looked uneasy, he didn't know anyone at the party and was content to play the shadow. Jay drank most of his wine and poured the rest over his head in a frenzy. This gained another cheer of applause, the notion of a great drinker had been forged. He took a beer and with his eyes dilating he suddenly shook the can and sprayed the contents over everyone laughing out loud. With menacing eyes, a rising destructive mode was forming and there was no way of avoiding it.

The music came loud and strong and the girls flocked to the edge of the room to witness what was supposed to be dancing but soon became a huge pushing and shoving brawl in the centre of the room. Jay, James and Den were loving every minute of it. Bottles smashed, girls screamed, even the kitchen door came off its hinges. This was the kind of stimulation and release he was looking for, the negative energy he had was pumping through him to all limbs. He stood in what he called his best John Wayne stance and sneered at Dean, a fellow student from his class who was shouting verbal abuse at him and charging at him like the rugby player he was. They clashed and both ended up on the floor. Jay, winded for a second, had taken half the mantelpiece with him on his decent.

'Getting pretty rough,' said James.

'Yeah... he punched me in the stomach.'

'Hit him back.'

Jay shook his head. 'No... no,' he muttered, 'it's just supposed to be pushing each other not punching.'

James steamed off into the darkness anyway to offer revenge. The party almost seemed out of control until the music was stopped and the lights came on. He saw Dean swearing, someone had tipped beer all over him and ripped his shirt.

'Phew,' Jay whistled quietly, 'that's worn me out,' and put his arms around Den and James.

Opening a can of beer he eased himself down into one of the corners of the front room, happy to soak up the atmosphere from there for a while when he heard his name being called, followed by a figure before him. He couldn't see the face, a light blinded his vision at that angle.

'I haven't seen you at college all week.'

'I was in on Tuesday,' he said as the figure slipped down beside him, and a small round fresh faced looking female came to his view that he was unable to recognise.

'You alright?' he mumbled.

'Fine,' she smiled. 'You're looking yourself.'

He pondered on what she had meant by that, then just smiled and tried to figure out who she was? Had he met her at another party? Had he been too drunk to recall? She finally introduced herself as Helen and still it confused him. Was he being chatted up?

She had a classic female pear-shape to her body, short blonde hair, great eyes and a strong northern accent that seemed to grate on him instantly, and the sky-blue knitted top she was wearing wasn't doing her any favours either.

'I'm in the year above you.'

'Oh right,' he replied, glancing around for an appropriate escape route and smiled widely as Den came hurtling towards him roaring, 'Jay, James is puking up.'

He patted her on the thigh and rose to his feet, smiled and said, 'I'll catch you later,' before dashing out into the yard.

'Waheey! Can't handle it,' spouted Den as Jay appeared next to him. Seeing the helpless figure of James hunched up onto his knees vomiting freely, he was struck dumb for a second or two before babbling, 'you alright mate?'

'I feel terrible,' came his feeble reply.

Friday, October 6

It had been a fairly heavy drinking bout and he failed to remember much, coming to the conclusion that he must of had a good time but for whatever reason deep down inside he wasn't really all that bothered. He'd been woke brashly at some cruel hour by the landlady who bawled at him for five minutes or more about the state of the hallway. He sat at the top of the stairs, head in his hands, taking the verbal battering. He blamed James for the plant being knocked over, in order to get some relief, but she chose to remind him of another time he reeled into the house, crashed into the wall taking a picture down with him. Not wanting to make the yelling last any longer than it had to, he repeatedly apologised for anything and everything in a soft aloof mumble until she had called it quits and left him to return to his woeful semi-comatose state for a couple more hours.

Hangovers are a mild form of poisoning, but that wasn't what was making him wince with pain, it was his throat. When fully awake he went to the kitchen and slid his breakfast from underneath the grill. The prospect of eating the food filled him with no pleasure, he felt hollow but it was not a hollowness that eating would sort out, more a feeling of low self esteem had taken route. He had to try and realise that you can't expect to party hard with a whole bunch of people and wake up the next day on your own and not feel some sense of abandonment... yet he simply put it down to yearning for Trac's presence.

James had left a note attached to a traffic cone in the middle of the room. It read; *Our front room is starting to look like the M25, gone to college see you later*. He trashed his breakfast and made some tea and sat in front of the TV flicking through the channels at speed, occasionally smiling to himself remembering bits of the party. Eventually realising he was still in the same clothes as the night before, he decided a wash was the first order of the day. He ran the bath and packed his laundry for his mum. His thoughts turned to Trac as he packed ready to set off home. The street outside was deserted wet and gloomy, and the rain increased its weight and speed. Staring he watched the pellets of rain squirm down the window pane, he turned as the kettle began to whistle and then checked the time with his watch. The approaching winter gave him a general feeling of depression. Days like these made him tired, even lonely for some reason. After finishing his tea he left a note for James and caught the bus to the railway station.

The train journeys, he decided, were awfully dull. After the first hour of passing countryside it became very plain and no-one seemed to talk. Unless you had a book to read or a personal stereo, all you could do was sit and stare at things; people, hedges, labels... boring! He had tried to make small talk with a complete stranger before, who responded with a look of shock and a verbal mumble that he couldn't decipher. 'Why do you give me a look as if I've just shagged your wife,' he said, but only in his head, for he knew that if he had said it out loud it would only cause more people to stare at him with disgust for breaking the silent train etiquette. And so he wandered to the buffet bar in carriage two for a can of lager, which was where he invented his new train game. The idea was simple, just by using your eyes you could make someone so self conscious that they'd have to go and make sure there was nothing wrong with their appearance. He would sit with a blank face in his seat and occasionally look at the person opposite in the eye, then glance up at their hair and pull an expression that said 'What is going on with your hair?' After a few goes, his victim would begin to brush their hair first, usually with their hand, checking that it's style hadn't fallen apart. The look on their face would be that of confusion. The biggest reward was after a few more flickers with his eyes, they would have to hurry to the toilet to check in a mirror and that was the point at which he could finally let a smile split his face. This train game and drinking lager were about the only two things he didn't get bored of. The most cans he had drank in a journey was about six and the most people he managed to irritate was about four, but he was always out to beat his record.

He sat, headphones on and eyes shut, for further sleep. The connection at Shefield ran smoothly and he was making good time. At half past six, *Welcome to Leicester Station,* was a nice sight. He waited patiently for his dad to pick him up, but nothing. Ten minutes later he was stood by the phone box on London Road occasionally jumping into the booth and dialling the same number over and over again.

'Bollocks,' he grunted slamming the receiver down and storming off. His anger subsided as he got on the next train to Narborough, all he could think about was Trac.

Home at last, sitting in The Beast filled him with happiness and contentment. Back in Trac's arms where he belonged he felt even better. Had she been able to encounter his eyes she might have seen how well the expression of heartfelt delight diffused over his face.

'How have you been?'

'I missed you,' he whispered as he released himself from the hug. 'Missed us.'

'You sound husky... it's very sexy,' she smiled.

'Really? I don't feel sexy,' he smiled. 'My throat's killing.'

He moved back in to embrace her further, concerned she was getting used to him not being around. 'You know what,' he said. 'I think the most important thing in a relationship is a good hug. I feel a whole lot better now.' He smiled not wishing to acknowledge it was a fix of security more than joy.

She gave him a happy face. 'What did you do last night then?'

'Went to that party.'

'I thought you would. Any good?'

'For the most part I had a good time.'

'And the rest?'

'A bit sketchy!'

Jay was laying on his stomach beside her, he told her that he was cold and she turned from the TV and pulled up the duvet, his duvet. He had forgotten this was his bed and he slipped under as she moved her warm legs in beside him. He gave a yawn followed by a sorrowful sigh, it was late. He cleared his throat. 'I still feel rough,' he said.

'You just need to go cold turkey for a few weeks.'

'Mmm... maybe?'

'I'm going to have to go home.'

'Can't you stay.'

'No, it's too late to ask Mum now.'

'Okay,' he said and idly pushed himself up into a sitting position, rubbing at his eyes. 'Come on then girl,' he chirped and patted her thigh.

She reluctantly climbed off the bed and began to dress. She repositioned her hair with a brush and spray. He picked up the keys to The Beast and they left.

Saturday, October 7

Jay gazed around Marks and Spencer's looking to treat Trac to a present. He trundled up to the ladies department to see if he could find something. He never normally got nervous or embarrassed but buying ladies underwear was a whole new experience. He wanted something elegant yet sexy at the same time. He stood biting at his thumb and pondered at the large displays, not knowing where to start.

'Can I help you?' came the voice of a young female assistant from behind him.

He turned to face her and she pulled a typical shop assistant smile.

'Er... I err, I'm looking for something for my girlfriend.'

Noting his discomfort she asked teasingly, 'something sexy?'

He rubbed at his forehead and looked about, 'Err, yeah sure,' he said as he drew his eyes back to the assistant and gave her a helpless shrug.

'Let me see if I can help. What cup size is she?'

He frowned, he didn't know what that meant, and avoided contact with her eyes.

'Do you know what her cup size is?'

'Yeah,' he said confidently. 'I mean no.' This time he gave her a pathetic shrug.

'Well her breast size. Is she small or large?'

'She's...' he began to feel flushed. 'She's about... about...' and brought his hands up and moved then round simulating her breast size hopelessly. 'About... about your size...' he smiled, 'I mean, your height and that... build you know.'

He didn't even bother to shrug this time he just took a deep breath. Shit, he thought. He didn't think it would be so hard, he felt a right fool standing there looking hopeless. The assistant felt sorry for him and took him on a short tour of all the different types of underwear, explaining as she went.

'There's so many different things,' he smiled and carried on looking, filling with confidence with every step. 'Oh I like this,' he said. 'She'll love this.'

'That's a basque.'

'Yeah, I'll take one of these.'

'Medium?'

'I think so.'

'If it doesn't fit she can always bring it back and exchange it.'

He nodded and gave a little sigh of relief and headed off to the till.

When he got to the café he could see Trac at the far corner table, squeezing her teeth into a doughnut. As he joined her she wiped a small lump of jam from her mouth and said, 'you caught me.'

'Does that mean I get to finish it then?' he smiled.

She nodded positively, 'I feel bad for just having the one bite.'

'Hey, this will cheer you up,' he beamed and plonked the M&S bag on the table.

'What's this?'

'Open it and see,' he replied excitedly.

She pawed at the light branded plastic bag and felt the soft silky material.

'Underwear,' she whispered.

Her lips curled slightly yet her eyes remained still. It was as if the defusion of joyful surprise was stalled by a hint of guilt. It was something she had never given him credit for. He put two lumps of sugar into his cup and stirred it slowly before tapping the spoon on the rim and tucking it in on the saucer. Her gaze remained distant, concerned he leaned across the table, took her hands in his and watched her eyes pool as a sense of sadness seeped from her.

'I've not bought it cos I'm seeing Adrian tonight, I'm not trying to buy you off if that's...'

She put a finger to his lips, 'shhh... it's not that... it's me. I'm being silly. I know how much your friends and everything means to you, it's...'

'It's what?... Tell me.'

'It's just there's times I need you and you're not here.'

'Hey... listen to me,' he said softly. 'It won't always be like this, I just need to do this right now.'

'Sometimes it's hard you being in York, it feels so far away and it hurts so much.'

'You know I keep asking... you should come up, it might help.'

'Mum won't approve,' she said softly as the first tears broke free. 'I just love and miss you,' she huffed. 'God, this is scary I'm only sixteen and I'm like this when I go out with my mates, there's at least one point during the night when I pine for you... usually more.'

In the hope to channel warm affection he mumbled soft and low, 'it's the same for me. I never counted on loving you so much. Maybe I should just quit.'

She moved her hands back to his. 'You can't do that Jay. I'll be okay, ignore me. I'm just at the vulnerable stage of the month so you have to be kind,' she got a tissue from her pocket and wiped her nose.

'I can cancel it with Adrian.'

She shook her head to say no. 'But you do look tired Jay,' she said. 'Maybe you should just stay in and have an early night.'

'I'm fine... I'm better,' he replied. 'Look I don't have to go out with Adrian till gone nine, so I can hang about till you finish work.'

'Pizza?'

He glanced at the bag and to her and smiled, 'I'm not sure I'm that rich.' She chuckled as she wiped away any built up tears.

He slurped on a can of Guinness and eased it back onto the window sill.

'In a moment,' he smirked. 'I think I'll have an unfeasibly large scotch.'

'Of course,' chuckled Adrian already mixing measures of scotch and Coke. 'Rat arsed we shall be.'

Jay held out a dark brown glass with small half spheres covering the base. 'Fill it up to the brim.'

'No problem,' he replied. 'I see we have new glassware.'

'Yeah, I'm afraid all the good glasses have gone, this is all that's left.'

Half a bottle of scotch in and they had passed from the sublime to the ridiculous. As Jay reached upward to his feet, he realised how drunk he actually was and in a soft easy tone muttered, 'need some fresh air.'

The pair of them staggered out the front door into the cool night air. Jay paused for a second, gained his balance with deep thought and concentration, and a quick shot from the bottle as he moved out onto the road. He heard his mum behind him shouting at them both from the doorway.

'Jason, get in here now. What do you think you're doing? It's gone two in the morning,' she wailed.

He failed to respond and looked out across the road and noted movement, a twitch of a curtain and a silhouette. He simply staggered away, falling on someone's car he just burst into hysterics. Adrian joined him as they pulled themselves together and wandered off down the road arm in arm singing as they disappeared into the dingy lit alleyway where adventure seemed to beckon.

The night breeze rustled through the trees while the two of them rambled through the streets. In a haze Jay tumbled into someone's back garden, laughing.

'Are you crazy or what? Come back,' whispered Adrian with a slur before following him.

'What's that?'

'Shhh cover me,' giggled Jay and he darted off in a funny direction bundling something heavy under his coat. Falling through a fence he struggled to get up. His pulse quickened, it was as if he had lost all sense of bearing, he was totally blitzed, wandering in a daze over unfamiliar territory. The two of them made it to the side of a house, not far from the street. Jay fell to the ground, this time caused by a flash of pain to his chest.

'Shit,' he groaned holding his chest in agony but grinning at the same time, following it with an unstable laugh.

'You alright Jay?'

'Yeah I'm okay,' he spluttered. 'I've got stitch or something.'
A light came on in the house. 'Shit scarper,' mumbled Adrian tugging at the collar of Jay's long coat.
Adrian fled with elegance while Jay did a half stagger, half run after him out into the street. As he did so the object fell from his coat. Adrian lurched to the floor and picked up an ornament and glared at it before laughing, it was a garden gnome.

Sunday, October 8

When Jay woke, he was filled with an urgent feeling that they must leave the house as quickly as possible before his mum got up, she had to be avoided at all costs. He became immensely amused after he rubbed his face and saw that his bedroom floor was taken over by Adrian hunched up in his sleeping bag among the empty bottles and cans. He decided to let some daylight in, pulled back the curtains and chuckled as he saw a large army of garden gnomes in line along his window sill.

'Adrian,' he whispered giving him a nudge with his foot.

Adrian squinted at the blur of gnomes, surprised to see them in full glory as they slowly came into focus.

'Oh no, we... we must of,' mumbled Adrian. 'This was one of your ideas.'

'Mine?'

'Yeah, it's got your name written all over it.'

Jay chuckled further as he picked up his camera and looked at the number of photos taken. 'Looks like we had quite an interesting time last night.'

'Looks that way,' smiled Adrian.

There was a certain amount of coming and going through the night, the eleven concrete garden gnomes and a windmill were quite big and heavy. After a cup of tea, aspirins and some Marmite on toast they parted company and Adrian jogged off up the walk way as he saw the bus in the distance.

'See you later,' shouted Jay after him.

He ignored his mum waiting in the kitchen, fingers stitched tight in front of her looking annoyed. He hadn't got the energy to be off-hand with her and made it halfway up to his room before she began yelling, calling him a thief amongst other things. Thus far, the memories of the night were at best intermittent only, it was obvious she was right, where else had the gnomes come from?

'I suppose you'll tell Dad?'

'I already have,'

'Right,' he responded mildly as he scratched the back of his head.

'Don't panic, I'm not impressed with him, he just thought it was funny.'

'Really?'

'Yes and he said if you can't remember where to return them then he'll have a couple of them and so will your grandad.'

Her face had lightened slightly from it's sternness, so he said, 'I got a windmill, that would look good on the rockery?'

'I don't see the funny side, so if someone comes to the door to complain you can explain yourself.'

He chewed on that for a moment or two, fair enough he thought and floated back to his room.

By night-time he took a turn for the worse, he was too weak to take advantage of Trac in her new underwear or to drive home, so she tucked him up in her bed. On the plus side she had found the previous evening's episode amusing and had found another home for a gnome.

'I told you, you shouldn't have gone out last night.'

'I had to see Adrian, he's off to London soon,' he mumbled.

'You could've done that without drinking.'

He just gave her a confused look that said 'don't be daft.'

'Any of it come back to you yet?'

'Nooo.'

'You still can't remember?'

He responded by shaking his head slightly.

'You know, if you just stayed in bed for three or four days you'd be so much better. Just slow down.'

Giving into her, he smiled at her with affectionate eyes. 'Okay.'

'Mum is getting you some medicine.'

'Ugh, no,' he scrunched his face up at her, 'I'm okay just give me some hot water, whiskey, a spoon of honey and a touch of lemon juice.'

'I don't think so Jay.'

'Yeah, it works.'

'How's that going to work?' quizzed Trac, looking unconvinced.

'The water warms me, the honey and lemon soothe my throat...'

'And the whiskey?' she interrupted.

'The whiskey lifts the spirit.'

'Well we haven't got any lemon.'

He blinked at her. 'Just whiskey and honey, better still a few warmed up whiskeys will do the trick.'

'Oh yeah right,' she said sarcastically. 'I can just see it now, Mum, Jason wants some whiskey!'

'Just sneak me some then.'

'Look if you want me to look after you then shut up.'

He was ready to scrunch his face up stick his bottom lip out and go into a stubborn mood but her mum came in. She was very caring, that was probably why she was a nurse he thought. Trac just sat on the edge of her bed smiling sweetly in a caring way too, as her mum sifted through a tub of different medicines.

'How do you feel then?' she asked soothingly.

'Awful, my throat hurts,' he whispered.

'Well I have some paracetamol, a Lemsip and some cough mixture.'

'Thanks,' he mumbled.

'If that doesn't sort you out, you'll have to go and see your doctor.'

'Okay.'

Her mum left them with Trac, now it was up to her to force all this medicine down him.

'Right, first drink this.'

He looked at her stern face for a second, then pulled his hand up from under the duvet. Swallowing the fizzing mixture his eye lids squeezed tightly together and he gulped loudly.

'Oh fuck...' he spluttered.

'Come on, drink up.'

'It tastes grim,' he muttered pulling an unsettled face.

'Come on, don't be silly.'

The rest of the concoction didn't go down with ease but it went down, that was the main thing and Trac adopted a more affectionate tone.

'There's a good boy,' she offered with a smile and passed him the Lemsip. He took it. 'Just don't go giving me anything else,' he snarled.

'You're such a baby.'

He held the warm mug in both hands and sipped, he cringed once or twice until he came accustomed to the taste, then it wasn't so bad.

'I bet I look awful.'

'You just look so tired.'

He felt his jaw line. 'Look at that,' he said, as he held his chin up to reveal a few dark bits of stubble.

'Oh, you man,' she said. 'You'd grow some messy stubble if you could.' He said nothing, just smiled and nodded.

'You could be a real slob then,' and she waggled his chin in her hand. He smirked and said, 'and what's wrong with that?'

The day, insulated by Trac and the duvet, had gone remarkably quick. He had the feeling of well-being staying at her house, in her room. Of course she had to sleep upstairs in the spare room and go to school the next day, but he enjoyed snuggling up in her bed, sleeping where she sleeps. Digging his head deep into her pillow, he fell asleep and Trac kissed him goodnight.

'I love you,' she whispered. 'Too much,' and switched out the sidelight.

Monday, October 9

The next morning he awoke to the sound of a hairdryer. He squinted up at Trac and she smiled back and mouthed the words, 'morning sexy.'

He watched her pull back her hair slightly and spray it firmly with a large can of hair spray.

'How do you feel now?'

'I'm not sure... A bit better.'

'I've put you some aspirins on the side there and make sure you drink lots of water.'

'I will,' he rolled over onto his front and rubbed his face into her pillow.

'Do you want something to eat?' she asked.

'No,' came a muffled reply.

'Are you going to be here when I get back?'

'Yeah. If I feel a little stronger I'll probably go home before you have your dinner.'

'Okay, I'll see you about four.'

He played her stereo softly most of the day and lay absorbed in thought, falling in and out of sleep. Her mum popped her head round the door occasionally and asked him if he needed anything. He didn't want to be too much trouble so he said, 'no I'm fine.' Yet she kindly made him some toast anyway. His loss of appetite continued and every bite was a task. His mouth stayed dry, not eager for anything, so he was forced into throwing the remnants out of the window for the birds.

At two thirty her mum left for work. He put the stereo on a little louder and fell asleep until Trac arrived home at five past four, slung her bag on the floor, kissed him quickly, mumbled something and went to make a cup of tea. She kept her distance from him, he noted she did this after a bad or long day, giving herself time to unwind until she could communicate freely.

'How are you feeling now?' she asked.

'Okay.'

'Like some tea?'

'Love some.'

He pulled his blue sweatshirt on, it hung below his bum so he didn't bother putting on his underwear or jeans in a hurry.

'What time does your mum get back?'

'About six, then she'll do the dinner.'

'I'll go before she comes back.'

'Okay, if you want.'

'Thank her for me won't you.'

She gave him a slow nod of her head, 'sure.'

Splashing water over his face and running his fingers through his hair, he tried to wake himself and find some energy. He did feel a little better being up on his feet, a few hours will do him good Trac advised him and gave him her grey scarf to keep him warm from the cold night air.

'Cheers,' he said lightly.

'You just make sure you tuck yourself up in bed early tonight.'

'Sure,' he smirked as he saluted her.

'Here take this,' and she gave him the small dark bottle of Sainsbury's cough mixture.

Tuesday, October 10

He lay on his bed motionless and, bored with overdosing on daytime TV and paracetamol, only the sound of the phone ringing again stirred him from a dream. Trac was coming over. He stretched out on his bed then embraced his pillow with excitement as if he had her in his arms, squeezing her tightly.

He changed the sheets and pillowcase and took a shower, sprinkled himself with powder, dressed and combed his hair. 'Uggh, too much, too smooth he thought, so he messed it up and laid back down onto his bed.

He woke with a tremendous sneeze and a diabolical pain in his head.

One end of his body was warm but the other half was cold and something was wet on his face.

'Sam,' he yelled shoving the dog on the floor.

He heard the front door close and Trac in the hallway talking to his mum. He sat up sharply and rubbed his eyes.

'Trac,' he croaked slightly going into the hall.

'Arrh how's my sexy pants then?'

'Better.'

'I've bought you some Lemsip.'

'Great,' he said in a dull tone.

'I've taken some tablets already.'

'You can still have one of these as well.'

'Suppose,' he moaned with little enthusiasm.

He was still thinking how a drop of warm whiskey would be nice. Just under his bed was a fresh flask sized bottle, an alternative pain killer, were you allowed to booze on tablets?

'What you thinking?'

'Nothing... I err,' he stammered and then a smile flickered across his face. 'You know what, I wouldn't mind a tattoo.'

Trac came alive and moved closer, her eyes were on him. 'Oh yeah, what of?' she hummed keenly.

'I don't know yet. I just want something to say what a great summer I've had, maybe a cartoon of The Yellow Fish would be cool.'

'Why the summer?'

'It's what I want back and can't have I guess.'

Standing up and looking into his mirror he muttered, 'do you think my hair looks okay? It's getting a bit long. Mum keeps telling me to get it cut and my dad thinks I look like a bum?'

'Yeah it looks nice,' she said with a strong tone of support.

'She's obsessed that I'm not eating too.'

'You look the same to me.'

'Maybe have the tattoo on my shoulder,' he said leaning towards the mirror. 'Everyone has them on their arms, mine are too skinny' he said putting another record onto the stereo.

'I wouldn't mind a rose on my shoulder, a black one or a blood red one.'

He turned to face her, 'I'm feeling a lot better now.'

'You seem a bit more active,' encouraged Trac gently.

'Maybe we could...'

'I don't think you've quite got the energy for that,' she teased. 'I'm a very demanding girl.'

'Well I do need to be fit now your mum and dad have gone away.'

'Yep,' she cheered.

'For two whole weeks,' he smiled

'You should be at college.'

'I've already told them I'll be off the rest of the week. May even get away with a few days next week seeing as it's your half term,' he said. 'Then, it will be my half term.'

She gave him a nod of her head, 'cool.'

'Shall we nip to The Bell on the way back to yours later.'

'The Bell's not on the way back to mine.'

'It can be,' he smiled.

'But you're meant to be ill.'

'Oh I am, but only in the head,' he said tapping the side of it with his index finger and she chuckled.

An early return to hers found him just leaning against her passage wall smiling, eyes bright and his face excited and overly animated. Eased by a couple of pints she liked him like this, he was honest and could say the most wonderful things.

'Big hug required,' he beamed opening his arms. She obliged and he uttered, 'you're crazy about me.'

'Might be,' she responded.

'Give me one of those looks of yours.'

'What looks?'

'One of those looks that say, screw me to the wall you big sex machine.' She chuckled with a teasing smile. 'Sorry, I don't know what you're talking about,' and he began to laugh.

Her room smelt of make up and White Musk perfume. He was hungry, his stomach was rumbling loud enough for her to hear.

'I'll make us some peanut butter on toast.'

'Lots, I've got some catching up to do.'

'Okay one mound of food coming up.'

He slipped his jacket off and glanced at her unmade bed, leaning over he kissed the aromatic pillow where she had recently lay and decided to stay there until she returned.

After their supper she washed up. On her return, she put her hand to her mouth and stopped talking in mid-sentence, he was naked, all he had was a smile, his earring and a hard on; she didn't hesitate for a second in undressing with a smile about her face.

'Little point in me slipping into my new underwear then is there?'

Sinking into the covers her head popped playfully from under the duvet smiling. Two weeks living together, this was going to be a whole new experience, a chance to say here I am... this is me at my worst.

Wednesday, October 11

Jay sat comfortably at the round dining table talking with his mouth full.

Trac couldn't understand what he was saying, so she just nodded with agreement to whatever it was and continued to wash dishes.

'Get us some ketchup girl,' he mused.

She moved her hand up to say okay and drifted off to the nearest cupboard.

'Here,' she said placing the bottle next to his plate.

'Cheers.'

'You can help yourself you know.'

She had the signs of another annoying day at school, so wasn't in the mood for much in the way of conversation.

'I can't wait till half term next week,' she muttered.

'I'll probably have to go back to college next week.'

She sighed, 'yeah I suppose you should.'

'Well I've had most of the last week off, then this week. It pisses me off that our half terms aren't the same week.'

Trac nodded lazily with agreement.

'I can't talk you into coming up to York for the weekend?'

'I so want to but Mum and Dad would go mad.'

'They wouldn't know if you came while they were away.'

'And you think my sister would allow that?'

'I guess not.'

The sky outside was darkening already and the room became dim. She had calmed down after a chocolate bar and a second cup of tea. She sat next to him with a still face that had forgotten how to frown, but was slowly producing dimples in her cheeks as a smile was on its way.

'Thanks for picking me up from school.'

In fact, what she had meant to have said was, 'thanks for putting up with my moods.' She slid over the gold wrapper of her chocolate bar that she had reworked into a heart shape.

He picked it up and smiled lightly. 'Anytime,' he said softly.

At the centre of the table he placed a bottle of vodka. There was little left in it but she wanted it as an ornament, something to remind her of him. It had been rattling about in The Beast for ages.

'There you are then babe,' he said as he slid the bottle towards her.

'Thanks.'

'I don't know why you want to keep it?'

'Oh it's just a keepsake thing.'

'So... what are we going to do tonight?' he sighed.

'We could get a film.'

'Yeah we could get a couple.'

'Or we could watch one of mine,' she suggested.

He replied, 'yeah right,' sarcastically and she nudged him. 'Oh come on, you know all the words to it.'

'No that's only *Back to the Future*. I've got *Grease*.'

'Which we've watched twice before.'

'*Teen Wolf*?'

'I take it that's a joke.'

'You watched it with me before.'

'Yes... yes I did and you know what, never again!'

'You're just mean'

'No I'm not.'

'I tell you what I have got, some *Red Dwarfs* on tape.'

'Umm...' he uttered, 'better but I'm not in the mood for it.'

She offered up a couple more things but his face began to scrunch up. 'I don't know then?' and gave him a lazy shrug.

'Right' he clapped his hands. 'Why don't we celebrate and go down the pub for a few drinks.'

'Nooo!.'

'Oh come on, why not?' he said and nudged her with his arm.

'You'll ignore me.'

'No I won't,' he said pulling a face.

He stood tiredly, arms folded with his shirt rolled up at the sleeves, buttons undone and the ends of the shirt untucked from his jeans, waiting for her to make her mind up.

'What about just us two down the pub on the corner here. I don't fancy driving all the way to The Bell anyway, besides I'm running out of petrol and...' he smiled raising a finger in the air, 'for the record I don't ignore you.' Just as he reached the point of deciding whether he would go with or without her she agreed.

'Great,' he chirped. 'So are you getting them in then?'

'That'll be right.'

'Sorry, I haven't got any cash,' he admitted and splayed out his arms as a sign of apology.

'You should take me out.'

'I do...' he frowned, 'I will.'

She extended a murmur he couldn't quite catch.

'Look I'll take you out soon. When I've got some money. I've still not had my grant come through yet and I'm well overdrawn.'

She gave him a disbelieving glance and stood from her chair and walked towards the kitchen.

'I know,' he said quickly, 'we could go for a pizza.'

'Why don't you save some of your money instead of blowing it all on drink, petrol and music.'

'What?' he chuckled to himself. 'Stay in... do nothing. No chance.'

'You will have to slow down sometime.'

'Never,' he smirked pulling on his boots and wrapping the laces round the ankle leather, bowing them at the top to save time.

'Right let's go.'

Trac gave out a little sigh as she moved her feet towards the front door. He was into his usual fast marching mode and made it to the bottom of the drive before she closed the front door. Jogging lightly, she caught up with him and skipped along behind him the rest of the way to keep up. In the Queen Arms they positioned themselves near the bar and stayed there comfortably for a few hours, sipping halves and talking freely.

'Move over,' she told him pulling the bed covers and shoving him slightly.

'Move where?' he laughed, 'If I move any further I'll be outside.'

She was exhausted and he was excited. He pushed himself into her a few times to make sure she got the message.

'Oh... I can't live with you, you're too much hard work,' she said in a hushed tone as she eased round, laying into him she idly played with his cock.

'I'm sooo tired,' she yawned.

'But... but.'

'It can't happen everyday,' she mumbled burning her head deeper under the covers.

'I'm going to sleep,' and she stopped all movement in her body. He was nearly at the point of total relaxation and tried to revive her hand. Trac tried for a short second or two but he had to take matters into his own hands.

'Can I cum on you?' he asked cheerily.

'Umm... I don't know,' she mumbled not really listening to him. 'No,' she then muttered but it was too late.

'Thanks,' she sighed. 'Feel better for that?'

'Mmm.'

He felt happy now, and a bit mischievous. He liked the feeling and pulled the covers up, curled round her and slept.

'Oh fuck, I don't believe it,' groaned Jay as he rolled away from her.

'What is it?' she asked yawning, 'it's two o'clock in the morning.'

'My leg's killing. I've got cramp or something?'

'Oh, great,' she moaned softly.

'It's being cramped in a single bed, have you got any Deep Heat?'

'In the bathroom.'

She heard him stumble through the doorway violently.

'Shit!' he snapped.

He disappeared making a racket as he stumbled through the darkness. He sat squinting in the toilet rubbing the cream into his legs.

'The stuff stinks,' she mumbled as he clambered back into bed.

Within a few moments something unpleasant was happening between his legs, his eyes opened and he lifted his head slightly from the pillow.

'What is it now?'

'My bollocks are roasting.'

Trac managed a soft laugh.

'I don't believe how hot they are.'

'Stop moaning and go to sleep.'

'I can't... I'm going to have to splash some cold water on them.'

He disappeared into the bathroom again only this time he cracked his leg. He swore and then grasping at his shin he lost his balance and fell to the ground for some further bruising. Trac began muttering something as she got out of bed.

'What are you doing?'

'Going to my sister's room,' she replied flatly.

'Why?'

When she failed to reply he let out a pathetic groan as he slipped back into her bed.

'Look, it's nothing against you,' Trac encouraged gently. 'I just need some sleep.'

'Okay,' he yawned.

He tried to drift back to sleep but it was no good, he needed her back by his side.

'Come back to bed with me,' he persisted as he pulled at her nearest arm.

'Jay,' she tutted.

'I can't sleep,' he confessed, 'not until you're there.'

Trac gave in and fumbled her way back, flopped an arm over him, spooned him and they slept like that for the rest of the night.

Thursday, October 12

Sunlight slowly began to glare through the gap in the curtains, Jay was wide awake in thought. He turned to Trac who was snuggled up in the quilt and pillow. He touched her hair, lightly brushing it above and behind her ear. He began talking softly, saying he loved her and cared for her. Her face stayed the same, deep in sleep, expressionless. Things were so much better together yet he had a terrible sensation that he had to pay attention to the now, that it would have to last him a long time as though he could sense they were drifting away from one another, a feeling that he thought might disappear if he refrained from saying it out loud.

The alarm clock sounded and awoke her for school with a jerk.

'Did you sleep well?' he asked softly.

'Umm yeah. Until about three when you took all the covers.'

'Yeah as if!'

'What are you doing so awake?'

'Don't know,' he shrugged and kissed her forehead. 'I was watching you sleep. You looked so peaceful.'

She smiled at him. Nothing was quite so pretty to him as she was in the morning. She nuzzled herself snugly against him and he held her in his arms.

'Are you going to school?'

'No,' came her reply and she rubbed her face into his shoulder and kissed him lightly. 'I want to stay here with you.'

The doorbell sounded and Craig appeared and made himself at home. He had nowhere to go, he had bunked off school and was looking for somewhere to spend his time.

Jay yawned loudly, eased himself out of bed and shuffled off into the bathroom. Reaching for the soap he saw the most horrible sight that he ever could of imagined. Trac heard a scream and ran to his aid.

'What is it?'

He was jumping up and down on tip toes whooping and shouting.

'There's a fucking massive spider in there,' he jabbered.

Trac put her hands on her hips, 'you big kid, I bet it's only small.'

'No I'm not joking it's massive. It went for me.'

She giggled, 'don't be so daft,' and proceeded to glance around the bathroom.

'Where?'

'On the sink.'

'Oh,' she said. 'It is pretty big.'

'See, I told you.'

When Trac came out of the bathroom pretending it was in her hand, he squealed, ran off into the lounge, slid across the glass door and locked it. She found all this vastly entertaining, it was so funny she looked like she might wet herself. When he had calmed down and his heart had resumed to its usual beat he still sat on the other side of the glass door looking subdued, peering over at her occasionally with one eye just to check to see if she made any advances. Trac got a big glass jar and disappeared, all he could hear was, 'come here my cutey.'

'A spider... cutey?' he bellowed sarcastically.

She ignored him and held the jar up to the light to inspect it in greater detail.

'It's bigger than your usual house spider.'

'I know it is, kill it,' came his muffled voice.

'I'm not killing it. I'll put it outside.'

'Make sure you lock all the windows and doors, it will probably come back and get me in the night.'

Craig was lurking about the garden drawing desperately at the remainder of his last cigarette, when she opened the back door.

'I take it he's not that keen on spiders?' he said.

She watched the spider scurry away down between the slabs of the patio and frowned up at Craig. 'You heard all that then?'

He smiled, nodded and put out his cigarette.

Jay had forgotten about the spider and was glued to some wildlife programme on the TV when Craig joined him. Trac made some rounds of toast and a large pot of tea. She couldn't help but continue making jokes about his fear of spiders, so he agreed to wash the pots in the hope her teasing would fade. She watched him proudly as he pulled on the marigold gloves and eased his hands into the sink. Three cups into the washing up he was bored and his thoughts turned to other things. He glanced at her out of the corner of his left eye then began to grin expansively.

She knew that look. 'What are you planning now?' she asked firmly.

'I might have a shower is all.'

'I'm first,' she informed him.

'We could both...' he smiled and gave a positive nod of his head as he pulled off the gloves.

'No,' she said firmly interrupting his keenness.

'Oh come on,' he smirked splaying out his arms as if to say 'why not?'

'We're not having a shower together.'

'Come on,' he mused and gave her a couple of friendly nudges and flashed a cunning smile.

'Okay, we can't while Craig's here.'

'He's watching telly.'

It was too late, he had made his move, he had got her locked in the bathroom. As her bathrobe slipped to the floor, so did Jay's jeans. The shower was an ongoing craving, Trac gave into all too easily.

'You're terrible,' she chuckled delightfully.

'You're just as bad.'

'And you didn't even finish the washing up.'

They splashed about making love. Jay stood with his mischievous grin once he had got his way with her. Trac looked up into the jet of water, her eyes closed she ran her fingers through her hair, she looked so beautiful he thought, so natural.

'I love it when your hair's wet,' he whispered into her ear as he moved closer.

The drumming of water and a squeal of feline excitement from the bathroom was all that could be heard.

For an hour or more, Jay sat at the dining table trying to sort out some of his college work, projects on top of projects, it all seemed to be getting out of control and all he was getting was a headache. He drank down his tea, put his pencil in his top pocket and stared into space, waiting for an idea.

After solving a number of design problems to a reasonable point, he stood up. Stretching out in all directions he gave out an exaggerated yawn.

'All done?' asked Trac.

'Yeah not bad. I've scamped out this brochure for Pira RSA, just going to keep it jet black, nice and slick with no photos, bit of clever typography and maybe a few spot UVs'

'What are they?'

'You know when you get glossy shiny areas on stuff.'

She gave a nod. 'I like this,' she said picking up a few sketches.

'Yeah that's an M&S Christmas window promotion. I'll actually cut all this out of lino and print them down from that.'

'Very clever. Have you got much more to do?'

'I've got to do an animation storyboard. I'm thinking cartoon so that will be easy. The title's *Love is Blind.*'

'Isn't it just.'

He gave out a yawn. 'I got loads more, but I'm done for today,' he said as he gathered his papers and trotted off to The Beast.

17. Reeling

Furtive behind the steering wheel, Jay pushed on the accelerator and The Beast shot forward. When he hit seventy, he released the pressure from the pedal and relaxed his grip on the wheel, whilst impatiently drumming at it with his fingers. Adrian sat in the passenger seat spurring him to drive faster. The fact that they may have be nearing a bend in the road did not matter. The back end of The Beast slid and Adrian grappled at the dashboard for support while Jay quickly lined it back up.

'Wooo, that was close,' he chuckled.

He could hear the half empty bottle of vodka beneath his seat, clanking away as it rolled freely between the discarded empties.

'Are you ever going to clean The Beast, Jay?'

'Mmm, maybe once a year,' he replied.

The road ahead was wide, empty and dark. He drove faster and faster, the smell of vodka sat in The Beast like a third person. He rolled the window down a touch and felt the cool damp air pass over his hands and chill the steering wheel. They had spent the night at the Ritzy night club in Hinckley. It had been student night and had offered a discounted rate of booze. On entering the club they were blinded by all the neon lights, it wasn't at all like the dingy places he normally frequented. He was feeling particularly moody, a sense that Trac hadn't wanted him to go, that he had gate-crashed her night out with her mates. More than that, in only a few weeks people, friends... everything seemed to be moving forward without him and he didn't feel comfortable with that. What did he expect, everything to stop once he wasn't there?

Jay gazed at Trac, she had actually smuggled a small 20cl bottle of Smirnoff into the club for him despite her reservations. He saw this as a grand gesture and allowed his friend to consume the majority. He studied her closely, taking her in as if he'd forgotten how pretty she was until then. He watched other guys do it too, attraction achieved before she said a word. She could have any guy she wanted, why would she stay with him? Jealous of the attention that she was oblivious to, simply meant nothing, but burdened him to the opportunity it brought.

The music and what little alcohol he consumed made him feel better. It carried him through until closing time when his mood returned to haunt him, it fuelled a rising cruel streak that set its target on her. He made fun of her 'taking the rip out of her' she called it. He seemed capable of tenderness and cruelty to her in the space of only a few moments. She didn't know whether he was genuinely feeling the way he expressed or if he was winding her up and enjoying her reaction. Truth was, he was pushing her away for the first time. She looked so much stronger than him. Now he struggled to open up to her, he couldn't talk about his feelings so easily anymore. Teasing her, playing games with her emotions in some small momentary way quashed his weakening dominance in their relationship. She was quickly becoming more independent and he wondered how long it would be until he was no longer required. Confidence crumbling and with a lack of faith he allowed the uneasiness to grow, fueling the fear, the fear that had haunted him since before their first kiss... she loves me, she loves me not?

He hit the accelerator and flew round the next sharp bend. The Yellow Fish dangled vigorously in the corner of his eye as The Beast picked up speed.

'Turn the window up Jay, it's freezing,' muttered Adrian hugging his baseball jacket around himself.

He rolled the window up then grabbed the vodka from under his seat. Loosening the top he took a short swig and saddled the bottle up tightly between his legs.

'Do you want a swig Adrian?'

'No I'm cool.'

'Oh come on. What you need is a little hint of death,' he grinned impudently and switched the head lights off.

'Fucking hell Jay!' retorted Adrian in a blind panic grappling for the dashboard again. 'You're fucking mental.'

The road was pitch black, and Jay swerved The Beast from one side of the road to the other, cackling with laughter as he did so. He finally switched the lights back on.

'Jesus Christ!' muttered Adrian feeling his heart pound.

Jay laughed a little more and took another swig of booze. 'I can't believe you're off to London.'

'First of November I'll be there.'

'What about us... The Beast.'

'And The Yellow Fish,' smiled Adrian giving it a tap. 'You'll have to come down and get pissed. I will know Soho inside out within a few weeks.'

'I'm sure you will,' he mused. 'You be okay on the sofa?'

'Yeah that's fine,' replied Adrian. 'Unless you need it.'

He looked at Adrian with an expression that said 'you might be right' as he brought The Beast to an abrupt halt and the two of them clambered out. As they walked up the steep drive to Trac's house he could see her with her two friends at the kitchen table. He tapped on the window and she stood up and came to open the door. As she did so, she said nothing, even her face was void of any kind of expression.

He wandered over to the kettle and made himself and Adrian a cup tea. Trac just glared at him occasionally which served only to generate an uneasy atmosphere until one of her friends broke the silence.

'Well...' she said moodily, 'I am going to bed then.'

'Yeah,' said the other girl, 'me too.'

Trac ushered them away to her sister's room, leaving him leaning against the sink, one hand in his pocket the other holding a mug.

'So what's up with her?' asked Adrian.

'What do you mean?' Jay replied plainly.

'Well she's not speaking to you for a start.'

He looked away to his left and thought about what to do, as he did so his eyes rolled around the room. 'It's nothing,' he said softly. 'I just took the mick out of her a little outside the club, just messing...'

Adrian warned him with a cough as she returned to the kitchen.

'I'm going to bed,' she said. 'Adrian I've put a sleeping bag on the settee in the lounge.'

'Thanks,' he smiled awkwardly.

'Am I in with you then?' asked Jay so softly you could hardly make out his words.

'I don't know... I'm thinking about it.'

He pulled a sorrowful face at her before sipping at his tea and smiling, a display that had won her over a few times in the past but was becoming predictable.

'Wash the cups up when you've finished,' she said and turned away and disappeared into her room. He tipped the rest of his tea away down the sink, swilled out the mug and upturned it onto the draining board in one swift movement.

'I'll see you in the morning,' he said and gave Adrian a friendly tap on the shoulder.

'Yeah, night.'

As he entered her room she was undressing. 'Can I help you with that?' he asked but she pulled a face that said a sarcastic, 'yeah right, as if!'

'I...'

'Don't say anything Jay,' she said. 'I'm trying to keep my temper, I love you a lot and I'm not going to stop unless you drive me crazy with all this stuff... you don't own me.'

'I know that, nobody owns anybody, I'm not putting a gun to your head.' She frowned at him as if wondering if the statement was a way of bating her, to make her push him away. He felt as though he had dug his own grave.

'Okay, okay,' he stammered, 'erm... I'll put some music on?'

'If you want.'

He shuffled over to the stereo pondering as to whether she loved him or simply loved the idea of him. He resolved to put something on she liked, INXS and realised she was only upset because she loved him. There was no other way to shed the guilt but to apologise.

'I am sorry,' he whispered. 'Don't be mad with me.'

Trac chose to ignore him until he reached for her arm.

'What?' she scowled pulling away from him.

'Look,' he said, in a tone that she'd recognise as another excuse for his behaviour. She would probably try and force him to admit he was wrong, but she looked worn out, worn down even.

'I'm sorry, I got carried away.' He shrugged his shoulders and splayed open his arms as if to welcome her into them. 'Don't be mad,' he repeated softly.

Trac rolled her eyes in exasperation. 'Why do you do this to me?'

'Do what?' he shrugged again and she went to walk away. 'Okay, okay I'm sorry please stay, I promise I'll make it up to you.'

She folded her arms and exuded a sigh as he looked down and pushed his hands into his pockets. There seemed little point in arguing, the louder she would get the softer his tone would become, quite easily to the point at which he would switch off altogether.

He raised an involuntary smile and lifted his head to speak. 'I do love you more than you could know, it's just sometimes I know I'm rubbish at showing it,' he said calmly. 'I'm really sorry... please won't you stay in here with me,' and placed a kiss onto her cheek. 'I was just trying to have a joke and I know I went too far...'

She looked at him squarely in the eyes. 'You... Why are you so nice one minute and a twat the next?'

He gave her an ingratiating smile. His eyes dilating almost doubling in size as he moved closer still. 'I guess that's all part of being a piss artist? and he gave her a confused shrug. 'I'm mean and pathetic... but I hope I'm fun too.'

'You don't deserve me,' she said flatly.

'I know, you're right,' he replied and his eyes began to shine. 'Maybe I'm just jealous?'

'Jealous of what?'

'I don't know,' he muttered vaguely and turned from her slightly. 'It's like your friends... family... they all get to be with you and I don't.'

'Well then, you shouldn't waste the time we do get being mean to me.'

He wanted her, he wanted the fun, he wanted the music, he wanted the parties, he wanted no responsibility, in short he wanted the summer back. Things weren't what they were, his life was changing and if he needed to move forward he had to accept it.

They cuddled up in a small ball shape, her bed dipped in the middle so it was crucial to have made up as they ended up wedged together regardless. There would however be a certain amount of frenzied pushing and shoving and she would claim that he was stealing all the covers. He could be so grumpy when needing sleep and Trac could get just as grouchy for the very same reason, a single bed it seemed was only good for occasional use, on a regular basis it was hard work.

Jay drove his hands through his hair as he wandered up Trac's drive. When he found the door ajar he called out, 'hello.' No-one answered. He nudged the door open freely and called out again.

'Who is it?' replied Trac with a playful eagerness in her voice.
In a simple lightening-swift movement he entered and closed the door behind him.

'It's Jay... the man of your dreams,' and he waltzed in, ready to play the fool. Being slightly drunk and unsteady, his coordination was off-beat but he tried his best to look sensual and endearing, to his enjoyment she found him amusing.

'Hello babe,' he said giving her his best smile as he thumbed open his collar.

'You shouldn't be driving... ever.'

'Why?'

'You're pissed again.'

'No... no, I'm not, merely merry is what I am,' he boasted.

'If I had my own place you'd do this all the time wouldn't you.'

'Do what?'

'Come over here with a drunk head, put some music on and crash out on my bed.'

'No... no,' he waved his finger at her pathetically. 'I'm not going to crash out. I've got far more energy and...' he hic-cupped loudly, '...and just to totally confuse you I'm not going to put any music on,' he grinned still waving an index finger at her.

'So how was Alton Towers?'

'Absolutely fantastic,' his voice bellowed, as he held a poise like a Shakespearean actor.

'Suppose you've been drunk all day then?'
Jay's brow wrinkled, was she policing him he thought? 'Wooo,' he replied amiably. 'I have a good time and you presume I've been drunk.'
She hugged her bathrobe around her body tightly as she reacted to the sexual mischievous glint that began to flutter in his eyes as he floated towards her.

'I love you,' he whispered giving her a hug.
With some of his shirt buttons wrong, half cut and emotional he looked sweet. She slipped her arms round him and enlightened him to the fact that she liked him like this but still doubted his ability to drive.
Trying to hitch open the material of her robe he uttered, 'are we going to have a good time then?'
She smiled up at him attractively as his hands followed the shape of her bum and contours of her hips, slowly making his way up to her exquisite breasts.

'You can't keep your hands off me.'

He gave her a kooky smile. 'That's a good thing right?'

Spying her glass of wine he let her go and reached for the fridge, helping himself to a can of beer.

'Thanks, now my mum will think I drank it.'

'It's but one can,' he said, with a now relaxed but smug smile.

'You had a can yesterday.'

'Did I?' he pulled a puzzled face then chuckled knowing full well he had.

'And...' she continued, 'you had one the day before that too.'

He shrugged his shoulders blithely. 'Oh well,' he smiled. 'So...'

'So?'

'Are you going to let me taste the wine on your lips.'

'I'm still thinking about it.'

Focusing on her slender legs, which she now dangled in front of him, he undid his belt and his jeans dropped to the ground. He took a swig of beer smiling constantly. With his brain not quite in gear with his body he slipped to the floor as he tried to pull his feet out of his jeans.

Trac looked at him quizzically, 'what are you doing?'

His laugh was more of a cackle, 'I... I fell.'

'Don't spill any beer.'

'As if,' he laughed.

As he over exaggerated his tangled trouser predicament, she caught his humour and joined him in laughing quite loudly. He looked like he was doing an escapology routine, rolling around the floor playfully. By the time he had wrestled himself free he was worn out.

'That's it, I'm not in the mood now,' he panted pushing his bottom lip out as he lay in a star shape on the floor.

She eased off the sofa, readjusted her gown so he caught a glimpse of what lay beneath and said, 'well I'm off to bed.'

He slipped in beside her and drifted into thought while absently combing her hair with his fingers. He remembered how he felt when he first began to fall in love with her, it was a feeling he missed terribly, the falling. He put his mouth to the nearest bear's ear and whispered softly.

'You see that girl. You see her, that's the girl I'm in love with, but shhh! it's a secret.'

Trac smiled at his childishness and spooned her body into his and he released a large sigh.

'What is it?' she asked.

'I don't know?' he paused, 'it's nothing.'

'Oh come on tell me.'

'All these feelings I have for you... I just don't want them to go, you know what I mean... don't you?'

She paused for a moment then said, 'yeah I do,' softly. 'I'm happy too. Don't worry, we will be okay. I'm not going anywhere Jay.'

If he was honest, the thought of losing her had began to grip him. Anxiety, he was developing too much of that, and hated his own vulnerability to it. He slipped out of bed, put the stereo on and picked up the remote control. As he approached the light switch he said, 'wish I could just stay here.'

The light from the stereo came on and she could hear and see the silhouette of his body fumbling its way towards the bed. His thumb felt the remote control and managed to press play. She enjoyed making love to music and told him it was the closest you could get to love in a movie, but she couldn't fall asleep to it like he did. She reached out and touched him, lightly running her fingers down his back she moved closer kissing him on the neck and gliding her tongue round his ear. His hand found her thighs, massaging them and slowly snaking up her hips and resting there. He felt comforted by the warmth of her flesh, he kissed her lips tasting her tongue. His body seemed to sink into a vast warm sea as they rolled from position to position.

'Sixty nine,' he whispered huskily.

He felt close, safe and undiscovered until he felt confident again. He had wanted to give himself to her body and soul to please her, to give everything and hold back nothing, as he lay there in the afterglow nestled somewhere between lust and self doubt.

Saturday, October 14

As they parted Jay became immediately saddened at the sudden loss. His pleas for her to stay with him bordered on desperate.

'Throw a sickie.'

'I need the money.'

'I'll give you the money.'

'Jay, you haven't got any money.'

He could have kicked himself for being so pathetic and returned home with every intention of sleeping until noon. He was already dreaming of her before his head hit the pillow.

At twelve he put the *Chart Show* on, but his mind was elsewhere, his lack of commitment to college, in fact it was the lack of commitment to Trac too. Caught in the middle, he felt futile, life didn't seem to hold what he expected it to, the unfairness grated at him. He'd spent quite a bit of time with Trac the last few days, in fact the last few weeks. It was nice though to be alone at home, he'd not been used to being with her all the time. He began to feel guilty about his behaviour and the future, the lack of being unable to be there for her and a sense of holding her back. He came to the conclusion that she deserved more, more than him. Everything seemed to be turning into a routine and he hated that. As time pressed on he felt more and more differing emotions, a sense of being trapped, his freedom was slipping. He needed space so that he could take control. He phoned her a little past six thirty.

'Hi,' she peeped. 'I thought you might be here when I got back.'

'Er... I'm going to see the lads tonight.'

'But you saw them all day yesterday.'

'Yeah, I know I just... I can come over after.'

'I don't want you crashing in here late.'

'I'll leave the pub about half nine... Yeah?'

'Okay fine,' and she put the phone down.

Jay was settled on a padded leather stool at the bar. He took a long pull on his pint of Guinness and glanced at the Red Stripe promotional clock on the wall. Ten thirty six, he ordered a whiskey and ice with a dash of water. He was happy to watch Nick and Rob play pool, arguing about who had the most flair at the game. He nursed the last few mouthfuls of beer, his shot and pondered as he watched the clock now blur before his eyes.

As the bell rang for last orders it startled him. He thought about making a move and turned to ease himself off the stool when Rob came up behind him and leant him back to the bar.

'What are you having Jay?'

'No, I'm going. I've got somewhere to be.'

'Oh come on... one more for the road.'

'No, I'm leaving. I told Trac I'd stop over.'

'It's last orders,' goaded Rob. 'Final round and I'll walk back with you.'

'Okay, a quick one... whiskey... ice.'

Only after he'd stood and began sifting through his pockets for the keys to The Beast did he realise he'd never be able to drive, Trac would go mad if he did. He stumbled to the pay phone in between the entrance and the bar area and dialled her number. She answered right away, halfway into the second ring, a bad sign.

'Trac?'

'I was expecting you ages ago.'

It was clear from her tone she was pissed off.

'I stayed longer than I intended,' he replied and made the effort to sound casual in order to play down the situation or at least defer any argument, but alcohol had rinsed the sparkle from his tongue.

'You said you'd be over at half nine.'

'Did I?'

'Jay you sound drunk.'

'A bit.'

'You better not even think about driving.'

'I guess I'll see you tomorrow then.'

'You could get a cab?'

He didn't trust himself to open his mouth at all, dreading this suggestion and felt happier in the silence.

'Well?' she prompted.

He scratched at the side of his head and mumbled, 'I'm not sure I have enough money.'

'Just forget it then.'

'Don't be like that.'

'Jay what do you expect.'

'I don't know?'

'I'm not bothered if you make it over. I'm going to bed,' she stated, and disconected.

He walked unsteadily away from the phone, back to where he came from, to be a barfly and drain off his final shot.

Sunday, October 15

In the morning he was still drunk and felt no better than yesterday, if not more disillusioned and with the added burden of having to go down to The Bell and apologise for his behaviour, vaguely recalling himself leaving the bar flicking his Vs and mouthing the words 'fuck off'. He didn't seem to have a grip on his life anymore, it felt like he was being pulled along by an outside force. If it wasn't the separation of York driving them apart, then his hiding from his feelings were causing more distance. The fact was he was drunk most of the time and he no longer seemed to have or want any control of it anymore, he simply suppressed reality and began to freefall. The summer had faded fast and the fun seemed to have faded along with it, and he didn't understand why. He no longer felt creative, his interest in college was dwindling, in fact, interest in everything from filling in his diary to taking photos had faded. All he did know was that the only thing he did care about was Trac, perhaps too much.

He reached for the phone and rubbed at his head thinking about what he should say to her, but it just made his brain hurt all the more so he just dialled.

'Trac.'

'Yeah.'

'It's me.'

'Yes I know. Why don't you come over?'

His voice rasped thick with emotion blurted, 'I don't know?'

'What's up?'

'I think...'

'What?'

'I think you should find somebody else.'

'What are you on about?' her voice raised in tone.

'I mean, I'm no good for you.'

'I don't understand?'

'I'm just not worth it. Fall out with me Trac.'

'Don't be silly. I don't want to fall out with you.'

'I'm not good enough for you, I'm rubbish, useless... less than useless.'

'You're not that bad.'

'You should be able to do whatever you want to do, I don't want to hold you back or drag you down.'

The phone line stayed silent for thirty seconds but it felt much longer. He wondered was she truly someone who refused to be distracted by his piss head persona he'd spent such a long time creating, to see nothing but the real him.

'So you want to finish with me?' she croaked, 'what about everything we've shared?'

'I know but at the start I felt I could give you something no-one else could give you... the fun, excitement and teach you stuff.'

'And now?'

'Now... I just... I just feel like you want more than I can give. I've nothing left to offer you. I'm... I'm all spent.'

He wasn't sure what he was doing, he was in love with her, far deeper than he had been with Shelley. Maybe that was the problem; he knew how he was going to feel and this time he would have no-one to help him through it. He wanted to say 'you're going to leave me someday and it's going to hurt far more. If I go now I can do it on my terms and maybe it won't hurt as bad.'

'Jay, talk to me.'

'I don't know what's going on... I'm... I'm just not worth it,' he said softly. 'I should be in York. I'm way behind on my work, I'm in debt, I drink too much and make you worry all the time. I'm just not there for you when you need me... I'm not there to love you like I need to.'

'I decide whether you're worth it or not. I know you like getting drunk I accept that, but I don't have to like it. Maybe you should just stop for a while. And I can't say you don't make me worry now and again, but you make me laugh too, and I do feel loved.'

What he wanted to say was 'I'm not there to feel you, and... it's crushing me' but instead he blurted, 'I'm nobody.'

'You are, you're somebody to me Jay.'

'Walk away from me.'

The phone line was silent for a few moments. 'Trac, you're beautiful, smart... you're the kind of girl that guys never get over.'

'But I love you.'

He failed again to say what he wanted to say, that he loved her too much it hurt. Instead he sighed, followed by a large in take of breath he barely whispered, 'you'll meet someone else.'

'Jay, I won't.'

'You met me didn't you.'

'That was different.'

'It wasn't, it's just a matter of time.'

'Come over to see me.'

'I don't know... I don't know what the fuck I'm doing anymore. You just shouldn't care. You need a guy who takes you out and looks after you. I'm sorry... I'd better go,' and he hung up.

He stood with his hands on his hips, to his greater surprise he felt even worse than before, it was as if someone had kicked him in the guts. What am I doing? he thought. What the fuck is up with me?

For two hours he sat restlessly in front of the TV feeling worse with every second that ticked by. Where was the relief? Was he being stubborn? Or noble, that loving someone that much meant you wanted what's best for them... even if it means you have to lose them. Too weak to cope with the huge void he felt, he pushed himself up onto his feet and snatched at the keys to The Beast and went to her.

When he got there, the front door was open so he went straight in. He could hear the shower running and tapped on the door and called her name.

'Yeah,' she responded.

'Open the door.'

She unlatched it and moved back pulling a towel up over her breasts. He stood leaning on the wall, raising the first true smile of the day as he didn't even try to push out or suppress the desire that were swamping his head.

'Drop the towel,' he whispered persuasively, and his eyes squinted softly. 'Drop the towel,' he repeated again faintly.

Moving closer to her smiling ruefully. 'Don't you get it, all I care about is you,' he said resolutely. 'So much so I don't even care about me anymore and I want this... you, more than anything. You're the girl I could never have. The kind of girl I've wanted to meet for what seemed forever.'

'Since Shelley you mean.'

'No... no.'

'You don't want me do you? I'm just here.'

'It's not that, it's... it's the opposite... you're everything.'

He placed his hands on her shoulders and her towel fell to the floor as he kissed her. 'I just don't want to lose you to someone else.'

'Now I don't know where I stand.'

'I don't either,' he said softly as he moved to wrap his arms around her. 'I'm here for you though.'

'You'll get wet,' she said nervously.

'I don't care,' he whispered, and moving closer he began to kiss down her neck before taking a step back to get a good look at her form.

'You're gorgeous,' he smiled.

She stood naked in front of him, biting at her lower lip. She glanced at her pile of clothes on the floor.

'Don't put any clothes back on,' he whispered, 'I love it when you're wet.' She shivered a little as he pulled her towards his chest and kissed her again. He nibbled at her ear and glided his tongue down her neck, the sensation spreading through his chest was warm. He found her bum and squeezed it gently.

'Do you still want me?' he whispered.

'Yes,' she said faintly.

'I'm glad. I would've missed you... terribly.'

Taking her to her bed, he lay her softly down on the duvet. As he joined her she rolled over onto him firmly as they both slid down into the bed. His mouth moved around playfully. He was conscious now of his erection, pushing up to get her attention.

She smiled broadly and said, 'does he want to come out and play then?' She stripped him slowly, keeping him on edge until he penetrated her. The warmth saturated his body, his hands slid through her hair as they kissed. The spiral of pleasure spread up his belly, as his muscles tightened. Their hips moved rhythmically, slowly without effort. The sensation built irresistibly between his legs. There was a sweet aching in his ribs, his hands swung out to seize her bum once again. He thrusted hard inside her until she was tight against him. She fell into his shoulder, her arms wrapped around him, around his neck. The tugging between them eased, then tightened again. 'I love you' spilled from him as he let go. The explosion made him shudder, he moaned softly into her ear, she bit into his shoulder and gave a growl. He caught his breath. Stroking her hair and stretching back the pleasure slipped away, but his heart continued to race. He wondered if the love making initiated by him was a way of feeling loved, to banish insecurity, enough to make him feel overly desirable again. Loving her and losing her? A single tear formed in the corner of each eye and he wiped them free before she noticed.

'I want it to stay like this,' he whispered as the urge to sleep began to take over. He closed his eyes and realised how out of control his feelings for her were, the vulnerability undermined him.

Trac eased her legs off the bed and began to blow dry her hair. As he followed suit he insisted on doing it for her, he had a softer touch until he got cheeky and gave her a playful blast of air between her legs. She squealed, 'get off,' and began to flap her arms at him trying not to giggle. He chased her round the room grinning and threatening to tickle her.

'Stop... Stop I haven't got the energy.'

'Okay,' he smiled. 'I'll stop.'

'I don't understand you,' she panted.

'I don't understand me either,' he smirked as he ran a hand through his hair.

'What are you thinking?'

'Nothing,' he dismissed. 'I'm fed up with thinking,' he said tonelessly.

Standing there he felt suspended somewhere between happy and sad. His eyes sparkled as if the surface had just had a fresh flood of tears and he looked away.

Trac pulled him back to her and smiled at him sympathetically.

'Jay talk to me.'

He stopped her short with a little shake of his head and a fast exhale of air. His eyes rolled as if he were trying to stop his eyes tearing further.

'But...'

He put his index finger to his lips, 'shhh.' He smiled lightly and added in a softer voice, 'I don't want to talk.'

He cupped her face and they kissed. When he finally pulled back away from her, his eyes were soft and he smiled positively. 'You going to make us a cup of tea then girl?'

'Don't know,' she teased, sensing his mood was about to change for the better. 'I'll think about it.'

'I wish I knew what you see in me,' he asked plainly.

'Oh, you're looking for a compliments now.'

'Not necessarily.'

'Lots of things,' she nodded. 'I like your eyes, you'll age well.'

'Well I hope you're around to see it.'

She stroked his face, glad that he was with her. 'What am I going to do with you eh?' she mumbled.

'I'll be alright,' he said.

'You know, I don't think anybody can tell what you're really like except me. You're always pissed or hung over.'

'I'm not always drunk, that's like a myth.'

'Hmm... you drink, you stay out late. You think pleasure is an occupation.'

'It's a tough commitment with a full time girlfriend.'

She shoved him lightly. 'Trying to get rid of me?'

'Nooo, but if you think about it, absent girlfriends don't get in the way of a man's drinking habits the way ever present ones do.'

'Tell me you haven't thought about that.'

'No,' he chuckled. 'It was merely an observation.'

'Hmm,' her eyes narrowed as she studied his face.

Watching her read him he leant forward, 'I fell over the other night,' he said softly. 'I forgot to tell you. Look, you can see the bruises.' He moved his hair out the way to reveal a small graze. She really didn't notice his cuts and bruises anymore, he always had some kind of small injury. He rolled back down onto her bed and made a request for a massage and she obliged.

'What would you do without me?'

'The truth?'

'Course.'

'Get drunk even more.'

She beat his back with her hands and quickly followed it by a soft sweeping motion from the base of his spine up to his shoulder blades.

'Umm, that feels great.'

'You're spoilt.'

He agreed by letting out another delighted moan.

'If you had one wish what would it be?'

He repeated her question in a silly sarcastic tone of voice, so she gave him a fun-loving thump to the ribs, to which he gave a groan and rolled onto his back to face her.

'Come on,' she said. 'What would you wish for?'

'Another million wishes.'

'Oh come on,' she nudged him. 'You can't do that.'

He chuckled, 'why not?'

'You,' she said nudging him cheerfully again.

'Okay... Okay. I wish... erm to be happy more often than not.'

'Wouldn't you have money.'

'Money... no, saving to do what you want is half the fun isn't it?'

'Well I guess it makes you appreciate it more.'

'I wish that me, you The Beast and The Yellow Fish live happily ever after.'

'I tell you what,' she said. 'I'll earn the cash and you...'

'Can get drunk?' he suggested.

'No just... I don't know, like you've said before be free, be creative.'

'Sounds like a plan.'

With the sky becoming moody and the days slowly becoming shorter, he didn't fancy the dark coldness and isolation of a train journey back north when he could comfortably lay all night with her and return in the morning.

'Are you sure?'

He placed his finger to her lips, 'shhh just say you'll love me forever.'

'Forever is too big a word Jay.'

He withdrew from her, like he had just taken a low blow and sank into her bed like a deflated balloon.

'Don't go all funny on me.'

His only response was a muffled wheezing noise.

'I can't say forever, just like you can't say I'm the only thing you love.'

With another muffled groan he rolled over rubbing his face frowning.

'I'm tired,' he yawned hoping to drop the conversation.

'Do you want something to eat?'

'Sure,' he murmured, 'anything will do.'

'The things I do for you.'

Trac woke him from his daydream. As he raised up off her bed looking back at the warm pillow, he wanted to sink back but she called him again.

'What's up.'

'It's for you'

'What's for me?'

'The phone.'

'Who is it?'

'Who do you think?' she said passing him a plate.

'Nooo,' he reverberated and took a slice of pizza off his plate and took a bite.

'Jay,' her voice became impatient, 'it's your mum.'

His face scrunched up and he waved a dismissive hand at her showing his disinterest in taking the call. Trac stood with one hand on her hips and the other still holding the phone, only then she added a stern face that he deciphered as 'take the fucking phone will you... now!'

With that, and the fact that the receiver began to almost look like a weapon he snatched it from her. 'Okay... Okay,' he grumbled. 'I know exactly what she's going to say.'

'Hello... yep... I know... No... No... No... Don't worry about it.'

He frowned and rubbed at his forehead before putting his head against the wall. 'I can work from home... at Trac's then... so why are you giving me shit?'

He pulled the phone away from his ear and pointed to it shaking his head at Trac and she smiled at him, shook her head back at him and mouthed, 'you,' and wandered back to the kitchen.

'Look I'm going... because... because I've got stuff to do. I'll go back tomorrow or something,' and with that he put the phone down and followed Trac into the kitchen.

'Here, I swapped your tea for a beer.'

'Cheers.'

'Well you might as well finish the last one.'

Sipping from the can he began to relax and the reality of the conversation stroke lecture he had received from his mum was now a mere fading memory. He was mellow enough now to sink into the sofa and watch some TV.

Monday, October 16

Jay stood in the kitchen looking down into a mug of hot water, watching the tea bag work its magic and slowly turn the water darker and darker. He sighed a couple of times without realising and it roused his mum from the paperwork sprawled out across the kitchen table.

'I've got quite a bit of work to get done before I set off to Bedford,' she said. 'So if you can avoid playing your music at full volume I'd appreciate it.' He gave her a frown and a slight nod of the head and returned to his thoughts. Where was the fun going? Was it as simple as Trac verses York? Now he had to be glad he was able to talk to Trac regarding just about anything and everything, but who did he have to talk to about him and Trac? And this wasn't that simple a problem to work out, he had been trying for what seemed like weeks and gave into the fact that he needed some help, he needed advice. Now his sister was good support when it came to matters of the heart and had been a good listener regarding Shelley's emigration, but what he was in need of was an experienced head, and that meant talking openly to his mum.

'Do you want a coffee? he asked softly.

'No I've got one thanks.'

He gave another sigh and lingered over squeezing the tea bag to the side of the cup as he tried to make sense of the scrambled thoughts and emotions inside and find a way to begin a heart-to-heart conversation. This is tough he thought, maybe it was just teenage rebellion or simply the fact that he was male hindering the process. From previous experience he knew starting and finishing would be the hardest part. He let out another quiet sigh just before he poured in the milk and took his first sip of tea.

'Do you want a hand with that?' his mum asked.

'With what?'

'That huge weight on your shoulders?'

He grunted something as he put his tea bag in the bin, pissed off that he was now so obvious.

'What's up then?' his mum continued staring up from her paperwork.

'Nothing,' he muttered in a feeble reply.

'Look, I know you well enough to know you've got something on your mind.'

He gave her a shrug and gazed back into his tea. 'It's just...'

'What?' she replied quickly with a tone that said 'come on I'm busy just spit it out!'

'It's just... York's not for me, I want to leave.'

'And why is that exactly?'

'It's just not where I want to be right now.'

'And Leicester is?'

'All my friends are here.'

'You'll make new friends, it just takes time.'

'That's not it, it's more than that.'

'Where are you going to live? Not here.'

'I'll find a new college somewhere nearer.'

'You've already applied to three of them and you didn't get in'

'There's others.'

'You're not dropping out,' she said sharply.

He wanted to snap back but decided it would be an unwise move and instead he said coldly, 'why not?'

'You can go and live with your dad then,' she uttered as she shuffled some pieces of paper abruptly.

He turned away, her direct manner was noted and unappreciated, giving him nothing more than the urge to throw his mug into the sink and have a mini tantrum. He would have done it had it not been for the pain held like a knot in his stomach that needed to unravel, be removed or at least tamed somewhat. He felt himself just wanting to slide to the floor and remain there until he felt better about things.

He rubbed at his ear, clearly agitated by the situation. He leant into the kitchen worktop as if he was struggling to stay upright. His deflated aura did not go unmissed and his mum in a softer tone of voice asked, 'what are you going to do if you leave college?'

He frowned and gave little energy into the shrug of his shoulders and replied, 'I don't know?'

'You've been drawing since you could pick up a pen... you get yourself into a good college and now you want to throw that away?'

He hesitated a moment then blurted, 'I'll be crazy to do that right,' feeling increasingly uncomfortable. 'You just... you just... don't understand.'

'You're not going to settle there at all if you keep coming back at weekends.'

He bowed his head, he had no fight back on that, she was right.

'We both know who this is about,' said his mum plainly.

He threw a glance over his shoulder, 'what do you mean?'

'Has Tracey asked you to stay in Leicester?'

He shook his head, 'no,' he replied aggressively.

'You're going to have to let her go, enjoy what you had and move on.'

He shook his head slowly, this was not what he wanted to hear. 'I can't do that,' he said.

'You need to think about your future.'

'Trac's the best thing for my future.'

'Is she? When's the last time you thought about Shelley?'

He bolted upright defensively. 'What's she got to do with it?' he muttered shaking his head in confusion, why did his mum have to bring her into it. He thought for a moment at how unfair it all was.

'I had no choice,' he said softly. 'I couldn't stop Shelley going to Australia, not even if I tried.'

'There will always be other girls.'

'No there won't.'

'You found Tracey didn't you.'

'I know, but... but I'm still left with knowing that... that I can't go through what I went through with Shelley again. I just... I just can't.'

'If you give up everything for her, she might not always be there for you in the future. Look what's happened to me and your dad.'

'All I want to do is hold onto what I have, not just her... everything, all my friends and that. And that's not asking too much is it?'

'Then carry on as you are, see them at weekends.'

'Yeah but, I feel like so much stuff happens and I'm like... out of the loop or something.'

'You've got to stop doubting yourself and realise that you're both young and she will change, so will you and all of your friends.'

'I don't want anything to change.'

'You have to choose your own path.'

'That's what I'm trying to do.'

'No you're not, you're following Tracey down hers. I know how much she means to you but you can't make major life decisions based on someone else.'

'Why not, people do it all the time?'

'You can't put that kind of pressure on her, she's only sixteen.'

'I know... I know,' he grumbled feeling a rise in frustration.

'Then make the right decision.'

'I wish it was that simple.'

'I don't know what you quite expect me to say?' There's no right or wrong answer, all I can do is give you the benefit of my own experience.'

'If I make a mistake it's my mistake,' he said, and gave a reluctant shrug. 'At the minute I've got to ask myself is a career really everything?'

His mum exhaled expressively, 'is she the kind of person that you are willing to take a very big leap of faith for?'

Feeling no better he didn't want to talk anymore, as the shutters began to come down he was glad to see his mum begin to move paperwork about. He had a romantic streak a mile wide and she expressed her wonder at where he got it from.

'You need to think about getting yourself back to York,' she said. 'You've got your half term coming up so don't be so impulsive, just sit on it for a while.'

He looked into his murky tea, now cold, and mumbled, 'I'll go tomorrow,' and poured it down the sink. In a lighter tone his mum said, 'if you're at home all day maybe you can do some washing up.'

He gave her a half hearted smile and thought about his workload that had mounted up, making him feel even worse. Avoiding everything seemed a solution but that found him wrestling with a darker side, he wanted a beer, he wanted to get drunk.

Tuesday, October 17

Jay sat methodically tearing a sheet of layout paper into tiny squares and dropping them one by one into Trac's bin, trying to put a braver face on everything. She was in a mood still from his short sharp behaviour on the phone the previous night, but having failed to return to York, opened up the short opportunity in which to make up for that. Yet with so much time off recently he was going to have to make an appearance up north sooner rather than later.

'Can you stop doing that?' said Trac irritably.

'Why?'

'It's annoying.'

He rasped his tongue and dropped the rest of the paper into the bin.

'You pair catching up on your homework?' came Trac's sister's voice.
Jay looked up and replied, 'sort of.'

'Well I'm just putting the kettle on.'

'I'm okay.'

'Trac?'

Trac gave a quick nod and returned her focus back to the folder she was
holding, biting on the end of her pen.

'I'm going to have to go back to York,' he said in a low tone, and she
gave him a light hearted smile that said 'I don't want you to go but you're
probably right.'

'Hey, look on the bright side, at least I won't be around to annoy you for
a few days.'

He hoped she would reply with something along the lines of 'I'd rather
have you around to annoy me than have you not here at all' but instead she
just gave him a frown.

'I think I'll be back on Saturday. Mum's on about picking me up so I
could meet you out of work?' and she replied with a nod of her head.

'Maybe invite Adrian and a few people round Saturday night?'

'What and have you two steal all of Mum and Dad's booze!'

'As if,' he chuckled. 'You can get a few friends round, have a bit of a party.'

'No.'

'Oh go on, it's your last Saturday night before your parents come home.'

'Jay, it's not going to happen,' and she waved a hand at him, 'so forget
about it.'

'Typical,' he remarked looking down himself.

'What's up now?'

Jay's lip curled. 'I've spilt ink all over my jeans now.'

'You're so clumsy,' she laughed. 'Come here.'

He rambled over to her, watching the ink slowly soaking into his best jeans.

'Take them off,' smiled Trac.

He lookws puzzled. 'What?'

'Take them off. We'll need to soak them.'

He pulled them off and watched her whisk them away.

'What am I going to wear to go home in?'

'You'll have to borrow a pair of mine.'

'You look after those,' he said looking anxiously at his jeans being
plunged into the sink forcefully.

'Don't worry I will.'

He put on a pair of her jeans, they fitted a little uncomfortably around the groin and a bit high above the ankles but they'd do, he thought as he slipped on his jacket.

She slapped him on the bum decisively. 'I guess I'll see you at the weekend then sexy pants,' she said as she followed him through the door.

They stopped in the middle of the hallway, his hands on the top of her arms, hers playing with the zip of his jacket. He took in the fresh scent of her hair and cupped her chin, raising her face to his.

'I hate goodbyes. I never know what to say.'

'Just say the three special words.'

'More scotch please,' he coughed and she dug him in his ribs with her elbow.

'I love you.'

'I love you too so keep him out of mischief,' she said rubbing his cock through his jeans.

'You make goodbyes even harder don't you,' he grinned. 'I'll see you.'

Time flew by too quickly but, with his half term break looming, it didn't seem so bad going back for a few days. He was doing his best to cheer up but the grubby cold station, with a strong smell of engine oil, was a lonely place at night. He checked his food parcel his mum had given him, but with most of it being in tin format, it was no good to him now. He put his personal stereo on and began to daydream, taking him from reality to a pleasant land. He sat on the train watching the day turn into night, the journey itself went swiftly except for the half an hour wait at Leeds station. He stared at a screwed up crisp packet, trying to focus on something, anything to stop the dull thoughts trying to take over, were all stations grim and this bleak at night?

He pulled his bag over his shoulder as the train pulled into York, it looked even more gloomy than he had remembered, a deep mist hung in the air. He jumped onto a bus and soon arrived at his digs. It was cold, and unconvinced by the dangerous looking calor gas heater, it pleased him that James was there. He was in a chatty mood and filled him with tea and even a small amount of hope, enough to spark his confidence.

Wednesday, October 18

As dawn broke glaucously over Clifton he sat at the breakfast table, he was still half asleep and looked isolated as he flipped through his diary pondering at the empty dates he had failed to fill. He trundled out the front door at eight fifteen, head down, art folder in hand and stood at the bus stop impatiently.

Back at college he became bored, almost instantly, and began making paper airplanes and chucked them across the room. Wednesdays were always the same, middle of the week and shit he thought.

By the afternoon things had picked up and he was in a better frame of mind as the company around him was stimulating, it charged him up with positivity. Thursday was being taken up by a visit to the Leeds art gallery, and Friday was the end of term party, so it had the makings of a speedy end to his week.

18. Last orders

Friday, October 20

Jay was broke, he had drawn the last twenty pounds of his overdraft limit from a bank in Leeds and used up pretty much all the cash his mum was prepared to give him. It was looking desperate for the end of term night out. James toyed with fifteen pounds almost handing it to Jay then retracting it again swiftly.

'It's not going to be enough to get you drunk anyway,' he babbled.

'Yeah it will. We are going to raid the landlady's drinks cabinet.'

'She'll know if we take a bottle,' replied James hesitantly passing him the money.

'We don't need to take a bottle,' he said as he snatched the cash. 'Cheers. I'm just going to make us a cocktail.'

'What kind?'

'A lethal one!' he replied, giving James a razor sharp grin.

'What are you mixing?'

'Shhh!' He smiled as he eyed the wooden cabinet, full of anticipation and excitement at what he might find.

He opened its door so slowly that it creaked marvellously, much to his enjoyment. He giggled like a juvenile who knew he was up to no good and beamed expansively at the array of bottles and glasses dotted about in no particular order.

'You just wait till you get a load of this, you'll glow like a lamp.'

He pawed each different bottle, inspecting its level and alcohol content, looking for the strongest liquor to form the base.

'Gin, scotch, vodka, Bacardi, tequila ... Malibu... too weak,' and shook his head.

'I'm not really used to spirits,' James murmured.

He placed two tall glasses on the sideboard and began mixing, whistling with excitement as he loaded them up. Over the years, he got down to a fine art the watering down of alcohol to give the appearance of not being tampered with. He was always careful never to add too much nor to dilute any bottle more than once. He paused for a moment, 'no scotch... bottles not been opened... that's okay,' he said casually using a finger to stir the contents a little.

'There you go,' he smiled passing it to James. 'Rocket fuel!'

A complete spirit mix, James began to look worried. He puffed out his cheeks as he took the glass from Jay's hand. Taking in the strong scent of the mixture he pulled his face away sharply.

'Go on, you'll be alright,' Jay whispered, twirling the concoction in his glass and holding it up to the light. 'It's pretty clear... that's good.'

He took his first sip and made a drawn out wheezing sound. Raising a fist to his mouth, he gave a little cough. 'On second thoughts there's a can of Tizer in the fridge.'

James acted upon this information with enthusiasm.

'See if there's any ice too.'

James returned swiftly and handed over the can and a glass with frosty looking ice that he'd scrapped from the side of the freezer. It looked like snow apart from the large piece he'd snapped off which was sticking out of the top. Stirring in a small amount of Tizer with a plastic stick, and adding in some of the frosty ice, he held it up to the light once more. Seen from outside, he might have been confused for a chemistry student, were it not for the mischievous expression about his face.

'Bubbles will help the speed of entry,' he muttered and began knocking his concoction back. The sharpness took his breath away and his eyes watered as he wheezed excitedly, as if the alcohol had began to seep its way into his bloodstream already. James held his glass uneasily. Looking into the potent liquid, he looked back to Jay who was making a slight whooping sound after each shot, feeling the pressure as he was already close to finishing.

'You'll be fine, just take a swig and then another,' goaded Jay.

James exhaled a huge amount of air as he prepared to take the plunge, first sipping a little and wincing slightly before knocking a gulp back, swearing repeatedly.

'I... I can't drink it.'

'Sure you can... and when you're jumping around to The Wonder Stuff with a big grin on your face you're going to thank me for it.'

The phone rang and Jay leapt at it like a cat, in no time at all his body felt warm and his limbs loose, he was ready.

'Hello.'

'Jay it's Anthony.'

'Alright Den.'

'You going to the party tonight?'

'Of course I am,' he replied, baffled by the question.

'I thought you were skint? How are you going to get pissed?'

He held up his glass with a last sip remaining and winked at James, 'Don't you worry about me, with any luck I'll be seeing double before I even get there.'

James slowly teased the fluid from his glass with a reasonable amount of muttering, spluttering and taking furtive swigs at the remaining can of Tizer in between. Jay accepted he wasn't a compatible drinking partner much easier than he accepted the winging.

'Oh, I'll drink the fucker,' he roared, snatching it from him.

Den's ability to play The Cult's 'She Sell Sanctuary' was overwhelmingly impressive thought Jay, as he moved from chair to chair until he was finally close enough to the guitar.

'I'll show you how to play it,' chuckled Den.

After twenty minutes he had only grasped the first couple of cords. His beer was getting flat and the frustration at not being able to grasp it entirety was turning to torture.

'Fucking hell,' he muttered for about the fifth time.

Den chuckled. 'Don't worry about it, you'll have to come round and have some lessons.'

'Really?' queried Jay.

'Yeah.'

'That'd be cool, cheers,' he said and played the only snippet he could from The Cult's 'Lil' Devil', gave the guitar a friendly tap and left it at that.

'We better get going if we're meeting everyone else,' said Den pulling on his long coat.

'Where we going?' James asked rising to his feet.

'The Bonding Warehouse... it's not far from here.'

'Cool,' said James excitedly jumping to his feet.

'Hey a load of us are going over to Manchester tomorrow night, you up for that?'

'I'll be going back to Leicester.'

'Are you sure? I mean we're planning on going to the Hacienda?'

'The Hacienda!'

'Yeah,' Den nodded. 'And you a New Order fan.'

Jay rubbed at his chin as he thought about Trac. 'I'm... I don't know? I wouldn't mind going but...'

Den, noting the discomforting expression across Jay's face said, 'don't worry about it, maybe next time.'

The Bonding Warehouse was on the edge of the River Ouse, with a couple of small balconies that took in a decent view of the river during the daytime. The bar area was fairly wide so you got a good view of what was happening. His group had found a corner to occupy, and the beer seemed to be flowing easily. The girls had ditched drinking halves in favour of pints and slowly seemed to be shredding their nice school girl persona for a more 'I don't care, I'm up for a good time,' attitude. Jay felt further excitement, as if feeding on the positive aura, as he strolled to the bar rubbing his hands together with glee.

Half an hour before time was called at the bar, the group began to split as they headed off to the club.

'Shall we make a move?' said Den finishing his beer.

'Den, you see that fish?'

'What are you on about?'

'That... that,' Jay pointed behind the bar.

Den looked up to see the shape of a fish attached to the wall. 'Yeah what about it?' he responded slightly confused.

'Is that like real do you think... like stuffed or something?'

'Eh... why?'

'It's cool. Would look good in my room is all.'

Den shook his head, 'come on we're off.'

Dissipated, he didn't look up from his pint. 'Yeah,' he mumbled as he raised the glass to his lips and knocked the remaining liquid back. 'I'm with you.'

As the three of them entered Keaton's nightclub, the dance-floor was huge, the Happy Mondays' 'Wrote For Luck' throbbed and oozed substance, lights flickered between the smoke and silhouettes on the dance-floor shuffled. Manchester was taking over, drugs and music entwined stronger than ever, young scruffy kids with no hope had seemed to have found unity and salvation, the sight revived Jay.

'Do you want a drink?' he jeered as he produced a ten pound note.

'Cheers.' responded James looking at the tenner in his hand, wondering if he would ever get his money back.

'Den?'

'Yeah, cheers.'

It was eleven thirty and the club was full. He surveyed three hundred and sixty degrees, smiling comfortably and leaning back into the bar before pushing himself off opting for one of the small black leather sofas.

'Hiya,' came a voice behind him. He looked away from Den and slightly over his shoulder, his eyes landed on Helen in a red shirt, her red lips smiling at him.

He returned the smile. 'Hi, sit down here,' he said patting the space on the leather sofa next to him. Her large round face and straight blonde hair styled in a bob were becoming familiar, and her accent was becoming less painful. She caught him gazing at her breasts for a few seconds or more, but she didn't look incensed or intimidated, she gave more of a warm look as her hand wandered from her lap to his knee.

'Hey, come on, now that's not fair,' he said sharply, feeling immediately uncomfortable and chuckling at her forwardness. He realised that her breasts were to him, perhaps not so much objects of sexual desire, he just longed to lay his head between them to sleep.

'You fancy coming out for a drink sometime?' she asked sliding her hand further between his thighs.

'My girlfriend won't be pleased,' he replied in a softer tone, and showed no outward emotion.

'Where is she?'

'Back home.'

'Right,' she nodded without too much concern.

'You know I like going out drinking, but you and me,' he shrugged, 'we can't.'

'Oh go on,' she said, placing a hand on his arm she let her top slip from her left shoulder. 'Your girlfriend doesn't have to know now does she.'

He rubbed his brow firmly and replied, 'I don't know why you like me? I drink too much, I've got no money, I'm hardly at college... lazy, I hate to dress smart, I'm not even hunky...' he said. 'In fact, I'm a nightmare.'

'I can't tempt you then?'

He smirked. 'Be fair, I'm attached to someone else.'

'Come on. Come back with me tonight,' her hand moved further up and cupped his crotch. He found himself lifting up from his seat.

'Why don't you show me what you're made of,' she growled.

He choked for a second on his drink, confused. He had never been so blatantly chatted up before, was this what girls up north were like? He looked around for help.

'I... I... I'm a bit busy at the minute,' he muttered, and moved her hand away. 'Maybe some other time.'

Helen slipped her top back over her shoulder. 'Your loss,' she smiled and disappeared into the crowd.

Den immediately pounced on him. 'Waaaaheyyyy!' he roared. 'You're in there.'

'No,' he said shaking his head and taking a sip of whiskey from his glass.

'Oh come off it, she's all over you.'

'No, she's just having fun.'

'Don't give me that shit.'

He chuckled, 'she got bored.'

'Look, I know what you're thinking, but your girl back home, she don't have to know.'

'Yeah, but I'd know.'

'How do you know your girl is behaving herself?'

'It's called trust.'

'You're crazy. You don't trust none of them,' he spluttered, 'They're devious. You use women, you don't get involved with them.'

'Forget it,' and with that he stuck his fingers in his ears.

'Under the thumb?' jeered Den pushing his thumb down on his head.

Jay ignored this and went over to the bar to drool over the optics and ordered a double Jim Beam, no ice. The barmaid turned and pumped his request. I could marry a barmaid he thought, placing a crumpled up five pound note into her hand. James gave him a friendly whack on the back. 'Are you coming to have a dance in a bit.'

'Yeah, sure... waiting for the right songs to come on,' and raised his glass with a gleeful expression that said he was looking forward to it.

A tinkering of notes raised a smile as The Wonder Stuff vibrated the room. Jay spied Den on the far side of the dance-floor as he began to weave about, bobbing up and down through the crowd to team up with him. A wave of popular tracks had the dance-floor spilling out beyond its boundaries. A haven for venting frustrations led to an immanent onset of a bout of wilful craziness as 'She Sells Sanctuary' belted out the large Marshall speakers. They enjoyed every second of boisterous fun, the pushing, leaping and singing into the air.

'Yeah-yeah hey-hey... yeah-yeah-hey heeeyyyaaay!'

Exhausted, the three of them collapsed and sprawlled out on the sofas.

'Wooo! I'm knackered,' Den panted.

Jay wiped at his face as he could feel his body shutting down, fast becoming oblivious somewhat to his surroundings, whiskey had pleasantly numbed his fears. He was in his own world now where he had no concerns about anything or anyone. Mixing drinks was never a good idea, the darker side of him was emerging, his attitude altering, the sense of devil-may-care had never been stronger. With little energy he drifted in an out of consciousness, he was like a corpse, porcelain white skin, red lips with no expression. Den woke him about an hour later. His eyes opened slowly and looked blood shot, he still couldn't function his body correctly, his lack of care an energy immobilised him.

'Come on. It's nearly two o'clock.'

'Where's James?' he sneered as he reached out to the table and drew off a glass of unclaimed wine.

'I think he's gone.'

This sparked an unexpected and hasty motion. 'The bastard!' he muttered as he pulled on Den to get to his feet groggy and weak.

'I'm... I'm going,' he slobbered in Den's ear as he continued to use him for support as they moved towards the exit.

'Don't go yet.'

'James has got the money for a taxi. Now he's fucked off.'

'He might be around somewhere.'

He rubbed his head desperately trying to get his brain to work. He tripped on a table leg and dropped to the floor, still holding his head he hadn't noticed.

'Look, why don't you sit back down. You're all over the place.'

'No... No, I'm... I'm going.'

Den helped him put his long coat on and showed him to the exit reluctantly. The cool fresh night air was a relief and brought him round just enough to enable him to stumble up the ally among the other piss heads relieving themselves indiscriminately. James was perched on a bench at the side of the road chatting to a girl he didn't recognise.

'James,' he hollered lurching towards him. 'Who's that then?' he asked squinting at the girl.

'This is Kerry, she's a student nurse.'

'Kerry, I'm afraid I've had a little too much to drink,' he whispered at her. 'Do you think you can help me get my cock out so I can have a pee.'

James stood up abruptly. 'You can't say that.'

'I just did.'

'That's bang out of order Jay.'

'She's... she's a nurse, they do it all the time,' he sniggered rising from his crabby mood momentarily.

James took him to one side and whispered, 'Jay, we can go back to her place, don't blow it.'

'And why would I want to do that?'

'You know so I can...' he frowned.

'What?' he rubbed at his temple in confusion.

'Get my leg over,' he nodded.

'Oh right...' he glanced over James's shoulder at her. She was sat searching in her bag for some cigarettes, cursing as she couldn't find any. His eyes began to focus better. 'She's ugly,' he said abruptly.

'No she isn't, she's fit.'

'Yeah for a goat,' he growled at him.

'Oh come on, I don't want to walk back on my own.'

'Has she got a full fridge?'

'What?'

'Ask her... ask her... if she's going to cook some food. So I can at least eat while you're shag... shagging her.'

'I can't do that.'

'See you then,' and he shuffled off in the wrong direction.

'Oh come on Jay,' he yelled.

He stopped and placed a hand on the wall to his left and turned slightly back to James. 'Has she got any whiskey?'

'I doubt it.'

To that he turned, lurched forward, scraping his left check against the rough edge of the wall and then rambled on.

James looked back to Kerry and shrugged apologetically.

'Jay you're going the wrong fucking way,' he yelled after him.

Jay lay comfortably numb, half in the gutter and half on the pavement. It was a quiet street, only the sound of the rainwater rushing down the sides of the road and trickling down the drain could be heard.

'Fucking hell Jay. Are you alright?'

James began to yank him upward by the collar of his coat. Slowly but surely consciousness came back to him.

'Fuck... Jay,' he muttered as he struggled with his weight. He gave him a soft slap across his cheek and he reared up and took a pathetic fisted swing outward that missed him completely, causing his knuckles to scrape painfully along the wall.

'What the fuck are you doing?'

'Uh... what?'

'Jase, it's James.'

Staring through the fog of alcohol, the flesh around Jay's eyes was so dark, he didn't look at all well.

'You look like shit,' said James as he helped him to his feet and leant him against the wall. Jay rubbed at his face hard, ran his fingers through his hair and twisted his neck a couple of times.

'I'm okay,' he smiled feebly. 'I'm okay. Just... just get me home.'

He saw a taxi come into view and rambled towards it, James quickly sprang to help him into it before cursing as he watched his girl drift away with her friends.

'Well cheers for that,' he spat and clambered into the cab behind him.

'What's... what's up with you?'

'I was well in with that girl.'

'What girl?'

'Oh, forget it.'

He felt pissed off that James wasn't a kindred spirit like Adrian, maybe that's why he and Adrian were such good party mates, they would jointly drink until they dropped and didn't care where they kipped. He lunged forward and opened the car door in a defiant response and caught sight of Vince walking along the pavement, hands in his pockets.

'Vince you twat,' he barked.

Vince looked up to see the taxi screech to a halt, with Jay half hanging out and James trying his best to wrestle him back.

Jay heard Vince cry, 'waheey,' as he stooped back into the cab speechless. Tired and weak he gave up and leant his head back on the seat, sleep was on its way and he was looking forward to it. Whatever was going on inside, the booze was making him worse. Whether it was simply fatigue or even guilt, it prompted the long silence until he was out cold.

Saturday, October 21

He woke from a dream in which he had broken into the Bonding Warehouse and took the stuffed mounted fish from the wall, only then to be surrounded by the police upon his escape. Fish under his arm he froze like a statue in the searchlight. 'Put... the... fish... down!' was being shouted through a megaphone. Someone was persistantly banging on his bedroom door. It was mid-morning, the sun was seeping around the edges of the curtains and James was calling.

'Jay, get up. Your mum's here.'

He heaved himself out of bed, his head pounding inside, his eyelids almost glued together as he wearily pulled on his jeans and shirt. He felt fragile but on the whole not that bad he thought, considering the mixed choice of drinks he'd made. He heard his mum call, 'come on Jay, I thought you'd be ready.' He grabbed for his bag from under the bed and began stuffing his clothes into it. As he retrieved the last loose sock from the end of the bed, he already began to feel the rising joy of returning.

'I'm off then,' he called out as shuffled down the stairs. 'I'll catch you later.'

'Okay,' replied James appearing from the kitchen with a piece of toast.

He opened the front door to see his mum sitting in the car with the engine running. He pulled the door to and jogged down the path and through the black metal gate. He was looking forward to seeing Trac. Work-wise his couple of days had been slow and unproductive, yet the amount of work he had to catch up with was enormous. Sitting in the car on the way home, he held a letter given to him by Jim Deans, the course leader, listing the following subjects he had been referred in; drawing, art history, image animation, typography, computer aided design and graphic design. Pretty much everything had, *work not submitted* written on it. He tried to figure out what he was going to do. The start of his half term holiday marked the end of Trac's. The plan had to be as simple as to work the hours she was at school and catch up. The only real problem was committing to it.

It was good to see The Beast and take it for a burn round the block, but beyond that it was a waiting game. The *NME* he bought to fill some of this time was a pretty boring read, with the likes of 'That's what I like' by Jive Bunny and the Master Mixers at number one. He found it a sad state of affairs, although he had to agree that it seemed the Stone Roses were now running the end of eighty nine and could do no wrong. The only saving grace was a photograph of Wendy James from Transvision Vamp holding the microphone in a very suggestive way. After a few minutes, he pondered as to whether it really was suggestive or not, maybe, if honest he was just in dire need of a damn good blow job?

The rain swept down High Street in sheets. Shivering in the doorway of the jean shop, he leant against the large glass window, occasionally running his hands through his hair as the wind displaced it. He thought about Trac and a warm bed as the cold began to bite, he was freezing. The rain became heavier and heavier, pelting forcefully and attacking him. With all the shops around him closed he had nowhere to hide and watched the shimmer of light in a puddle below. Loneliness began to creep up and surrounded him with the drop in temperature, he felt no ambition and no direction; he was fed up, tired and drenched. He moved grudgingly as the door opened behind him. Every second she was late his anger escalated, normally it came in a flash; a verbal or physical flurry. He rummaged furiously for the right words to vent it out and spat, 'fucking hell,' under his breath as he wandered about, up and down past shops in an effort to keep warm, glaring at people almost wishing he could have an argument with someone to relieve himself of his anger. The big steel shutter rose a little and Trac finally emerged and jogged towards him.

'I've been waiting fucking ages,' he bleated.

She could see he was cold, wet and pissed off and acted accordingly.

'Sorry,' she said softly.

He shuddered a little. 'It's freezing as well.'

She sighed, 'I couldn't help it. I had to wait till we cashed up. Here,' and she handed him a small piece of paper. It read;

To Jay, Soz I'm late, do you still love me? Trac.

She noticed the slight raise in each corner of his mouth.

'Awh, you're smiling,' and she jumped and clapped her hands.

'How can I stay mardy at you?'

'It's because you love me.'

He couldn't stop the grin splitting his face, he tried to, but it was impossible. She filled him with such joy, it was hard to stay angry for long.

'So, what did you do at college?'

'Nothing. Wasn't worth going back, all I got was hassled about the damage to the house after that party. Typical I get all the blame.'

'The photos did show you weren't innocent.'

'I know, but I wasn't the only one.'

'That's not like you to bother about something like that.'

'Yeah, I don't know,' he shrugged, 'ignore me... it's just that I've not been there a term yet and I'm being barred from almost every party.'

'Well I for one, think that's a good thing.'

He scrunched his face up at her.

'Maybe they're just not ready for someone like you?'

Jay smiled to himself from inside. He locked his bedroom door, Trac stood with a blank expression on her face. She watched him unbuckle his belt and take his jeans off. Without moving he continued to undress in the half light of his TV set. As he slipped off his shirt and T-shirt he slowly began to smile broadly. He approached her, with a moment that did not come often enough, she was fully clothed and he was fully unclothed, and he could see it excited her. She sat on his bed and removed her first layer of clothes, treated him with a smile, landing him with desire. He thought for a moment.

'I've got to take a picture of you,' he said, eyes studying her legs closely. Trac leant forward clutching her black T-shirt to her chest slightly as the camera clicked, before un-clipping her stockings as he edged towards her.

'Corr,' he chuckled lightly.

'You don't like stockings.'

'I do, all I said was I liked woolly tights. I like these too.'

She stretched her arms as far above her head as they would go as he moved closer to her. His face lit up with delight as he stroked at her thighs.

'I'd like to watch you do it yourself,' he murmured softly.

'No,' came her reply.

He eased back into a sitting position, leaning on the bed's headrest, comfortably, one leg over the other. She showed no sign that she had rejected his desire and pulled at his knee to goad him close again. Instead he remained motionless for a few moments until just his eyes looked away to the far right and fluttered a few times as they moved up and down before drawing back to her. The muscles around his mouth slightly moved to reflect his disappointment as he whispered, 'do it for me,' and he reached for her hand and placed it between her thighs.

She reddened terribly. 'Jay?' she uttered looking up at him with a confused expression about her face.

'Does it embarrass you?'

She avoided his gaze. 'You just want me to be your dirty slag.'

His eyes narrowed as he smirked slightly, 'yeah,' he whispered, 'yeah I do.'

'Give me some vodka then.'

He tilted his head in surprise to that and she leant forward.

'What's up?' she smiled, 'cat got your tongue?'

Sunday, October 22

Sunday, day of rest. They slept until nine, had some light pillow talk, moved positions and slept further until about eleven twenty before Jay got restless and began to fidget.

'Come on,' he said positively. 'Shall we get up then?'

She would not budge. She looked so attractive he didn't want to argue. He got back into bed and began to massage every part of her body. She lay contented and let out the odd subtle moan, with her face buried deep into his pillow.

At lunchtime, and with artwork sprawled across Trac's kitchen table, he tried to engage his brain into generating ideas for the last couple of hours. All he seemed to achieve was a stinking migraine. He meandered back into her room to see what she was up to. She was sat on her bed, faded grey T-shirt, white cotton knickers, a pair of thick black socks loose by her ankles, feet pointing inward slightly, thumbing through an *i-D* magazine. He gave out a long sigh and sat down, his chin resting on the back of the chair, and began drumming his legs impatiently, letting out deep breaths that puffed his cheeks out.

She peered over at him. 'What's up sexy pants?'

He gave her a shrug of his shoulders. 'I'm just fed up, I just don't seem to have a creative spark and the problem is I can't force it.'

Stretching her T-shirt and hooking it over her knees she said, 'it'll happen.'

'I'm just so behind as well which doesn't help.'

'How many subjects?'

'All of them... well except photography.'

'Maybe if you're not feeling so creative you could do some writing?'

'What writing? Oh... that. I thought you were going to help me with that?'

'You know I'll do anything for you... except write that damn art gallery essay.'

'I thought you said you would?'

'No. You asked me and I said no... remember?'

'Yeah but?'

'Nooo.'

'Oh go on.'

'Jay,' she sighed. 'I've never even been to Leeds.'

'That doesn't matter.'

She shook her head at him and put a hand up as if to say end of conversation. He shrugged, stood up slowly and wandered back to the kitchen lethargically then on into the lounge. Glancing at a baby photo, he smiled and picked it up, as she walked past to the kettle.

'Look at you here.'

'I know,' she shouted.

'Big cheeks,' he turned the photo slightly. 'Well, one big cheek.'

A sudden wave of sadness washed over him, as though he was disappointed that he had never grew up with her. In that moment his love felt unconditional. She was his little baby. Confused, he felt his brow contort slightly as he submerged into a sinking feeling, a hopeless lack of control.

He moved towards the TV set in a subdued manner and switched it on before slumping onto the sofa. Flicking through the channels he found nothing of interest. He muttered, 'shit,' to himself and reached for the *Radio Times*, thumbed through a few pages then yawned and tossed it towards the coffee table and missed. He stood up and began to mooch again. Restless, he returned to the dining table and pawed effortlessly at the paper strewn across it. Rattling a pencil between his teeth he rose and circled the kitchen, squeezed Trac's bum and made a rasping noise, to which she told him too behave. He slumped once more into the sofa and went through the TV channels again.

'I keep hounding Mum to get Sky, we could have MTV on.'

He made no reply just continued to flick through each channel again and again and finally tossed the remote towards the coffee table and missed.

'I'm going to put the washing machine on, do you need anything doing?'

He didn't verbally reply to that either, just wandered off into her room to collect some of his clothes that could do with a wash.

'Found anything?'

'Yeah, I've found something but I'm not sure what it is,' he said with a low chuckle, as he held up a pair of larger than life knickers. 'Tell me these aren't yours,' he said and she snatched them from him bringing an amused grin to his face.

'Does this mean we've been seeing each other too long now, I will start seeing less of you in the skimpy stuff like last night.'

Her stone face didn't falter, she just turned and marched off in the direction of the kitchen cursing as she went. When the gap between them exceeded a yard, he skipped a little to catch her.

'Come to think of it,' he sniggered. 'Can't you put them on for me, I think they're beginning to turn me on?'.

'Oh bog off.'

'What,' he replied with fake innocence. 'I'm being serious,' he said.

He considered putting his arm around her waist but as he moved closer to her she stepped down into the lounge and slid the internal patio door across and locked it.

'Oh, come on I'm only messing.'

She ignored him and slumped onto the couch. Retaining her blank face she picked up the *Radio Times* from off the floor and began thumbing through it.

'You're not grumping at me are you?'

He put his hands on his hips and stood for a moment or two thinking of a plan, but it came down to one of three simple things; leave, go off and listen to some music for half an hour, or grovel like mad for the next fifteen minutes. He looked at his watch and decided there was enough time to listen to some music, then treat her like a princess there after. Going home was not an option for the fear that the grumpiness would only amass to an almost irreparable proportion. The forth option that began to creep into his head made him chuckle again, as he imagined himself finding another pair of big pants and parading around in them, if Trac was one of his mates, a bloke mate that is, they would appreciate the humour, but Trac's face had frozen. Yep, he decided, the new Wonder Stuff album was up for another play.

An hour later he woke to find a post-it note stuck to his chest. *Needs tidying up!* was written in capital letters in red felt-tip pen, below which in smaller lower case letters; *just a note to say sorry for being grumpy. Love you very much xx.* He emerged from her room to find her doing the ironing. He gave a soft smile as he wafted the note and said, 'tea?' She gave him a nod of her head. He did the washing up and then went off to see if there was anything better on the TV just as the phone began to ring. When Trac failed to answer on the seventh ring he picked up the reciever.

'Hello.... yeah... not bad... I know I said call... yeah but... nothing just something to do with pants... don't worry about it... I'll tell you later...'

When Trac appeared with another pile of clothing, she stopped and studied him. He put the hand over the mouth piece. 'It's Adrian asking me to get drunk,' he smiled.

Her face transformed from the soft gaze to that of a very stern look.

'Hi... yeah sorry mate can't do it... Really?' He turned back to Trac with a smile, 'he's only gone and got a bottle of tequila.'

Her stern expression remained.

'Adrian, I can't tonight... come on, that's not fair,' he looked over at Trac one more time to see if she would give. 'He said I can have the worm.'

Her eyebrows raised as she frowned and shook her head lightly as she moved off to the dining table. 'Look, keep hold of it mate.... yeah... okay... yeah see you.'

He put down the phone and gave a slight shrug as he moved back to the sofa. Trac appeared sharply at the doorway.

'You're not going to sulk all evening are you?' she asked calmly.

'No... I'm fine... what about you?'

'Mmm. You still haven't noticed then?'

'Noticed what?' he mumbled as he slouched a stage further into the sofa. Trac gave her thigh a light slap and smiled broadly at him.

'My jeans,' he bellowed.

'All nice and clean for you.'

'Get them off then.'

'You're supposed to seduce a girl.'

'Umm?'

'So do I look good in them or what?'

'Yes, very sexy, but they're mine.'

'Can I keep them for a bit.'

He puffed his cheeks out. 'Alright go on,' he mumbled, 'just look after them.'

'That reminds me, I've got something to show you,' and she rushed off. With a yawn he sprawled out along the sofa and plumped a cushion under his head. He was just thinking about the possibility of another snooze, when she came twirling into the room happily. Not quite sure what was occurring he remained silent but for a smile and flutter of his eyes.

'So?' she said.

'So?' he answered.

'Do you like my new top?' and she twirled again.

'Perfect,' he replied softly, trying to stretch an arm to reach the remote.

'What's on your mind?'

'Nothing.'

'Well you haven't even looked at my top.'

'I told you, perfect.'

'But do I look good in it?'

'Yeah great,' he said flatly.

'What's up?'

'Nothing.'

'God, why are you so restless?'

'Ugh!' he grunted still stretching for the remote.

She looked at her watch, 'you hungry?'

'I'll be alright in a minute,' he mumbled.

She put her hands on her hips, frowned at him and waited for a proper answer to the question

'Er... no... not really. I'll just have a bit of Marmite on toast,' he said as he fell from the sofa to the floor.

'We haven't got any.'

Looking up at her he said, 'you must have.'

'Nooo.'

He got to his feet and headed for the kitchen.

'You won't find any,' she said confidently as he passed her.

In the last cupboard a shelf swung out and there at the bottom, at the back was the little black jar he was looking for.

'Marmite,' he said plainly, 'there you go.'

She glared at him, 'look at the state of it. It's been in there years.'

'So...' he chuckled. 'It'll be alright.'

'I'm not kissing you if you eat that stuff,' she pouted quickly, as he reached for the bread.

'Why not?'

'I don't like it. I told you it's awful stuff,' she replied in a voice as petty as the situation.

'You smoke and I don't like that,' he mumbled casually.

She turned her nose up. 'Well you don't have to kiss me,' she said spitefully to contrast his tone, but he failed to rise to it.

'I really would like some Marmite and then afterwards I'm going to kiss you, and if you don't let me I'll have to give you a slap,' he said in jest, grinning inanely.

She ignored the remark, stretched out her leg and wiggled her foot, narrowed her eyes and asked him if he was capable of making something decent for tea. Still feeling a slight amount of guilt about the mood he was in, the big pants incident and the bizarre effect she knew her feet had on him, he put down the Marmite and replied, 'I reckon I can manage that.'

Monday, October 23

Jay was sat on a fence sharpening a pencil. The sky a brilliant orange as the sun shone down creating a humid and rich glow all around him. An earlier shower had kicked up the smell of grass and rotting leaves. October was nearly over and he was dreading the clocks being changed, making the days way too short. As he made an assortment of different sketches, he found himself studying the leaves falling from the trees, some drifted right down while some swiftly descended. Watching one particular golden orange and brown edged leaf hanging on by a thread, he began to wonder when it might fall. Before he could finish its outline on paper the wind had taken it away, he couldn't help but think that it was somehow symbolic, a sign that the summer had well and truly vanished, a new page had well and truly started, new decisions. Whatever the future may bring, it couldn't ever change the summer. With his creative urge lost, he became fed up with the paper in front of him. He packed his kit away and began to stroll back down the lane. He returned the slight bluntness of his pencil back to a point again and slipped it behind his ear. Stopping, he wanted to appreciate this place before it was fully lost to the autumn and, as he stood there soaking it up through all his senses, the memories he had with Trac flashed into his head randomly. As he twirled the knife in his hands a couple of times he noted a tree to his right, set back a little from the worn pathway. He stepped towards it and began to carve into it.

He walked back into her house, into the kitchen where Trac was at the sink washing up. She glanced over to see him in a kind of lost trance, deep in thought he was pottering around in a circle, tapping the end of his pencil on his forehead.

'What have you got all over your mitts?'

He drifted out of his trance and looked down at his green covered hands and before the excited part of him could say, 'I've carved a heart on a tree with our names in it,' a sense of vulnerability washed over him. Instead he mumbled, 'I don't know... nothing,' and shuffled towards the sink.

'So did you get all the references you needed?'

'I think so, I had a couple of ideas going round my head walking back. I can't quite picture how it's going to look yet, but I'm going to keep it simple, clean and use natural colours.'

Trac simply nodded.

'I guess I better get them down on paper before I forget,' he smiled, opened up his art box and sat down at the dining table and set to work.

Tuesday, October 24

It was here, their last day of freedom before her parents arrived home. Jay was more than eager for her to stay home as he was in a seriously horny mood. He teased her by whispering suggestions in her ear.

'It's your last day of freedom,' he said. 'You've got to stay home. Go on, say yes,' he goaded.

'Oh... I don't know... Okay then,' she said.

He gave her a big grin that split his face. 'Give me a hug,' he demanded. She made a strained groan and shifted herself to him. 'God you're always so warm.'

'We can spend the whole day in bed,' he said, and felt her nod against his side.

At nine fifteen Trac sat up abruptly and bit on her finger. Jay gave out a yawn, stretched a little and rubbed his face into the pillow to try and bring himself round before squinting up at her.

'What's up babe?'

'I feel a bit guilty, I should have gone.'

'Too late now.'

'I'm going to get a bollocking if I don't go.'

'Don't worry about it.'

'I've had loads of time off already.'

'What's done is done,' he said. 'No point in worrying about it.'

'I'll have to get my sister to write me a note.'

'I can write you one. I'll say you were too sexy to attend.'

He pulled the bed covers around himself. 'It ain't half snug in here.'

'Lazy bones.'

She ran a hand down his stomach, 'you didn't have that when we first started going out.'

He looked down to see she was referring to the caterpillar of hair that had grown up to his belly button.

'Really, I never noticed.'

She stood up out of bed, slipped on her dressing gown, and disappeared. Picking up her underwear, he looked at it, smiling with satisfaction at the thought of taking them as a souvenir and for some reason unknown to him put them on his head and started reading her *Face* magazine.

'What are you doing with them on your head?'

He looked up at her puzzled expression, 'I err... I was...' he gave her a lethargic shrug and shook his head lightly.

'So,' she smiled, 'are you going to wash me?'

He closed the magazine and said, 'I'll give it a go.'

They showered; washed each other slowly and fully. He tried to hold back his surge of excitement but it was too strong and within moments had wrestled her to the bathroom floor. Once inside her he felt enormous relief. They lay there for a long while, until she eventually got cold and the spark of energy returned in his eyes.

'Beautiful,' he whispered and picked her up by the hips and swung her round. She giggled, wiping her hair away from her eyes.

Placing her carefully onto her bed and looking down on her he smiled gently. He was entranced by the picture of her naked body spread across the covers. He kissed her stomach, she tasted fresh. Luxuriously he began to slide his lips over the tips of each of her toes and slowly up her legs. Her smile changed to a slow wondering delight before she leant back and gripped hold of the pillow with pleasure.

'There she is,' he smirked, 'all excited.'

He kissed her slowly then fast, with perfection in mind. Clenching her fists she began to breathe deeper and heavier. They rolled around the bed in sequence as she began to caress him back. He moaned softly and then gasped as she took 'Him' into her mouth, his face flushed instantly. She rolled onto her side and he met her, moving gently they stayed in the sideways position before she moved on top. He felt his climax, thrusting her onto her back, perspiration plastered her hair to her forehead and he squeezed her bum into his orgasm. Collapsing on her, his face against her chest he whispered, 'you get me going so much.'

She let out a panted sigh and stretched her arms. Smiling she asked, 'do you get excited thinking about me in York?'

'Yeah,' he murmured lightly, still basking in the afterglow.

'Sorry you have to sort yourself out.'

'I don't think about you that much,' he chuckled.

The front door then clicked and Trac jolted forward. 'Oh my God!... Must be my sister... It's got to be my sister!'

Jay froze in the most uncomfortable position ever, what if it was her mum and dad? He cowered below the covers as she got up. Her sister popped her head round the door and studied Trac carefully, 'and what have you two been up to?' she asked in a accusing tone.

Her fella John, appeared and thrust his hands to his hips and spluttered, 'your mum wouldn't be pleased if she knew we let Jason stop over all the time.'

Jay felt his face scrunch up, what the fuck has it got to do with you? he thought and considered bursting out from under the covers for a confrontation but opted to stay where he was as leaping out at them all naked with a still semi-erect cock would probably just cause an initial shock, quickly followed by a ripple of laughter.

'You two fancy a cup of tea?' asked her sister lightly, offering a way forward that wasn't going to result in bad feeling or Jay making a spectacle of himself. Trac rolled out of the bed looking more than a bit fed up. Disappointed in her change of mood, he wanted to challenge her and the lyrics to the song playing seemed to fit how he was feeling. He needed to push her as if to test her love and loyalty hoping she would take the bait and rise to it, maybe put pay to or defend the increasing undercurrent of self doubt that bubbled beneath the surface. He started to sing along to The Wonder Stuff's 'Golden Green' and dance upon her. *'And if she loves me... she'll say that she loves me... lies will shine in her eyes!'*

Trac was blind to his presence. He watched her intently, he enjoyed the way she moved as she shuffled around her room until finally resting in front of her mirror and began brushing her hair, probably the most womanly action of all he thought. He wished for the heavy burden of York, his education and his future would disappear. She dabbed a few bits of make up on and sipped her tea in between dressing. She kissed him and grabbed her bag and left for school.

'I'll see you at four.'

'I thought you weren't going to go today?'

'What, and put up with John giving me a hard time all day?'

He looked to the ground, 'what am I going to do?'

She gave him a shrug. 'Sleep, draw, watch the telly... I don't know?'

Catching her arm he followed her into the hall. There followed a silence, a relaxed one as she sat on the bottom of the stairs and allowed him to put her feet into her shoes and tie the laces.

'Do you want me to wait?' he whispered.

Slipping her into her jacket, she flicked out her hair over the collar and replied, 'sure,' giving him a quick kiss.

He resided back to her pit rubbing his face into her pillow, finding it pleasingly aromatic he opted for further sleep. Hours later he got up and hunted through the kitchen cupboards for a snack.

'Magic. Brandy snaps,' he said to himself.

Best just have one he thought, five minutes later the box lay empty and he was back in her bed. The thought of quitting York and everyone, to just live in her room appealed to him, he liked her room, her bed, her environment it seemed a strange sense of escape, he felt safe there.

The next time he woke was to the sound of hoovering, Trac's sister and John had began the task of tidying the house from top to bottom before her parents arrived home. He lay for half an hour listening to them cleaning, before he began to feel a little guilty, so he began to tidy Trac's room. He dusted, hoovered, he even ironed some of her clothes, folded them up neatly and put them away. He studied the various photos of the summer on her cork notice board with pride, it helped to block the impending dullness he began to feel about being apart from her. Every life has its holidays, he thought, and this summer of '89 was assuredly his as he remembered what he had told her before he had left for York for the first time.

'Whatever happens, we will always have this summer,' it made his eyes narrow, mouth widen to a smile... he felt as spirited as he had ever been.

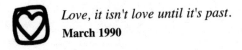 *Love, it isn't love until it's past.*
March 1990

Epilogue. Standing on your own two feet.

York, Late October, 1990

It was a crisp and bright October day. Jay appeared at the top of Gladstone Street with a brown grocery bag wrapped in his arms. Fumbling with his keys he entered home. It was great to have a place outside the city of York, and independence for once seemed to be agreeing with him. Placing the groceries onto the kitchen worktop James came bouncing through from the lounge.

'What did you get?' he asked looking into the bag furtively.

'Milk, bread, half a chicken, some veg, a few tins of rice pudding and a bar of Milka chocolate.'

'Cool,' he smiled as he happily packed some of the food away while Jay began to prepare the chicken for dinner. Gone were the days of beans on toast, he was actually turning out to be something of a cook. He spent much of his time reading, watching films and drawing, even his college grades were on the up too. The odd visits to the pub were few and far between, and when he did go, he often only drank blackcurrant and soda. No longer living beyond his means helped him towards his goal of taking a year out abroad once he had graduated. He cut pictures of America and Australia from magazines and travel brochures, placing them around his bed to help keep him focused.

'So, you decided if you're going back to Leicester this weekend?'

'Yeah,' Jay nodded. 'I reckon so.'

There was a slight mist in the air so he pulled his jacket closer to keep his warmth. He'd not been back to Leicester for quite a while, and now didn't seem to miss it so much. He wandered through the doors of the Helsinki bar looking rested, even a little younger than his years and felt fresh and smart in his highly polished boots, black 501s, black polo neck and dark brown suede jacket. It caught him a little off guard to see that Trac was there. Although he would deny it, or try to hide it, the poignant sensation within let him know he still felt for her.

He made his way to the bar and got a drink. With a fixed-smile he tapped the bar lightly and leaned into it and waited as the familiar drunken silhouette jeering, 'DDDEEE!' rambled towards him.

'Adrian. Long time no see,' he smiled.

Behind him Dave appeared in a better state. 'How are you doing Jay?'

'Yeah, I'm good,' he nodded with an easy smile. 'You?'

'Not bad. What's that you're drinking?'

'Coke.'

'With what?'

He tilted his glass. 'Nothing...' he replied. 'Just Coke.'

Dave gave him a puzzled look, then began to study his clothes. 'What's all this?' he asked pulling at the collar of his jacket. 'How can you afford this?'

'I've been doing quite a bit of freelance work, you know in between college stuff.'

Pointing at his feet Dave smiled. 'Still got your Docs though.'

'Yeah, my old faithful DMs they're still going.'

'So why aren't you drinking then?'

'He's really calmed down,' interrupted Adrian.

'Yeah,' smirked Jay. 'I'm retired. Purifying myself,' he chuckled lightly.

'I can't believe it, you've still got those mad dog eyes.'

'Well thanks for that Dave,' he replied with a pat to his back.

'So you don't drink at all?'

'Yeah, I have the odd pint of Guinness now and again but that's about it.'

'Can't believe you're not getting legless!'

'It's a weird thing,' said Jay sipping at his drink. 'For all the boredom of being normal, it's not that bad.'

To be truthful he thought, the irony of it was fucking brilliant. He raised his drink and they chinked glasses.

'It's really nice you two inviting me down here,' he smiled looking round. 'I've not been here in ages.'

Between the soft and loud music, snatches of conversation became more sketchy and difficult. He wondered if he should leave and catch up with the guys down The Bell before the place descended into chaos. His eyes wandered over the crowds of people around him, avoiding faces and shapes he didn't recognise until his eyes fell on Trac. He studied her as she pushed her hair outward; long, mousey coloured and straight again, how he liked it. She looked beautiful, even more so than he remembered. When she realised he was watching her, she stepped out slightly from the shelter of her new friends and smiled across at him. It was a genuine smile. She was visibly pleased to see him, she lifted her hand slightly from her glass and gave a wave. For a fleeting moment he felt as though they were going to walk out, round the corner and jump into The Beast, but that was gone too, crashed, far from a blaze of glory. He wanted to walk over to her, be bright and confident and ask her how she was and what she was she up to. The butterflies in his stomach wouldn't pass which made him question how far he had got to forgetting her. There was also an underlining touch of guilt that palpably squeezed at his heart. What else would he say? 'Hello, I miss you.' Did he have the right to say that, that he missed dancing, talking and especially the other. She was all the things he wasn't or had somehow inadvertently drifted from being the promise of, smart, sensible, stylish... sexy. It had made him feel like a fraud and in the long term he guessed he couldn't quite get comfortable with that, still there was relief thrown in too. She was still looking at him, he was drawn into her gaze. Looking right through him she was letting him know that she could still read him. He realised then that in this thing they shared called a romance, some things just don't have to, or need to be said, it's just in the air... a feeling, he didn't quite know how it worked? You just know. He realised then that he had to be happy just to see her smile.

Adrian whooped as he prised his way through a narrow gap of people, clanking the glasses he was carrying.

Jay took his drink. 'Cheers mate,' he smiled and gave his pal a light squeeze of his shoulder before looking back to see Trac was once more engulfed by her new crowd in a different place.

Profound moments affect people in different ways. He fell in love with Trac, with drinking, the ridiculous highs and lows, the impulsiveness and the unpredictability of it all. He had an inability to cope with any prolonged absence from his loved ones. For him the summer of '89 was one of those big moments in life that you wish you could catch in a bottle and store, something to soak up sometime down the line. It was a time of excess, experimenting, annoying the middle-aged and for making mistakes. A time when anything was possible, and for a short time it was. They were rites of passage, part of growing up that had grounded him, mellowed him and gave him a strength of focus and a calmness he didn't have before. Without consciously thinking, he patted The Yellow Fish tattoo over his left shoulder, wild and free? He took a sip of his Coke and allowed the memories to come flooding in, feeling elated and liberated he smiled broadly and wondered, if it were ever possible to have a summer like '89 again and he were to ask the girl he loved to join him... would she?

ACKNOWLEDGMENTS

Taken directly from my diaries and supported by letters, photos and friends (for the times I was too inebriated to remember). This book was written in the summer of 1990, edited in 2008 and recalls my eighteenth year as I saw it at the time.

Thank you to everyone at Star Publishing, to my editor Lindsay James for all her hard work in helping to edit and shape the work. Also to Marc Taylor for all his help during the proofing process. Further thanks also goes to the Arts Council, East Midlands for all its advice through the Critically Write scheme.

Thank you to the following for their permission to reproduce copyright material:

Golden Green by The Wonder Stuff
Words and Music by Malcolm Treece, Martin Gilks, Robert Jones and Miles Hunt.
Lyrics reproduced by permission.
© Copyright 1989 PolyGram Music Publishing Limited.
Universal Music Publishing Limited.
Used by permission of Music Sales Limited.
All Rights Reserved. International Copyright Secured.

Where Egos Dare - The Cult Ride The Rainbow to the Headquarters of Evil. Story by James Brown.
NME. 23rd September 1989.
Extract reproduced by permission.
© Copyright 1989 IPC Media.
Published by Holburn Publishing Group.
All Rights Reserved.

Any other third party correspondence has been recreated.

Every reasonable effort has been made to contact all copyright holders, but if there are any errors or emissions we will be pleased to insert the appropriate acknowledgment in any subsequent printing of this publication.